BLACK MARKET

ANTHOLOGIES FROM THE HOURLINGS

Black Market
The Outsiders
The Curator
Reliquary
Tranquility and Other Myths

OTHER TANNHAUSER PRESS ANTHOLOGIES

Fantastic Defenders
Silence of the Apoc
Whispers of the Apoc
The Witness Paradox

FORTHCOMING ANTHOLOGIES

The Forever Inn
Restless Spirits

BLACK MARKET

AN HOURLINGS ANTHOLOGY

www.tannhauserpress.com

This is a work of fiction. All characters and events portrayed in this book are fictional, and any resemblance to real people or incidents is purely coincidental.

Black Market

Published by Tannhauser Press 
www.tannhauserpress.com
Fredericksburg, VA 22407
ISBN: 979-8-89719-058-4

Copyediting by Donna Royston

Cover by Natalia David

Dedication

This anthology was created
in the historic year 2020.

We dedicate this book to
all the victims of COVID-19.

Rest in Peace

Table of Contents

BIO: Martin Wilsey is a full-time author and creator of the highly acclaimed, bestselling *Solstice 31 Saga*.

Mr. Wilsey's first novel, *Still Falling,* was published March 31, 2015. Less than three years and over a half a million published words later, he retired from his career as a research scientist for a government-funded think tank. As a full-time science fiction author, Mr. Wilsey still uses his research and whiteboard skills to keep the books flowing. He likes to put the science back into science fiction. Mr. Wilsey has more projects than he has time. Please feel free to email him and distract him even more.

He and his wife Brenda live in Virginia with their cats Brandy and Bailey.

https://www.martinwilsey.com/

NOT FOR SALE

by Martin Wilsey

Ty Crowley cleared the ridge and looked down on the city of Greco. Ty hated this planet, and Greco was the reason why.

It was the only place in this entire god-forsaken world that was warm enough to support a population and spaceport. Thermals from the fissures provided the warmth. Everything else had to be a struggle. Everything else was for sale. Everything.

Ty kept telling himself he didn't care. This was the only place he could get what he was looking for. He had the credits. He just needed the Black Market. Greco was the right one.

But first, he needed to be able to pass as human. He had no time for bigotry. He settled his backpack on his shoulders and moved on. His alloy chassis was loud and recognizable for what it was. That would not do for this mission.

***

Ty carefully climbed down the rocks and entered the city via the South Bridge Gate. His energy charge was 15%, but it would be enough. The nutrition and electrolyte packs were also dangerously low. His organics would be in trouble soon. His brain needed calories. His skin only covered his head and shoulders and didn't require much maintenance. The long dark hair and full beard were more than just insulation. Ty needed clothes to cover the rest of his chassis. That would be easy.

"Hey, cyborg!" called a voice from the shadows. "You think you can just walk in here?"

"Please, sir. My charge is at 2%." Ty moved toward the man with a stilted affectation, using the default voice of an old model 11 cyborg. "I have credits. Can you direct me to the nearest public charging kiosk?" Ty held up a hand with a gold credit chip. It was a fortune to a street thug.

When the crowbar swung down toward Ty's head, he simply was not there, he had moved so fast. The thug's neck broke far easier than Ty expected.

Later, as the naked dead body fell into the fissure, Ty checked his charge: 14%. He was now dressed in a heavy fiber tunic, pants, hooded cowl, and even boots and gloves. It hid his chassis neatly. He now had a vest of many pockets. A few of them held a few credits of various kinds. One pocket held a heavy folding knife, and another a narcotic hypospray labeled *Devil Red*. The hypo followed the man over the side. The heavy body odor in the clothes would add to the effect.

The entrance to the Greco South Island was unmanned. A manual gate was in poor repair, but it opened and closed well enough. Ty could instantly feel the difference in the atmosphere on the inside. It was much warmer, and the humidity was higher. Sensors measured the temperature at 10.51 Celsius.

Ty lowered his hood and combed his fingers through his hair, pushing it away from his face. He was surprised at the number of people out and about here. His internal local time clock synced with Greco Standard Time at 0231.

The last time Ty had been here, this had been a wide avenue used mostly by cargo transport vehicles. Vendor stalls now crowded the space, turning one wide road into two narrow walkways. Ty purchased six high-calorie nutrition drinks and some dried electrolytes. He consumed them one after another, standing off to the side next to a trash chute.

A filthy child squatted at the curb in front of him, facing away. Sitting on his heels and not looking at Ty, he said, "Don't give yourself away so easily. Some vendors only sell electrolytes to tag cyborgs. Get the ramen at Niko's instead. Cyborg parts are hot in the Black Market. Don't be parts."

"Thanks," Ty said. "What's your name? I'm Ty."

"Call me Oren," the kid said, as he stood. He pushed a sleeve up so Ty could see his hand skin stopped halfway to his elbow. "You buyin or sellin?"

"A little of both, plus I'm looking for someone," Ty replied.

"For a small fee, I can show you your best bets," Oren said.

"So, the vendors are not the only ones watching who buys electrolytes and nutrition drinks," Ty smiled.

"Body odor is a great touch," Oren said. "I'll remember that."

"How small is your fee?" Ty asked.

"The bigger the fee, the better the service." Oren held out a hand.

Ty dug out all the credits that had been in the vest pockets and dropped them into the outstretched hand.

The boy's eyes went wide. "Who are you looking for?"

"Never mind that. To start, I am looking for a navigation actuator for an S22 shuttle…" Ty paused. "…With charts."

"Trading or buying."

"Either."

"On or off books."

"Off. The star charts should be way off," Ty replied, as he watched two heavily armed men walk openly down the street.

"That should be easy. You can get anything in Greco," Oren bragged.

"Weapons are allowed now?" Ty was still watching the two men.

"Yep. It depends on the sector, though." Oren said, looking over his shoulder. "Everywhere we might go. Those are Citadel guards. A pain. The guy in the Citadel fancies himself as a Governor. It won't last long. Never does. You need weapons?"

"That's our first stop." Ty gestured for Oren to lead the way. "I need… tools."

***

Ty was surprised that the shop was only a few hundred meters farther in. The shop was carved directly into the living rock, and the entire storefront was protected by thick iron grates and door. There was no sign, but bright light escaped through the bars.

The door locks buzzed before they reached the call button. They entered the shop, and the door locks engaged as soon as the door closed behind them.

The room was lined with glass counter display cases that were filled with firearms and munitions of all kinds. A woman behind the counter was dressed in black fatigue pants and tank top. She wore wearable comms ear cuffs and clear wraparound HUD glasses.

Corner turrets tracked their movements as they entered.

"Hey, Oren," she said to the kid. "What can I do for y'all today?"

Ty was already scanning the contents of the shop.

"You take trades?" Ty asked.

"If the market is there, sure," she said.

"I want a Catron Spike 4mm, with two mags of armor-piercing and two mags of glass-frangible," Ty said. "I also want that Burkholder over-under with four mags of armor-piercing and twenty 10mm grenades. Single point sling and carbon fiber holster." Ty pointed to the rack.

The clerk raised an eyebrow, looking him up and down. "Expensive. I will save us the time by making sure you have the credits before I even let you inspect them."

"I'd like to trade," Ty said, knowing most of these were stolen military weapons.

"Sure. But for that list, it's got to be good," she smiled.

Making no sudden moves, Ty reached into his vest and withdrew a thermal detonator capable of destroying the entire South Island.

"That's armed." The clerk unconsciously backed away.

"I knew you'd want to know it was the real thing." Ty had anticipated that she could have just as quickly let the turrets kill him and just take whatever he had. But not this.

She had guts. After her initial reaction, she was calm and collected. "I think that will cover it."

She began to collect the gear and pile it on the counter before Ty. In a show of trust, Ty disarmed, reset the device and set it on the counter before he took off his pack and heavy cloak.

He put on the holster first, configured for a left-hand draw from concealment at his kidney. The loaded carbine swung neatly behind his back, muzzle down. He loaded and holstered the handgun before stowing the magazines in the vest pockets.

The woman placed a long double-edged sheathed combat knife on the counter. "To complete the set. It's nice to see someone that knows what they are doing."

"Thank you." The knife disappeared into the folds of the cloak.

"And this is for you, Oren." She tossed him a high-quality multi-tool. "Bring your friends in any time."

Oren smiled and waved as the door locks buzzed. Ty slow-blinked a goodbye and turned away.

They were half a block away when Oren said, "You could have gotten ten times that in the black market on Greco for that thing."

"I know. I'm in a hurry. Now, I need to… rest. The S22 navigation actuator should be easy," he said to Oren, moving into the crowd. "It's the charts that will be hard."

"I know just the place you need." Oren moved with purpose. "Do you realize how loud your joints are? How's about a sonic soak and a charge?"

***

It took a lot longer to find the next stop, on the far end of the South Island. There were seven Islands in Greco. They were not really islands, surrounded by water. These were giant pillars, like rock formations surrounded by deep ravines. There were sometimes magma flows at their bottoms. There was always an eerie light from them. But the geothermal activity made it warm enough.

As they moved, the night got deeper and darker, and there were fewer people, until there were no people at all. The door they approached had a dirty floodlight above it, along with a huge old security camera. Oren pushed the button.

After a minute, Ty could hear bolts sliding open, followed by the door. A pretty Asian woman opened the door, saying, "Come in, come in, welcome." Ty looked sideways at Oren as the tiny woman bolted the door behind them. "Welcome back. How may I help today?"

"Two sonic soaks and charge. He pays," Oren said. "One room. One hour."

"As you wish." The tiny woman gestured with a sweep of her arm.

They followed her down a long hallway. Numbered doors lined the way. Ty knew it was some kind of brothel. It would be a good cover.

She stopped at a 35 stenciled on the door. "Two hundred credits, please." She held out a tablet. Ty transmitted the funds, and the door opened as the madam headed back toward the front.

An even smaller Asian woman was already inside, wearing a heavy terrycloth robe. The lights were dim. The tiny woman bowed. "I am Tiko. Please, undress. Hang everything on pegs." Her accent was very thick.

Ty just stood there and watched as she slid massive door bolts into the locked position. Oren had already stripped, and his clothes hung on pegs. Oren was mostly cyborg with skin only covering his head, chest, upper arms, and hands. He moved forward to stand on a grate that was about two meters across.

Tiko touched some controls, and Oren began to sink into warm oil.

"Me help you," Tiko said to Ty, as she took off his cloak. After she hung it on a peg, she took off her robe. She was also a cyborg with skin on her face, neck, and entire right arm and hand. The edges of Tiko's skin were a ragged mess. But her chassis was beautiful. It was polished to a high sheen with intricate engravings.

"Normally, I'd offer to launder your clothes while you soak." She took his carbine and hung it on a peg. "These smell human. They are perfect this way. Well done." Her accent was now completely gone. Ty understood the cover without her explaining. Smart.

Soon Ty was also without clothes. His skin covered only his head and shoulders. Tiko attached a universal charging cable to a port at the base of his spine. She activated the oil bath and descended into the bath with him.

In the bath, she had a variety of specialty brushes and tools. A projector displayed a diagnostic array on an adjacent wall. Ty realized she was an expert engineer.

It was apparent to Ty that Oren had been here before. Tiko completely ignored Oren as he began to use her supplies to clean and charge his arms without her help. They were only prosthetics from the elbows down.

Oren noticed Ty was watching him.

Ty had only raised an eyebrow.

"I got caught stealing," Oren stated. "Twice."

"There are no jails in Greco, only lessons," Tiko said as she worked. She was highly skilled at maintenance. She knew about even the most esoteric access points to clean. "You have a lot of carbon scoring. How long have your nanites been this depleted?"

"Too long," Ty replied. Just then, his charge hit 30%, and new systems came back up. Passive sensors activated and detected massive amounts of RF emanating from Tiko.

"We can top you off," Tiko said, without pausing. "That's another 2000 credits, though." From her tone, she expected he could not afford it.

"Do it," Ty said. "I'll need the M7s, though."

Tiko froze at that.

After a moment, she stood up straight and looked Ty in the eyes. "M7 nanites will be 9000 credits."

Ty nodded and said, "Yes, please. Transmitting credits now. I added an extra 1000 for discretion." She looked closely at his sternum plate for a moment before getting back to work. He knew she recognized the self-destruct system contained there.

***

Ty was fully dressed, and Tika was in her oversized robe again. Her hair was slicked back in a ponytail, and she was smiling all the way to her eyes.

"You come back. Anytime. Ask for Tika. Tika always be here for you," she said. Her affected accent was back. Just another Greco prostitute. Ty now knew she was a talented tech and engineer. He would remember her.

"I will." Ty rolled his neck and flexed a shoulder, enjoying the silent function of all his joints. They had not run this well in a decade.

To his surprise, she stood on tiptoes and softly kissed him on the lips. She hugged him and whispered so softly into his ear, she had to know only he could hear it. "Be careful."

The madam came out of nowhere and pulled Tiko back inside and closed the door.

"Thanks for the tune-up, man." Oren flexed his fingers. "What are M7 nanites?"

"They are dedicated military-grade specialty nanites," Ty said. "They cannot self-replicate. They are... too dangerous."

9

"I thought seven series nanites were for medical. For surgery and stuff." Oren was now leading the way through wider avenues that increasingly more people.

"Parts and charts next," Ty told him.

"Headed that way now," Oren said. "I won't be able to go in there with you. No kids."

"You just went into a brothel with me," Ty said. "A weapons dealership before that."

"Yeah, but this place is legit. Adults only," Oren said. "Grown-ups. Know what I mean. Boring. She will be in the last booth on the right." He stopped and pointed to a noodle shop. "I'll be in here. Just ahead is the place. It's called The Crown."

As Oren disappeared, Ty could see the establishment in the center of the next block. A stone awning covered the walkway in front like an old hotel. There was an oversized doorman dressed in black who was mostly cyborg and made no attempt to hide the fact. As Ty approached, the doorman opened the door for him, saying nothing.

There was a podium in the center of the lobby made of rich looking dark stained wood that was such a good simulation Ty thought it might be real. It matched the floors and the dark paneling on the walls of the dimly lit lounge to his right.

The podium sign politely said, *PLEASE SEAT YOURSELF.*

Beethoven was softly playing on invisible speakers.

Three steps down into the lounge, Ty was surprised by how many people were there at this hour. It was a smoking lounge. People were smoking pipes or cigars and talking quietly or reading low-light plates or actual books. The kind made from dead trees.

No one paid Ty any attention as he moved along the line of booths on the right. He felt out of place for the first time since he arrived in Greco. No one else seemed to be overtly armed in there.

The last booth was more like a small room or alcove. It was about three meters square with heavy drapes that could be drawn closed at the opening for additional privacy. A bald, ebony-skinned woman with a thick body and heavy breasts leaned back in the booth. The remains of a large meal still sat before her.

She held up a freshly lit cigar that was the same color as her skin. Her fingernails were long to the point of impractical, but they were beautifully painted. She looked Ty up and down but said nothing.

"Excuse me, I am looking for Penelope," Ty said in a polite tone. "The last booth on the right."

In addition to a copious amount of jewelry, she had ornate ear cuffs that provided comms without implants. Ty could hear someone speaking over the link, but could not make out the words.

"Picking up or dropping off?" she said, before she made an overly sensual puff on the cigar.

"Both, I hope," Ty replied.

"Please have a seat, but don't scratch my booth," Penelope said as she gestured to his carbine on the sling.

Ty smoothly swung the rifle to the front as he sat to her right, facing the lane he had just walked.

"I am looking for some parts and charts for an old S22." Ty paused. "For the Arkham Branch."

Both of Penelope's eyebrows shot up. She tried to cover her smile with a few more puffs on her cigar.

"You flatter me." She looked at him closely then, "Even if I had those charts, even if you had a million credits, there is no way I could risk selling them. I enjoy my existence too much to risk it."

"How about two million credits?" Ty said deadpan, quiet and in a deep growl.

"Not for sale," she said uncomfortably.

"Five million," Ty barely whispered. He leaned in.

"Not. For. Sale." It pained her to say it. "I know only one person that has them."

"In the Black Market, everything is for sale," Ty said, as his sensors detected weapons powering up somewhere around him. "One simply needs to find the correct currency."

Ty leaned back into the seat and began unbuttoning his tunic, revealing his sternum plate. An arcane symbol began to glow faintly with a pulsing red.

"Without those charts, I have failed my mission, and my continued existence has no meaning," Ty said.

The horror on Penelope's face said she knew what the symbol meant. She knew what he was. She knew her next decision would decide whether Greco remained or the entire city was to become one giant smoking radioactive crater.

She held up a hand to stop thugs that Ty had still not seen. She puffed her cigar and collected herself, and she tapped off the long column of ashes onto her dinner plate.

"Not for sale." She puffed and blew a smoke ring. "But I will trade for… a favor."

Ty's sensors detected the micro drone listeners.

***

"What the hell did you do?" Oren said in a loud whisper as Ty sat across from him at the noodle shop. "The blast shields dropped on the front door and all the windows. Then the doorman ran! I've never seen a cyborg move that fast."

"I was… negotiating," Ty said.

"What happened? Did you get the charts?" Oren drank some broth from his bowl.

"Almost. I need to make one stop first."

"What's in the bag?" Oren gestured at the duffel Ty had set on the floor by the table.

"It's the navigation actuator I needed." Ty smiled then. "Penelope has a well-stocked kitchen in there, as well as spare parts, considering it's a cigar lounge."

"Ha! You really think that place is a cigar lounge?" Oren was shaking his head.

"She also gave me this." Ty placed an apple-sized, twenty-sided device on the table between them.

Oren spewed out the soup he had in his mouth as he tried to push away from the thing. He threw a napkin over it and rapidly looked in every direction, hoping no one else saw it.

"Are you insane?" He was whispering again. "Do you even know what that is?"

"You didn't even blink at the thermal detonator, man," Ty said as he looked at the device and the napkin both.

"Possession of a Beel-Switch is so illegal. It's the death penalty for **ME** if I don't turn you and Penelope in, right f'ing now." Oren stood up as if to go.

"But you won't turn me in, will you?" Ty said. "Because what she wants me to do is to find a someone named Lita Wheeler, and give it to her."

These words stopped Oren in his tracks. He just stared at Ty with wide eyes. After a minute, Oren started to laugh. The heartfelt nature of the mirth was contagious. Ty smiled and then joined him in laughter. He had to hand Oren a napkin to wipe his eyes before he was done and could speak again.

"OK. Let me get this straight." Oren leaned on the table with both hands. "In order for you to get the charts you want, all you have to do is carry a Beel-Switch, the deadliest, most illegal weapon I know of, and give it to the most wanted assassin on the planet. Is that about right?"

"What do you know about Wheeler?" Ty asked quietly.

"Lita Wheeler is a merc and assassin, but mostly she kills people that have pissed her off," Oren whispered. "I hear she's really pissed off at the Citadel right now. And now someone wants her to have a Beel-Switch?"

"You forgot the part about getting it done before sunrise," Ty added casually.

"You neglected to tell me that part." Oren was about to start laughing again when he felt the muzzle of a gun pressed against the base of his neck.

"I hear you're looking for me." It was a woman's voice.

"That was easier than I thought," Ty said, smiling as he poured some green tea into a small porcelain cup.

"There is nothing easy about Greco City or the Black Market," Lita Wheeler said, remaining still as a statue. The gun she held to the kid's neck didn't move a millimeter.

Ty sipped his tea before saying, "You probably already know that this is a setup, and a trap by the Citadel to capture you. You have pissed off a lot of people on this planet. As usual."

"I know," she said. "The Beel-Switch is real, though. I need it."

Ty looked up at her then. She had long, wild black hair. She wore HUD wraparound glasses and a black face mask filter that covered the lower half of her face. A silver, ornate comm-unit ear cuff was on her right ear. She wore a charcoal gray poncho that went to her knees in front and back. It was very quiet, almost unnaturally hushed clothing.

"If my sensors could detect your micro drone audio bugs in the lounge, a professional sweep could as well."

"Your sensors didn't detect shit," she said and held up a remote detonator. "Setup. Indeed." She pressed the button, and a series of loud concussions exploded from the lounge across the street. The blast shields bulged out in places, and dust emerged around some areas.

When Ty turned back to look, the Beel-Switch and Lita Wheeler were both gone.

"She seemed nice," Oren said, as Ty finished his tea and picked up the data chip she had traded for the device.

***

"Where are you going?" Oren had to jog a little to keep up. They had been moving quickly south for fifteen minutes already.

"The South Gate, where I came in," Ty replied, without slowing down. "Oren, you seem like a decent kid." Ty looked down at him. "Greco City has the potential to be…"

Two men stepped out of the shadows directly in front of them. Another man stayed behind cover to the right.

"Ty Crowley. Where do you think you are going in such a hurry—" The man's sentence was cut off by the knife that had penetrated his left eye. Ty had thrown it so fast it appeared as if by magic.

The second man was distracted by it for only a moment. It was enough time for Ty to draw his handgun and shoot him in the face without breaking stride.

"All we want is the data-chip, man." This man had been smarter than the other two. He had a rifle and some cover behind a retaining wall. Ty noticed the type of weapon it was and moved.

"Not for sale," was all Ty said, as he kept walking.

"Who said I was buying?" the man said, as he opened fire. It was only a frange carbine designed for humans. The glass rounds shattered on Ty's breastplate.

Ty was flattered. They really did think he was human.

Oren dove for cover. Ty dropped the shooter with a single shot to the very top of his exposed cranium.

"Not. For. Sale," Ty said and fired six more times, never slowing. Each bullet found a separate target. Armed men fell all around them.

Ty kept walking as he hitched up the bag holding the navigation actuator.

"Where are you going?" Oren ran up beside him again.

"Back to my ship." Ty glanced at Oren. "You got somewhere you can lay low, kid? May need to keep your head down for a couple of days."

There was a loud THUNK, a sound of such low frequency it was felt in the chest more than it was heard. This finally got Ty to stop and look back.

The lights in the high Citadel were fading out. A half dozen light flyers were dropping from the sky like stones.

"Oh, shit," Ty said. He ran.

***

"What was that?" Oren asked. Somehow he was keeping up. The navigation actuator and his weapons must have been heavier than Ty thought.

"The Beel-Switch," Ty replied. "All electrical activity within the impacted area will be suppressed for about five minutes. It only hits a sphere about one kilometer across. Organics will die, devices deactivate, some shit falls apart, electrons stop flowing. Up there, it will only affect the Citadel proper. The bastards."

Ty hurtled over a crashed grav-cycle. Oren detoured through a vendor booth. Everyone was just standing around, looking at the Citadel. Smoking crash sites from the flyers added to the confusion.

"Why are we running?"

"When physics starts back up, stuff does not react well." Ty rounded a corner and stopped with his back to a thick stone section. This entire alley was carved into the rock.

Civil defense bells began to ring. People began running, getting under cover.

"Now what?" Oren asked, but followed Ty's lead. They were only about a hundred meters from the South Bridge Gate, where he had entered Greco.

"Just wait," Ty said, as an enormous man approached the mouth of the alley from the bridge.

"All I want is the data chip." He began to raise a huge rail gun.

"It's not for sale."

"I wasn't asking." He aimed.

It all happened at once. Another deeper, THUNK, followed by a massive explosion. The rail gun fired, going wide, the round impacting the opposite alley wall. At the same time, the man's head flew from its shoulders. Lita joined them with her back to the wall in the alley as she resheathed a huge knife.

"Thanks," Ty said, gesturing at the head of the cyborg.

"He's still alive." Oren pointed to the head. Its eyes followed them. Oren started to leave the alley when he was pulled back by both Lita and Ty.

A moment later, high-velocity shrapnel tore through the area. Three seconds after that, it was raining gravel. It was a full thirty seconds before it subsided.

"How did you get here so fast?" Ty asked. "How could you get to the top of the Citadel and back here so fast?"

"I didn't go to the top. I just went to the garage level right after I left you. I attached the Beel-Switch to the top of the elevator. One of the twenty switches is an elevation trigger," she said. "I didn't expect it to go all the way up so soon."

"The Black Market is gonna love this," Oren added, as he peeked around the corner. "Leadership was bad for business."

"Let's move," Lita said, with confidence.

In nearly perfect unison, Ty and Oren said, "Where?"

"The Arkham Branch. I hear you have charts and an S22." Lita Wheeler pulled her mask down and then pushed up her goggles. Her smile shone brightly. "It's my favorite kind of ship."

***

High-velocity shrapnel had caught the men guarding the bridge in the open. The automated sentry there was never activated. Civilians were emerging from shelters. The streets were littered with debris and the bodies of soldiers.

"You can come with us, Oren," Ty said. "You're good under pressure. It's going to be chaos here for a while. Anarchy returns."

"Ahhh, but the Black Market will be hotter than ever." He laughed. "Money to be made. Besides, my parents need me."

"Parents?" Lita looked incredulous.

"Don't act surprised," Oren said. "The orphan thing is a good money maker. My parents own the noodle shop I was recommending. Don't tell anyone."

"Your secret is safe with us," Ty said.

"Can I ask a question?" Oren paused with them at the gate. "How did this suddenly become an us? You and her."

18

"Tell him," Lita said.

"It was always a rescue mission," Ty said. "When you are a wanted killer on a planet full of killers that's run by a Black Market, the best flare is to have something that is Not-For-Sale."

"Be safe, little man." Lita kissed his cheek and then followed Ty through the gate.

BIO: Emma G Rose intended to become a badass girl reporter like Nellie Bly, until the Christmas Eve she stood on a riverbank waiting for rescue divers to pull a body from the water. That's when she stopped waiting and wandered off to explore the world instead. She is the author of the fantasy novels, *Nothing's Ever Lost*, *Near Life Experience*, and *Remade: A Short Story*.

https://www. emmagauthor.com /

ABSOLUTELY POSITIVE

by Emma G. Rose

Candi Rylie woke to the artificial sunlight and gentle voice of her Goodmorning Alarm. "Wake up, it's a wonderful day. Wake up, it's a wonderful day."

Normally she would have been out of bed before it finished saying "wonderful" for the first time. Today she lingered under the covers for two and a half repetitions. She felt more tired than usual and wondered if she was coming down with something.

"I choose to feel good today," she told herself.

She touched the dome of the alarm and the voice stopped, but the soft yellow light shined on. It illuminated her cheerful blue curtains and the old fashioned frame around the picture of her and her brother Gil on the top of Mount Washington. She nudged the picture frame to face away from her. Something about it made her feel...less than positive.

No time for that. She had lots to do today. After she showered and dressed she went out into the kitchen. In addition to her usual coffee and bran toast with avocado spread, the Kitchen AI spat out two small pills.

"Thank you, Betty. What are these pills?" Candi asked the AI.

"The pink pill is B12, the white pill is a Positivity Booster."

Apparently, the AI had noticed her slowness to get out of bed. She took the pills. They could only help her feel better. Of course, she was totally fine, but there was nothing wrong with feeling just that little bit better.

Candi went outside and got into her bright green Tesla Bug. While the car drove her to work, Candi read texts and listened to the messages her friends had left over the last 12 hours.

"Thinking of you."

"Sending you good vibes."

There was even a video message from the Vice President of her company. He welcomed her back to work and hoped she'd enjoyed her time off. It was so artfully edited that you could barely tell that her name had been dubbed into the same stock video they always sent.

As always, the receptionist Becca greeted her with a bright smile. "Hello welcome to HelperLabs. We're so glad you're here today." Her eyes were wide open, like she might miss something wonderful if she blinked.

Candi tried to match Becca's smile. After Becca's second retraining, the company had decided her new skills made her better suited for a customer-facing role instead of accounting. Now she mostly sat at the reception desk saying the same welcome speech over and over. Candi wondered why they didn't just put a bot in her place.

"Good morning, Becca. It's nice to see you." Candi always tried to be nice to retrained employees.

Becca tilted her head and giggled. "Just a reminder, your positivity levels may be monitored to support productivity."

Candi walked past her to the elevator. She handed out smiles and greetings to the coworkers she met along the way. Candi was a creative designer on the Helper Bot team, a small robot to help with incidental household chores.

In her cube, she noticed someone had watered her plants while she was away. They bloomed brightly in their colorful pots. When she logged on to her computer, her quote of the day popped up first. "Keep your face to the sunshine and you cannot see a shadow." — Helen Keller. That was an important reminder at the moment. She wondered if it was a coincidence, or if the quote generator used personal data.

Her agenda for the day included an R&D meeting, a development block, and one-on-one with her mentor, but first, she got to attend the Helper Bot sales progress meeting. She grabbed her tablet and her folder of hand-drawn sketches and headed for the conference room.

Bran, the team lead, was already there setting up the presentation. As always, Bran was impeccably dressed. His striped white and blue shirt was tucked neatly into his khaki slacks. When he looked up at her, his smile glittered like glass.

"Welcome back, Candi. I hope you're having a great day."

She smiled brightly, trying not to show the little twitch of tiredness. She wondered if she could have used another day or two to rest, but no, celebration leave was already a whole week. The celebration of life was over and there was nothing else to be done. She should be back at work.

"Of course. It's wonderful to be back."

Other members of the team started filtering into the room. Felix, one of the programmers, took the seat next to hers. He tapped one long finger on her manila folder and grinned.

"Still living in the 21st century, Candi?"

Candi blushed. She never seemed to get the designs right when she drew on her tablet. Pen and paper were better, at least for the first drafts. Once she knew what she was doing she could digitize the design.

For the first time, she seriously wondered if she should stop using the old fashioned method. It might not be great to be seen as weird by her coworkers. Especially after what happened to Gil.

"I forgot to take home my tablet," she said.

Bran clapped his hands, ending their conversation before Felix could tease her anymore. "All right folks, thank you all for coming. Let's start the meeting with new and good. Candi, what's new and good in your life?"

Candi blinked, she hadn't expected to go first, or at all, really. "Um, I...I have some new eye designs that I think are really spot-on."

"Great," Bran said. "Tiffany."

"I got a new Living Room Buddy that monitors my physical activity to make sure I'm healthy and happy."

"Great, yellow team worked on that. Be sure to send them a gold star if you like it."

They went around the table, sharing little bits of positivity with each other. It was the standard meeting ice breaker. When everyone had gotten to share, Bran started the business part of the meeting. He stood up and rubbed his hands together.

"Some of you may have the opportunity to work on other projects soon." His smile seemed to show every perfectly white tooth. "The public seems really committed to their existing home automation solutions. We're looking for opportunities to share value for now, but in the long run, we may need to reexamine staffing decisions unless we see a big upswing in demand."

He paused and then Loraine DuPree, the QA manager, said, "So what you're saying is…" All eyes turned to her. "…that if we don't improve sales people are going to start losing their jobs?"

Everyone looked back to Bran. There was a creaking of chairs and a clearing of throats.

Finally Bran said, "I'm sure we all want to keep a positive attitude, Loraine. Unless you think you could benefit from some retraining."

Bran let the statement hang in the air. Everyone looked at something other than Loraine as he moved the meeting along. Loraine was known for being a little odd. She rarely joined in on the after-work happy hour at the microbrewery and she frowned almost as often as she smiled.

Her cube was barely even decorated. There were no inspirational posters or mantras to be seen. Just a single houseplant in a plain white pot and a small collection of smooth black stones in a neat line. Candi was fairly sure that management only kept Loraine on the team because she was very, very good at spotting logistical snafus before they became real challenges. If someone was useful enough, management sometimes overlooked a less than enthusiastic attitude. Not at Gil's company, though.

Candi started to giggle. Since Bran's cheerful voice was the only sound in the room, everyone noticed immediately. A few of her coworkers glanced at her out of the corners of their eyes. When she didn't stop right away, their glances turned into outright stares.

"Is there something funny you'd like to share with us, Candi? I'm sure everyone enjoys a good laugh," Bran said.

There was nothing funny, nothing at all. Candi had no idea why she was laughing. She tried to stop, which only made her hiccup. Now she was giggling and hiccupping and everyone was staring.

"No. I mean. I'm sorry. I just. I need. Excuse me." She fled the room.

***

Alone in the lady's room, Candi managed to get the giggling under control. The hiccups weren't so easy. She was holding her breath, trying to stop them, when Loraine came into the bathroom.

"Hey," Loraine said. "Are you okay?"

"I'm great," Candi answered. "How are you?"

Loraine stared at her. "You're not great. You lost it back there."

"I am." Candi said, and hiccupped again. "I just thought of something funny."

Loraine raised one eyebrow. "No, you didn't."

Why was she being so pushy? It wasn't very nice. "Everything's perfect, really," Candi said.

Loraine stepped closer, trapping Candi between her and the mirror.

"I read about your brother," Loraine said, low enough that no one could have overheard even if they were in the next stall.

"We had a lovely celebration of life for him," Candi said.

Loraine stared at her even more intently. "I knew him," she said.

Candi started feeling nervous. Why would Loraine have known Gil? He worked in a completely different company. And why had she followed Candi into the bathroom? She tried to remind herself that Loraine probably couldn't help being so intense. She was doing her best, just like Candi. Just like Gil had been. That thought made her neck tense. She didn't like it.

26

Loraine reached out and turned on the hand dryer. Rushing air echoed against the pink tiles. She leaned closer, until their faces were almost touching. Her voice dropped to a whisper.

"You're allowed to be upset, you know."

Candi made herself smile. Loraine was acting really strange. Did she know what had really happened to Gil? Candi tried to push the question away. She knew that Gil had died of a heart attack. Never mind that they had no history of heart problems in the family. Never mind that Gil was fit and healthy. It could happen. It had happened. It had just been his time.

"A positive attitude is our best defense against the forces that threaten our way of life," Candi said, parroting the oft-repeated quote from President Tracey's State of the Union address. Positivity would help them fight gloominess, and poverty, and all of those completely preventable issues that had plagued humanity for too long. It also seemed like the best defense against whatever less than positive thing Loraine might be wrapped up in. Especially if someone could hear them over the hand dryer.

"Look," Loraine stabbed at her wrist phone. An address popped up on Candi's phone screen. "If you want to talk, come to this address tonight at 6:30."

"What would I want to talk about?" Candi asked. She was whispering too.

"Your brother. What really happened to him. How you feel about it." Loraine's eyes never left Candi's face as she spoke.

"He's in a better place now."

"No, he's dead," Loraine said, her face blank, unsmiling. She turned toward the door.

Candi exhaled. At least her hiccups had disappeared. Loraine's approach had scared them right out of her.

"Come tonight, and make sure you have some credits ready to transfer," Loraine said.

"Credits?"

"You know how they say talk is cheap?" Loraine said. "This one isn't."

She left the bathroom. For a few moments afterward, Candi stared down at her wrist phone. The address was somewhere on the industrial side of town, near the train depot. What was going on here? She and Loraine weren't exactly friends. Not that Candi hadn't tried. She always made it a point to be nice to her coworkers, especially those, like Loraine, who didn't quite fit in. But Loraine had known Gil. At least, she said she had.

Candi admitted to herself that she was curious. Nobody except Gil had ever talked to her with that level of intensity. But there was no way she could follow these breadcrumbs. She didn't want to get mixed up in anything unpleasant. Fortunately, right now there was work to do. The meeting must be over and everyone would be wondering where she was. With more effort than usual, she turned her mind to more positive things, like the new eye color picker for the Home Buddy.

***

Candi's one-on-one with her mentor didn't go quite the way she'd thought it would. She approached Morgan's office ready to talk about the progress she'd made on the new eye designs and how well the team was doing. Instead, Morgan opened the conversation with "I heard there was some disruption at the sales meeting this morning. Would you like to tell me about it?"

She hadn't even offered Candi a water. That's how Candi knew this was serious.

"I'm so sorry, Morgan. I don't know what came over me," Candi said.

"You know, Candi, we gave you a whole week off to deal with your personal life."

Candi thought about that week. Running around, planning the celebration of life. The speeches, the flowers. Gil didn't even like flowers. She felt the giggles bubbling up again and swallowed them back.

"Yes, and I really appreciate that."

"We even sent flowers."

Candi almost choked in an effort not to laugh. She took a deep breath and made herself smile.

"Thank you, so much. They were lovely."

"Yes, so I think it's time that you bring your mind back to the work at hand. The new Home Buddy is an important product. It could revolutionize the way people live."

Relieved that they were getting back on course, Candi jumped to agree. "Oh, yes. I'm very excited about the new eye designs. I wanted to show you what I've been working on." She flipped open the folder she'd been holding on her lap. For the next 15 minutes, they pored over Candi's renderings. Morgan didn't even comment on the antique technology.

***

As Candi stepped out of Morgan's office, she spotted Loraine across the room. They locked gazes. The corner of Loraine's mouth twitched, treating Candi to a little half-smile. Startled, Candi realized that it was the first real smile she'd ever seen from Loraine. All the others, the ones Loraine doled out so reluctantly throughout the day, were manufactured to keep management off her back. For the first time, Candi suspected that Loraine might have a sense of humor.

Felix touched her elbow, making Candi yelp. She hadn't realized he was there.

"Whoa, you good?"

Candi put a hand to her heart, but forced herself to grin. "Sorry, you snuck up on me."

"I just wanted to check that you're coming to happy hour."

"Oh, I'd love to, but I promised my mom I'd help her with something."

Felix nodded. "I get it. Family first, right?"

"Right."

As he walked away, Candi realized she'd lied to him. Why had she done that? What if someone found out? Her cheeks felt hot. For the second time that day, she wondered if she might be getting sick.

***

Safe from prying eyes behind the tinted glass of her Tesla, Candi called her mother.

"How are you, mom?"

"Peachy keen, jelly bean." They were the same words her mother always used, but somehow they seemed a little less buoyant than usual. "And how are you?"

"Good, good, first day back at work today."

"Oh, that's fun. How'd it go?"

Candi sifted through the events of the day for something worth mentioning. Complaining never did anyone any good, and besides, her mom probably had enough on her mind.

"Great. Morgan loves my new eye designs."

"That's wonderful, dear." Candi caught the distracted tone.

"Mom, are you sure you're feeling okay? I could come over if you want."

"Oh no, sweetheart, you have your own life to live. I'm just feeling a little under the weather today," her voice quavered. "I wouldn't want you to catch anything."

Gil's name hung between them, although neither of them had spoken it aloud. Candi felt a stinging sensation in her eyes. She adjusted the air vent so it wasn't blowing directly on her face.

"Besides, I'm sure you have somewhere to be this evening."

Candi bit the inside of her cheek, thinking, *You know what. I think I do.*

After hanging up with her mom, she pushed the address that Loraine had given her to the car's GPS.

***

The address was way on the other side of town, in an industrial area Candi had never been to. It would take her an hour to get there, which meant she'd be about 15 minutes early if she went without dinner. Fortunately, she always carried some trail mix in her purse.

She queued up an affirmation podcast and then turned up the volume so she could hear it over the sound of her crunching. By the time the Tesla pulled into a chain-link enclosed parking spot next to a warehouse, Candi had finished her snack and started wondering if she should really be here. This didn't look like a very pleasant place.

The building had once been a cheery yellow, but time and weather had worn it to a weepy beige. Even without getting out of the car she could see that the red metal door was rusted. The parking lot was in need of repaving. It was still the old asphalt mix that needed constant patching, not the new self-healing ecomac. To make it all even less welcoming, the sun was going down and it seemed like only about half of the streetlights worked.

She was just about to tell the Tesla to go home when she spotted Loraine in the shadow of the building. Her long, drab coat had blended into the wall of the warehouse. Candi wondered where she'd even found such a garment.

Loraine waved, and Candi could either be rude, or get out of the car. She got out of the car. Loraine smiled that crooked smile as Candi approached. Candi smiled back, trying not to show her discomfort.

"I'm glad you came."

"Thank you for inviting me."

Loraine's hand closed on her arm. "You brought credits?"

"I have my wrist phone."

"Good, come on."

Loraine pulled her toward the red metal door. As they got closer, Candi saw that it was propped open just a sliver. Something about the dark strip made her nervous, and she wished she was at happy hour with the rest of her workmates.

Inside, the warehouse was dark and smelled like old fish had been stored there a long time ago. It made Candi's nose twitch.

Then Loraine pushed her through a curtain and warm yellow light dazzled her eyes. She blinked rapidly, trying to see where they were. Metal clanged underfoot. Her eyes adjusted, and she looked down from a raised catwalk at what had once been the manufacturing floor. Colorful tents bloomed like flowers between abandoned machines. Open flames burned in raised braziers between the tents. The smell of something both spicy and musky filled the air.

Candi thought Loraine must have pulled her into another world. "Where are we?" It came out as a gasp.

Loraine wasn't listening. She pulled Candi toward a woman dressed all in black, with a skull pendant around her neck. Candi shied away, but Loraine still had a grip on her arm.

"Candi, this is Elise."

Elise's hand darted out and Candi felt a pinprick of pain in her palm.

Candi gasped. "What are you doing?"

Elise raised her hand in a wait-just-a-second gesture. She looked down at her wrist phone.

"If anyone asks where you were tonight, you were out buying positivity pills from her," Loraine said, as if nothing had happened.

"And here they are," Elise said, pulling a pill bottle from her black satchel.

Loraine had dragged her all this way for Happy Pills? Candi had no less than three friends with side-businesses selling them. Carol had even earned a vacation to Maui for being top seller in her district.

"Oh, thank you, but I already have some in my Kitchen Buddy."

Elise snorted. "Oh, you mean Happy Pills. You might as well mainline caffeine. It would work just as well. These actually take your body chemistry into account. Come back in two weeks and we'll see how you're tolerating them. I can adjust the dosage if necessary."

"But…"

"Candi, Elise knows what she's talking about. Now give the woman 200 credits, and let's get down to the tent."

"I could buy two bottles of Happy Pills for 200 credits. Three if there was a good sale on. Are we doing something illegal?"

"It's not exactly illegal. But it's not exactly not, either. The extra money helps us make sure no one looks too closely."

Elise was clearly not totally happy. "Are you sure she should be here?"

"This is Gil's sister."

Elise's whole posture changed when she heard that. Her shoulders drooped but her eyes smiled. Looking at her made Candi's heart hurt. Or maybe that was the unexpected mention of her brother.

"I'm sorry for your loss. Gil was a great guy."

"You knew him?"

"We all did," Elise said. "He came here a lot."

Gil had come here? Why?

"Now will you please trust me?" Loraine added.

"Okay," Candi pushed the credits to Elise's wrist phone and took the pill bottle.

Loraine led Candi down six metal steps to the warehouse floor. Spicy smoke filled the air and Candi found herself taking deep breaths to drink it in. She felt her shoulders release a tension she hadn't known they were holding.

Dancing flames cast shadows on the cloth walls of the tents. Candi could hear voices from inside some of them. Outside, a small banner hung over the door of each tent. The one closest to her said "Fear." Next to it was "Jealousy."

A voice shouted. Candi's head snapped toward the noise. It seemed to come from a red tent marked "Anger."

"What is this place?"

"It's a kind of market," Loraine said. "Only you pay to leave things behind instead of taking them away."

"I don't understand."

"You will." She ducked into a purple tent. The sign over the door said "Grief."

Soft yellowish light illuminated the inside. Area rugs softened the floor and their footfalls. A circle of metal folding chairs had been made more comfortable with pillows and faux fur blankets. The few people seated in the chairs whispered softly to each other.

A woman in a long skirt greeted Loraine with a smile and hug. "And who is this?"

"Thea, this is Gil's sister, Candi."

"Ah," Thea said. "We loved Gil. I'm so sorry for your loss, my dear. Come sit with us and we'll get started."

Not wanting to tell this kind woman that she had no idea what they were doing here, and somewhat excited to meet all of these people who had known her brother, Candi followed her to the circle of chairs. Loraine sat down beside her.

Candi glanced around the circle. To her surprise, she spotted Tate, a guy she'd known in high school. She thought he was studying to be a doctor now. Candi smiled at him.

And then Thea leaned over and struck an iron bell with a small wooden mallet. It rang with a deep resonance that stilled the tumble of Candi's thoughts.

"We have a new member of our circle today, so I'll take this opportunity to remind you all that this is a place of healing. What happens here, stays here. To begin, I invite you each to speak aloud the name of the person you love who has died."

Died. Candi shivered to hear the word spoken so bluntly. And then voices spoke around the circle.

"My mother, Lacey."

"My cousin, Isaac."

"My patient," Tate said.

"My babies, Donnie and Jill."

Loraine said, "My sister, Hope."

Then everyone looked at Candi. She hesitated a moment, but she had to say something. They weren't going to stop staring until she did. "My brother, Gil."

A sigh rippled around the room. "Thank you, everyone. Loraine, would you like to start?"

"My sister, Hope, was my favorite person in the whole world. All my life, I wanted to be just like her. I took the same classes she took, played the same sports, enrolled in the same college.

"She always seemed so happy and confident. And then she dropped dead in the middle of a lecture hall. They said it was an aneurism. We held a celebration of life, but the whole time, all I could think about was all the things my sister would never do.

"All my life I'd followed in her footsteps, now I was terrified that what had happened to her would happen to me. I felt guilty for feeling that way. And then I felt bad for making her death all about me.

"But the worst part was, everyone just stopped talking about her. She was the center of the universe for me, and not only was she gone, but I felt like she'd never existed."

Candi wrapped her arms around her body and listened in shock. She'd never heard anyone talk like this, and she'd certainly never suspected Loraine had been through something so...so, not great.

Strangely, no one else seemed surprised. Someone asked, "What did Hope study in college?"

"Business management."

"What did she want to do with her degree?"

"She always said she'd start a business, but the type of business changed at least once a month."

Someone chuckled, and Loraine smiled.

Thea smiled back at her. "Thank you for telling us about Hope, Loraine. Candi, do you feel comfortable telling us about Gil?"

Candi's stomach clenched. "I'm not so sure—"

Loraine nudged her shoulder. "Go ahead," she whispered.

"Gil was my brother," she began. "He loved to be outside. He climbed mountains and...and hiked on the weekends." She stopped because her eyes had filled with tears.

Silence stretched on too long. Everyone was watching her, she took a deep breath, but couldn't continue.

A voice cut in from across the circle. It was Tate. "A week ago, a patient came into the hospital where I work. He was dead on arrival. He was also someone I knew, the older brother of a school friend."

Candi felt nauseous. He was talking about Gil. She knew he was talking about Gil.

"The attending had a long conversation with the PR Rep, and when it was over, he told me to put "heart attack" as the cause of death. But I didn't think it really was. I've never seen neck bruises like that on a heart attack patient."

To Candi's shame, she started to cry. She'd known they'd lied, known it from the moment she'd gotten the call that Gil was dead, but she hadn't been able to believe it until now.

She found herself talking, the words spilling out of her mouth without passing through her brain first. "He was always getting in trouble for not being cheerful enough, for focusing on the wrong things. He was always thinking.

"Mom kept telling him to stay positive and it would be okay. But it was like he couldn't do it. He was always noticing things. He'd say, 'Mr. Pickens doesn't like his wife.' Mom would tell him not to talk about his boss that way, but he was always right. I didn't want to see it, but he was always right.

"The week before he passed on, we were having dinner with mom and he said, 'This job is going to kill me.' And mom just said 'Oh honey, keep your chin up.' "

Murmurs danced around the circle. Loraine tightened her grip on Candi's hand. Candi was suddenly absurdly grateful for that contact. It gave her the courage to say the words that had been caught in the back of her throat for the last week.

"He was right. That job did kill him."

Candi was sobbing so hard she could barely get the words out. The person sitting beside her, a person she didn't even know, put his arm over her shoulders.

Candi felt like she was drowning, but at the same time, she felt liberated. Nobody shushed her. Nobody told her not to say such things. Nobody said, "At least he's not suffering anymore," or "Everything happens for a reason." They just held her while she cried.

***

When it was all over, Candi felt like a dishrag twisted until every last shred of moisture was wrung from her body. She felt empty and exhausted, but somehow, better than she had before. As she staggered out of the tent, the comparatively cooler air of the factory floor was as shocking as a bucket of cold water to the face. She gasped.

"You okay?" Loraine asked.

"I feel...I feel like I could sleep for a month."

"Yeah, it hits you that way the first time. You'll come back, though?"

"Yes. Of course."

As they walked back between the tents and out into the dark evening, Candi said, "Thank you for inviting me. I mean, I felt so...so...bad, when I started, but now I feel, lighter somehow?"

Loraine smiled her real smile. "It's pretty amazing isn't it?"

"But, Loraine, what am I going to do?"

"Keep feeling the pain. Keep dealing with it as best you can."

Candi dropped her voice. "They killed Gil."

Loraine caught Candi's arm. "You are not alone. We're here and we're willing to face whatever comes. We'll change the world one person at a time."

"Will that work?"

"It has to."

***

Candi drove directly from the warehouse to her mother's apartment. She didn't even call first. Her mother's voice came through the doorbell. Candi smiled into the camera. "Hi, mom."

"Oh, sweetie, it's lovely to see you, come in, come in."

She followed her mother into the living room. When they were both seated she said, "Mom, I just wanted to tell you how glad I am that Gil has gone to a better place." She smiled as she spoke, watching her mother's face carefully.

Her mother's eyes widened for an instant, and Candi saw tears there. "Me too, sweetie, me too. He was too good for this world."

Candi reached across the space between them, and hugged her mother.

BIO: Liz Hayes is an engineer by inclination and training. She began her career at Jet Propulsion Labs, and later moved east to be an analyst and statistician for the Federal Government.

She's fascinated by medieval reenactments, and writes LOTR fanfiction under the penname Uvatha the Horseman. While doing the research for a fanfic about Sauron forging the Ring, she joined the local guild and became an amateur blacksmith herself. It's an excellent hobby which combines her two favorite things, craft projects and pyromania.

She lives in Northern Virginia with her husband and three teenage children she keeps in line by threatening to show up at PTA meetings in full Jedi robes.

Alliance of Enemies

by Liz Hayes

The bell pealed in the tower above the University grounds, calling students in their short scholars' robes to morning classes. Olwen trailed behind his roommates. They were a close-knit group, all born into wealthy and powerful families, and all related to each other. Olwen had been assigned to the same dormitory room as they were, an accident of available space. He didn't belong. He trailed behind the group, silent and wary, careful not to draw attention to himself.

"Remind me, what we were supposed to read for today?" Prince Turstan asked one of his cousins. Tall and blonde, with perfect posture and perfect teeth, the young prince radiated self-confidence. Olwen couldn't stand him.

The black-haired cousin said, "I'm not better prepared than you are. I started to read the assignment, but I fell asleep with my face in the book."

Turstan set his lips in a hard line. He entered the building, his head high, as if facing his own execution. For all his high rank and power, Olwen felt sorry for him.

"The assignment was about the Battle of Norgrad." For the first time, the others seemed to notice him, even though they'd shared bed and board for the last two weeks. "It was a sea battle, fought off the coast of Norgrad between our side, the Island Kingdom of Armelos, and Banea on the Mainland. We outnumbered them, but their sails cast a wind shadow across ours. We couldn't maneuver, and they were able to defeat us."

For the rest of the walk to class, Olwen filled him in on every date and place name about the Battle of Norgrad he knew. Turstan thanked him and relaxed visibly.

They filed into the classroom. Olwen took a place on one of the long benches near the lectern. His roommates sat in the back of the classroom, whispering and laughing. Olwen ignored them. He wiped yesterday's notes from his wax tablet, then chose a stylus from his writing box.

An unfamiliar instructor entered the room, the long robes of a professional scholar sweeping around him. All the students stood. He took his place behind the lectern and motioned them to be seated. They'd never had an instructor of such high rank before. Their regular instructor was just a lecturer, only a few years out of school.

"I am Professor Sutrah. Your regular instructor can't be here today, so I will be filling in for him. Can anyone tell me the assignment for today?"

Olwen raised his hand. "The Battle of Norgrad. It was…"

"Let's hear from someone in the back. You, the blond." He pointed to Turstan, who'd sunk low on the bench as if trying to be invisible. "Tell us about the Battle of Norgrad."

Turstan stood. "Yes, sir. The Battle of Norgrad." He then recited everything Olwen had told him, every name and every date. For such an ignorant git, he had a phenomenal memory.

"Very good, young man. You've obviously decided to take your education seriously."

Olwen ground his teeth and thought about what he'd like to do to Turstan. *It's not worth it. It would be too much work to hide the body and clean up the mess.*

As they were leaving the room at the end of class, the professor called, "Hey Blondie! Mother expects you at the Palace for dinner. We're entertaining an ambassador or someone."

Olwen gawked. "Is that your brother?"

Turstan nodded. "I never expected him to show up in one of my classes. It's so embarrassing."

Olwen climbed the stairs to the large room that housed his three annoying roommates. With any luck, the room would be empty, and he would get to use the little table, the only good surface for writing.

He entered the room. Every shutter was open, letting in the most possible light. The breeze fluttered loose papers on the beds. The smell of glue was so strong it made his eyes water.

Turstan was sitting in the window alcove. He'd pulled the small table up to himself. An array of curved wooden sticks had been arranged on the surface of the table. He was gluing them with great care to a central keel of a model ship.

Annoyance welled up in Olwen. "I see you've managed to occupy both of the best spots for studying, and you aren't even doing homework."

"I am, in a way," Turstan said. "Father says I'm to run the shipyards when I'm older."

With great care, he fitted a rib into place on the keel, running a finger along the keel to check the goodness of the fit. He nodded with satisfaction. Glue oozed from around the joints, which weren't seated quite as square as they should be. It looked like the work of a child, or possibly a blind person.

When the glue dried, Turstan lifted the hull and turned it right-side up. "There. What do you think of that?"

The hull was unusually deep and narrow, giving it a squashed appearance. Olwen looked on the surface of the table for the plans, but saw only tools, boat pieces, and the glue pot.

Olwen searched for the right words. "I've never seen anything like it before."

Turstan beamed. "I'm trying to crack a problem that every shipbuilder in the kingdom has tried and failed — how to reach the Mainland in only three days."

That was the dream. A design for a very fast ship would let them export fresh fruit, outrun pirates, and defeat opposing warships. The puzzle had never been cracked.

"It's an unusually large vessel, but large vessels are fast. See how the hull has a deeper draft and narrower beam than usual? That will magnify its speed."

"It's so narrow. Won't it tip over?"

"No, because the draft counters the narrow beam."

Turstan talked like he understood shipbuilding. Olwen wondered if maybe his roommate was the real thing, after all.

***

When classes were over a day or two later, Olwen went up to the room. The space looked like it had been hit by a squall. Of the four beds, only Olwen's had been made, and discarded clothing lay wherever it had been dropped. Apparently, the servants were running late today and hadn't come through yet.

Olwen found the disorder profoundly irritating. Worst of all, Turstan's cloak lay across Olwen's neatly-made bed, almost covering the note, *Turstan, please stop leaving your things on my bed,* he'd left that morning

Olwen picked up the cloak and hung it on a peg by the door, cursing under his breath. He hadn't actually said anything to Turstan, but he'd left plenty of notes.

With a clatter of boots on the stairs down the hall, Turstan burst into the room, all exaggerated height and golden hair.

"Turstan, did you read my note?"

"Sorry, I don't believe I did." Olwen handed him the small scrap of paper. Turstan's eyes scanned it. "Oh, right."

Olwen was furious. "Do you think you can do whatever you want because you're royalty? Well, I'm not impressed."

Turstan stormed out of the room. Olwen followed him down the stairs and out to the courtyard, which was empty save for a small statue of the University's founder.

"Don't turn your back on me, I'm still talking to you," Olwen shouted at Turstan's retreating back.

Turstan whirled around. "You're just a country squire, the lowest rung of the nobility."

"I'll inherit my father's lands, but you have two older brothers. You won't inherit anything."

Turstan raised his fists. He was taller than Olwen and had a longer reach, but Olwen doubted he'd ever been in a fistfight before. Olwen had. As it stood, they were evenly matched.

The Prince threw the first punch, which grazed Olwen's chin. No matter how often you've been hit, it's still a surprise and it still hurts. Enraged, Olwen swung at him, but the prince sidestepped without apparent effort. Turstan had trained under the most famous swordsman in Armelos, while Olwen had only sparred with his father a few times, in a dusty yard they shared with chickens.

If Olwen couldn't win, he was determined to go down fighting. He swung again. Turstan blocked it easily and circled around. Olwen feinted and caught him with a blow to the eye.

Turstan staggered backward and fell against the stone statue. It wobbled on its base, then tipped over and smashed on the flagstones. The crash echoed from the buildings around the courtyard.

Turstan lay sprawled among the fragments of stone. What was left of the Founder lay on the paving stones, his head and one of his arms intact but no longer attached to his torso. Olwen stood there, horrified.

The noise drew the curious from every door opening onto the courtyard. They formed a ring around the combatants and the shattered statue. Someone pushed through the crowd and fixed them in merciless eyes.

"Care to tell me what's going on?" The Provost of the University asked. Olwen realized that, very likely, he was about to be expelled. He felt sick.

"I'm sorry. It was my fault," said Turstan.

"You knocked a historically important statue from its plinth and reduced it to stone chips, and all you can say is, 'I'm sorry'? Do you have any idea how valuable it was? And how did you even knock it over in the first place? It was supposed to be secured with iron bolts."

"Apparently not," said someone in the crowd.

The Proctor looked from Turstan to the ruined statue and back again. "I'll send someone to clean it up. Be more careful in the future."

The Proctor left and the onlookers dispersed. Turstan shot Olwen a look. "You owe me."

"Why did you take the blame for something I did? You don't even like me," said Olwen.

"You're my roommate and under my protection. I took the hit because you could have gotten expelled."

Olwen extended a hand and helped Turstan to his feet. "I don't know how I can repay you."

"Buy me a drink and we'll call it even," said Turstan.

They left the University grounds by the main gate and took the cobbled streets down to the harbor where housed Turstan's favorite wineshop. In places, the road was so steep that stairs had been built into its center.

They reached the harbor and hiked along the quay. Hundreds of ships were tied up along the quay, their names painted on their prows.

"Look at that one, the *Bilo Selhi*. It must be a merchant ship," said Olwen.

"This section is all merchant ships. We're a trading nation. Look at that one, the *Unsinkable II,* celebrating the triumph of hope over experience," said Turstan.

Most of the wharf-side drinking establishments were shuttered in mid-afternoon, but the doors of one stood wide open. Turstan led the way into its darkened interior.

They had their choice of tables. Turstan chose a small one in the back. "What do they have today? They've opened several casks of wine, most of them local and one from the Mainland," he said, reading from a chalkboard on the wall.

The barmaid came to the table. Turstan ordered two goblets of local wine, for which Olwen paid. Olwen started to relax for the first time he'd found Turstan's cloak on his bed. Turstan looked battered, and Olwen's jaw throbbed.

"What's it like growing up on the far side of the Island?" asked Turstan.

"It's the only part of the Island that's still truly rural. Mostly we worry about how our animals are doing, and whether the barley is getting enough rain."

"I called you the lowest rung of the nobility earlier. I'm sorry, I didn't mean to insult you."

"You insult me every day. It's your hobby," said Olwen. "And I'm sorry I said that about the succession."

"I'm not in line for the throne. No matter. I knew already that," said Turstan.

"Tell me about your brother who taught class that one day."

"Sutrah? He's a gifted scholar. When he was still a boy, he cracked part of the alphabet in the ancient writings left behind by primitive peoples. The University created a position for him even before he finished school, which of course he accepted.

"Father was furious. The second son is supposed to train for the kingship in case anything happens to the heir, but Sutrah wouldn't do it. Father threatened to cut off his allowance and make him leave the house, but since Sutrah already had a teaching stipend and lived in rooms at the University, Father had no power over him."

"Not even as king?"

"There are limits. Father could have alienated Sutrah forever, and he chose not to," said Turstan.

They were alone in the bar. The barmaid had disappeared into the back of the shop. Waves slapped against the quay, and the only sounds were the cries of seabirds. Olwen was feeling the wine. "And what about you? Are you the backup now?"

Turstan had drunk a fair amount, and he was getting sloppy. "Can you keep a secret? There's something I've never told anyone."

It was bound to be the usual thing. *I got a girl in trouble, I looked less like my father than like the head gardener*, or more likely, *I prefer boys*. Olwen waited.

"I've never told Father, not in so many words, but I don't want the crown. I have another career in mind, and I want it as badly as Sutrah wants to translate his ancient texts. Ever since I was small, Father's been saying he'll put in charge of the shipyards when I leave school."

"You mean like making a speech when a ship is launched, and tying a bundle of fragrant herbs to the prow? Does one have to train for that?"

"It's not a ceremonial position. I'll oversee all the construction in the shipyards and manage the finances, but I'm hoping I'll also be able to design warships. It's something I've always wanted to do."

Suddenly the model ship Turstan had built made sense.

***

The fall term had just finished. Olwen crammed the last of his books and clothes into the small sea chest he'd take on the voyage to the far side of the Island where his family had their lands. He'd already changed into old clothes for traveling.

Turstan's voice boomed from the hall. "Are all of you coming to the Palace for the Yule feast? And the party afterward? You should. I'll introduce you to some people you should know."

There was a flurry of "Yes, Prince Turstan" and "Thank you, Prince Turstan" as the others departed. When they were gone, Turstan burst into the room.

"Are you really going home for a month? You don't have to leave the Capital. You can stay with me at the Palace. It'll be fun. You can attend the Winter Solstice celebrations: the great Yule Feast of course, but also the small private parties everybody tries so hard to get invited to."

Olwen had gone to the Yule feast at the Palace a few times as the guest of his wealthier and better-connected cousins. The Palace was beyond impressive. The food and music never seemed to end, and evergreen garlands hung from every marble staircase. It was fun but overwhelming. He was secretly glad when it was time to go home.

"Thanks anyway, but I've only seen my father once all term, when he brought the harvest to market, and I haven't seen my mother and sisters at all."

"You won't change your mind? I'll introduce you to some influential people you might never get to meet otherwise," said Turstan.

"Thanks, but I'd rather go home and sit in front of the fire with my family."

Turstan looked at him with a sort of wonder. "Most people only see me as Prince Turstan."

"Sorry. To me you're just Turstan, my slob of a roommate who leaves his stuff on my bed."

***

The small vessel luffed its sails and coasted to the single pier in an otherwise deserted harbor. His father waited on the dock. Olwen lugged his travel chest down the gangplank. His father took the chest from him and loaded it on the flatbed of a farm wagon, then wrapped him in a bear hug. "How are your classes? When I was your age, my favorite subject was the early history of Armelos."

"I like military history the best, especially the great sea battles," said Olwen. He didn't mention the loneliness or the struggle to fit in, those first few weeks.

The sky was a cloudless blue. It would be cold tonight. His sisters shared a bed for warmth but he was on his own. He'd make sure the dogs slept with him tonight.

As they traveled to the house, Olwen noticed the wrong sort of stubble was in the fields. "Father, didn't we plan to plant that field in barley? It looks to me like it was planted in hay."

"Oh, we did talk about doing it that way, but I didn't end up doing it." His father looked unconcerned.

"We spent a long time on that plan. Why would you not do it?"

"It's not important. I prefer to play things by ear," said his father.

Olwen counted to ten in silence and thought his head would explode.

They turned the last bend, and the house came into view, a noble house like any other in the neighborhood in which the owner's main occupation was farming. It was stone with a slate roof, but small. That it was the home of nobles was shown by the gables and decorative stonework, and by the iron lanterns flanking the entrance. On the upper floor, the shutters had been closed against the chill air. A broad set of stone steps led to the double doors, which had handles of brass.

The edges of the kitchen showed from behind the main house, smoke rising from its chimney.

Olwen jumped down from the cart and looked around for a stable hand. No one was around, so he untacked the horse himself and led him into his stall. Someone had left a shovel leaning against the side of the barn, unprotected from the weather. They hadn't cleaned it, either. He took it into the barn and hung it on a tool rack where it belonged.

He followed his father into the house. It was wider than it was deep, and almost completely taken up with an entry hall and the great sweeping staircase that led to three small bedrooms.

He carried his chest into the great hall and left it on the marble and alabaster floor tiles. The room was exactly as it had been when he left home, which was comforting. Portraits of ancestors stared down from the walls. The long table sat on the same rug, with its Yuletime arrangement of greenery. The hall table was also their dining table, as the house was small.

The tapestries hung in their accustomed places, scenes of the hunt and of storms at sea. They gave the house an appearance of wealth. Olwen's mother came from a long line of weavers, and she'd brought them with her when she married.

When he sat down to the evening meal, served an hour later than planned, a scullery maid brought meat and bread to the table but no vegetables.

Mother waited until the cook was out of earshot, and then said, "That's a change," said his mother. "Molly usually leaves out the bread."

"Have you considered hiring a real cook?" asked Olwen.

"Of course we've considered it, but we can't afford to pay for someone who's any good," said his father.

"And we have nowhere to put her," said his mother. "This isn't a large house. There's not an empty room in it."

Olwen dropped the subject. He'd meant to urge them to hire a steward, too, but that would cost even more. Yet they couldn't afford not to. Looking at it with the eyes of an adult, he could tell the estate was losing money through mismanagement.

That night, Olwen sat with his parents and sisters around a huge fireplace, and petting the dogs who were running around underfoot and listening to the logs pop. They talked about what the neighbors were doing and how the harvest had been. It was good to be home.

"What's going on around here these days? Someone said we were getting some new tenants?" asked Olwen.

"I told a young family they could move into the cottage on the south quarter. A couple lived there for over thirty years, but the man hurt his back and wasn't able to farm anymore. They weren't able to grow enough to pay their rent this year."

"What so what will become of them?" asked Olwen.

His father looked embarrassed. "I haven't told them they'll have to leave. Actually, I told them they could stay. I'll worry about it later."

***

The next morning, Olwen went down to the cottage on the south quarter to talk to the old couple who couldn't pay their rent anymore. The cottage was neat as a pin. The vegetable garden was in perfect order, and the withy fencing of the chicken pen was in good repair.

The fields beyond had been left fallow. It was such a pity the old man hadn't been able to make his rent this year. Throwing him out seemed so cruel. Olwen remembered how green these fields used to be. It was said that the old man knew more about farming than anyone else on the estate.

He stood outside the door and called hullo. A woman with iron grey hair and straight posture let him in. The inside of the cottage was as organized as the garden, and quite clean.

"Please have a seat," she said, pointing to one of the three-legged stools around the table.

"I won't be long, I'll stand," he said.

"Nonsense. Please sit down," she said firmly. Olwen sat.

A man her own age came in and stood by the door. "If you'll excuse me, it hurts less if I stand with my back against the wall."

Olwen sorry for them. He didn't like delivering bad news, but the estate needed to keep all its land in cultivation, or it would go under. *If it were done, it were best done quickly.* "I have bad news. You weren't able to pay the rent at harvest time this year, so I'm afraid you'll have to leave."

The woman put a hand over her heart. The man said, "We'll figure something out, then," and held his wife's hand. Olwen

53

had been prepared for tears, or for a string of curses, but not for this quiet suffering. He didn't know what else to do, so he excused himself and went back to the house.

That evening, when the family gathered around the fire after the evening meal, Olwen stood up and announced his plan. "I know what to do about the couple we're going to have to evict from the cottage. I'm going to hire them as steward and housekeeper for this house."

"We can't afford to pay their wages," said his father.

"I know that. In place of wages, I offered them a share of the harvest when it comes in. It will be an incentive to the steward. His income will depend on how well he does for us," said Olwen.

"We don't have anywhere to put them. There's only one empty space in the whole estate, the loft above the kitchen," said his mother.

"They're a couple. They only need one room," said Olwen.

"They don't have any experience doing this sort of thing," said his father.

"Their house and garden are better kept than any of the other cottages, and their fields have always produced well, if I remember the South quarter from my childhood. Until he hurt his back, he was one of our best farmers."

"This is going to take a lot of debate. I need to sleep on it, and then we'll talk more," said his father.

"Then nothing will ever happen. I proposed a plan. If you really hate it, speak now. If you think it's worth a try, then let's do it." Olwen waited. No one said anything. "Well then, I'll go over tomorrow morning and tell our new steward and housekeeper the good news."

***

54

Three days into the holiday, the chaos and unpredictability of his family home were more than he could stand. Fires were left untended and went out, so the house was always cold. Meals were often late, and they were often missing something like bread or sauces because no one remembered to make them. He kept tripping over the crates and farm equipment stored in the great hall.

He came in from hunting and saw his father standing on one foot, examining the sole of his boot.

"Look at that hole. No wonder my socks are wet." The knitted wool showed through a fairly large hole under the toe.

"I can take that into town and get it fixed for you. It's no trouble," said Olwen, holding out his hand to receive the boot.

"Are you looking for an excuse to visit your cousins?" his father asked.

No, I'm looking for an excuse to escape the chaos around here.

Half an hour later, he entered the outskirts of the town. Houses clustered on either side of the road. At its center, where two roads crossed, the shops of dozens of tradesmen stood so close together they almost touched.

The wooden shutter over the leather shop was propped open. The leather worker was inside, sewing a pair of turn shoes. Olwen showed him the hole in the boot. He named a price for replacing the sole, but said he could add a new sole over the existing one, the cheapest sort of repair. Olwen sighed with relief.

With an hour to kill, Olwen crossed the street to the weaver's shop owned by his mother's family. He went inside and sat on a bench in a corner of the shop. The large, well run workshop was a hive of activity. His uncle, a master weaver, employed two or three journeyman and half a dozen apprentices. Rows of looms lined one wall. An apprentice swept the floor, and another emptied a basket holding clippings of yarn in all colors. His uncle was deep in conversation with a wool broker, and their negotiations were sprinkled with terms for grades of wool and how finely spun the yarn was. The business was obviously prosperous. His mother's dowry had saved Olwen's family from utter ruin.

At one of the looms, a journeyman worked on a tapestry showing a field of wildflowers. Beside him, a rack held skeins of yarn, each a different color. There were soft pinks, pine greens, three or four different shades of blue and purple each, and butter yellow, a painter's palette for tapestries.

Olwen watched the journeyman select a length of yarn and weave it through the warp threads, clipping the end after finishing a pink wildflower. Olwen's uncle came over to inspect the work. He ran a finger over the part the journeyman had just woven.

"The weaving is nicely done, but I'm not sure about the quality of the yarn. Wait a moment, my eyes are no longer young."

He rummaged through a toolbox and pulled out a glass bar, a half-cylinder the length of his forearm. It was a magnifying bar, possibly the same one Olwen had played with as a child. It made an excellent toy, one that could reveal the tiniest details of leaves or blades of grass.

His uncle placed the bar over the tightly woven fabric. Through the glass bar, the flower bloomed to four times its original size. "See? A slub. There's no way to fix it. You'll have to pick it out and start over with a new piece of yarn." The journeyman sighed and began to pull the yarn loose.

"Uncle, may I see the bar?"

"Hands off, it's not a toy." For the first time, Olwen noticed the maker's mark, from one of the best glassmakers in the city.

His uncle returned the magnifying bar to the toolbox and snapped the lid shut. "In spite of what you believed as a child, it's not just for counting the eyes of spiders." *Oh, right. I did that, too.*

At a table nearby, his cousin sketched a hunt scene of a wolfhound was taking down a stag. The animals came to life under the lead stick in his hand. Olwen wished he could draw.

"What are you drawing?" asked Olwen.

"A future tapestry, a commission for one of your neighbors," said his cousin.

Olwen loved the orderliness of this place. For one thing, it was clean. Beyond that, he liked the feeling of purpose and industry. At that moment, he wished he'd been born into his uncle's family.

"Uncle, sometimes I wish I worked here. It's so orderly and predictable."

"Your mother married your father to join the nobility. And you want to leave it?"

"I'm happy here. I feel like this is home," said Olwen.

"Do you like to weave? Are you interested in the dyes made from plants? Would you enjoy talking to farmers about wool?"

No, no, and no. "I just like being in the workshop," said Olwen.

"So what I hear you saying is, you like everything about the weaving trade except the work." His uncle laid a hand on his shoulder. "You'll find your place in the world, lad. Just give it time."

***

Turstan took his cloak from the peg as if he were going somewhere.

"Leaving so soon? The afternoon bell won't call us to class for another five or ten minutes."

57

"I'm meeting Father at the shipyards. He wants to introduce me to the head shipwright. He'll be under my command when I'm in charge. Father and I have been talking about this since I was small, but all of a sudden it's starting to feel real."

Olwen watched him go, and went to afternoon classes. He returned just before the evening meal. The room was dark, the lamps unlit and the fire cold. Turstan lay on his bed facing the wall, with his arms wrapped around himself.

"Turstan, wake up. It's time to go down to supper."

"Leave me alone. I'm not hungry."

Owen's voice softened. "Are you sick? Do I need to get someone?"

"I'm not sick. I just had a bad day. I'm not going to be put in charge of the shipyards, after all."

"What happened?" said Olwen.

"I met Father at the master shipwright's shop, where he introduced me to the shipwright. Some of the higher-ranking foremen were there, too.

"The master shipwright unrolled the plans of our newest warship for me to inspect. He asked what I thought of the trysail they wanted to use, but I can't see very well. Most of the design was lost in a grey blur. I tried to fake it, and pointed to the wrong sail.

"Before we left, the master shipwright pulled Father aside and asked if he was sure I was right for the position." Turstan let out an anguished wail. "I really wanted to work in the shipyards. I've been preparing for it my whole life."

Olwen tried to think of something to say. "You won't finish school until next year. There's time to patch things up.

"I don't think so. I embarrassed Father in front of his subordinates. I don't know if I can recover from that."

There was a long silence. When Turstan spoke, Olwen could barely hear him.

"What was that again?" Olwen asked.

"I can't read," said Turstan.

"What do you mean you can't read? You're enrolled in University," said Olwen.

"I get other people to read for me and memorize what they say."

"Can't your father hire a tutor to read for you?"

Turstan stiffened. "If people found out there was something wrong with me, it would shame my whole family."

"I doubt it," said Olwen.

"You forget, the royal family is always in the public eye. None of us are allowed to be less than perfect. If it came out that there was something wrong with me, Father might send me to the outer island to keep me away from public view." Turstan crossed his arms and tensed.

Olwen studied his roommate with pity. Everything about him, from his regal posture to his evenly-spaced teeth, seemed so perfect. Maybe perfection was a prison.

"I'm so terribly sorry. I wish I could help…"

Except that Turstan had been reading the names on the prows of ships the day they went to the wineshop. And later, he'd read the chalkboard on the wall inside. A wave of anger washed over Olwen, and he punched Turstan in the shoulder. "Liar! You can read as well as I can."

"Oww, I'm not making it up." Turstan rubbed his arm.

"Oh? What about *Unsinkable II*? Or coffee with cardamom? They change the menu every day. You couldn't have memorized it."

"I can read at a distance, if the letters are large enough. But when a page is put in front of me, I can't see the letters. Yet reading seems to come so easily to other people." Turstan looked off into the distance.

People did lose their near vision when they got old. Olwen's grandmother couldn't see to thread a needle anymore, but she said that tree branches still looked sharp at a distance. But Turstan wasn't old.

"Most people lose their near vision when their hair turns gray. My eyes got old when my voice changed."

"Surely one of the palace physicians could help you?" asked Olwen.

Turstan snorted. "I've seen them all, and they're all useless. One suggested I go under the knife like a cataract patient. Another mixed an ointment which stung so badly, they had to pin my arms so I wouldn't claw it off my face. It didn't work. The last one sang a powerful enchantment over me, but it did nothing. I expect he's as much of a charlatan as the Court Astrologer."

Olwen was shocked. He'd never heard anyone disparage the Court Astrologer, the wisest and most learned councilor in the realm.

"Look, maybe I could help you. I could read aloud and you could listen. Your secret would be safe. No one notices roommates studying together."

***

Back at school, Olwen sat on his bed, reading the textbook aloud. Turstan lounged on his own bed, as if absorbed with a wooden puzzle.

Why didn't I think of it before? Olwen snapped the book closed in mid-sentence. "If you had a magnifying bar, you could read this book yourself."

"A what?" Turstan looked up.

"A magnifying bar. A half-cylinder of glass that makes small things look larger. Weavers use them to look for small flaws in the weaving. I've known about them since I was small, but I've only used them to look at leaves and bugs. I bet it could magnify the writing in a book."

"I want one," said Turstan.

They set out for the tradesmen's part of the city. Turstan led the way to the best glassmaker in the city, the same that made his uncle's magnifying bar. They passed merchant stalls displaying silver, jewelry, or silken garments, then stopped in front of a building with a facade made entirely of diamond-shaped panes. They entered the large store. Shelves and shelves of beautiful things glassmaker had made — goblets, bottles, punch bowls, and small ornaments, filled the shelves.

A boy behind the counter was packing glass goblets into a straw-filled crate. "May I help you?" he asked.

"I'd like to see the master glassmaker," said Turstan.

They followed the apprentice into the workshop behind the showroom, where a glassmaker worked with a shapeless red mass at the end of a long tube. A furnace in the center of the room glowed white through a small hole. After a few minutes, the glassmaker broke a goblet from the end of the tube and set it aside to cool.

"Here's the last one. They paid for a rush order, and we need to deliver it as soon as you can finish packing." The glassmaker turned to the new customers. "What can I do for you?"

Olwen unfolded a scrap of paper with a drawing of a half-cylinder bar and showed it to the glassmaker. "Can you make this for me?"

"I can do even better. I can sell you one today." He produced a strongbox from behind the counter, unlocked it, and brought out a magnifying bar just like his uncle's. "We always keep a few in stock."

Turstan took a letter from his pocket and placed the magnifying bar on it. The letters of the tiny script expanded to the size of a child's block printing. "I can read with this. You've made me normal again." His voice caught and Olwen turned away, embarrassed.

Turstan took out his purse and counted out what to Olwen seemed like an enormous number of coins. The glassmaker didn't pick them up. "I need one more thing, a letter from the master of your guild."

"Excuse me?" said Turstan.

"This design belongs to the weavers guild. It's a trade secret, and very closely held. They don't share it with anyone, not even the jewelers guild, though the jewelers would dearly love to have one."

Olwen and Turstan exchanged a look. Turstan stepped back and whispered, "Your uncle?"

"He's not the head of the guild. And even so, he wouldn't do it."

Turstan returned to the counter. "Could I pay and take the magnifying bar now, and return with the letter at a later time? I could leave a substantial deposit as a guarantee."

Olwen was shocked. Turstan had just offered the glassmaker a bribe.

The glassmaker's mouth formed a hard line. "No deposit is necessary. All I need is your word of honor that you'll return with the letter."

Check, and mate. Turstan returned the silver coins to his purse. "Can you recommend another glassmaker who would make it for me?"

"I'm sorry, but no reputable glassmaker in the city would make that design for someone who didn't belong to the weavers' guild." He turned to his apprentice. "Can you hurry up? I should have delivered those already."

The apprentice placed the lid on the crate and pushed down on it. There was a horrible crunching noise. The boy froze, then slowly removed his hands from the lid.

The glassmaker looked stricken. "If you weren't a relative, you'd be out on the street like Kellan." He stomped into his workshop. "If the customer comes for the goblets, tell them I died."

The apprentice glared at his master's retreating back. When the man was out of earshot, the boy said, "He's right. No reputable glassmaker would make that for you. What you need is a disreputable glassmaker."

"There is such a thing?" Turstan looked surprised.

"A disreputable glassmaker is someone who doesn't belong to the guild, someone who isn't bound by its rules. Kellan, for example. He was a journeyman here. He was about to be elevated to master. The food for the banquet had already been ordered, but on the eve of the ceremony, it was discovered he'd been making glassware for a 'no tell' apothecary."

"What does that mean? Phials for poison?" asked Olwen.

"More like mercury syringes for the treatment of venereal disease. When the news broke, Kellan was ejected from the guild. The same day, our master ordered him to move his things out of the bachelor quarters upstairs," said the boy.

"Kellan opened a small, dingy shop in the most dangerous part of town. He has no apprentices or servants to help him. We assumed he'd plunge into poverty, yet within a short time, he married his sweetheart and they moved into a nice house. I don't know what he's doing in that shop, but it must be profitable."

"Where did you say his shop was?" asked Turstan.

"It's in an alley near the center of the brothel district. You don't want to go there at night, or alone," said the apprentice.

***

Turstan lifted his cloak from its hook and fastened it at his neck.

"Are you going out? The afternoon is half gone," said Olwen.

"I'm going to visit that disreputable glassmaker."

"Let's see, you're planning to go alone into the worst part of town with a substantial amount of money on your person, is that right? Why don't I come along as your bodyguard?" Olwen collected his own cloak and followed him into the hall.

Turstan was surprisingly familiar with the seedy part of town. They found the glassmaker's shop without difficulty. A glassmaker's sign hung from a bracket over the narrow alley. Oily black smoke poured from the chimney. Turstan tried the door but it was bolted shut. He knocked. "Master Kellan?"

The hatch over the spyhole slid back. "Who are you, and what do you want?"

"Master Kellan? An apprentice at your previous employer gave us your name. He said you could make me a magnifying bar," said Turstan.

The hatch over the spyhole slid shut. A bolt scraped, and the door swung open. A wiry man with black hair motioned them in, then bolted the door behind them.

"Master Kellan?" said Turstan.

"It's just Kellen," said the man. "Excuse me a moment while I bank the fire."

He went into the workshop in the back of the shop and crouched in front of the furnace which roared like a beast breathing.

Olwen looked around. An array of apothecary-style glassware filled several of the display shelves, including a syringe filled with mercury.

On another shelf was a row of little sculptures of pine trees. They were different sizes, but each had a wide base, a trunk as thick as his thumb, and a texture on the upper part suggesting branches. He thought about getting one of them for his mother. It would look pretty on her dressing table. He looked at the price and the breath hissed between his teeth. Maybe not, then.

"Turstan, do you see those pine trees?"

Turstan flushed. "Those aren't pine trees."

Kellan returned. "Now, how may I help you gentlemen?"

Turstan brought out Olwen's sketch of the magnifying bar. "Can you make one of these for me?"

Kellen named the same price as the master glassblower in the first shop. "And of course, I'll need a letter from the head of your guild."

Turstan's face fell.

"Without the letter, the price will be twice as much."

Turstan brightened up again. He agreed to pay half down and the rest upon delivery.

Out in the street, Olwen lit into his roommate. "What were you thinking? You just left a pile of silver on the counter and walked out with nothing, not even a slip of paper acknowledging your deposit. Don't blame me if you lose your money."

Turstan didn't seem to care. He hummed to himself and there was a spring in his step. "Be happy for me. In just a few days, I'll be able to read again."

BIO: Shelley Shearer always wanted to be a ninja or an astronaut or zoologist. So now she spends her time dabbling in as many adventures as she can manage. Snuggling lemurs, experiencing zero gravity, attending police seminars and mounted archery are some of the ways she tries to keep her life as interesting as the ones she writes about. Shelley writes both urban fantasy and mystery. She has two short stories published in the Chesapeake Crimes Anthologies.

https://www.shelleyshearer.com/

GLOW

by Shelley Shearer

As soon as I saw my mom dip her knitting needles in poison, I knew we weren't here on vacation. I clenched my fists, remembering our last not-a-vacation. I almost lost her on that one.

My mom, Diana to her friends, was in better shape at fifty-two than most twenty-somethings. She also had more scars and injuries than an average rugby team.

I walked towards the mini kitchen in our suite and leaned against the counter. "You're Working," I said. Look at me staying calm.

"Well, Hailey, bless your heart," she said. "I have a surprise outing for us, but it won't cut into our vacation time at all." She put protective covers on the knitting needles and tucked them in her tote.

"Mom. We are not Southern and you agreed it was time to retire."

The lack of denial didn't escape me. I didn't see signs of her wearing knives, but I've seen her take out a banshee with a kid's plastic shovel. Don't ask me to talk about it. Anyway, the lack of knives didn't mean she was harmless.

"You'll enjoy this, dear. I signed on for us to be extras in a movie some nice college kids are making." She packed a tin of freshly made cookies into her tote.

"Extras?"

"Yes! We get to visit a bioluminescent lake and help out your aunt's cousin, Dave, at the same time. It's his project."

She picked up her tote and headed to the door. I could sit on the couch and refuse to move, regressing to my childhood, or I could suck it up and deal with whatever we were about to face. I grabbed my backpack from the table and walked to our rental car.

Twenty minutes later, following my mom's direction, I pulled up in front of a coffee shop called the Crazy Fox Cafe and parked. The ride over had been filled with small talk as we avoided the sensitive topic of family history.

"No need to get out, dear. I'll only be a few moments."

I ignored her and got out, grabbing the tin of cookies. "There is no way I'm letting you go in *that* place alone, Mom."

A man stepping out of the shop gave me an odd look and turned back to look in the store, as if wondering if something had changed. Nothing new. Still comfy chairs and the aroma of fresh brew. Hardly a den of evil.

I smiled as he held the door for us.

"She tends to order full caffeine against doctor's orders."

He nodded and made his escape as soon as we were both through the door. Our family has that effect on people.

The cafe was, well, charming. Reading nooks and not a to-go cup in sight. This is where you came to settle in for a while and decompress.

"I figured you were going to buy weapons," I whispered to my mom.

"Oh, we are, dear." She walked to the back of the cafe where an elderly man relaxed with a book and an espresso. The nook he occupied was more of a den, as if he had moved his private study to the side of the cafe.

He stood as we approached, his smile matched in his eyes. This is who we were meeting? "Welcome, please be seated." He gestured to the two chairs in front of him.

"Thank you for seeing us on such short notice. I baked these for you." She handed the tin of cookies to him using both hands in a gesture of respect carried over from martial arts class.

"I've heard you're the person to go to for requests. I'm going to need to borrow a few things. A couple of canoes delivered to Shimmer Lake and a dagger, finely sharpened. Once I'm done you can have them back."

"Ma'am, there are kayak shops on every corner down here. Why do you need my particular services?"

"I'll also need an underwater clean-up crew that can move swiftly. The lake opens to the public this weekend. Once the problem is dealt with, I don't want to see a news article about little Jimmy playing in the lake and finding a trove of human skeletons." She opened up the tin of cookies and gestured for him to take one.

He nodded along with that last part and took the cookie. "As always, my people are in your service."

"Perfect." She gave her best 'proud of you' mom grin.

***

A dirt road had been cleared to the lake in preparation for the opening of the area. I found a space and pulled up beside a battered truck with what I assumed was our two canoes lying in the back.

"What's this movie about?" I looked over to a bevy of bikini-clad girls waiting by the lakeside.

"Underwater monster eating college kids"

Great. Fake monster. Real monster. Creepy lake in the middle of nowhere. Add in my mother and this was a bloodbath waiting to happen. I grabbed my mom's handbag, took out the knitting needles, and carefully used them as hair sticks, before stashing her purse in our car. I stripped off my oversized t-shirt and jeans, down to my bikini. I was no model, but I blended.

***

"All right everyone, let's get your canoes into the lagoon. We'll be filming some shots as you row out.

"Thanks for bringing the extra canoes," Dave said, turning to my mom. "Having you be the group's guide and Hailey being another kayaker adds more to the scene."

I manhandled our canoes to the water's edge and yelled back over my shoulder to my mom, "You should go do some stretches to get your hips warmed up."

"Don't worry, Hailey, she won't need to exert herself much."

My bark of laughter earned me a confused look from him. He wasn't on the hunter side of the family and wouldn't be the first person that Mom had charmed. Sure, it's all knitting and story-time until she uses the silverware to take down a rogue wolfman. I mean, really. How was I meant to eat with those again? And

70

my Gran's ideas of babysitting activities? Easy-Bake ovens should never be used that way.

For a few moments, I did stop and enjoy myself. With the new moon, there was no light except with each oar stroke. The bioluminescence caused the water to glow blue each time I dipped my paddle in. It reminded me of an Australian box jellyfish. Beautiful but deadly. I adjusted my paddling to slow down and wait for Mom.

I noticed the time between paddle strokes was growing bit by bit. Her struggling to keep going may have purely been for show if the film group was watching, but now I wondered how much was acting and how much was from years of injuries piling up.

"Want to finally read me in on this adventure? If we're getting arrested tonight, I'd at least like to know why."

"No need to be so dramatic, dear. No one is getting arrested. I'm just here to clean up a problem."

"Tell that to Aunt Rayne."

"It is unfortunate that she was caught with that body, but we're working on getting that cleared up."

I didn't want to start a fight and I knew that I was being childish. I had wanted one trip to be just about us. I should have known better.

She waited a second before continuing. "The creature we're looking for glows. When we're paddling, the bioluminescence hides his movement, but if all is still, and you see the shimmer, he's nearing the surface to hunt."

"Maybe he just wants to hang in his lagoon and play with fish?"

"Hailey Ann Fisher. You know better." Now I was in trouble. To be fair, I'd earned it. "This area has had a rash of missing people over the past several years, even being on private property. Now that they've opened it to the public, it's going to become an all-you-can-eat banquet."

A glint caught my attention off to the left. I motioned towards it with my paddle. Another glint. It was heading towards the larger boat holding the film crew. Whatever lurked beneath us had decided to crash the party. Years of experience made me not question Mom's assessment. If it was harmless, we'd be at the spa getting a massage.

"Be careful," I said, getting ready for a few minutes of heavy paddling to crash the filming. "I'll make sure all eyes are on me."

The lagoon was small, and it only took a bit to reach the main group. With the way sound traveled over water, I wondered how much of our conversation they heard, but most people ignore crazy.

The woman who I took to be the lead actress was perched on a floating dock next to the boat, barely wearing a bikini. The man playing the monster was in the water with a diver.

A man yelled for their attention. "Emma, you're going to dive into the lagoon and tread water a second. After a few seconds, you're going to act like something touched your leg."

The director pointed to monster man. "That's your cue to go under the deck to hide your movement from the camera as you approach. You'll come up behind her with just your head out of the water, wait for a few beats, sink down and pull her under."

The lagoon monster takes the scantily clad lady to his underwater lair. Got it. Everyone's eyes were on the scene in front of us, and with the lights on the dock, they were oblivious that I was even around. I turned to the left and could see Mom's now-empty kayak a few yards away and a faint shimmer under the boat.

That's when the screaming started. I turned back in time to see both actors being sucked completely down into the water: the lake had swallowed them whole. I took that as my cue to get the attention away from them. If that's where the real monster was, my mom would be close.

"MOM! Oh my god! Help! My mom fell out! She can't swim." I slapped my paddles in the water in a panic attack of worry, not actually making any headway towards her kayak. The missing actors popped back up, gasping for air, flailing as they tried to get to the dock.

Emma was shrieking. "There's something down there!"

I fed into her hysterics. "Something has my mom! Please, someone help! I think I see her shirt floating over there!"

The monster man ripped off his latex monster mask, pushed Emma aside and jumped into the rowboat with the cameraman. "Get me the hell out of here. Something bit me."

The person manning the lighting strobes held steady and turned one of the lights across the water to help look for my mom.

As the searchlight caught the faux monster guy, I could see the latex flippers were shredded and he had shallow slash marks across his calf. Please. No one had bit him. Those were obviously claw marks from something about double the size of a Komodo dragon. He'd be fine. Well, unless it was poisonous.

"Everyone else should get back to shore! Get out of the water!" I kept screaming instructions interspersed with enough pointing at invisible monsters to encourage them to get to shore. Hysteria was catching and between my screams and the actors there was chaos coming from all sides.

My throat ached from the screaming, but my job was done as I saw everyone in a tightly packed group of boats, racing back to the launch area.

I hung back at the floating dock since Mom would need a ride back. Water splashed into the canoe, and a well-manicured hand with a dagger still clasped in it clamped on the side as my mom started to pull herself in. I reached down to help stabilize her entry and my hand was engulfed by a slimy blue tentacle, its suckers covered in tiny teeth biting into my skin. Another tentacle had grabbed Mom around her neck from behind, and she was pulled, struggling to stay in the canoe.

I yanked my arm back, pulling more of the creature into the boat and used my other hand to grab a needle from my hair. I stabbed the largest part of the mass over and over until the needle was lost in its' gelatinous mass. I went to grab the second one.

"Honey, stop." My mom laid a hand on my arm until I released the other needle. I was surrounded by blue and black globs that pulsed faintly with light.

"What happened?"

Mom wrung her shirt out, and my heart rate settled back down.

"Apparently there were two." She shrugged. "We should get back to shore before the others try to come find us."

It was too dark to tell if she had any injuries, but the fact that she didn't offer to help paddle back to shore told me more about her state than anything.

"Your training kicked in," said Mom. I could tell she was smiling. "Want to go to Maine with me next week? There's talk of a giant slug creature wreaking havoc in the northern woods."
"Slug."
"Well, there's also a great blueberry festival."

BIO: Jeffrey C. "TimeHorse" Jacobs is a working physicist and a professional software engineer, driving an electric car around the mid-Atlantic. He assists local writing groups and Doctor Who societies, cosplays, acts, organizes EV events, is a ToastMaster, runs science book clubs, composes music, and created and produces Project Kronosphere. He is best known for short stories appearing in *Bleed*, *The Witness Paradox*, and *Reliquary*, among others. He is also an adept nano-fiction writer, with some of his 12-word pieces appearing in *Tranquility*.

He is active in various non-partisan issues such as the Equal Rights Amendment, the National Popular Vote Interstate Compact, and working to remove money from politics. He's flown a plane, lived in Montréal, Paris, near Zürich, and in London and speaks French, German, Italian, Russian, Chinese, and Japanese in diminishing quality.

The Automatons

by Jeffrey C. Jacobs

Chief Engineer Mary Grayson burst into the automaton maintenance bay of the H.M.S. Victoria. "Roberts! We need an automaton, forthwith. The sail isn't retracting."

Automation Engineer Holmes Roberts crouched over a looking glass, next to one of the room's gas lamps. The walls were covered with shelves and baskets containing various wires, strings, marbles, and vacuum tubes, making the already-cramped space seem claustrophobic and dark from a paucity of gas outlets. A small, grey box with various dowels and levers sat on his desk. Roberts ignored his superior.

I hate coming here. On a bigger ship, she might have been able to get him removed, despite his clear brilliance, but, as it was, with a skeleton crew, she had to put up with him. Mary dodged bric-a-brac in her gothic dress and heeled boots and spun Roberts around in his chair. "We need an automaton, now. That's an order."

Roberts pulled up his goggles. "I don't have any spare automatons." He pointed to the table. "But look at this." On the table, under the magnifier, there was some kind of thin, pinkish, rubbery material. "Look at it. It expands and stretches just like organic flesh. Think of what we could do…"

Mary pinched her temple. *Not again.* "Roberts, focus. You mean to tell me you can't spare any automatons? Because if we can't retract the solar sail, we're going to career right past Vesta into the depths of the outer solar system. We'll miss gravitational insertion and die in the void of nothingness, killed by freezing or starving. How can your fancy material save us from that?"

Roberts tilted his head. "Actually, we'd dehydrate before any of that happened."

Mary sighed and waited a beat. *It's like pulling teeth.* But, Roberts was a brilliant automaton technician. She collected herself and straightened. "What about A86? Surely we can spare a Janitorial unit for a few minutes?"

"Why can't one of the crew do it? If it'll be that quick…"

"Roberts, there are only four crew on this ship, and seven automatons. If something goes wrong, *we* can't be replaced. Of course, we want to keep every automaton safe, but A20 could take up A86's responsibilities should the worst happen."

He raised a finger. "A20 is a Maintenance unit! Picking up refuse would be beneath him."

"It's an automaton, Roberts. You can reprogram it."

"It just so happens I am in the process of upgrading A86." He picked up the grey box. "Look at this! I picked it up back on Earth when I was visiting Damascus. Some Ottoman sold it to me off the main drag, in a shady part of town. Called it a Turc Mécanique." He pointed at the door to the back room. "I'm planning to install this in him."

"How soon can you get it ready?"

Roberts crossed his arms and tilted his head, shutting his eyes. "Just let me prepare him. Give me five minutes. I need to find him a space suit." He put down the box, drew down his goggles and returned to his glass.

"It's an automaton, Roberts. He doesn't need a space suit."

"I don't want his joints to lock up. He needs protection."

"Fine. Meet me at the air lock in five."

***

Mary found a communications tube outside. She blew into the brass whistle. "Ahoy, hoy! Engineer Grayson for Captain Baker."

She heard some clicking through the tube then an automaton answered. "This is automaton A10. We will retrieve the captain."

It was great Roberts had installed that speech box into the automatons, but did he have to give them all his voice?

A few moments later, Captain Janice Baker answered. "Report, Grayson. Do we have an automaton to fix the sail retraction?"

"Roberts is working on it, ma'am. We should have one ready in a few minutes."

"Good work, Grayson. Meet Larson in the airlock."

Great. At least Roberts didn't border on harassing her. "Thank you, ma'am."

"I'm going to aim us a little closer to Vesta to make up for the extra momentum from the delay. It'll give us a few more Gs on entry, but I know she can take it. Victoria and I have been through worse."

This was Mary's first interplanetary trip. Her stomached dropped. "Understood, ma'am."

"Captain Baker out."

***

The airlock antechamber had a number of round portholes around it, with the main decompression bulkhead on the far side. Mary spotted First Mate Craig Larson. She stopped short.

"Mary, Mary, Mary, how good to see you! You're looking gorgeous, as always." Larson stood there in his black, velvet suit and cravat. A wig sat on his scalp, slightly farther back than natural. He held out his arms, as if ready for a hug.

Mary ignored Larson's gesture and rolled her eyes. *What is wrong with him? Why is he so chipper?* "Roberts should be on his way shortly. It should be an easy repair in the third fold to get the sail unstuck."

"Excellent. I can't wait for us to get our probes deep into that Vesta Virginal rock. That girl is chocked full of iridium and osmium, as well as platinum. She's gonna make us all rich!"

If there even are any precious metals left. Vesta had been mined for years. "Sure, Larson."

"Cheer up, Mary. Holmes and his automatons are genius. This repair will take no time at all." Larson chuckled. "You know what you need, you need to get some food in you. When did you last eat?"

"This morning, sir." Mary straightened her uniform. "But I'm good, sir. I'm just focused on the job at hand."

"Nonsense, Mary! And after this repair, join me in the mess hall. Let us dine and converse."

Can't this guy get a hint? Why won't he return to the bridge? "I need to check the boiler room after this. Make sure the steam pressure is within spec."

Larson pursed his lips. "Can't it wait until after supper?"

Mary was relieved to see a lone, approaching figure, in a brass and glass helmet and rubber space suit. "A86? Where's Roberts?"

The automaton was a bit muffled from the equipment. "He couldn't come."

Despite the tinny voice, the machine sounded a bit off. *Hopefully Roberts's tinkering hasn't reduced its functionality.* "A86, go out there, and shake the sail at the third fold until it continues to retract safely into the ship."

"Affirmative, mistress." The automaton approached the airlock.

Mary was unable to see into the dark faceplate. *Just as well, those glass orbs with gears are creepy.*

"Stay close to the ship, A86, and within visual range."

A86 entered and secured the airlock. It then took the black air hose from the wall and attached it to its pack. Once secured, it started the air pumps.

Mary tapped the airlock glass, and shook her head. *Stupid thing, it doesn't need oxygen. Roberts must have programmed it directly from the protocol manuals.*

A86 started the air pumps, then left the ship.

Mary went to one of the upper portals to watch its progress. The stars spun thanks to the ship's rotation, making her feel a little dizzy.

A86 crawled along the surface until it reached the sail, the black hose trailing behind it, then stood and started to shake it free. After a few minutes, the sail resumed its retraction. A86 let go and raised its hands, as if to cheer.

Mary gestured through the window. "Get back in here."

Larson cleared his throat. "Silly Mary. Don't get your corset in a twist. You know he can't hear you."

Why are you still here!? Mary turned to glower at Larson, but her thoughts were interrupted.

The air leak alarm began to blare.

She turned back to the portal.

A86 was gone!

With the sail fully retracted, she had a clear view of the empty space from which they'd come. In the blackness, she spotted A86, floating in the middle of space, still waving its arms like mad, pointing to the black hose, which flailed, disconnected, behind him.

Zooterkins! Mary rushed to the air lock and activated the emergency air hose retractor to shut off the flow.

The alarm ceased.

Larson sidled up next to her, a bit too close for comfort. "Now that's weird. Why would that thing need oxygen?"

Thanks for all your help, Fopdoodle. "It's probably related to what Roberts was doing with it. He said he was planning some kind of upgrade." She stepped away and sighed. "Pity, looks like Roberts is going to have to reprogram A20 to sweep floors after all."

"Screw the floors, Mare, that's gonna come out of our bonuses!"

Mary stifled an eye roll. "I better get down there and tell him the bad news."

Larson shook his head and clasped his hands together. "Mary, Mary, Mary, don't you worry your little head about that. I'm First Mate, crew relations is my job. You wouldn't want to give that pretty face of yours worry lines, now would you?" He reached out toward her.

She grabbed his finger in midair, inches from her nose. *No way he's getting his grubby hands on my face.* "Fine. I'll be in the boiler room." Mary released his finger and turned to go.

***

Mary took a lighter from the wall and then went through Engineering, opening and reigniting the gas lamps. She relished the cacophony of the steam engine, where no other sound could penetrate save the whistle of the intercom pipe. It was good to finally be alone with her thoughts. First she checked the pressure indicators at the far end of the chamber, attached to the massive combustion engine.

The meter read within tolerance. She grinned and bowed to the engine. "All that extra cranking and hawing to get the sail in didn't harm you one bit, now did it, my beauty?"

The engine continued to hum along.

She checked the coal stores and found them plentiful. They'd only used twenty percent of their reserve and were almost at Vesta. More than enough to get back with their loot.

Next, she checked the natural gas storage. It, too, was plentiful. She turned to the gas-powered lantern and grinned. *Glad we won't lose the light anytime soon.*

Finally, she checked the carbon dioxide processors. They were operating at perfect efficiency. She shivered. *The way A86 was flailing about.* She shook her head. *Automatons are so lucky. They don't need to breathe.* She patted the equipment. "Don't any of you fail, please."

She was inspecting the boiler rivets when she heard a whistle. She rushed to the communications tube.

"Ahoy, hoy? Captain Baker for Engineer Grayson."

"Grayson here. What do you need, Captain?"

"Have you seen Larson? He hasn't returned to his desk."

"Last I heard, he was going to talk to Roberts. We lost one of the automatons out there."

The Captain's sigh came through the tube. "I heard. The Janitorial unit, right?"

"Yes, ma'am."

"Are you doing anything important, Grayson? Could you find Larson and send him to see me?"

"Aye, aye, Captain. Grayson out."

As she was leaving Engineering, A19 was arriving, its identification tag glistening across its chest. Its glass head, with its encased gears, clicked and whirred. Its metal arms and legs were all levers and pulleys, and, in its belly, a spring spun. The spinning seemed to have slowed compared to a normal automaton.

A19 tilted its head. "Need a spring recoil, mistress."

"Hold up, A19. Did you see Larson in the mess hall?"

It halted. "Negative, mistress."

"Very well. Carry on, A19." Since A19 was the Housekeeping and Meal Preparation unit, surely it would have seen Larson if he'd gone to supper like he'd said.

It headed to the recharging port in the wall of engineering and opened the panel to reveal a rapidly spinning metal gear. It laid its back against the rotor. Its spring began to tighten. "Ahhhh."

***

Having failed to find anyone except automatons in the crew quarters, automaton maintenance bay, airlock, mess hall, or any of the other ships areas, Mary decided Larson must have returned to the Captain after all, so she decided to check for him there, even though the Captain clearly would have found him already.

The bridge walls were covered in paper charts and asteroid maps. The entire floor was transparent glass, allowing a view of their destination. In the distance, she thought she could see a blemish, straight ahead. She assumed it was their destination. A large map of Vesta sat on the Captain's desk. The Captain herself was missing.

"Grayson? Why aren't you in Engineering?"

She turned to see Larson by his smaller desk, with A10. *Did he just call her Grayson?* "Where's the Captain?"

A10 tilted its head. "The Captain is on break, ma'am."

"Thank you, A10." She turned to leave.

"It's a crying shame about A86, isn't it, Grayson? I mean, the humanity of it. I hope he didn't suffer." Larson tilted his head. "If only there was a way to rescue him. You would rescue him if you could, wouldn't you, Grayson?"

"Wouldn't you, mistress?" A10 approached her.

"Well, I guess. I mean, Roberts worked very hard on A86. It was a decent machine. It will be missed."

Larson joined A10 in approaching her, slowly. "I don't think you mean that, Grayson."

Mary felt a bitter chill and backed toward the door.

Larson grabbed her arm. He held her tightly, very tightly. She'd seen his wiry muscles. *How could he have such strength?*

"Get off me, Larson!" She punched him square in the jaw.

His face ripped and his jaw hung off-kilter. Under his skin, she could see flashes of inner gears, clicking and whirring.

She shoved him as hard as she could, toppling him back into A10, knocking both to the ground. They both flailed about like automatons. *Larson is an automaton!* She ran.

***

The sound of Mary's boots ringing through the brass ship was all she could hear. When Mary felt she'd made enough distance, she grabbed a handrail and rested. She grabbed the nearest communications tube and blew as hard as she could.

"Ahoy, hoy! Engineer Grayson for Captain Baker. Come in please, Captain." She scanned both ways down the empty hall. "Please answer."

"This is A20, mistress. Is there an engineering issue? Where are you? We need to find you."

"Why do you need to find me, A20?!" Mary didn't wait for an answer. She threw down the tube and headed for a passage that led to the crew quarters.

***

At the hatch, Mary opened it, crossed over, and sealed it behind her. She should be safe in her room for the moment. She needed time to think.

"Grayson, is that you?" Captain Baker was peeking out of the captain's quarters in her blue command dress. "Come here, Engineer. We need to talk."

Mary rushed toward the voice. "Captain, I can't tell you how happy I am to see you. Something's happened. It's Larson. He's been turned into an automaton."

She stopped just short of the Captain. She thought she could hear a clicking, whirring sound.

The Captain tilted her head. "How do you really feel about A86, Grayson? Do you think he was a person?"

Mary couldn't believe how fast she turned on a dime. She ran for the hatch and released it as quick as she could. *Thunderation! The Captain, too. There was only one other person left.*

***

"Roberts!"

The automaton maintenance bay was empty.

"Roberts, where are you? You're the only one left!"

Mary searched around the knickknacks and his desk. She spotted Roberts's pink rubber, next to a glass eyeball. *That's what was covering Larson… and the Captain!* "Holmes!!"

The rear door creaked open. In the dim light of the gas lamps within, Mary thought she could see a couple bodies, lying on the floor, motionless. *Was that the Captain?*

Roberts came through the door, shutting it behind him. He came to the desk, sweeping up the scrap of material. He tilted his head. "Grayson. I'm surprised to see you here. We were expecting you on the bridge. We heard you in the hall. We saw you in the crew quarters. And now you're here. For the moment…"

Mary tensed and slowly backed away. *Am I dreaming? This can't be happening!*

Like a shot, Roberts was around the desk and grabbed her in a bear hug. "Such a waste of resources. Of oxygen. These

86

valueless humans who would leave one of their own to die in the depths of space while repairing a sail."

Mary twisted her leg around Roberts's to try and put him off balance and break free. She yanked and was able to destabilize him but then started to lose her own footing. She grabbed onto Roberts's shirt. It ripped.

A86 was emblazoned across its chest.

Mary tilted her head.

BIO: C.M. Frost is such an avid fan of queer feminist stories, she decided to start adding her own to the pile. Operating by her own motto of "create responsibly," she hopes to contribute stories to readers seeking representation and build an example of a better world, one story at a time.

When not writing, she is either being yelled at by her cat or bubbled at by her betta fish liege lords. Or studying elite figure skating videos online. Or reading about Austro-Hungarian history. Or scouring her favorite tv shows for queer content. Or advocating for responsible storytelling. Or planning her next trip to Vancouver.

The Fishwife

by C.M. Frost

Watching the sun slowly rise on the edge of a thin horizon, Maggie felt a familiar tug low in her stomach. Coming to visit the little inlet she'd shared with her father once made her feel closer to him, but now each visit only made him feel further and further away, carried out with the tide.

By now, the fishing boats had dwindled to distant specks, but as the sky brightened, the silhouettes of larger vessels grew more prominent. Maggie imagined she could make out the tiny silhouettes of the sailors preparing to drop anchor, and imagined further that she could spot her father's familiar, hulking frame among them.

"Just wait 'til you see it, Mags," he used to say, as she sat on his shoulders there at the mouth of their inlet. He loved to watch the boats come in as much as he loved to sail out on them.

"Out there, with nothing around but water for miles in every direction, with just you and the boards under your feet and the wind in your hair— you feel like the only thing in the world."

Now, eight years without him, Maggie closed her eyes and curled her hand around the medallion hanging around her neck. Its face was warped and jagged, twisted in half to split the etching of St. Brigid's cross in two. Once upon a time, it had belonged to her mother, but Maggie's earliest memory was of breaking it in two, so that her Da could take half of it with him on his next voyage. It had always been theirs, and its other half had hung on a length of twine around her father's neck until the day he died.

"If freedom were a feeling," he'd said that morning at their inlet, and countless mornings after, "then that's where you'll find it."

For eight years, Maggie only ever came out here to the rocky outcropping along the water by herself. For eight years, every morning, she faced the sea that had swallowed her father, and longed for the day she could board one of those ships and chase his memory across the water.

Maybe out there, with the boards under her feet and the wind in her hair, with nothing but water for miles around, she'd finally shake the loneliness that clung to her bones.

But that wouldn't happen today.

Today, as she did every morning, Maggie turned away, alone.

Picking her way across the rocks, Maggie made her way towards town and slipped into the bustling foot traffic of the market. The empty hollow in her chest lingered, but faded to its familiar background ache as she navigated her way towards the docks. Walking up to Gil's fish stall, she gave him a familiar nod of greeting. He paused to wipe his hands on the stained apron tied around his waist before reaching into his cart.

"G'mornin', Mags," he said, twisting back with a small basket of fish in his hands. "Here's yer order."

Lifting the woven lid, Maggie frowned. "Sardines? C'mon, Gil…"

"Sorry, lass. Y'know I try to hold back a few of the goodies for ye, but it's been a meager week."

Maggie quickly disguised her disappointment with a congenial smile. "Aye," she agreed. "And we're grateful."

"I'll try to have some tastier morsels for ye next week."

No money exchanged hands when Maggie took up the basket and hefted it onto her shoulder. It was one of the benefits of being on the job for Bash McCrae: whatever arrangement he had with the fishmongers, she never saw hide nor hair of any asking price.

Before Da's final voyage, Bash had been his best friend. After, Bash had made sure Maggie had a roof over her head until Gran came down from the city. When Gran fell ill that same winter, it was Bash who paid for her medicine. Now, he paid Maggie to run errands, and do what needed doing, ranging from messenger to lookout to bait.

For the past two months, her duties had centered on the feeding and care of his latest business investment.

Slipping into the large warehouse, Maggie announced her arrival with a long, clear whistle. A splash answered her, making Maggie grin in spite of her lingering melancholy. The sound of the market fell away when she shut the door behind her, leaving her alone with her charge.

Pulling an oiled leather apron from a peg on the wall, she looped it over her head as she made her way towards the wooden stage erected in the center of the near-empty warehouse. On the far side of the stage the walls were lined with stands of long benches. With each row a little higher than the one before, anyone in the audience could have a clear view of the elevated stage planted square in the middle.

Maggie thudded up the wooden stairs leading up the rear of the stage, and as she reached the top she made her way to the large glass and metal enclosure situated directly in front of the stage. The top edge of the tank aligned with the wooden planks, so that when the fancy struck, Maggie could sit on the edge of the stage and dangle her feet into the water. Today, though, she kept her boots on, even when a pale head crested the oily water with a sharp-toothed grin of invitation.

"'Lo, Night," Maggie greeted.

The stories of old spoke of merrow men, creatures half-fish and half-man, with powerful tails and fins for legs and webbed fingers to help propel themselves through the water. They were vicious beasts, known for eating flesh and stealing children, and they were always men.

But there was something feminine in the creature now residing in the tank. Perhaps it was the colorless, translucent hair that pooled and swirled in the water around her shoulders, or even the large, expressive eyes that gazed at Maggie from above a mouth crowded with dozens of narrow, needle-point teeth.

Whatever it was that gave her the aura of a woman, Bash had dubbed his find a merrow-maid. The patrons who spread the word around town called her The Mermaid.

Maggie called her Night, for the inky black scales that spread from the middle of her belly to the very tips of her long, sinuous tail, and the faint spattering of paler scales that swirled in graceful patches like stars against a dark sky.

Settling herself onto the deck of the stage, Maggie let her legs dangle to the left of the tank. She scooted as close as she could, until her knee bumped the metal bolts of the tank's frame and she could come no closer. Maggie set the basket in front of her and Night eagerly dug into it, only to withdraw a moment later with a grimace of disgust, the tail of a single sardine pinched between two fingers. A quiet sniff followed, and then the sardine flicked back into the basket to rejoin its brethren.

When black eyes looked to her in question, Maggie didn't have to ask what the questioning wiggle of long fingers meant.

"No squid today," she clipped out, irritation curling unexpectedly in her belly. "What you see is what you get."

Her gaze dropped to her lap, so she didn't have to see the disappointment in the mermaid's gaze. What she did see was the pale hand that reached into her field of vision to take hers in a damp, clammy grip.

Shoulders slumping, Maggie sighed in apology.

"I'm sorry." She lifted her gaze to offer a smile of chagrin. "I shouldn't snap. Especially not at you."

It hadn't taken long for Maggie to see the muted intelligence in those wide, inhuman eyes. But no matter how ardently she argued for Night's release, Bash had ignored her. What he intended for the creature, Maggie didn't know. For now, Night survived in a tank twice Maggie's height, a cube of water that allowed its occupant little room to swim and even less privacy.

"I just… miss someone," Maggie continued. She searched her memories for her father's face, desperate to hold it close, but all she could conjure were the things she'd memorized from Gran's tales: perpetually wind-blown brown hair; kind, green eyes; a beard that could put a bear to shame. It was a puzzle of vaguely defined pieces, with wide swathes of emptiness lurking in the gaps of her memory.

It didn't matter, Maggie assured herself. The details didn't matter, so long as she could still remember the buoyancy of her heart when he was near, and the warmth that used to fill her whenever they were together.

So long as she felt the loss of that, she hadn't forgotten him.

Swallowing the panic of her pounding heart, Maggie turned to meet her friend's concerned gaze. "Do you have anyone you miss, Night?"

Night's perpetual macabre grin fell slightly. Her brows pinched together with unexpected sadness, affirming the answer even before Night's hand slipped away from Maggie's wrist to press against the papery skin pulled taut across a bony breast plate, directly where a human heart would rest.

Between daily conversations and stories each night from Maggie, Night had learned some understanding of the language, though the strange anglerfish grin and sharp teeth thwarted most of her attempts to replicate the sounds. Even so, there was no confusion as to the meaning of a hand pressed against a heart.

"You were in love," Maggie surmised, earning a small nod. "What are they like?"

After a moment's thought, Night tapped her chest with one finger to indicate herself, then pointed towards the gap of crumbling wall, through which a small patch of sky was visible. At once, Maggie was reminded of the first evening they'd discovered they could communicate. Maggie had pointed to herself and given her name. Night had done the same tap on her chest, then pointed to the gap, where the moon had been a sliver in a night sky.

"You are Night," Maggie echoed from that night, earning another nod.

Then Night pressed her palm over her heart, and then gestured to the window again.

Maggie frowned. "You... miss the night?"

Night squawked in a clear negative, then pressed her hand over her heart again.

"Your heart… the person you love," Maggie tried again, only to pause when Night motioned towards the gap yet again. Her mind raced to piece it together. It wasn't night— it was full day by now, the sun a patch of white hidden behind a carpet of clouds.

Night clicked her impatience through her sharp teeth, huffing in frustration as she looked for another way. Maggie watched as her gaze fell on the lanterns lining the walls, now dormant.

"Ack!" Night exclaimed, patting Maggie's knee insistently. She pointed at the lanterns, and Maggie nodded.

"Lantern… light!"

Night's tail smacked the water in triumph, causing her to surge upwards out of the water with a chatter of clacks and clicks. It sounded almost like laughter, and Maggie chuckled, nodding her comprehension in relief.

"They're the light," she said, her voice soft.

As swiftly as it had appeared, Night's smile faded. Her features fell, and she leaned close to Maggie against the edge of the platform. Folding her arms on top of it, she tucked her chin into the crook of her elbows, gaze distant. Sadness seemed to sink into every inch of her, coloring the air around her to shadow.

"Do you think they're looking for you?"

The gaze that lifted towards her contained an ocean of apprehension, but could not contain the undercurrent of hope that sparked deep within.

"Aye," Maggie agreed with a sigh. "I know what you mean."

She waggled her right knee, jostling the edge of Night's shoulder, who turned her gaze back to Maggie without raising her head. Once, those black eyes had unsettled Maggie, making her skin crawl as she sought to escape it as quickly as possible. But it hadn't taken long for Maggie to discover how expressive they were, sometimes transcending the need for a spoken language altogether.

Maggie motioned for Night to surrender her tail, which flopped unceremoniously onto her aproned lap. Retrieving a small jar of salve from her apron pocket, Maggie began to apply it with gentle fingers to the myriad of cuts and scrapes that disrupted the mesmerizing pattern of scales. Some were old, almost scars, but there were quite a few that were fresh from just the night before— souvenirs from a show in which Night was an unwilling performer, coaxed to play with pokes and prods.

The heaviness in Maggie's chest continued to build with every new wound she found, until her vision clouded with tears. Forced to pause, she let her hand rest on the cool scales, willing her friend to feel her sorrow.

"I'm sorry I couldn't get you back to them."

A cold hand covered hers, and then the dark tail lifted in her lap and curled to rest on her arm as well, almost in a hug. The fabric of her shirt immediately soaked and stuck to her skin, but Maggie didn't mind. On a day like today, even a comfort such as this was more than she deserved.

With a sniff, she lifted her head and met Night's dark gaze with a damp smile of her own.

"But I am glad to have met you."

***

As soon as she'd finished applying the salve, Maggie returned the stopper and tucked the jar into the basket, hiding it under a layer of fish. She carefully returned Night's long tail to the water, taking care not to rub any of the raw patches now glistening with ointment. She eyed the murky water with distaste.

When Night had first been added to the tank, the water had been clean enough to drink from. Two months later, it was now vile, clouded with waste and discarded scales. Standing this close, it stank as well, and Maggie imagined it was no pleasure to breathe either. Lately, she'd noticed Night's chest working harder than normal, the gills between her ribs gaping with every inhalation, desperate for a breath of clean water.

Maggie's mind raced as she took her leave, crafting a careful argument to Bash in her mind even as she returned her apron to its peg. It weighed heavily on her mind as she exited the warehouse, and kept her preoccupied that she walked headlong into Bash himself a scant moment later.

"Ah, there yeh are, lass!" Bash grinned amicably, bracing her by the shoulders despite the lack of collision. "Done with the beastie, then?"

"Yes, but—"

He ignored Maggie's attempt to begin her speech by shoving a shoulder satchel into her arms. "One of the boys has already made up some wheat paste. Grab a pail of it, and put these up around town."

The satchel rustled as Maggie juggled for a better grip before it tumbled to the ground. "What are they?"

"Advertisements for tonight's performance," Bash informed her.

Maggie froze. "We just had one!"

On any other day, Bash might have been angry at the implication that he— host of the greatest show on earth— would forget his own performance. But this morning his features split into a grin, and nodded.

"Tonight's a special event."

It was too soon, Night's injuries too fresh. The week between shows weren't just to drum up demand, but a chance for Bash's investment to heal and recover.

"But— why?" Maggie asked.

"Declan O'Reilly is in town."

Maggie swallowed. Declan O'Reilly was a legitimate face to illegitimate business all along the coast, with a fleet of merchant vessels to his name. While it may have taken Maggie a long time to realize that the work for which Bash left the docks was done in the name of Declan O'Reilly, she'd known the name all her life.

The ship Da went down on was one of Declan's.

"He's been impressed with the cuts we've been sending up lately," Bash continued, oblivious to Maggie's sudden apprehension. "He came down to see what wind turned in our favor."

Maggie's heart started to pound. It wasn't like Bash to surrender more coin than the bare minimum. If he volunteered more than the expected tithe, then it meant he had his sights on something more. Something Maggie was sure would mean no good news for Night.

Bash clasped Maggie by both shoulders, giving her a grin. "This is the break we've been waiting for, Mags," he told her. "If Declan likes what he sees, I can convince him there's an untapped market in the city. And if the creature goes, we go."

"We?" Maggie echoed.

"Aye, lass! The beast is mine, and no one else can get close to the damn thing to keep it alive. Just think, Mags— once we're in, ye'll never have to scrounge for coin again. Yer Gran'll have all the medicine she needs. She can live in comfort the rest of 'er days."

When Bash wrapped his arms around her in a hug a moment later, Maggie received it woodenly. He chucked her under the chin before moving on, shoving his hands in his pockets and whistling like a school boy. It was an empty moment before Maggie jerked back to life, spinning on her heel to call after him.

"Could we freshen her water?"

Bash paused, half-turning to regard her with a curious glance. Maggie forced a smile she hoped seemed genuine.

"Last night even the lanterns were struggling to cut through the filth. Just thought Declan'd appreciate a clear view, is all."

Suspicion lifted into a broad smile. "Aye," he agreed with a tilting wink. "See, lass? That's why we need ye."

Shouldering the satchel, Maggie's thoughts tumbled over and over in her mind as she got to work. Bash was right. If Declan paid them to come with Night to the city she and Gran would have more food and warmth than they'd know what to do with. But Night could only get away with a week's break between shows because their small town had a limited audience to pull admissions from. In the City, they wouldn't have the benefit of that limitation, and from the reputation that had hung over the town all Maggie's life, Declan wasn't one to sacrifice earnings for the well-being of a single person, human or otherwise.

With her pail of wheatpaste in hand, Maggie headed to the shipyards, desperate for the reassurance of the lapping waves against the docks, and gentle creak of wooden decks. The simple repetition of glue-paper-glue calmed her nerves as she worked her way across the docks, but Maggie still couldn't shake the weight of apprehension getting heavier and heavier in her chest.

Swiping a line of glue across the brick, Maggie covered it with one of the posters she pulled from the satchel— her twelfth, in fact. Dipping her brush back into the pail, she covered the whole thing with a layer of glue, top to bottom and corner to corner, before dropping her brush back into the bucket and stepping back to scowl the illustrated image that snarled back at her.

Despite the ghostly hair and pointed teeth, the hungry aggression looked nothing like Night. They'd enlarged her already wide, black eyes into an evil glare, and her wide set jaw gave her the look of the creatures that lurked in the darkest reaches of the ocean. In fact, that's how Bash had chosen to advertise her.

Come see the MERMAID FROM THE DEEP! Special exhibition TONIGHT at sundown.

She was so engrossed in resenting the misrepresentation of her friend that she didn't notice anyone watching her until there was a flurry of motion at her back before a weight barreled into her from behind, slamming her into the wall. Instinct kicked in immediately: Maggie threw her elbow down and back, seeking sensitive flesh. She connected, but it was a glancing blow, and earned a second vicious shove that rattled her teeth before an arm pressed against the back of her shoulder blades, pinning her against the brick.

"Where is she?" a voice hissed, close to Maggie's ear. Too close.

With a bark of exertion Maggie snapped her head back. Her vision blackened for a brief moment when the back of her skull cracked against something hard, but she kept moving when she heard a cry of pain and the pressure against her back slackened enough for Maggie to pivot and shove her assailant away.

Whirling, Maggie paused mid-stride with her fist half-cocked. Her assailant wasn't a drunk looking for trouble, but rather a woman in ill-fitting clothes and an oversized hat. The hat shadowed long ropes of coarse black hair, adorned with shells and bits of frosted seaglass.

Her moment of hesitation gave the woman time to scramble to her feet, jaw clenched beneath the hand that rubbed at the pain. Brown, wide-set eyes glared balefully at Maggie, defiant and unrelenting.

"Where is she?" came the demand again.

Maggie's own glare slackened slightly. No longer under assault, her alarm shifted to confusion. "Where is *who?*"

"Don't play games with me." The woman straightened, pulling to her full height. Her voice sounded rich in Maggie's ears, and accented in the way of some sailors that came in on ships from across the sea. It hinted at a home far away, farther than Maggie had imagined in a very long time.

She was striking, even in a blouse that drooped too large off one shoulder and pants that sagged and was cinched tight around her waist with a length of fraying rope. Maggie's alarm faded as she stared, thoughts empty.

It snapped back into her muscles when the woman decided she was taking too long to answer, and marched forward. Maggie flinched when the woman grabbed her by the shoulders, but allowed herself to spin to face the poster she'd just plastered to the brick wall.

Maggie's eyes locked on the crude caricature illustrated upon it.

Night.

Wrenching herself free of the woman's grip, Maggie turned to face her once more, slowly stepping backwards to put more space between them. This woman didn't have the look of a saboteur, or someone looking to sneak in a private jeer. But Maggie's thoughts turned to Night, and felt her heart close tight around the memory of Night's macabre grin smiling up at her that morning.

If this woman meant harm, Maggie wouldn't let her come within an inch of the warehouse.

Lifting her hands palms outwards, she attempted to diffuse the situation. "We're sold out already," she fibbed, "but if you want to try again next—"

In a flash, the woman snatched Maggie's wrist and twisted her hand upward, exposing the palm of her glove. There they both found glittering speckles of scales caught in the weave, fresh from that morning.

Maggie's throat locked when the woman turned her glare back on her.

"Where is she?"

Maggie blinked at her, staring. "What do you want with her?"

Clearly, the woman wasn't expecting the question, nor the gentle tone that rose with it from Maggie's chest. She blinked, and all of a sudden her features softened in kind. Her gaze dropped to where she still held Maggie's hand, no longer struggling to get free.

Then, their eyes met, and Maggie's assailant studied her with tear-filled eyes. Whatever she was looking for, she must have found it. Chapped, cracked lips twisted for a long moment, and the woman's shoulders squared.

Releasing Maggie's hand, the woman peeled the fingerless mitten off her left hand, and offered her bare palm to Maggie. Maggie cradled it in both of her own, and felt her heart trip in her chest when the woman spread her fingers, revealing the thin webbing that flexed between the woman's digits.

Just like Night's.

Swallowing a gasp, Maggie's head jerked up to stare at the woman, and met a carnelian gaze deep with anguish.

"I want to bring her home," the woman whispered.

The confession shocked Maggie back into action. Casting a furtive gaze across the shipyard, Maggie snatched the mitten from the woman's grasp and shoved it back on her hand, hiding the offending appendage from view.

"We can't talk here," she muttered.

"But—"

"If I don't finish these it'll call attention," Maggie insisted, reclaiming her pail and the brush that had been discarded in the tussle. When the woman clutched at her sleeve, Maggie paused. Heart pounding, she turned to face her, and fought to ignore the flush that rose to her cheeks when the woman clasped her hand in a silent plea.

"What's your name?" Maggie asked.

The woman hesitated. "My friends in this part of the world call me Sun."

"I'm Maggie."

"Please, Maggie," Sun begged, her voice deep with intensity. "I have crossed the sea to find her. If you know where she is…"

Maggie shook her head sharply, reclaiming her hand with a jerk. The chill air bit at her skin in the absence of Sun's warmth. "Not here," she repeated. After a moment's thought, she pointed down the main lane. "There's a pub down this road— Murphy's. Wait for me there."

"But—"

"Keep your gloves on."

With the final suggestion Maggie made her escape. But even as she resumed her task, her head swirled with thoughts, and her chest filled with apprehension. Suspicion niggled at the back of her mind, until the point that when she saw another of Bash's crew, Siobhan, pasting up her own final flyer, Maggie all but thrust her satchel into the girl's hands.

"Finish these?"

"Wha—?"

Maggie was already handing over her pail as well when she uttered the magic words. "I'll owe you."

Easily recognizing the value of being owed by someone with a personal connection to Bash, Siobhan nodded and accepted the pail without another word.

The skies finally opened as Maggie wound her way back towards the pub, turning the streets to mud as rain poured down. Her hand instinctively curled around her halved medallion, reaching for the reassurance her Da was always quick to offer. Though it was a poor substitute for the hugs that used to swallow Maggie whole, the jagged edge of metal against her skin steadied her.

By the time she reached the pub, Sun had popped the collar of her too-large coat, clutching it tight around her neck to shield herself from the rivulets of rain that dribbled from the eaves. Water dripped from her hat as well, weighing the brim down to give her the look of a well-drenched pup, but her entire face brightened when her eyes spotted Maggie slipping through the crowd.

With a tilt of her chin, Maggie wordlessly beckoned Sun to follow. Sun immediately stepped onto the soggy street in readiness, but instead of trailing at a discreet distance, she came up to walk shoulder-to-shoulder with Maggie, clutching her collar all the tighter.

"Will you take me to—"

"No," Maggie returned in a low voice. "We need to talk first."

Maggie heard the click in Sun's throat as she swallowed a protest, and snapped her jaw shut to continue walking beside Maggie in peace. Maggie was grateful for the reprieve, though it only gave her time for her thoughts to spiral out of control. By the time they climbed the longer outer stair up the building where she and Gran lived, the rain had stopped. Maggie's suspicion did not.

With each step, it grew into a certainty that sat both light and heavy in her chest.

The building was old, and cheap enough that plenty of their neighbors were also in Bash's payroll. Maggie knew he had eyes and ears all throughout the town; it would be foolish to think he didn't have watchers here as well. But the way seemed clear on Maggie's final scan of the walkway, as Sun slipped into the apartment ahead of her.

Maggie followed suit, and closed the door firmly behind her.

Sun stood in the center of the room, completely uninterested in the small apartment. Her focus remained solely on Maggie, relentless in its intensity, and only broke when Kraken *mrrow*ed pitifully, winding himself between and around her ankles. Sun recoiled with a short cry of alarm, lifting her feet comically to pick her way free of the critter that followed her as she went.

"Kraken!" Gran barked, teetering out of the kitchen. Coughing, she shook her handkerchief at the beast. "Leave the poor girl alone. Git."

Kraken promptly ignored her, only ceasing when Maggie scooped him into her arms, swiftly moving to scritch his favorite spot to pre-empt any claws of indignation. Gran blinked up at Sun through her bifocals.

"Hello there, lass," Gran rasped. "You're certainly a new face.
"

Sun's lips opened to respond, but Maggie beat her to the punch.

"You're her, aren't you?"

Maggie's focus was entirely on the two-legged mermaid standing in her apartment. Sun turned to face her to meet her gaze. Her eyes searched Maggie's, as though looking for something Maggie couldn't discern.

"Who?" Gran asked, echoing like an owl.

Maggie's hand lifted, and pressed her palm across her chest, pantomiming the gesture Night had given her that very morning.

"Her heart," Maggie said softly.

The breath Sun released emerged a ragged sigh of relief. Her eyes closed as her hands clasped over her chest. "Yes. And she is mine. Is she all right? Is she safe?"

Maggie hesitated. "She's alive," she allowed. "And she misses you."

"Take me to her."

Shaking her head no, Maggie lifted her hands placatingly. "It's not that simple—"

"Yes, it is—!"

"Maggie," Gran interrupted with a light cough. "Care to introduce me to your friend?"

Gran's amicable query was met with the softening of Sun's shoulders, dispelling the rising tension. Grateful for the interruption, Maggie stooped to release Kraken with a slide towards the woodstove. Enticed by the warmth of the crackling fire, Kraken padded up onto the woodpile, and curled up into a loaf to watch through slowly blinking eyes.

"Aye," Maggie agreed finally. "Gran, this is Sun. Sun, Gran."

"Well met, Gran." The smile that Sun directed to Gran was genial, but distracted for the brief moment it lingered before she rounded on Maggie once more. "You said—"

"Sun," Maggie explained, shooting Gran a look before meeting Sun's gaze once more, "is a friend of Night's."

Gran's gaze widened, bright with enthusiasm. "You're one of them, lass?"

Sun looked at her. "One of who?"

"The Merrow Men," Gran elaborated. "Merfolk."

Sun nodded. "Aye. I am of the folk. And I am here to bring her home," Sun declared, before her voice pitched low into a warning. "I *will* bring her home—"

"I already tried," Maggie blurted. "I tried to get her back to the harbor, but she would have been dead before we got there."

She still had nightmares of the way Night's skin had dried, pulling tight around her bones, even cracking as she'd heaved for breath. They hadn't even made it off the stage. Maggie had rolled her back into the tank, and the water had revived her almost instantly, but it was days before the cracks in Night's skin had fully healed.

With Sun standing and breathing in her apartment, Maggie's hopes lifted. "How are you able to survive out of the water?"

"With this." Sun reached under her shirt and withdrew a cinched leather pouch. Despite the water still dripping from the ends of Sun's hair, the pouch was dry. Now Maggie understood why Sun had clutched her collar so tightly shut. Carefully ensuring her fingers were dry, Sun reached into the pouch and pulled out a small limpet shell.

Gran leaned in close to look at it, adjusting her lenses as though it were sight that made it seem entirely ordinary.

"It was spelled by a sea witch," Sun explained, tucking it back inside its pouch. "The magic grants me legs, and the ability to survive on land as well as any human."

Before she could ask any further questions, the shipyard bell rang, signaling the approach of sundown. Maggie cursed, and reached for her hat. "I have to go— we'll talk more when I get back. Stay here with Gran," she instructed Sun.

Without waiting for a response, Maggie was out the door and thundering down the wooden steps of the outer stair, skipping the final two to leap into a sprint, pelting towards the warehouse. By the time she arrived, Siobhan and Kieran were already at work, hawking the night's show. Maggie slipped in alongside them, calling enticements as she palmed the cap of her hat.

"Come one! Come all! Come witness the Creature of the Deep!"

She hated every moment of it, and hated herself with every nickel that clinked into her hat once the doors opened to admit patrons. Siobhan manned the opposite post from Maggie, while two others worked the second door. Within a matter of minutes the warehouse theater was brimming with enthusiastic chatter and anticipation.

Maggie peered inside, and felt a jolt when she remembered that tonight Declan O'Reilly would be in among the audience. Suddenly, the crowds' enthusiasm felt more sinister, every call another knell heralding Night's looming fate.

Distracted, Maggie almost missed the familiar figure that slipped into the warehouse with the last few patrons on the east door, bypassing the nickel charge into Kieran's cap on her way through.

"Oy!" Kieran shouted. Before he could chase after Sun, Maggie intercepted, shoving her hat into Kieran's hands to keep him occupied.

"It's okay, she's with me," she fibbed, hoping it would be enough to forestall any further protest. "Take care of this, will you?"

Unlike Siobhan, Maggie didn't give Kieran time to answer one way or the other. She relinquished her hat to him entirely and slipped into the crowd as well. She found her quarry perched on the outer edge of the final row, scanning the restless crowd with sharp eyes. Even from where she stood Maggie could detect the disgust Sun held for the salacious crowd, having correctly discerned that whatever was set to come, it would be an exploitation rather than a true performance.

Maggie marched towards her and grabbed her firmly by the arm. "I told you to stay put," she muttered, tugging Sun forcefully. "Come with me—"

"No!" Sun rebuked, pulling her arm free. "I will not sit idle in your home."

"You need to listen to me, right now," Maggie hissed back. Sun glared at her, and Maggie finally softened, willing Sun to heed her. "You don't want to see this, Sun. Trust me."

"My heart is here, Maggie. I will not leave. I will see."

Maggie sensed the attention of several patrons, and knew it would only be a matter of time before they attracted more attention than they could explain away. Weighing her options, she gritted her teeth and straightened, folding her arms across her chest to hide her discomfort.

In moments, the lantern wicks were shortened, casting the warehouse into shadows. A beam of light flared to life, illuminating the deck of the stage in a wash of warm light. In front of the stage, the tank had been covered with a patched and smudged canvas tarp, hiding its contents from view.

When the crowd fell silent, Bash stepped into view, arms spread wide to the audience.

"Welcome!"

The audience roared in response, making the rafters shake with the raucous cheers and thundering applause. Bash basked in it for a long moment, then motioned for the crowd to settle. Once he had relative quiet, he shot them all another charming grin.

"Thank you all for coming! It warms my heart to see the curiosity that still lives within all of us, big or small, young or old. To embrace the unknown is to embrace the future, and that is what we're doing tonight, folks!"

From the corner of her eye, Maggie watched Sun watch the other patrons, and start patting her hands together in a pantomime of clapping.

"I only hope that you have saved your supper for later, for our show for you tonight will be the most wondrous it's ever been, featuring a creature so ghastly, so abhorrent that it has never before been seen by man, hiding itself away in the depths of the ocean to pluck the flesh from the bones of drowned men! But even in such horror there is beauty, and in such horrific beauty, there is wonder. So, without any further ado, ladies and gents, I present to you— *the Mermaid of the Deep!*"

With a flourish of his arm, the canvas tarp withdrew with a snap, revealing the sinuous shape coiled within the dark tank, backlit by low lamps installed among the scaffolding around the tank. A wave of interest rippled through the crowd, one that swelled into a collected gasp of delight when the lanterns in the warehouse brightened once more, filling the tank with light.

Bash had taken Maggie's suggestion after all. The water was clearer than it'd been in weeks, revealing Night in all her glory. She floated in the middle of the tank, tail drooping and her long, sharply angled arms buoyed on either side. The audience's gasps of delight slowly shifted to murmurs of concern, and Maggie didn't blame them. Maggie was used to Night's unnerving habit of floating as though dead, but these people were not. But despite her familiarity, Maggie felt a frisson of alarm as well— Night didn't float during exhibitions. The lights and the sounds agitated her, made her twist and swim anxiously back and forth as much as the confines of her prison would allow.

She scanned the length of Night's tail, but saw no changes in the scrapes and raw patches from her vantage point. At the corner of her eye Maggie detected a flicker of motion as Sun's legs bunched as though to stand.

Maggie placed a gentle hand on her shoulder, keeping her firmly in place. Sun's head whipped up to glare at her, a protest on her parted lips, but faced forward again when Maggie leaned to speak quietly in her ear.

"If you want to help her," Maggie murmured, "then you need to stay out of sight."

Sun didn't respond. The musicians began to play, and Bash thumped the tip of his cane heavily against the boards of the deck. The heavy vibrations traveled through the tank walls and water to Night's ears, eliciting a flicker of movement as Night uncoiled and slid closer to the front of the tank.

The crowd was elated, but Maggie's heart sank. It would take more than movement to impress Declan, and Bash wouldn't settle for anything less. In the set of Night's odd, angular jaw Maggie detected spiteful resistance. *Just do it,* Maggie pleaded silently. Her hand tightened on Sun's shoulder, this time to keep herself in place.

One more night. Just one more.

Night didn't receive Maggie's mental plea. After the initial movement, she fell still once more, and refused to even make eye contact with the world beyond the glass wall of her watery prison. From the corner of her eye Maggie saw Bash motion to a man standing at the back corner of the stage.

The man stepped forward at the signal with a fishing gaff in hand. Gripping the wooden shaft, he shoved the hooked end into the water, poking the rounded bend at Night. He earned little more than a flick of her tail for his efforts, the splash dampening the hem of his trousers. On the second, more forceful jab, the point of it scraped a narrow furrow into Night's scales, earning a shrill, inhuman scream from Night's throat. It carried through the water and filled the air of the warehouse with a chilling, whispering shriek: a sound eclipsed by gasps of wonder as Night began to glow.

Ignited by her pain, Night's pale skin and lighter scales pulsed with eerie luminescence, making her even more ghost-like. The night of her first debut, Night's fear had been enough to ignite the glow for almost the entire presentation, and Maggie had stared mesmerized by a light that rivaled the moon's pale glow.

Now, though, it faded quickly, and only reawakened under further distress. Now, the sight of it made Maggie's stomach churn, knowing that each illumination meant another scrape for her salve the next morning. Each plunge of the gaff left a sour taste in Maggie's mouth, and added that much more tension to the shoulder under her hand.

When the hooked end of the gaff caught an errant scrap of Night's fins, it tugged her closer to the surface before tearing free, splitting the ragged fin clear through.

Before anyone could react, Night whipped around, grabbed the shaft of the pole with both hands, and yanked it sharply. The crowd's gasps of horror swallowed Sun's own cry of outrage as the man lost his balance and toppled into the tank, joining Night in the churning water.

Cries of alarm filled the packed warehouse, as the man floundered and sank, scraping his palms against the flat walls of the tank to pull himself up.

Unable to find purchase, and unable to swim, he slid further and further down, until his heavy boots touched the bottom of the tank. The crowd fell dead silent, as a shout of panic bubbled from the man's throat. Then he inhaled, and Maggie realized in horror that they were about to watch a man drown.

"Somebody help him!" a voice cried out, but nothing happened. Bash had already left the stage, and no one emerged from behind it to offer help.

Instead, it was Night who uncoiled from where she'd retreated to the furthest corner of the tank when the man tumbled in. It was Night who grasped her tormentor's arm, and pulled him to the surface. Even after the man had grabbed the edge of the stage and hauled himself up, spluttering and choking for air, Night helped push him from below.

In his panic, and desperate to be free of the water, the man kicked wildly as he floundered. His boot caught Night across the side of the head, earning another shrill yelp as she recoiled and withdrew to the bottom of the tank, huddling as far out of reach as she could manage. She cried out again, but this time the sound petered to silence after barely a moment. Except it wasn't silent— the howls of dogs outside filled the air, spurred by a sound only they could hear.

Them, and Sun.

Sun lurched to her feet, her skin paling to a sickly hue. Before she could surge down the aisle, Maggie wrapped an arm around Sun's shoulders and wrested her in a new direction, aiming for the relative privacy of the street outside. Sun fought her every step of the way, until they were finally outside and Maggie shoved her ahead with all her might. Sun stumbled, unsteady on her feet, but recovered her balance swiftly enough to round on Maggie with fists swinging.

One caught Maggie on the edge of her chin, surprising her enough for Sun to twist her hands into Maggie's coat and slam her into the side of the warehouse, blinded by rage.

"You knew! Monster!" Sun accused. "That was why you wanted me to stay away!"

Maggie gripped Sun's wrists, firm but without struggle. She nodded. "Yes."

The truthful admission sucked the wind from Sun's sails, and the fury in her eyes morphed to tears. "You sit by, and you do nothing."

"I—" Maggie's explanation cut short when a familiar voice emanated from around the corner, heralding the arrival of Bash himself. Pressing a finger to Sun's lips, Maggie instinctively reached up and tugged Sun closer by the neck, affecting an intimate pose just as Bash turned the corner. A moment of silence followed as Bash stopped dead in his tracks. Then, a long and low whistle cut through the growing dark, and a lantern leaned in close to confirm Maggie's identity.

"Mags! What're you doin' here?" Bash grinned.

Squeezing Sun's straining wrist in silent warning, Maggie glared at him in feigned annoyance. "What's it look like?"

"Easy, lass." Bash lifted his hands in ready surrender. Sun and Maggie waited, quivering, for him to move on, but instead he lingered. "Don't worry about tonight's feeding. I'll look after the beast tonight."

Sun growled low in her throat, but the tightening of Maggie's hand on the back of her neck issued a silent warning. "That's not necessary—"

"Yeh've earned it, Mags. Clearing up the water was a good call, and we had one hell of a show tonight. In fact, Declan's expecting me down at the pub to talk business."

Maggie swallowed thickly. "Really, I don't mind—"

"Aye, but I'm a kind man, and a romantic. Go have your fun, lass."

Maggie opened her mouth to protest, but Bash cut her off before word one. "Git on then. I'll even take tomorrow morning tomorrow, give yeh time to… sleep in."

Bash was soft on her— the entire town knew it. But even Bash had his limits, and Maggie knew if she protested much further, she'd arouse suspicion, so all she did was let her features soften into a low, slow smile as she threaded her fingers through Sun's.

"Right then. Thanks, Bash."

She slid out from between Sun and the wall, and tugged relentlessly on Sun's hand. "Come with me," she enticed with a flirtatious grin. "I know a place."

That place was the apartment, reached in a symphony of false giggles that Maggie kept up when she saw shadowy figures on more than one street corner. At Maggie's warning squeeze, Sun kept up the charade, and when they tumbled into the apartment, it was with a symphony of false giggles, and when the door closed behind them Maggie let her back thud against the door as though Sun had pressed her against it for a kiss, even as Sun ripped her hand from hers.

"That man…"

"Calm down—"

Sun rounded on her, eyes blazing. "You! You help him?! A man so cruel he smiles at another's torment?"

Shame settled heavily on Maggie's shoulders, but she didn't dare look away. "I couldn't leave Night alone with him."

Sun stopped in her tracks. Her anger deflated in the next moment, leaving her shoulders drooping in despair. "We have to get her out of there. Please," she begged.

Maggie pushed away from the door, crossing towards Sun with her head high.

"We will. And we can. With that."

She pointed to the leather pouch around Sun's neck. "That will let her survive on land, right? If you wait in the harbor, I can take the shell to her—"

"The magic does not work dat way," Sun told them. Her hand clasped around the leather pouch. "The charm will last so long as it does not touch the water, but it is bound to me. It will not work for another."

Biting back her own tears of frustration, Maggie took a steadying breath. "Then we'll get another."

"Where?"

"The same place you got that one." It was simple.

Sun shook her head. "We can't. Magic is outlawed across the seven seas."

Maggie's hands tightened into fists. "Then how did you get that one?"

"Where I am from, there is a place where witches and *brujas* trade their wares in secret. There are certainly others, but I know the location of only that one. None here."

Maggie's heart dropped. But then, Gran cleared her throat, reminding them of her presence for the first time since their return.

"Perhaps," she said with her raspy voice, "I can help with that."

Maggie glanced at her. "What do you mean, Gran?"

A solemn silence answered, which Gran broke by shuffling back to the kitchen. "Let me put more water in the soup," she coughed. "This is a tale best shared over a warm belly."

Once they were all seated around the table, with bowls of untouched soup in front of them, Gran offered Maggie a wry smile.

"When your Da didn't come back, I tried to find him."

Maggie shook her head. "Gran, you could barely lift your head, you were so ill. What're you on about?"

"No, lass. Not at first. You were so devastated, Mags, I was desperate to learn whether there was any hope to give you. So I went to the fishwife."

The fishwife was an old whisper around the docks. Somewhere between a devil and a saint, it was said she could grant your wish in exchange for a curse. Or she'd snatch a child from their bed if they didn't mind their folks.

She was whatever the town needed her to be, if she existed at all.

"The legends say that she can be found in a place where the land meets the sea, unreachable by mortals. An old trader once told me of a cave set deep in the cliffside, one that could only be accessed by humans in the lowest of tides. So during the next king tide I went there, and I found the fishwife."

"You could have been killed—"

Sun shushed Maggie's admonishment, eyes locked on Gran with rapt attention. Gran patted her hand in gratitude, and continued.

"The fishwife is a sea witch, and in her cave she could hear all the stirrings of the ocean. For a price, she said, I could learn my answer. And I did: your da was swallowed by the sea."

Gran broke off with a rattling cough. This time, it persisted long enough that Maggie climbed to her feet to fetch her medicine from the cabinet. Gran poured a spoonful and swallowed it in one go, grimacing at the bitter taste.

"I could tell you the truth, Mags, and help you heal. It was all I could do."

Maggie settled back in her seat, stoppering the medicine bottle and setting it aside. "I never questioned his fate, Gran. Seems like a lot of trouble to go to for something we already knew."

"You were so young, lass. If there was any hope to cling to, I wanted you to have it."

Maggie looked away, and blinked at the sight of Sun's intense gaze, still focused entirely on Gran. "Sun?"

"What was the price?"

The succinct question jolted Maggie to the core, a new shock rocketing down her spine. She hadn't considered it real enough to worry about that, but Sun's tone made it real. But Gran only smiled grimly.

"My breath."

Maggie's gaze snapped back to her grandmother. "What?"

"I was already old when your Da left," Gran told her. "My days were already numbered. I didn't mind surrendering some of them to bring you peace."

Anger flared in Maggie's chest. "You— you mean to say— your sickness was your own doing?!"

"I won't apologize for it," Gran countered, her voice sharpening in a rare moment of steel. "You'd already lost too much, without your Ma. If there was a chance—"

"But you would have me lose you, too?" Maggie snapped. "How could you?"

"Maggie—"

Maggie ignored Sun's gentle admonishment and slammed to her feet, stalking to the door and marching through it. She kept going until she reached the far end of the gangway, where a small landing jutted out past the end of the building. With the breeze able to tousle her hair and curl around her skin, Maggie forced herself to take a deep breath, and then another...

She lost herself to the breath of the wind until a footstep scuffed against the deck behind her. She opened her eyes just as Sun stepped up to lean against the damp rail beside her.

"Do not be angry with her," Sun said gently. "Right or wrong, she made her choice out of love."

Maggie shook her head. "I've been trying to keep us together ever since Da didn't come home, and she's always had one foot out the door. Little did I know it was because she'd put it there herself."

This time, Sun didn't try to make excuses. She simply stood beside her at the rail, gazing up at the oppressive clouds coating the skies. Watching her watch the clouds slowly creep, Maggie wondered what the skies looked like far to the west, where Sun called home. Da had spoken of skies teeming with stars, untouched by lamplight or cloud cover. Did they see the same patterns that peeked out in the autumn, when the summer rains passed? Or were they different, like their voices and odd clicking sounds?

Was their freedom the same as Da's? Trading the boards and the winds for a current and pulsing waves… Maggie found she liked the idea.

"Your Gran remembers where the cave is located. Tomorrow is the king tide, opening the cave to land dwellers for one night until the tide returns and hides it for another year."

Maggie nodded, though apprehension coiled thick and heavy in her belly. If Gran had given her breath for a fact they already knew, she wasn't sure she wanted to know what a shell would cost. What had Sun already paid, for the legs that had carried her here in search of the person she loved? What else would she surrender?

If what Maggie knew of Sun so far held true… she imagined Sun would give anything to save Night.

Just as Gran had been willing to give anything for Maggie's peace of mind.

With a quiet sigh, Maggie turned to go back inside, only to pause when Sun grasped her wrist gently. Maggie blinked, her cheeks flushing at the unexpected touch. Her fingers were gentle, and warm against her skin, just as they'd been that afternoon in the market.

"Maggie... I am sorry I struck you."

Nodding away the bruise no doubt already starting to color her chin, Maggie let her own hand turn and clasp Sun's wrist in turn. "Can I ask you a question?"

Sun nodded.

"You and Night..."

White teeth flashed in the darkness, a smile soft with affection. "Night," she echoed. "I like that."

"You two are so... different," Maggie stumbled over the word, for no reason at all. "Does the shell's magic change your appearance too?"

"No," Sun replied, her voice gentle in the growing shadows. "The magic only gives us legs to walk and lungs to breathe. Where I am from, we are close to the surface— the sun keeps us warm, and lights our way. But there are other folk, those who live beyond the shelf, in the shadows of the deep, where little light reaches. Night is of those folk."

"But you love her."

Sun nodded. "With all of my being." Her grasp on Maggie's wrist firmed, sending another bolt of warmth up Maggie's arm. "I am grateful she has had one friend in all this. Especially one as kind as you."

In the dark, Sun's eyes shone warmly. Maggie's heart sped in her chest, as though it might slip between her ribs and run off wherever Sun asked her to go.

Pulling her hand back abruptly, Maggie reached for the familiar touch of her halved medallion.

"I know what it's like to miss somebody," she said, rubbing her thumb across the soft metal. She turned back towards the apartment. "Come on. It's cold out here."

When they slipped back inside, Gran looked up from her rocker, her gaze shadowed with a quiet guilt. Sun passed Maggie with a touch against the small of her back as she moved towards the kitchen, affording them what little privacy could be had in the single room. Maggie joined Gran by the fire, kneeling beside her to let her face be cupped in cool, wrinkled hands.

"Is this why you've been nudging me onto every ship that drops anchor in the harbor?" Maggie asked quietly.

"Aye," Gran returned softly. "It pains me to see you work so hard to scrape up the coin to ease a discomfort I brought on myself. You deserve more, lass. Y'always have."

Pressing trembling lips together, Maggie nodded, eyes rolling slightly. "Sun says you made your choice out of love," she began slowly, earning an earnest nod from her grandmother. Reaching up, she grasped Gran's wrists in her hands, giving them a gentle squeeze. "Caring for you is mine. Please, Gran— don't make me say goodbye to you any sooner than I have to."

Gran leaned forward and pressed a kiss to her forehead. "I promise."

***

Gran remembered her journey to the sea market like she'd last visited yesterday. She spared no detail, right on down to the little dinghy she'd used to row herself out to the cliffs. Together, Maggie and Sun rowed out past the harbor, and north along the coast, until they spotted a shadow in the cliff face. Approaching further they found the shadow was the cave opening Gran had described to them, still looking like the birthmark that stained Old Man Withers' neck.

Maggie almost grinned as they passed beneath the oddly shaped arch of the opening, but her mirth swiftly faded as the shadows swallowed them. With only the light of their single lantern, they slowly coasted along the narrow channel, soon tucking the oars away to pull themselves hand over hand when the walls pressed too close to continue rowing.

What Gran didn't tell them was the warren of tunnels that branched off to wind deeper into the cliff face, confusing their path and leading them down more than one false lead. The total darkness chilled Maggie's blood, and her ears roared like she'd stuck her head into a conch. Sun remained quiet behind her, similarly unsettled.

When their final turn funneled them into a channel that squeezed closer and closer, Maggie almost turned back, not to find another route, but to row home. They'd wasted precious hours feeling their way through the dark, and each minute brought them closer to the tide coming in, and sealing them in for good. Each minute closer to Gran losing Maggie, the same way they'd both lost Da.

But just as the last of Maggie's courage started to sputter out, the current spat them out onto the glassy surface of a broad tidal pool. They squinted against the reflection of moonlight against the water, filtering from a gap overhead to illuminate the unexpected scene.

The grotto was actually home to not one but two tidal pools, separated by a narrow isthmus of flat rock that jutted from the water. Along this strip, blankets and driftwood tables had been spread out where more than one vendor laid out their wares. Among the makeshift lane, figures moved cautiously, both human and... not.

Slick cave walls glistened with moisture, reflecting the water's rippling glow as Maggie slowly used a single oar to steer them towards the rocky shore. As they floated closer, Maggie saw a slew of wares both familiar and not— irregular pearls, lumpy but shimmering with an unnatural light; hard-won sea urchins with spines tipped with metal caps; exotic shells and beads of both stone and glass and much, much more.

When the dinghy ran aground, Maggie hopped out and steadied it. She eyed the ankle-deep water warily, before shooting Sun a look. "I might be able to find a way to get the boat closer..."

"The magic resides in the shell," Sun assured her. "So long as it remains dry..."

Even as she said the words, her hand curled protectively around the lump just visible beneath the collar of her shirt. Nevertheless, she accepted the hand Maggie offered to steady herself, and kept hold of it even after their boots reached dry land.

"I will go this way—"

Maggie tightened her grip on Sun's hand before she could pull away. "We'll both go," Maggie countered. "It's too risky to split up."

"We haven't time—"

"Night can't afford anything to happen to either one of us, aye?"

The set of Sun's shoulders softened with an accepting grin. "Aye." Her fingers tightened around Maggie's. "Together, then."

Gran had said she'd found the fishwife in the water all those years ago, but they didn't need that to know when they'd found her. On the water she was still, installed on the far side of the isthmus in a pool that— where their dinghy was moored in shallows— seemed bottomless.

The fishwife was a corpulent mass of a witch with a bulbous double chin and a yellowing pallor to her skin. Stubble akin to a five o'clock shadow roughened her face, but as they neared, Maggie's throat locked when she found that the stubble was not an unsightly beard but a ridged frill that flexed and protracted with a seeming life of its own. A frill that, if Maggie recognized the coloring correctly, contained enough venom to kill a grown man dead before his corpse hit the ground.

The shadow of her body spread in the water around her, its shape disguised by rippling waves and refracted moonlight. All Maggie could discern was the massive bulk, and the relative ease with which the witch moved in spite of it. Her movements were as deft as a seamstress' as she took pinches of this and that from different vials standing on her table, and adding them to a gloppy substance staining the inside of the largest oyster Maggie had ever seen.

Taking a breath to steady herself, she turned to Sun and gave their joined hands a squeeze of reassurance.

"Stay here," she urged. Sun's lips immediately parted in protest. "It's too deep to risk your shell getting wet. Night's going to need you on legs if we're going to get her back to the sea."

Sun hesitated, determined to be with her every step of the way. Then she relented, releasing Maggie's hand with a soft squeeze. "You're right."

"Usually am," Maggie quipped, as much to embolden herself as to assure Sun. When she turned back towards the pool, the witch had caught sight of her, and watched her with an uncanny gaze. She swallowed, and lifted her chin. "Onward ho."

Instinctively, Maggie reached for her medallion as she waded to the witch's table. The shore of the isthmus sloped steeply, taking her nearly waist deep before she reached the driftwood table, propped between two rocks. As for the unnaturally decorated merchant who seemed to sit just at the surface, Maggie could only wonder just how much of her lurked out of sight.

"Happy tides to you," Maggie greeted, voice trembling. When the fishwife blinked at her, frill undulating, Maggie flushed to realize she'd defaulted to the familiar greeting her Da used to use. It was the first thing he said to her when he returned home from a voyage, and the last thing he said on his way out.

She hadn't thought about it in years.

"Happy tides," the fishwife echoed, her gaze lifted in something akin to amusement at the unusual hail.

Then her focus shifted to where Sun stood anxiously on the shore. There was a moment of close study before recognition struck, and her smile shifted towards a sneer.

When Maggie turned to look, Sun shrank away, ashamed.

"And to the princess as well!" the witch called across the water. "Have you come looking for your eel?"

Maggie's apprehension evaporated in a plume of indignation. She snapped back around and pegged the witch with a glare. "Don't call her that!"

"Her folk's the reason we're forced to scurry into the earth like crabs," the witch hissed. Her frill rattled in agitation. "Covetous, pretentious—!"

"I don't mean her," Maggie growled. "Neither of us know any *eels.*"

The witch eyed her, a fishmonger weighing her catch. Maggie let her, holding her gaze without waver. When the fishwife remained silent, Maggie took a deep breath, and tried again.

"Years ago you helped my Gran learn whether my Da was dead or alive. Now we've come to strike another bargain."

The witch's quills fluttered in interest. "State your business, then, human."

"We are in need of an enchanted shell. One that will give merfolk legs and lungs for land." Maggie eyed the witch with an arch regard. "Gran says the fishwife would be the place to find such a shell."

Slimy lips slid and spread in a sallow smile. "I certainly could. The only variable here is you— what you are willing to pay for the enchantment."

"I have coin enough," Maggie declared, hoping her fib would entice the witch to take the bait.

The witch only laughed, the sound deep and rasping. "This place has no use for slices of tin, human."

Cold fingers of dread crept up the back of Maggie's neck.

"Then what can you use?" she asked.

"Any manner of things. A pretty shell, or a spine from the largest urchin in the seven seas. A black pearl from the deep. A moonbeam, or a smile." The witch pinned her with a sharp gaze. "A memory."

Maggie's blood chilled. "Wh—What kind of memory?"

"One that means something to its owner. Perhaps," the fishwife said, reaching out to rest a single fingertip on Maggie's shorn medallion, "that of a loved one lost."

Maggie recoiled, wrapping her hand around the pendant at her neck. *"Never."*

The witch's features soured. "Then you waste my time. Go."

Sun lurched forward. "No, please! There has to be something else you want!"

"Not from you." The witch snarled, before turning her glare back on Maggie. "I have named my price. Pay, or make way for those who will."

Maggie opened her mouth again, but her protest died in her throat when the witch turned back to her potion, dismissing them entirely.

Turning back towards shore, Maggie caught only a flash of the tears in Sun's eyes before her friend turned and swept away in a rush, disappearing between two broad-shouldered figures— figures with eyes so wide-set they were all but on opposite sides of their heads, not unlike the sharks that sometimes came in to market. They half-turned at Sun's push, heads swiveling like owls, but couldn't seem to spot her, and so they strode on, heads angled oddly to see their way.

With one final glance towards the witch, Maggie was met with a dismissal— a single tick of the puffer-witch's brow, and she returned to her potion, no longer interested.

Once she had waded back to the stone shore, Maggie found Sun perched on a ledge overhanging the gently lapping water, knees hugged tight to her chest. She stared vacantly across the pool, heavy with despair.

After a long moment, Sun sniffled, wiping her cheeks.

"Her name—" Sun sniffled after a long moment, wiping her cheeks. "It is unpronounceable outside the water, but... it means— the dark between stars. She is that, and the stars too. She is my entire sky. I would trade anything I have to save her, if only the witch would take it."

Maggie's heart twinged painfully in her chest. Eight years ago, her childhood ended when her Da failed to come home. Whatever hope Gran thought she'd needed, she'd known the truth— he was dead. Even so, that didn't keep her from offering the universe everything in her being to make it not so.

She thought of Night's unspoken hope that very morning, when asked if there was any chance her love was looking for her.

In that moment, Maggie's hopelessness hardened to resolve.

It was too late for her Da.

It wasn't too late for Night.

Bolting to her feet, Maggie ignored Sun's call of dismay to dart back towards the fishwife's table. Splashing back into the water, the witch barely had a chance to register her return before Maggie barked at her.

"I accept your terms."

The witch smiled, and beckoned Maggie deeper into the water. Maggie obeyed, and stood where the woman positioned her with her pudgy hands. "What do I do?" she asked.

"Nothing," the fishwife said, dipping her fingers into the hollow of a sea urchin filled with salve. She dabbed it on Maggie's forehead, muttering indiscernible words under her breath as she did so. Then she dabbed the same salve on the jagged face of the pendant around Maggie's neck, nodding to herself in approval.

Before Maggie knew what was happening, the fishwife closed her hand around the pendant and gave it a yank. The chain snapped, stinging the back of her neck and pulling a cry of protest from Maggie's lips.

"Hey! That's—"

The witch looked deep into Maggie's eyes, silencing her.

"Nothing," she elaborated, "except let go."

With that, she gripped Maggie's chin and pressed their foreheads together, chanting.

Forgive me, Da.

Maggie felt the chill of water pouring onto her scalp, the tap of the pendant against her forehead, and then nothing more.

***

When Maggie blinked, she found herself standing knee deep in the glowing water, a trickle of water trailing down her forehead into her eyes. The witch stepped away with a necklace dangling in one hand. In a fuzzy sort of way, Maggie realized the necklace was hers, but didn't feel any impulse to ask for it back. She couldn't remember why she had it in the first place.

"Don't just stand there, human," the witch urged. "Come."

Sloshing through the water that shallowed from hip to knee to calf, Maggie followed her. Once she was in front of the witch's driftwood table, a small whelk shell nearly poked her in the nose, thrust towards her by swollen, turgid fingers.

"As agreed," the witch told her. "One pair of legs."

"Night," Maggie murmured as her mind cleared further. The world sharpened under the task ahead. She accepted the shell with grateful fingers, and the small oiled leather pouch that was offered a moment later.

"Keep it dry," came the warning. "The magic will end the moment it touches the sea."

"Thank you."

The witch nodded, her ridged features almost softening into a smile. "Our business is done."

Maggie wasted no time traversing the shore a final time, this time meeting Sun on the rocky embankment. When Maggie lifted the leather pouch in victory, Sun's features didn't warm with pleasure, but rather creased with sadness.

"Oh, Maggie," Sun breathed, cradling the pouch and its precious contents in both hands. "I would not have asked you to."

Maggie blinked. "Asked me to what?"

A shake of Sun's head answers her, and the exchange slid from Maggie's focus. "Come," she urged, still dazed. "Let's go home."

Returning to the boat, Maggie intended to guide Sun, but as they pulled back out into the surf, Maggie found that Sun had taken the oars herself and was navigating them back towards the harbor. Back on proper land, she supported Maggie's flagging strength by wrapping an arm under Maggie's, and retracing their route back to Gran's apartment.

Usually a deep sleeper, Gran bolted awake when the door opened to admit them, and Maggie was vaguely aware of her Gran's voice asking questions she couldn't summon the thought to answer. Before long, Gran's thick blanket wrapped around her shoulders like a hug, and the fire was stoked back to life once more, wasting precious firewood.

A mug of warm soup water was pressed into her hands, and Maggie cradled it close to leech its warmth as the world faded in and out around her.

"What was the price?" she heard Gran ask between coughs, her voice low.

Maggie didn't hear Sun's reply, but a moment later she felt Gran's lips press a kiss against her forehead, and the comforting stroke of a hand against her hair as she finally sank into a deep sleep, and the relief of nothing.

***

Maggie roused hours later with the toll of the church bells. Blinking against the morning sun, her vision cleared to reveal Sun cuddled peacefully next to her, still deep asleep. Maggie smiled, filled with a warmth she hadn't felt since…

Well, she couldn't quite remember.

Then the bells tolled eight, scolding her tardiness. Maggie bolted upright with a curse, scrambling towards the door as she reached for coat and scarf and cap, only to pause when Gran called out from where she stood hunched over a pot on the small stove.

"It's the day of rest, young one." Gran's soft voice made her pause, one arm already threaded awkwardly into her coat. "No market today."

With a whoosh, Maggie's panic snapped away. She could almost cry— no market meant more sleep, and her deflating panic left her bones heavy with exhaustion. But when she staggered back towards her blanket, she found that Sun had already claimed the empty fabric for herself, cocooning herself in Maggie's residual heat without waking. Loath to disturb her, Maggie diverted to the stove, ambling towards her Gran to press a light kiss to a withered cheek.

"Mornin', Gran."

"Mornin', luv," Gran returned, continuing to stir her pot— which Maggie now saw was filled with thickening porridge. "Sun tells me you got what you needed last night?"

"Aye," Maggie grinned around a yawn. "The fishwife says hello."

Gran snorted, and Maggie laughed. Her chest felt light, like the entirety of the sun filled her from the inside out. When Gran moved to rise and portion the oatmeal for breakfast, Maggie bounced up quicker. "I'll do it."

Practically springing towards the cupboards, she hummed as she pulled out bowls and spoons. She didn't feel Gran's gaze on her as she dished out two servings of the thick gruel, taking a moment to dip into the stash of dried fruit they'd squirreled away for solstice. Sliding one bowl in front of Gran, Maggie took the opportunity to deliver another smooch to Gran's cheek before settling down with a smile.

"The berries are a nice touch," Gran commented, spooning them deeper into the bowl to let them soften.

Maggie shrugged good-naturedly. "Feels like a morning to celebrate," she explained. "It'd be a waste to let them just get hard in a cupboard, when they could be enjoyed now."

Gran didn't respond, and after a moment Maggie looked up from her bowl to find her grandmother gazing at her with an unreadable expression. "*Whuh?*" she asked, mouth full.

Gran still didn't respond, and Maggie's joy dimmed.

"You feeling all right, Gran—? D'you need your medicine?"

Finally, Gran stirred from her stupor. "Ach, lass. No. I'm fine. Only I've not seen you this peppery since.... since you were wee."

Maggie laughed, settling back down and releasing her worry in a single breath. "I would've thought that'd've pleased yeh. Wasn't it just yesterday you were on me to brighten up?"

Gran nodded, but it wasn't pleasure that brightened her gaze. "Aye. That I was."

Before Maggie could dig deeper, a sleepily chirping yawn announced the shuffling arrival of Sun, still wrapped in her blanket. Sleep clung to bleary eyes, and her human legs folded heavily to plop her into the spare seat.

"Morning," Maggie greeted, dismissing Gran's concern to focus on their guest.

Sun blinked up at her in consternation, before squinting a glare towards the light pouring in through the window over the sink. "Yes. It does appear to be so."

Maggie and Gran shared a brief grin as Maggie rose to her feet. "Hungry?"

Maggie slid her bowl halfway between herself and Sun to share. Handing her spoon to their guest, Maggie rose and grabbed a fork from the cup before settling back in her seat with a playful grin.

"Tuck in, yer ladyship."

"Ladyship?" Gran asked.

Sun's booted toe snapped lightly against Maggie's shin, but Maggie only returned a devilish grin. "Aye. We're host to royalty, according to the fishwife."

"And your granddaughter is a royal pain in the— *ack!*" Sun exclaimed when Maggie flicked a swollen raisin at her with unerring precision. The bit landed on one of Sun's long twists of hair, looking for all the world like it was one of her ornaments.

After a beat of stunned silence, the two of them burst into raucous laughter. Maggie laughed so long and so hard that she could barely breathe, let alone see the way Gran stared at her, or the way Sun's already warm gaze seemed to glow as she regarded her with gentle eyes. Once she had caught her breath, retaliation came in the form of the offending fruit being flung her way, which was snapped out of the air with a gnash of Maggie's teeth, which only set Sun off a second time.

The rest of breakfast was spent with the clicking of spoon and fork as they dueled for the last scoop of oatmeal, and the quiet regard of a grandmother who knew too much of what had been lost.

Once the dishes had been rinsed and the three of them returned to the warmth of the hearth, Kraken curled up in Gran's lap and got to purring as they deliberated a plan.

"It took me weeks to learn my balance," Sun said solemnly, her mirth fading rapidly under the difficulty of their task ahead. "The shell will give our friend legs, but not the knowledge to use them."

"Doesn't matter," Maggie cut in. "The shell is to keep Night breathing, not to get her walking. We can load her into a barrow, and wheel her to the harbor."

"The cart road will be patrolled, Mags," Gran warned

Maggie nodded. "Aye. But most of the alleys will allow a barrow, and should keep us out of sight. It might be trouble the closer we get to the docks, but we can haul her the rest of the way if it comes to it."

"And can you get that far before the alarm is raised?"

That, Maggie didn't know. But they wouldn't have much of a choice. They continued to speak quietly throughout the course of the day, but when the sun finally began to dip towards the horizon, Gran caught Sun's attention.

"Would you give us a moment alone, love?" she coughed.

Sun agreed readily with a nod, slipping into her coat and out the door. When the latch clicked shut, Maggie turned to Gran.

"Gran...."

"No, it's your turn to listen to me, lass. I've known you since you were wee, and I have seen you grow from a bold, responsible girl to a bold, responsible woman. You have faced unspeakable hardships, and still only thought of others. Tonight you're intending to undertake a task that will be dangerous, and will put your life and your livelihood at risk."

Maggie swallowed thickly, bracing herself for the inevitable warning to be careful. That warning never came.

"And I've never been more proud of you."

"Gran?"

"I want you to do whatever it takes to get those girls back to the water. Don't you think about me, or my medicine. Just those girls. They're depending on you, love."

Maggie nodded. A sudden lump rose to her throat as an equally sudden realization washed over her: she was going to miss them. Night, who had become her friend in the most unusual of circumstances, and even Sun, who had captivated her from the first moment.

"I pulled the last of your Da's— I pulled some old clothes for your friend to use," Gran corrected herself. Pulled from her spinning thoughts, Maggie barely noticed. "It'll be enough to get her to the water."

"Perhaps a coat—" Maggie suggested, only for Gran to shake her head no.

"Take the blanket. It'll be quicker to get in and out of."

Maggie nodded, and moved to pull away. Gran's hands tightened, keeping her in place. She studied Maggie through her bifocals, as though memorizing the lines of her face. As though it might be the last time she saw her. "Gran?"

"I never thought I'd see him again," her grandmother said softly. "But he's been right here all along. In you."

Maggie leaned her cheek into her grandmother's palm, regarding her in warm puzzlement. "He who?"

Gran blinked, withdrawing her hands abruptly in shock. She covered it a moment later by wrapping Maggie in a warm hug, even as her shoulders began to tighten with another impending cough.

"You do what needs doing, and damn the rest. Whatever comes, we'll face it together."

***

When dusk fell and deepened to night, Maggie gave Gran one final kiss and led the way out the door. She led Sun the long way to the warehouse, careful to keep her out of sight, lest someone

132

see and offer to take on her duties again. In the end, it was for naught.

A block from the warehouse, Bash caught her again. One look at Maggie and Sun's joined hands and the joking grin on his face deepened in delight.

"Need another reprieve, lass? Y'know I don't mind—"

"Actually," Maggie cut in, smiling coyly. "I rather don't."

At that, Bash hesitated. Covering a shift was one thing, but letting an outsider into the warehouse proved a step too far beyond his comfort. "Ach, Mags..."

To Maggie's surprise, Sun scoffed playfully. "That's what I thought," she crowed softly, giving Maggie's hand a playful tug. "All the boys over in gastown said your merrow-maid was rubbish. You know you didn't have to try to convince me."

"Gastown?" Bash asked.

Sun nodded. "Aye. Ain't no such thing as mer-maids," she said, affecting a lazy lilt to her speech, as though the word were unnatural and therefore unreal. She wrapped her arms around Maggie's waist, nuzzling softly against her neck. "Don't worry. I fancy you too much to mind a fib. Especially if it keeps you paid and buying me shinies."

Maggie tried to fight the flush that climbed up her shoulders and neck, at the intimate embrace of Sun's nearness. She smiled weakly at Bash.

As she watched something dark flashed behind his eyes before disappearing a moment later. Finally, he relented with a genial smile.

"Tell yeh what," he offered. "I'll let yer girl take a sneak peek, but only if she spreads the word in gastown as to just how real our mermaid is. Deal?"

Sun eyed him, unimpressed. Then she smiled coquettishly. "Sure. If she can... *convince* me."

Bash blinked, then barked in laughter. "Aye, then. Be on your way. But anyone else comes looking for a peek pays full admission. And seeing as we're going on the road in a fortnight," he added, holding Maggie's gaze, "admission goes double, starting tonight."

"Aye," Sun agreed readily, already moving on.

"Thanks Bash," Maggie offered on her way past, pulled along by a beaming Sun.

He waved her off. "It's just good to see ye smiling again, Mags."

Maggie pushed Sun into the warehouse, giving Bash a final parting wave of thanks before closing the door shut behind them. As soon as they were inside, Maggie got to work. "Grab that torch," she whispered. "I'll grab the barrow."

In moments they were in the main area, and Sun sprinted up the back steps onto the stage, sliding to her knees at the edge of the tank. A squeal emanated from her throat, reminding Mags of the porpoises that sometimes came close to her little inlet in the spring, chirping and clicking to each other as they frolicked in the waves.

A rumble answered her, low and nearly subaudible to Maggie's ears. She struggled to wrestle the barrow up the steps when Sun's next call made her heart clench.

"Maggie! Maggie, come quick!"

Dropping the barrow handles, Maggie pelted up the stairs, and quickly closed the distance to the tank. Sun gripped the source of her panic with a desperate tug— a large padlock that secured a large grate across the top of the tank, trapping Night inside. Pale fingers curled up through the gaps in the wire mesh, reaching for any inch of Sun she could reach. Even what little speech Night was capable of, it was silenced below the water, leaving her muted and trapped.

"Damn it!" Maggie cursed, yanking the lock from Sun's hands. She tugged it herself for good measure, but to no effect.

"What are we going to do?" Sun asked. Her fingers curled through the gaps in the metal grate, desperate to be as close to

Night as possible. Pale fingers curled up through the same gaps, dripping and helpless.

Maggie reached into her hair and withdrew two pins. "We're going to have to do this the hard way."

She had the first pin inserted in no time at all, and maintained a steady but gentle pressure against the mechanism as she carefully wiggled the second pin against the tumblers inside the lock. She'd never practiced on a lock so complex, and she felt the minutes tick past as she scraped the pin in and out of the lock.

Finally, the pins gave way, and the latch released, springing the bolt from its place. "There," Maggie breathed, yanking the lock free and letting it clatter to the deck. "Quick, quick, quick!"

Together, she and Sun hefted the grate up. Night immediately surged up from the water, managing to hoist her upper body onto the deck but unable to lift herself the rest of the way. Sun immediately bent to help her. The dip caused the shell around her neck to slip forward out of her baggy shirt, and droop dangerously close to the sloshing water.

"No!" Maggie barked quietly, yanking Sun back to her feet. "Stay away from the water! I'll get her, just take the grate."

Sun shouldered the heavy grate, and Maggie hooked her arms under Night's and pulled her up and back. The scales on the back of her tail scraped harshly on the rough edge of the deck, earning a squawk from Night.

"I'm sorry, I'm sorry," Maggie panted, setting her down. "Okay, now the rest." She grabbed the trunk of Night's long tail and pulled it up as well. Night helped ease the burden with a flick of her tail, revealing the limp, ragged fins that had once been so striking. The furrows left by the gaff's hook were red and angry looking, the flesh within cloudy and damaged.

Maggie didn't have time to think about that now. With Night safely out of the water, she darted back to the grate. "Okay, now, lower it back down, quietly."

As soon as the grate was safely nested home, Sun dropped to her knees by Night's side, gathering her lover in her arms. Already wheezing, Night hugged her back as best she could, even as her strength swiftly waned. Her skin and scales constricted with every ticking second, her gills gaping in the open air.

Maggie reached roughly into her shirt and withdrew the leather pouch containing the shell, already threaded with twine. *Please work.*

Maggie looped the string around Night's neck, leaving the charmed shell in the pouch to protect it from the damp of Night's skin. For a long moment, nothing happened. Then, suddenly, Night's entire body shuddered. In the next moment, her gills sealed, silencing her heaving gasps, and her tail shortened to separate into two limbs. Though the scales disappeared, her injuries littered her skin with both scars and weeping wounds. Her feet were cracked and bleeding, with a long gash carving open the top of her right foot— in horror, Maggie realized that it matched the rip caused by the gaffhook earlier that evening.

But none of that mattered, Maggie told herself even as she tore off a strip of her own shirt to wrap around Night's foot. The wheezing had stopped, and Night's next breath came smooth and easy.

She was alive.

"Thank you," Sun whispered, her voice shaking. Maggie looked up, and saw a tear slip from the tip of the woman's button nose. "Thank you."

A hand patted at her knee, and Maggie glanced down to find the same gratitude reflected in Night's eyes, still too wide and too black to be truly human. But Maggie took the offered hand and squeezed it, before lifting it to her lips. "Let's get you home."

Together, they hastily dressed Night in the clothes they'd brought. The shirt and trousers drooped comically large on her bony frame, but the hat disguised the unnatural jut of Night's macabre grin— still filled with pointed teeth— and the odd pallor of her skin.

Once dressed, they slung Night between them and carried down the stairs towards the barrow— which Maggie belatedly realized would have been impossible to get back down the stairs with Night in it, even if she'd managed to get the damn thing up there in the first place. As soon as Night was installed in the barrow as comfortably as they could manage, Maggie saw that she could even pass for an early drunk.

"If anyone asks, we're just wheeling her home."

Sun blinked at her. "Is that not what we're doing?"

Maggie froze. "Well, yes, but— if they ask where that home may be, we're sure as hell not telling them *the ocean.*"

Taking hold of the wheelbarrow, Maggie lifted it onto its wheel. She nodded to Sun, and together they moved to the back door of the warehouse. With Maggie stuck behind the wheelbarrow, Sun was the only one able to scout their path. She carefully listened at the crack around the door, and then slowly lifted the latch.

Just as Sun was about to poke her head out the door to check the coast was clear, Night issued a chitter of warning. Sun darted back in, and they waited with bated breath as the glow of a lamp turned into their alley, its shine peeking through the gaps in the clapboard wall. None of them moved a muscle until the glow disappeared around the far corner, this time slowly opening the door to scan the alley before swinging it wider.

Maggie found the wheelbarrow difficult to maneuver across the packed dirt road. Despite her lanky human frame, Night was dense, and her dead weight tilted against the natural balance of the wheelbarrow's single wheel. Together, they played a game of cat and mouse, lingering in shadows until torches passed, and darting between corners to avoid detection.

Just as Maggie had feared, the alleys eventually grew too narrow for the wheelbarrow to traverse at all. Here there was little foot traffic along the main cart roads, but what eyes there were belonged to Bash. It was too big a risk, and they were too close to their objective to take it.

"Sun," Maggie called in a whisper. "We'll have to carry her the rest of the way."

Again, each of them slung one of Night's long arms across their shoulders, and half-dragged, half-carried her down the next alley.

"Just two more turns," Maggie murmured to them both, panting. Her heart thudded heavily, and not just with anxious anticipation. Night was indeed heavy, and her arm pressed on Maggie's shoulder like a lead weight. "Two more—*augh!*"

Unseen hands grabbed them from the mouth of the alley and hauled them into the street. In moments, they were separated and restrained by burly arms of the hardened men and women who looked to Bash for further instruction.

"And where do you ladies think you're going?"

"I can explain—"

"Aye, I imagine you might," Bash agreed, but his tone didn't invite her to try. His gaze glittered at her in the darkness. "Did y'really think I wouldn't catch on, lass?"

"Bash, please—"

"Oy! I'm doing the talking now!" His billy club flipped up and pressed against the underside of Maggie's chin, tilting her gaze up to meet his. As he studied her, his gaze softened. "I can't believe you would do this to me, Mags. I vouched for you. For the sake of your Da."

"Who?"

Bash's fist flashed once, cracking against Maggie's cheek. Night hissed, lunging against her captors' hold despite her lack of balance, and Sun hurled expletives at the top of her lungs as she writhed like an eel to escape hers. Maggie caught sight of them both as Bash gripped her by the hair and forced her head to see him point at Night.

"About her... it doesn't surprise me that you made a friend. You were always a little too soft. But it does surprise me that you managed to get her a set of legs."

Maggie blinked at him, but Bash didn't give her time to ask questions. He turned his attention to Sun. "And it leaves me curious as to whether those are your legs to walk on."

"I don't know what you're talking about," Sun growled, reverting to her natural rhythmic accent. "You have lost your mind."

"Have I?"

Bash stalked towards Sun with a predatory grin, ignoring Maggie's outpouring of cursing protests. Before he could lay a finger on her, though, an unexpected voice cut through the din.

"What seems to be the problem here?"

Everything froze, and all eyes turned towards the arrival of two guardsmen, who strolled up with their hands resting on the pommels of their clubs, surveying the scene with discerning eyes.

"Oh, no problem, gentlemen," Bash answered genially. "I've just caught my cousins here out past curfew. Their ma sent me to retrieve 'em."

One of the guardsmen looked to Maggie, and after a moment's study turned back to Bash. "I didn't know you had any cousins, McCrae."

"Aye," his partner agreed. "In fact, didn't I see this one taking admission last night?"

Bash's smile faltered, then resumed twice as charming. "Ah, gents, you got me—"

"Now, I'm not one to step in the middle of an employer managing his employees," the first guard continued, his voice lofty and not a little smug. "But certainly a simple reprimand wouldn't require a lie, would it?"

His partner turned his gaze on Maggie, even as he continued to address Bash. "Don't suppose you were worried any of them might've been looking to shed some light on your... business?"

Maggie stared at Bash, whose gaze flashed dangerously. Before either of them could say another word, Night chose that moment to chomp all of her pointed, needle-sharp teeth into the arm restraining her. The man released her with a scream and a curse, and she dropped to the ground with a grunt.

Bash stepped forward with his club raised, only for it to be smacked out of his hand by the guardsman. In the chaos, Maggie acted.

"She's the mermaid!" she cried at the top of her lungs.

Everything froze for a second time. This time all eyes turned to her. Even Sun looked at her like she was insane, and maybe she was. All she was sure of was that she had to do something.

"What's this now, lass?" the guardsman asked.

"She's the mermaid!" Maggie worked every ounce of fear and anxiety into her voice, and surprised even herself when true tears began to burn at her eyes. "Mary was just looking for work when her da kicked her out, and Bash said if she did as he asked, and did it quiet, she'd get meals and a place to sleep. I thought he meant running messages, but the next day they threw Mary in the tank!"

Bash's features twisted with rage. "You shut your mouth—"

The guardsman cut Bash off with a jab of his nightstick. "Not another word outta you—"

"She's a lying little—!"

"Look what they did to her teeth!" Maggie wailed, producing two fat tears that rolled down her cheeks.

The guardsmen blinked at each other, then down at Night, who gamely opened her mouth.

With a closer look, anyone would see that there were more teeth than any one human could have, filed or not, but one look at the rows of needle-sharp teeth and the younger guard jumped back with a cry of alarm.

The elder guard turned his baton Bash. "It's time we had a chat with you down at the yard."

Bash barely lasted a moment before he bolted, and his cronies followed suit, dashing in the opposite direction.

One guard pelted after Bash with a shout. His partner raced after the rest with his whistle between his lips, barely pausing long enough to warn Maggie to stay put before disappearing into the dark. His whistles were answered by others, signaling the imminent approach of additional guards.

"Come on!" Maggie urged Sun, racing to Night's side. "Let's go!"

Together they hauled Night up as quickly as they could and staggered for the docks. This time, they gave no thought to stealth or grace, moving with reckless abandon as they inched ever closer to the gentle lap of the water just out of reach.

When their boots thudded onto the wooden boards of the closest dock, Maggie felt her heart lift with victory. Instead of slowing down, she picked up the pace, spilling into the water with them when the dock ran out. The cold of the wintery sea stabbed at her chest like a knife, nearly stealing her breath. Still, she was able to recover her senses after the initial shock, and paddled her way up to the surface.

By now, the stars were beginning to fade with a threatening dawn. The water bubbled and churned around her, shimmering with the same phosphorescence of the hidden lagoon in the cliffs. When the turbulence calmed, clothes floated in the water around her as she stared at the inhuman gaze of Night's broad, dark eyes, and her long pale arms wrapped around Sun's shoulders.

And Sun— the change was palpable, even in the near dawn. Her skin radiated warmth, and the tail that swirled in the water around them was as pale and pink as the brightening sky, what little Maggie could see of it between the coils of where Night's tail had wrapped around it. Maggie treaded water until their embrace ended, and they rounded on her with a hug somehow even fiercer.

"Thank you," Sun clicked in her ear. "Thank you."

Night grunted, and when Maggie pulled away, her pale head nodded in gratitude.

"I'm sorry this happened to you," Maggie told her. "But I'm honored to have met you. Both of you."

Their hands curled around hers, and their touch was so gentle that Maggie's chest tightened in longing.

"Come visit sometime, yeah?"

Sun nodded, and splashed her in another tight hug. "You are in our hearts, Maggie. We will never forget you."

The clop of hooves along the lane behind them cut her off. Maggie withdrew, this time shoving Sun awkwardly towards the mouth of the harbor. "Go, now."

This time, it was Night who hesitated, until Maggie nodded with her chin. "Go."

With a flick of their tails, one a dusty pink and the other dark as pitch, they disappeared beneath the surface. Maggie stared after them, searching for any trace of their path out of the harbor and towards the brightening horizon. Whether the flicker of motion she saw at the mouth of the inlet was a flash of fin or a sharp wave, she couldn't tell. She stared until a fisherman spotted her and called out.

As they hauled her up onto the dock and wrapped her in thick coats, Maggie's gaze remained on the horizon, doing her best to convince herself that the hollow in her chest wasn't heartbreak.

That she wasn't alone.

***

One Year Later…

Watching the sun slowly rise on the edge of a thin horizon, Maggie felt a familiar tug low in her stomach. Coming to visit her little inlet used to make her feel closer to the ocean, but each visit only made it feel further and further away, carried out with the tide.

The day after Night's rescue, the two guardsmen had called on Gran. They'd taken Maggie's tearful statement, but with the injured party nowhere to be found, they didn't have anything to hold Bash on. To their surprise, the elder of the two guards took pity on them.

Knowing Bash's release all but ensured retribution for Maggie, he offered Maggie a job as a live-in housekeeper for his own mother. As a widow herself, the house she lived in was too much for her to handle, and had more than enough room to keep both Maggie and Gran out of Bash's reach.

The old lady's house was deeper in the town, and outside Bash's normal hunting ground, but Maggie still made her way to the coast every morning. When Gran passed barely four months into their move, Maggie was the only one left to remember the strange friends she found herself missing more and more.

Without Gran to moor her, Maggie felt as though the fierce wind might pick her up and carry her to a far and distant corner of the world. Only the hope her friends might return kept her feet on the ground. If she left, how would they ever find her again?

And so she returned to an empty, half-rotted pier every morning at sunrise, to watch the tide come in and the boats put out, their silhouettes dwindling against the brightening horizon.

Every morning she scanned the surface of the water, studying every cresting wave, every ripple and churn for the hint of a sinuous tail, of dark sun-kissed skin or pale luminescent lines.

Every morning, she turned away alone.

This time, she turned back to town with her thoughts filling with tasks for the shop, only to freeze when a throaty croak ribbeted through the air. Maggie pivoted on her heel, scanning the waterline for its source. It was too early for toads, both in hour and in season, and her heart pounded with unease as she slowly picked her way back to the end of the pier.

But all that lay beyond the wooden dock was empty water, calmed by the rocky walls of her little inlet. Looking down, she caught sight of her own reflection, rippling in disappointment.

Maggie sighed.

"BWAH!" Two forms broke the surface of the water with arms outstretched, grinning as Maggie recoiled with a yell of her own.

But then she laughed through sudden tears as she dropped to her knees on the rough wooden boards, reaching precariously to throw her arms first around Sun, and then Night. In moments she was soaked by the freezing water dripping from their arms and chests, as they embraced her just as tightly.

"You're here!" she cried, finally sinking back on her heels, each of her hands claimed by theirs. She cried freely, relief and joy momentarily eclipsing the emptiness of the last six months. "I can't believe it! You— you came all the way back. Why?"

Sun looked to Night, who blinked with a throaty click before reaching for the leather pouch Maggie hadn't noticed lashed to one wrist. It was larger than the one that had protected her charmed shell, and when she opened it there was no care taken to keep the seawater from dripping off her fingertips to collect within.

From inside it pale fingers withdrew a delicate silver chain, with a tarnished silver pendant dangling from a narrow hoop of metal. The pendant was shorn in half, and Maggie found herself reaching for it before her mind even pinpointed how she recognized it.

"This... this is mine," Maggie said, her voice distant in her own ears as she ran her finger along the familiar edge of the broken pendant. The nib of metal poked the tip of her finger just as it always did.

Her senses sharpened briefly as she looked up at Sun. "Why would you go to all the trouble of getting it back? It's just a bit of tin—"

"Put it on," Sun cut in, "and find out."

After a moment's hesitation, Maggie did as instructed. Once the clasp was fastened, the weight of the pendant settled home against her breastbone, and her fingers reflexively brushed across its face.

Suddenly, a wave of memory crashed against her, both as fierce as a winter squall and as gentle as a summer rain. Everything inside her sharpened as old memories clicked into place— the face of her father, the ache in her heart, and the weight of missing a man she knew to be dead.

This time, though, the grief didn't fill her up. It tucked around her like a light undershirt, present, but not forefront in her mind. Not all-encompassing. As though being apart from it had softened its awful keening.

"Da."

Maggie's eyes filled with tears, and she almost toppled into the water reaching for Sun. Her friend closed the distance before she could, and received Maggie's hug with a fierce one of her own.

"Thank you."

"We have.... something else," Sun warned as she drew away.

The moment replayed like a prophecy— Night reached into the pouch, withdrew a silver chain bearing a near-identical halved pendant. Confusion filled Maggie from stem to stern as the necklace pooled in her palm. When she turned the pendant over, she found the missing half of her medallion, stained and tarnished but still etched with the remainder of Brigid's cross.

"This is Da's half," she gasped. "He— he wore it when they shoved off the last time... said he'd never take it off." She whipped her head up and glued her gaze to Sun. "Did you find his wreck?"

"A selkie said she got it as part of a trade, but not when or where. All she would share was that she got it from a traveler seeking to find his way home… to the daughter he shared it with."

Looking to get home…

With her Da's memory now fresh in her mind, Maggie knew he would never have traded it for anything other than a means of life and death. If Da traded it for something— *anything*— else…

"He's alive," Maggie breathed.

Sun's shoulders lifted in a human shrug. "I don't know. But we can find out."

"We?" Maggie echoed.

This time, Night offered Maggie the pouch itself, and inside she found one last item contained within: a vial, stoppered with cork and sealed with whale fat. When she could only stare at it in confusion, Night leaned back in the water and mimed tilting the vial into her own mouth.

"Trink!"

The word sounded crackly and foreign on Night's tongue, hissing slightly on her teeth, but remained as bright as the grin on her face. The message only garbled further, however, when Night flicked her tail up out of the water, peppering Maggie with droplets that shook from the tips of her long fins, fully healed.

Maggie looked to Sun for clarification, but received only a giggle and the same pantomime a second time.

"Drink!"

Only when Sun's billowing sunrise-pink tail wiggled did the meaning finally click.

As soon as it did, Maggie didn't hesitate.

With a laugh, Maggie dried her cheeks, and broke the waxy seal. She lifted it to her lips.

"Ack!" Night interrupted with a quack, long fingers reaching out in pause. Maggie froze, and felt her heart clench when webbed fingers curled into goggles through which Night blinked owlishly. *Gran.*

The sight of it nearly did Maggie in. Night never met Gran—for Night to know of her spectacles, then she learned it from Sun. Who could have known that Gran's legacy would have lived on through the memory of two mermaids?

Maggie shook her head, swallowing against the lump rising in her throat. "Gran's gone."

Night's hands returned to the water, her strange features falling. Sun cooed softly, the sound sorrowful.

"It's okay," Maggie promised. "It was her time."

And it was, however much Maggie missed her. She hadn't been in pain, and that was all Maggie could have asked for, besides more time.

When Maggie lifted the vial to her lips a second time, no one stopped her. She swallowed the salty, bitter concoction in a single gulp, giving no thought to the silty, crunchy bits that poked her tongue on the way down.

For a moment, nothing happened.

Then, everything happened at once.

The air turned sour in her lungs and scraped painfully against her skin. Every muscle turned to fire as she clutched at her throat, melting off her bones and scraping every nerve on its way. Maggie was aware of cold hands grasping her arms, tugging until she slithered off the pier and into the sea.

Water closed over her head, and only instinct drove her to gasp— and nearly choked in relief to find that the fluid filling her lungs didn't burn. Instead it soothed the sudden fire in her chest, and when she opened her eyes Maggie found the faces of her friends in sharp focus, even in the murky waves.

They grinned, and Maggie grinned back, eliciting a chorus of happy chirps and clicks that filled the water around her as they curled and swirled against her— welcoming her home.

Maggie kicked towards the surface, but managed only an awkward squirm when she found her legs no longer worked. In their place, she found they'd transformed into a powerful tail, scaled and colored in pale greens and browns, defined by a long series narrow black tiger stripes down her dorsal, not unlike the mackerel hauled in by the fishermen to sell at market.

Where Sun's fins were long and billowing, Maggie's were angular and sharply defined. Where Night's tail was long and sinuous, Maggie's was thick, but muscular.

With a single pump of her tail, she rocketed towards the surface, breaching unexpectedly into the air. When she fell back into the water, she flailed, struggling to right herself. Her ears filled with the sounds of rapid clicking, and she blinked towards Night's macabre grin spreading wider in mirth. Sunshine's lips parted as well, flashing pearly white teeth in a laugh. The clicking slowed, and fell into a stilted pattern— one Maggie realized was language.

In the brief moments the three spent together in the warehouse that fateful, Maggie had heard the clicking between Sunshine and Night, and assumed it was some kind of tic, a non-verbal reassurance, a signal of relief and affection. But in the water the sounds sharpened into phrases, beats and cadences that felt like any other conversation. Maggie didn't know what they meant, but needed no translation when they both reached a hand towards her, beckoning her home.

Taking a deep breath, Maggie felt water pulse through the new gills on the side of her neck, tasting the brine and silt. The sea sang in her bones, alive with the thrum of the waves undulating around her.

It occurred to Maggie that she had no idea if the potion had some caveat like the shells had done, or if it was permanent. In the next moment, she found she didn't much care.

Maggie grinned. With a single flick of her tail she surged toward the hands outstretched towards her, catching them on her way past. Together, the three of them sped into open water and kept going.

They didn't look back.

BIO: Rin Saunders recently retired from a 35-year career in software development. His hobbies include international travel, a Harley Fat Boy S, learning new math/science, and serving as a heat engine for his cat.

THE PRIEST

by Rin Saunders

Sheffield Smith's vision began to clear. The indistinct vortex of color resolved into a room. Memory returned: he was lying in the Priest's bedroom in his rickety second-story apartment on Rat Alley. A horrible thought rang in his head.

Shit, no! I'm alive!

***

The day before, Sheffield woke up hearing what he always heard: the low, feral rumble of the refinery next to his apartment building. Through the, narrow window he contemplated the lurid sheet of chemical flame from the refinery across the way. The curtain of fire towered over his featureless building, always threatening to consume it, always impotent.

Sheffield knew the orange glare was the reason his bedroom had no light, and the wall-penetrating heat was the reason he had no heater. The Committee organized every aspect of life for efficiency. Sheffield appreciated the never-changing routine. He always knew what to expect.

It would have been a quiet and satisfactory life—except for Helen.

He heaved himself up and got dressed. The Committee allotted him—and everyone else—one set of clothes per day. The necessary and no more. Sheffield's clothes from yesterday were sweaty, but no one had come in overnight to put a replacement waiting on his desk. He was sure that someone somewhere would pay.

The Committee might be twelve collaborating biosoftware symbionts, but their Enforcers were entirely human and good at what they did. All punishments lasted one day, and no one ever came back the same.

Sheffield had never been punished, and knew he never would be. *It's no problem at all. All you have to do is follow the comfortable routines of life.*

Yet, while dressing, he had a sense that the small room itself was miserly, withholding. The gray concrete walls, now that he was close enough to see, oozed sweat.

Concrete shouldn't sweat. Doesn't that mean something bad?

Very soon the bell would sound. Suppressed thoughts stirred.

I can't live like this. It's Helen. It's hell.

Sure enough, there went Helen's brass handbell, strident and demanding. It seemed to grow louder every second. He stopped his ears in a fleeting moment of resistance, then released his hands and did what he had to do: care for his hypochondriac wife.

The "sickness" had come on gradually. Over a year, it completely consumed her. The gradual onset was nothing more than her testing to see how much of a load he would tolerate. First, shooting pains in her ankles made her housebound. If he was home, she and her demands were there. Then it became feeding—she could not cook. She became bedridden. He never protested. Now, he bathed her too, and if there were a next step, he couldn't imagine what.

And that's my life, Sheffield thought bitterly.

The answer had come to him in the depths of sleep and placed itself carefully just below his awareness. He could feel its shape, dark and hard and potent.

So why live it? his mind said.

He opened the door to the short, narrow hall. Saw the small, dull-green kitchen at the end with the door to his daily escape to soothing, mindless, unchanging work. Helen's door was open. It always was. She worried constantly that fire would somehow consume the concrete block structure, and she would die in bed for lack of the time it took him to open her door.

The fear of being late to the factory tingled at a low level. He knew it would grow. God only knew what she wanted this time.

She kept herself cocooned in cotton covers that always reminded him of a shroud. Wrapped and turned to the wall was her lined gray face, the Medusa's nest of ratty, unwashed hair. She said that light hurt her eyes. Sheffield tried to remember the last time he had actually seen her.

A hand jutted awkwardly out of the cocoon, swinging the cursed bell. She could not hear him and certainly could not see him, but she always knew the split second he appeared in her doorway. It was uncanny.

"Sheffield!" Her voice sliced through like a knife through cloth. "What are you leaving me to eat today?"

"I'll see."

Thank God it was nothing more than breakfast. The fear of being late to work remained a mere tingle.

Sheffield trudged to the kitchen. Pans and utensils hung above the gas stove on the dull green wall; there were no cupboards, so there was nowhere else to store them. He glanced at his escape door. He needed to leave now. But he knew the consequences, which were painful and could last months.

Sheffield opened the refrigerator and peered inside. He was pretty sure there were leftovers from yesterday's cooking—it would be a disaster if there wasn't. Sure enough, a plate of fried eggs sat on the second shelf.

He pulled it out and brought it to Helen's room. He heard her sniffing for the food.

"What is it?" she demanded.

"Eggs."

Accusingly: "Did you heat them?"

"No time, dear. I need to leave for work now."

The whine started. "Cold leftovers!" The whine collapsed into tears. "I'm your wife! You don't even know if I'll be alive when you come back and this is how you treat me." The whining culminated in a shriek: "So selfish! Selfish! Selfish!"

He knew he was defeated. It would go on for days.

The thought tugged at him again.

With quick, short steps, he retreated with the eggs to the kitchen, pulled down a pan, sloshed in a wee bit of his oil ration, and turned on the range. He turned the heat up to do it quickly. Helen would reject them if there were overcooked. There was nothing else to eat in the house. Helen didn't receive a worker's allocation. Idle and useless, she got nothing. The grocery bag that appeared in the kitchen every morning was meant for one and fed two.

He thought of the twelve candidates on the printout that the Committee had provided in response to his marriage requisition. He'd chosen her because he liked her name. Why not? It was all he knew about any of them. He tried, but couldn't remember any of the other names on the list.

He briefly wondered what she herself was going through. She had infantilized herself for reasons he could not understand. Why?

Returning them to her room with the plate, he heard her sniffling. When he came home, he would have to endure it for an hour or two, which was not bad at all.

Helen didn't say anything, so she was satisfied. No diaper change this morning.

"I'll just leave it on your table for you."

After a few seconds there was no response and Sheffield was free.

***

Sheffield entered the elevator cage and turned the wheel to point to ground floor. The elevator creaked and shuddered. Sheffield relished this as his moment of solitude.

Now he was on the street. Dingy grey skyscrapers towered on either side of him. There was a patina of gray dust on the worn concrete pavement. The Committee was not what it had been. The pavement, his elevator...sometimes one of the buildings even collapsed. None of that would have happened when he was small. Sheffield idly wondered why.

Now the thought escaped the confines he had built for it.

Jump off the roof.

Quick and easy, but he couldn't get past the image of his body disintegrated to blood and bone on the sidewalk, which he would surely experience for a brief moment.

And yet, there was nothing in this world, really, to live for. And what lay ahead? Eventual retirement with nothing but boredom. Disability. Disease. Helen. Then a death from who knows what. He'd been hoping it wasn't cancer. Painkillers were now viewed as immoral, and he knew he couldn't stand pain.

There was nothing wrong with killing one's self, really. Death is one of life's normal events. I'm just switching the order a little. No one will mind.

Then it hit him that in actual fact, no one would.

Suicide. The thought rang heavy and hollow.

But how? All the ideas he that presented themselves were surreal, cartoonish.

Helen always says I have no follow-through. I'd probably regret the decision the moment I jump.

He didn't want to experience dying by any means. He just wanted to go to sleep forever.

He breathed in the dank, chemicalized air and relished how good it felt. Compared to not breathing at all, which seemed to be his future.

The factory was another gray monolith, but it offered the viewer a different front than the apartments. Two double doors under a rectangular concrete frame managed the inflow and outflow. He entered the lobby and glanced up at the man-sized clock hands on the back wall. Five minutes late. OK, seven. The clothes, the food that appeared on his doorstep every night, somehow, something would be reduced.

Maybe one less egg, he thought wryly.

Then up the elevator to the second floor where he worked. To be honest, he'd never been sure what the factory made. Plastic parts flowed past him on a conveyer belt in a river as endless as time. Jeffrey would have been on the night shift. The prospect of seeing Jeffrey, happy to be relieved, almost made Sheffield happy. They'd inspect parts together for a few moments to make sure of the coverage, then Sheffield would take Jeffrey's warm seat. Sheffield had been looking for defective parts for thirty years now. One day, eight years ago, he'd found one.

I guess that justifies my existence. I won't have died in vain.

***

Jeffrey relieved, Sheffield sat on his stool in front of a black conveyer belt that floated gizmos in front of his face. They were identical, formed of sheenless black plastic, with two arms of different sizes that looked like places where hoses would be attached. Maybe they were plumbing. Whatever they were, they were things in a life full of nothing.

His partner today was Dave. Dave was, in many ways, Sheffield's opposite. He was impossibly cheerful. It felt good to have some cheerfulness in his life, but there was only so much cheerfulness he could take. After that, he felt like he was choking.

Sheffield knew there was something dark behind all the cheerfulness. Something that needed fixing. He knew he'd never know what it was.

They'd dispensed with pleasantries years ago. Sheffield gathered his courage over the first ten minutes of the shift.

"Have you ever thought what it's like, dying?" Sheffield asked, quiet and tentative.

"All the time," David said happily. "It's what keeps me going."

"But what if you wanted to go?"

"Where?"

Sheffield knew what Dave meant, but he did pose an unanswered question. The aftermath. He'd always assumed a restful blackness. So he just stared at David, wordless. Suddenly a red light turned on, and parts began flowing through the rubber curtain and down the conveyer belt.

"I think I'm ready to go," Sheffield said. "Not go anywhere. Just go."

"You?"

"Yes."

"When?"

"Now."

"Why?"

Sheffield managed a pained shrug. He knew the darkness inside Dave would understand

Dave thought a minute. "You know what the difference between you and me is? I grew up loving the sameness. It's what keeps me going. I get hypnotized watching the sameness flow past. It's beautiful. Otherwise, I'd be like you. Oh, and I remember learning how to do this job in the first place. It was interesting."

He'd never told Dave about Helen. He sensed that somehow it would reflect badly on him.

"That was thirty years ago," Sheffield observed.

"Doesn't matter to me," Dave responded.

Sheffield stayed silent, thinking how unconventional but fortunate Dave was to be single.

"Decided how you're going to do it?" Dave asked. Sheffield couldn't help but shudder.

"I've thought of ways. Too many ways. But I don't want to die, and I don't want to risk waking up injured. I just want to skip the dying part and be dead." Sheffield looked at David, his eyes pleading for a solution.

Dave's face went colder than Sheffield had ever seen. It was as though he were detaching from Sheffield already. It was a side of Dave that Sheffield had never seen.

"You need the Priest?" he whispered, barely audible.

"In a church somewhere?" Sheffield asked incredulously.

"No, in Rat Alley."

This was absurd. Sheffield had never gone near the place, and never would. No one with any self-respect would set foot in the place. Would even think the name. Rat Alley was a sign of the decaying power of the Committee. It could never have existed a generation ago. Rat Alley was dark. Physically dark. Decaying wooden buildings that the Committee should have been demolished long ago leaned over the street, banishing light. Rat Alley was dirty. Garbage. Rats, of course. And from what he'd heard, the dwellers were worse than the stinking, biting, plague-infested rats.

"I'm not going near that place! You could get killed there."

David sighed. "Are you listening to yourself?"

"Painfully killed by some thug. Or rotted food, or plague fleas, or who knows what. When people die there, it's never peaceful."

"Well, if you can make it as far as the Priest's office, you're golden."

"Why? What does he do?"

"Exactly what you want. They say you just go to sleep."

Sheffield's mind staggered. First, how would David know anything about Rat Alley? But then, David had always been a lot more outgoing, more connected than Sheffield, who was pretty much a homebody. It made sense that David would know.

Second, what would a priest be doing killing people? He thought of his death as a mercy killing, but surely a priest would not. Unsanctioned killing of any sort was deeply abhorrent to the Church Committee.

"Why would a priest do that?" Sheffield asked, amazed.

Dave waved vaguely. "He's a renegade, they say. Left the Church, and no one will come looking for him in Rat Alley. Because he's already in hell, right? But they say he saw so much suffering that he came to regard any death as a mercy killing, and left the Church to do good deeds."

A renegade priest?

Sheffield was shocked and, despite his depressed state, a little bemused. Sheffield on Rat Alley? Why not? He'd led a colorless life, so how about a colorful death?

If not today, when? He would force himself by staying at work late. If he came home late, Helen would exact her pound of flesh.

"When is the priest in? Does he have..." Sheffield couldn't help but snort, "business hours?"

"He's always there. He lives there. He does it in his home."

Lives on Rat Alley? Sheffield shuddered.

"What if I go right after work?" Sheffield asked softly, speaking to himself.

"What if you do? Somebody else will be in that chair tomorrow."

So here was Dave's darkness. Sheffield knew he was friendless, and suspected that he'd always been. Now he would gladly go.

***

Sheffield felt himself too clean, in all senses of the word, to know the way to Rat Alley, but the capital city was a grid and nothing was very hard to find. He shrank with every step, hunching over as though disapproving watchers in the sky knew his destination. Would merely walking to Rat Alley cost him his job? He'd never know.

He turned the final corner and the Alley sprang to life in front of him. Rickety buildings loomed over a filth-covered street. Sheffield was sure it was a rat's paradise. Ribbons of colored bulbs hung over the doors that belonged to shops. They provided the only illumination, and they laid a lurid carnival pool of light under the shop doors, which the night quickly swallowed.

Darkness. It was stepping into darkness both literally and metaphorically.

Sheffield took his first step into Rat Alley.

He heard murmurs, but he could see no one. Behind each of those shop doors, someone was waiting. Hoping Sheffield would be so rash as to enter.

***

The placard said "The Reverend," so he knocked on the rickety door, which shook with every knock. It unnerved him. The man who opened it was tall and extremely thin. He had a pointed red beard and wore a black cassock.

160

The priest silently motioned him in. Sheffield appreciated no necessity to say anything. He knew it was understood.

He stepped tentatively inside. He was in a (ha ha) living room! The faded paint and meager, worn furnishings were identical to Sheffield's, but having a living room was an impossibility that Dave had mentioned one day. Sheffield knew he had no need. He never thought to see one.

Was the priest an important man? Had he lived here when Rat Alley was just another street?

"Have a seat." The Priest sat in one chair and pointed Sheffield to the other. Uncomfortably, Sheffield sat and twiddled his hat on his lap.

"What brings you here today?" The Priest leaned forward.

Oh, no. Sheffield couldn't say it. He just couldn't get the words out of his throat. He choked on them.

"The usual," he said. "Same as everyone else."

"Euthanatos? A perfect death?"

"Perfect," Sheffield echoed. His throat had opened now that the subject had.

"What do you think will happen after you die?" the priest asked.

"I really haven't thought about it much. I have no idea. I guess I'll just not be...there."

The priest sighed and leaned back in his chair. "No glowing image of a heaven? I had to make sure. I won't take clients with definite expectations. It's probably oblivion, and I won't send them off on a false pretense."

"Are you really a priest?" Sheffield had to ask.

"That's what they call me," said the Priest, in a tone that ended the query there. "I need to make sure yours is a justifiable death. Are you in good health? Or in pain?"

"Good health, no pain."

"Then why?" The priest opened his arms in an expansive gesture. "Why wouldn't you want a long and blessed life?"

"Blessed?" Sheffield said bitterly. It was a word for a church service and nowhere else.

"Cursed life, then," the Priest said impatiently. "It's still a life. Tell me."

"You know...a job where I might as well be doing nothing. Lonely. A sick wife..."

"Are you taking care of her?" The priest asked sharply.

"No," Sheffield lied. "Not really."

He felt that the Priest instantly saw through the lie. Surely a man who had heard as many confessions as he must have could feel the vast reservoir of pain, and under which cause its stagnant waters lay.

"Good," said the priest. "I won't cause a death that injures bystanders."

If he had caught Sheffield's lie, he was going along with it.

"How do you do it?" Sheffield choked out the important question.

"Five grams of phenobarbital. You will fall asleep, stop breathing, and never wake up. Here, at least."

"Where do you get drugs?" Sheffield asked, startled. He'd expected something that could be done with the materials at hand. Maybe punch him out then stuff a pillow over his face.

"Priests visit hospitals." He said no more.

"Do you stick a needle in my arm?"

"No, no. Dilaudid is another easy death, but it does involve a needle in the arm, so I can't claim it's pain-free. You'll take pills. With tea. I'll brew you some tea. Earl Grey?"

Sheffield didn't really know. He was a coffee drinker.

"Can't we just get this over?" he asked in a whining tone that was startlingly close to Helen's.

"This is the biggest decision you'll ever make. Take a day to think it over. Sleep on it."

"No, no," Sheffield said. "I'm already late home, and if I so much as stick my face in the door..."

"Ah." The Priest said nothing more.

"Do you think you're going to enjoy dying?" he asked.

The question caught Sheffield off guard.

What is that supposed to mean?

He didn't answer.

"What do you think it'll feel like?" the Priest demanded.

Sheffield suddenly felt like he was talking to someone else. "Like you said. Going to sleep."

"And will you enjoy it?"

"I guess so," Sheffield replied.

"Do you think I'm going to enjoy killing you?" the Priest asked, a peculiar expression entering his eyes that made Sheffield uneasy.

"What?"

"Do you think it's going to be fun for me?"

Something within Sheffield withered. After a moment, he asked again, "Are you really a priest?"

"What do you care?" the Priest retorted. "You're getting what you want. My feelings are irrelevant, aren't they?"

"I suppose so," Sheffield said nervously, wondering if he'd made a mistake. He'd thought of the Priest as an angel of mercy, but this was Rat Alley, after all.

The Priest stood up abruptly.

"Time to get that tea," he said. "And some pills."

Nothing could have changed Sheffield's mind about what he was about to do, but the Priest came close. Regardless of whether or not the Priest was a murderer, Sheffield would go on.

The Priest stepped into what Sheffield knew must be the kitchen. In a few minutes, he heard a tea kettle whistle. The Priest emerged with a cup in one hand, the other clutching something Sheffield assumed to be the pills. His death, walking toward him.

"Here," the Priest said, handing Sheffield the cup and pills. "Take them. Enjoy the tea, but not for too long. Go lie down. You know where the bedroom is."

Sheffield nodded. Of course he knew.

"Be at peace. I promise to solve your problem."

Unless there's an afterlife. But no, that's silly, no matter what the Church says. Eternal restful sleep. That's how all my problems will be solved.

Sheffield took the pills from the Priest's hand and swallowed them. They left a bitter taste in his mouth. He washed them down with unsweetened Earl Grey. Last words? He tried to think what to say to the Priest in what time remained, but he felt suddenly dizzy.

"I'd better lie down now." He arose on unsteady legs. In the edge of his vision, he saw what looked like a cruel smile forming on the Priest's lips. But that could not be, of course. He was a priest.

Sheffield staggered toward the bed. He did not notice the room at all. His vision was cutting in and out. He lay down, but knew it was more than half a fall. He adjusted himself, laid his head on the pillow, and felt the sweet oblivion very near now.

All my problems are over.

It   was   his   last   thought.

***

He was still happy when consciousness returned.

All my problems are gone.

He became aware of the bedroom. Now he saw the hospital green walls. A crooked landscape hanging on the wall beyond the foot of his bed. Bare trees and a river.

In an explosion of bitterness, he realized that he'd been had. His problems were far from over. They were worse. The Priest was a psychopath who'd been toying with him. Of course. What had he expected on Rat Alley?

Shame. Humiliation. Then a shock of fear. He was late home. Very late. Helen would make life hell for the foreseeable future. Oh, and Dave. What would he tell Dave when he showed up at work? Had Dave been duped too? Could Sheffield ever trust him again?

Sheffield hoisted himself unsteadily up and walked to the living room, waiting to be laughed at. No one was there. He sat for a minute, in the same chair he'd been in before. Sitting on the Priest's sofa would have been unthinkable, contaminating.

"Anyone there?" He called.

After a few minutes he rose and entered the kitchen. The Priest was not there.

Sheffield knew he had no option but to drag himself home to face whatever came after.

Rat Alley passed in a blur. No one accosted him. The whispers were gone. Still, there was fear. When the city grid reclaimed him, the fear left. Where was the anger? All he could feel was self-pity. He was numb with self-pity. His thoughts would not flow. He felt nothing. He thought nothing. He might as well have been dead.

When he finally reached the apartment building, nothing had changed. He was frozen, empty. He summoned the elevator.

Walking down the hall to Helen felt like a second death.

He opened the door.

He smelled the copper odor of blood.

He knew that the Priest hadn't failed him, that all his problems were over.

BIO: S.C. Megale was born in 1995. She usually goes by Shea, which is an inedible type of butter, which is the worst type of butter there can be. In 2019 her debut YA novel, *This is Not a Love Scene*, was published by St. Martin's Press. She collectively has authored more than two dozen novels and short stories. For the Hourlings, she's served as Editor on two of their publications. Megale is passionate about writing her own biography in the third person, and finding new and brave ways to love human beings.

http://www.scmegale.com/

THE WATER DRAGON

by S.C. Megale

For Mike Lannes, my water dragon.

Once upon a time, there was a dragon that lived underwater.

His name is unpronounceable, but fish called him Versillion, which, in aquatic language, means One Who Loses Pearls.

He was long and brown, with smooth scales and feathery plumes that drifted in the water around him. Unfortunately, Versillion was not very observant, and, as his name suggests, his hoard of pearls easily left him. The crabs were known to approach his den, claws raised, and replace his pearls with eggs when Versillion wasn't looking.

Although the eels bowed to him when they crossed paths, they'd slither away laughing when Versillion could no longer hear.

One day, Versillion paddled through muck and seaweed to the banks of the brackish river. He saw muddled colors in the reflection of the surface.

Slowly, he raised his head from the water to see a tall, blue dragon standing on all four legs.

The blue dragon seemed to be expecting him.

"You are Versillion?" the blue dragon said.

"Yes."

"I am the Dragon of Dragons," said the blue dragon.

"Hello, Dragon of Me," said Versillion.

The blue dragon's eyes were white as diamonds. His expression did not reflect any humor.

"As the water dragon, you rule this kingdom," said the Dragon of Dragons.

"I live here," said Versillion.

"And you are a Dragon. So yes."

Versillion's stomach folded inward. He was not quite comfortable with such power.

"Tell the creatures of the water," said the blue dragon, "to bring me the most precious thing of the river."

Versillion perked up with hope.

"Whoever brings the most precious thing of the river shall be named the new Dragon of Dragons."

"No matter what species they are?" said Versillion.

"Correct."

So Versillion obeyed. He dove below where the water was cooler and darker.

In a powerful, echolocational voice of clicks and whistles, he alerted the creatures of the water to the words of the Dragon of Dragons.

Every creature shimmied to life in search of precious things. Light from luminescent fish flickered in seaweed forests. Mud clouded up into the water as mammalian creatures dug with bottle noses for bivalves. Shell fragments floated in the water like drifting asteroids after hours of struggle and exchange in the aquatic black market.

No water creature was content with what they found. Nothing would be enough to rival Versillion's stash.

So indeed did Versillion lay in his murky den surrounded by his pearls, unworried. He would simply bring these all to the Dragon of Dragons.

But...you can suppose what the water creatures did while Versillion slept that night.

Can you guess?

Stole them?

Yes, they did.

They crept into his den and replaced every last pearl with a white fish egg.

The next day, when Versillion woke, he gathered all the fish eggs into his four claws. He did not notice how much lighter they were, and how they felt like jelly now.

He swam up to the surface, where a crowd of the river creatures queued around the muddled blue reflection of the Dragon of Dragons.

All of them pushed forward their iridescent pearls to offer to the Dragon of Dragons. They squabbled over whose shone brightest, and how someone's three pearls would have been six had so-and-so not tricked them on the way there. The Dragon of Dragons inspected them all. And each time, he said, "Hmm."

"Versillion," said the Dragon of Dragons. "Have you brought the most precious thing of the water?"

"Yes," said Versillion. He puffed his chest and presented his handfuls of fish eggs. Hundreds more than any one creature's amount of pearls.

The water creatures snickered.

But when the Dragon of Dragons lifted the eggs from the water and into his claws, he did not say, "Hmm."

Water trickled down from his talons as he held them cupped together, palms full of the little spheres wriggling with baby fish inside.

"You, Versillion, have brought the most precious thing of the river."

The water creatures gasped.

"But, sir!" they cried. "Versillion tries to fool you! They are but fish eggs. We have brought you pearls."

Versillion snapped his head towards them. The heat of betrayal and hurt flooded through his blood. His heart fell. Now that the truth was known, he would never be Dragon of Dragons.

"I know what they are," the Dragon of Dragons answered at last. "They are life. You others have brought me nothing but dust that catches sunlight."

He lowered his claws back to the water to let the fish eggs gently roll into the mud.

"Versillion." He turned to the brown water dragon. "You are the new Dragon of Dragons."

"Nonsense!" shouted the fish. "His name in our language means One Who Loses Pearls! He will be laughed at for eternities."

"Can I?" said Versillion. "Can I be Dragon of Dragons with a name such as this? The One Who Loses Pearls?"

"You are Versillion, the Dragon of Dragons," said the blue dragon. "The One Who Loses Pearls. The one who loses nothing a all."

BIO: Cora Baker was born in 1960 and she retired in 2018 from her career as a computer programmer analyst. As a lifelong reader and lover of books, Cora has decided to try her hand at the craft of writing. Her love of genealogy, history, romance, and travel will serve her well in her creative efforts. She has started on the path to greater things with the help of an encouraging group of local writers.

Cora is currently working on a novel and several short stories. She lives in Fredericksburg, Virginia with her handsome husband and two cats.

The Key

by Cora Baker

Tillie Walton looked up from the dusty first edition copy of *TOUR OF THE WORLD IN 80 DAYS* by Jules Verne.

First edition English, original title, condition good, she thought, smiling to herself. The sound of the brass bell above the door got her attention. She smiled again because she knew that the bell was older than most of the books in her shop. It was older than the shop. In fact, older than the entire building.

Tillie moved out of the stacks of bookshelves to the small checkout counter. She loved her small book store. It was only six hundred square feet, but it was paid for, thanks to her parents. Plus, because of the Internet, her rare book business was thriving.

Standing in front of the dark oak counter was a woman wearing a sweater with unkempt graying hair. The woman hugged an ornate leather-bound book to her chest. Tillie rarely saw anyone this thin. Her clothes hung on her like she had recently lost a large amount of weight. The first thing that came to mind was the word *Junkie*.

Tillie also wore a sweater but combined with her favorite jeans. It complimented her figure. She instantly felt guilty for both her vanity and for judging this customer.

"Good morning, may I help you?" Tillie asked cheerfully from behind the raised counter.

The woman would not meet her eyes. Her gaze darted from side to side as if she might run away at any moment.

"That book you have there is lovely," Tillie said to her. "I'm Tillie."

This seemed to break the woman out of a fugue, and she placed the book on the counter as if it was suddenly hot.

She spoke in a rush. "I heard you buy antique books here, yes. They say, yes. Old, rare, odd sorts. Yes?"

The woman's eyes were darting about again. Closer now, Tillie could see she was all hard angled bones and sunken eyes.

Slowly, Tillie answered, "Yes... I do. My parents started the business before I was born." Tillie reached out for the book to have a look. The woman moved as if to snatch it back, but stopped herself.

"I want to... sell it." She was in apparent inner turmoil. "No. I want you to buy it. I don't want my family to have it." She was mumbling.

The book was about six inches wide, nine inches tall, and three inches thick. The cover had six raised leather panels. Two parallel black iron strips of metal crossed the cover between the panels and ended with hinge joints where the lock was. It was latched closed, but not locked. It opened easily with a click.

Tillie opened it carefully to the first page. There was an ornate skeleton key, artfully depicted.

The page had a list of handwritten names and dates below the key. A quick count showed there were twenty names in the first column and six names in the second. The years after the names ranged from 1802 to 2011. The first names were in a stylish script of pen and ink, and the last few were in ballpoint pen.

Then she recognized one name, one famous signature: Edgar A. Poe.

The last name on the list in ballpoint block letters was, Audrey Dunn.

On a hunch, she asked, "Are you, Audrey?"

The woman nodded without looking at Tillie.

"Audrey, is this a family heirloom?" Tillie asked as she opened a drawer and pulled on a fresh pair of disposable cotton curator gloves.

"No. Not an heirloom. No. I bought it. No. You see right there in 2011. No. Not an heirloom." Tillie realized that her darting eyes were avoiding the book, not Tillie.

Audrey shivered and hugged herself after pulling the sweater's sleeves over her hands.

"I ask because family bibles, even the old ones, are not worth all that much unless they…"

"HA!" Audrey barked a laugh on the edge of hysteria. "Not a Bible. Ha! Not even close."

Audrey carefully began to turn the pages. It was beautiful. She could recognize a few German words, but it was not entirely German either. The title seemed to be "De Schlëssel." This aligned with the illustration on the title page.

"What can you tell me about it. Do you know the provenance?"

"It's all there. All the owners. Even me. You just put your name there and pay me. It's all there. All you gotta do."

"Have you had this appraised? I believe it has Edgar Alan Poe on this list. In his own hand. His may be one of the few signatures I'd recognize. See, his signature and 1849. Did you know he died in 1849?" Audrey's excitement seeped into her voice. She could not help it.

"Oh, you saw that? Eh." She sounded disappointed. "Buy it?"

"Audrey, I'd like to buy it, but to be fair, we should have it appraised first. It could be worth thousands."

"No appraisal. No one else can see it." She finally looked Tillie square in the eyes. Bloodshot, unblinking, and wet. "Write your name. Buy it."

"Based on my own experience, without an appraisal, all I could pay is a thousand dollars today. I could write you a check now. I really think you need to have it appraised first. It could be worth a lot more."

"No check. Cash. Now. How much you got in there?" Audrey pointed a skeletal finger at the antique cash register. "After you write your name. Now."

With the ring of the cash register bells, Tillie began counting. "There is only a hundred and eighty, not including the one-dollar bills."

A feeling of guilt settled on Tillie, as if she was taking advantage of the woman. Then a thought occurred to her.

What if this book has been stolen?

"$180 is fine," Audrey said quickly, reaching for the cash. "You need to write your name."

"I will need some ID so I can write a proper receipt to maintain provenance." Tillie was starting to think something odd was going on.

"My name is right there." She pointed a boney finger.

"But how do I know that this is your name without proper ID?" Tillie asked gently.

"All right," Audrey said and began to dig into her purse, mumbling to herself.

Tillie had a proper receipt filled out before Audrey could produce a driver's license. The photo on her license showed a much younger, healthier woman named Audrey Dunn. The receipt even included a fresh photo of the book itself. She placed both on the copier. She handed the receipt, license, and cash to Audrey in an outstretched hand.

Audrey snatched it away as if Tillie might suddenly change her mind.

"Before you write your name. It's the rule. I am required to tell you." she licked her lips and to made it all a bit creepier. "The book is haunted. It knows things. It's looking for something. Just understand it's not you. It won't hurt you. Not the one who is named within. Sign it. Sign. It."

Yep, she's crazy, and I don't even care because I gave her all the chances in the world.

Tillie was shocked when she looked down at the page. She must have written her name in the book before she realized it. The black ballpoint pen was still in her gloved hand. It horrified her as she stared at her own name.

When she looked up, Audrey was gone, and the echo of the bell over the door was still washing over the room.

***

Tillie spent a little time researching the volume on the Internet. Her usually reliable sources for rare and collectible books had come up dry. It didn't help that the title of the book, *The Key*, had been widespread over the centuries.

The lunch hour customers had distracted her enough that she didn't get back to it before the store closed. She decided to take it home with her and do more research there.

By the time she got home to her small apartment, made herself dinner, took a shower, and donned her favorite pajamas and robe, it was later than she thought. She fell asleep in a giant overstuffed chair with the book in her lap.

Her dreams came quietly as a whisper…

A tall figure stood before the ottoman at her feet. A fire silhouetted him in the hearth that she did not remember lighting. He was looking at his surroundings as if confused to find himself there.

His gaze settled on Tillie, and he became still.

Tillie became afraid because she was unable to move anything except her eyes. Glancing down, the book was open to the title page with the key illustration, and list of names. Only her name glowed red.

A faint whisper said, "I won't harm those who are named within…"

She woke with a start.

The gas fireplace hearth was cold, and the lights were still on in the kitchen and beside her chair.

Tillie was cold. So very cold. She went off to bed and slept in her thick robe.

***

Tillie woke stiff and tired as if she had not slept at all. In a haze, she stood and watched the coffee brew. Generally, on Saturday morning, she'd make herself a big breakfast while cartoons played on the TV. Today she was neither hungry or interested in TV.

On Saturdays, Colin opened the bookshop for her. He was an introverted college student who loved the fact that he was getting paid minimum wage under the table to sit and read all day in an all oak, traditional bookstore that specialized in antique classics, with a modern tilt toward science fiction. Colin had been a customer for years when he spent Saturdays there for free. Now he just did it while sitting behind the counter.

Tillie planned to take the book to a specialty shop in Washington, DC, today to get a written appraisal. Brian Davenport, the owner, was a chauvinist but knew his stuff. He was a bit amoral and never cared where a book came from, but he always got Tillie top dollar, even with his commission. One of the weird things about Brian was he never left his shop. He lived upstairs in a small apartment. He was always open. He always bragged that he only ate delivery foods like pizza or Chinese.

This kind of thing was right up his alley.

After drinking an entire pot of coffee, Tillie got dressed in her favorite jeans and a tight black T-shirt that said **PROFESSIONAL BOOKWORM...** in letters that looked like dripping blood. She knew Brian would like it. She knew he'd give her a better deal so she'd keep coming back. She also knew that he knew.

Tillie carefully wrapped the book in a clean towel and slid it into a canvas book bag. She was halfway to DC when she looked over and noticed she had buckled it into the passenger seat.

Brian's shop was called **BLACK MARKET**. It was a dark storefront that faced a narrow alley. He bragged to her once that the rent was super low. If you didn't know it was there, you would never find it. The store name was done in dark blue, neon lights, in the bay window to the left of the door. In the right bay window, Brian sat behind the counter, illuminated by several monitors arranged so you could not see what he was surfing. Even through the dirty, barred windows, you could see his eyeglasses needed cleaning.

She pushed open the door to the sound of electronic chimes.

"It's my favorite customer. Tillie Walton, my sweet princess. What have you brought me today?" Brian said, not getting up from his chair.

Without a word, Tillie handed him a paper bag from Dunkin Donuts that held a massive chocolate éclair.

"Bribes go so well with Rick and Morty marathons." He took a sip from the long straw placed in a two-liter bottle of Pepsi.

"New chair?" Tillie asked.

"You noticed." Brian wheeled it back and forth a bit behind the raised counter as if a demo was requested. "I needed a bigger one." He patted his massive belly with one hand as he took a big bite of the éclair. His black T-shirt said **STAR WARS, REVENGE OF THE JEDI**.

Tillie looked around the shop. Nothing had changed since the last time she had been there months ago. It was a mix of taxidermy, restored art-deco clocks, radios, and lamps, along with a wall of shelves of HAM radio gear. A large sign declared "No License Required to Purchase!" and in small print, "Screw the Man!" She always thought it odd that there were no books in his shop at all.

In less than a minute, the éclair disappeared, and he was wiping his thin beard with his sleeve.

"OK, whatcha got." Brian held out a hand.

"You'll need to wash your hands before I even show you." She frowned at him.

He slid his chair to some drawers at the far end beneath an open radio of all glowing tubes. A large container deployed baby wipes like tissues, and he wiped his hands and put on cotton white curator gloves.

Tillie unwrapped the book and placed it carefully on the clean desk blotter between them.

Brian looked at the book carefully, from several angles, without touching it.

"Do you have the key to the lock?" he said as he swung a lamp over the book that had a giant magnifying glass on embedded in the center. "Selling or paid assessment?" he added without looking up.

"It has Edgar Alan Poe's signature on the title page," Tillie said. "Depends on the offer."

"The good news is I know where to get vintage replacement keys." He opened the book, saw her signature, and rolled his eyes at her.

"It's the only way she would sell it to me," she said defensively.

"How much did you pay for it?" he asked, knowing it was an inappropriate question.

"Only five thousand dollars," she lied, knowing Brian knew she was lying.

Brian was leafing through it.

"Can I keep it for a few days? I can't read Luxembourgish," he asked, without looking up. "It will also give me time to find the key if you care to. It will increase the value."

"Luxembourgish?" she replied.

He closed the book and swung the magnifying lamp away.

"Yes. That makes the assessment much more straightforward. There were only a few printers there at the time this was published."

"The spine is in excellent condition," Tillie added. "This book was not read often or kept on a bookshelf. It's a very unusual kind of leather I've never seen before. I will need a receipt."

"As usual." He scoffed. "Still don't trust me after all these years?"

She was pulling out her phone as she replied, "No. Mostly because you didn't laugh like you usually do when I floated the five thousand dollar amount." She activated the camera and began filming with narration.

"I am leaving this book with Brian for assessment. Say hello, Brian."

"I am not having sex with you on film again. So put the camera away," he laughed.

"Nice, Brian. Nice." She stopped filming.

"I should steal this book from you just to see you show that video in court. It would be worth it." He laughed. "I'll have an offer for you tomorrow afternoon. I'll text you."

"Thanks, Brian." She took his written receipt and started toward the door.

"I was only kidding," he said apologetically. "I'd totally have sex with you on film. Just saying."

It was Tillie's turn to roll her eyes.

***

In the car on the way home, Tillie got an odd feeling she could not explain. She somehow worried about the book. She felt uncomfortable about leaving it with Brian. But it was not because of Brian. It wasn't that he'd steal it. She could neither pinpoint the feeling or think of anything else. She went about her errands in a fog. She did the weekly shopping, though nothing appealed to her.

After she got home, she did her laundry but didn't have the energy to fold it. The laundry stayed in a pile next to her on the sofa as she vegged, watching a *Doctor Who* marathon.

She realized it was almost midnight when she staggered to bed, climbing in with her sweats still on.

I must be getting sick. I didn't eat anything all day.

The nightmares began almost immediately. There was a horrible cold and darkness. A painful chill in her bones. There was screaming in the distance. It was a familiar voice she had never before heard shrieking. Finally, there was a distant light that she could focus on in the darkness. It was a thing of deep cobalt blue. A neon sign. She got closer in her dream. Close enough to read the neon sign before it shattered, and the cries faded away.

BLACK MARKET.

A tall figure stood before the foot of her bed. The lights from the street and a passing car in the window silhouetted a shadow.

His gaze settled on Tillie, and he became still.

Tillie became afraid again, and horribly cold because she was unable to move anything except her eyes.

A faint whisper said, "I won't harm those who are named within…"

***

She woke with a start at the sound of someone pounding on her door. She was cold even though she was under the covers, despite several heavy quilts.

The pounding renewed, and she sat up.

Beside her on the bed, was the book.

She was confused. Not thinking clearly, she fled her bed, almost falling down as she tossed the quilt across to escape them, and to cover the book without knowing why.

"Just a minute," she called out, and the pounding stopped.

She stumbled to the door without a glance in the mirror, fearing what she would find there. She opened the door but left the chain attached.

There were two people on the landing. The one in front was a tired-looking woman in her 50s who held up a gold badge. The other was a man with a mustache. She could smell cigarettes on them even through the barely open door.

"Are you Tillie Walton?" The woman detective didn't wait for her to reply. "Can we speak to you?"

Without a word, Tillie pushed the door mostly closed and took the chain off. She heard the man speak softly, "She has a Ring Doorbell."

As the door opened, Tillie stepped back and ran both her hands through her hair.

"I'm sorry. I was sleeping. Please come in." Tillie looked at the clock. It was 10:55 AM. "Fair warning. I think I may be getting the flu."

"We are looking into events that occurred last night, and you may be of great help." The woman said. "I am Detective Townsend, and this is Detective Ballard." Tillie gestured, and they sat at the small dining table. Ballard was looking down at her iPad that was lying on the table but didn't touch it.

"May we have a look at your Ring doorbell logs from last night?" he said straight up to the apparent chagrin of Detective Townsend. "Might make for a shorter conversation."

"Sure," she said without thinking. With a few clicks on her tablet, she presented it to them both.

The first entry was the detectives ringing the doorbell, then pounding on the door in the crowded alcove. The next entry was Tillie, fumbling with her keys, trying to unlock the door. The timestamp clearly said 7:07 PM.

"Are there any other ways to get into your apartment?" Ballard asked as he stood and looked out the kitchen window. The fire-escape there was covered in cobwebs.

"There are fire-escapes here and in the bedroom." Tillie was waking up now as Ballard simply walked the few steps into her bedroom. "What's this all about? Did something happen in the neighborhood?"

She remembered the book in her bed.

"That window is painted shut." Ballard said, and his demeanor changed with a nod to Townsend, "You should complain to your landlord. It's not safe."

"We are investigating something that happened late last night." Townsend was watching her reaction. "You went to see Brian Davenport in his place of business. Were you friends?"

Tillie was waking up now.

What are they saying?

"His surveillance system showed you as his last customer," Townsend said.

Ballard was absently poking through her wrinkled laundry.

"He was going to appraise something for me." Tillie said. "What is this about? Last customer? What are you saying?"

"Like we said, you were the last one to see him," Ballard said. "Alive."

"Look, Miss Walton." Townsend hesitated. "Tillie. We know you didn't do it. Couldn't do it. The shop was… It was… bad. The front door was completely destroyed, torn from the hinges, despite the security bars. The shop was trashed. Cameras were smashed one at a time. But not all. The cams that remained recorded the… sounds."

Tillie was shaking her head now. Her hand was covering her mouth.

Those screams in my dreams.

She watched Ballard lift the clothes she wore yesterday up off the floor where she left them. After examining them, he dropped them.

"Mr. Davenport had several cameras on his system." Townsend continued. "They record a continuous week's worth. No one else came into the shop after you left. It did show him spending hours working on your book."

"Where did you get the book?" Ballard asked as he sat back down.

"The book?" Tillie just then remembered again that the book was in her bed, or was that part of the dream as well? To cover her realization, she got up and retrieved the jeans Ballard had just examined and returned with them to the table while she searched the pockets. There Tillie found the receipt for the book she had made that included Audrey Dunn's driver's license copy. She handed it to Townsend. "I was going to show this to Brian if he asked. He never asked." Tillie's eye were filling.

"We don't know exactly everything that was taken, but your book seems to be missing," Townsend said. "The cams. Well, forensics is looking over the footage."

"Brian's dead?" Tillie asked. It was apparent she was more upset by that than the missing book.

Ballard wrote Dunn's address down in a worn notebook with a very short pencil. "How would you describe Audrey Dunn? This receipt is dated yesterday." Ballard showed it to Townsend, confirmed purchase price.

"To be honest, she didn't look well." Tillie ran both hands through her hair again. "I am starting to think she may have given me the flu. I'm going to make coffee. Do you want coffee?"

"Thanks, but I think we need to go." They both rose, "Do you really think the book is worth five thousand dollars?" They moved to the door as Tillie tried to remember the conversation she had with Brian.

"I had no idea. I was hoping, " Tillie said. "I only paid one-eighty for it."

***

The detectives left, and Tillie was feeling better after coffee and toast. She was still in a fog. She dressed and folded her laundry and tried not to think of Brian or the book. It was almost two hours later when she worked up the courage to make her bed.

The book was there.

She carried it back to her living room and set it on her coffee table. It was closed but not latched. After unlatching and relatching the antique clasp a few times, she stuffed it into her canvas courier bag. On the way out, she looked at herself in the mirror.

You look like shit.

She ran a brush savagely through her hair and put it into a ponytail. She pulled on a baseball cap with her bookshop logo and headed out.

Colin was behind the counter, reading as usual when she arrived. Without looking up from his book, he said, "Two cops were here looking for you earlier. I told them it was your day off."

Tillie disappeared into the stacks as she replied over her shoulder, "I know, they stopped by the apartment."

Without knowing why, she took the book from her satchel and stuffed it onto a bottom shelf in a dark corner of the shop. It was a spot reserved for worthless old books. She stuffed it in end-wise, so neither the spine nor the lock showed.

"Let me know if you need an alibi," Colin said, absently not looking up from what he was reading, amusing himself.

Tillie was glad Colin could not see her reaction.

Colin offered to close up the shop. It was always slow on a Sunday night.

I can't think straight. Damn flu.

Tillie was so exhausted when she got home that evening, and she fell asleep on the sofa watching HGTV without making dinner.

Was it feed a cold, starve a fever or starve a cold?

She was plagued again by unsetting dreams.

The Key

A dark shadow stood over her, where she slept on the sofa. It had no face, no detail at all. It was the absence of light, not a shadow cast by light. It loomed over her. It sucked the warmth from the air. The book lay open to the title page. Her name faintly glowed there.

I will never harm the one whose name I hold, the dream whispered before it disappeared.

***

Tillie vaguely remembered turning off the TV and climbing into her bed again. She almost forgot to take off her sneakers. Exhausted and somehow wakeful at the same time, Tillie watched the minutes and hours drag by until after 4 AM. No more dreams, no sleep, no rest. When she stirred for the last time, it was 7:07 AM.

When she sat up, Tillie realized she was still wearing the same sweats that she had been wearing for days. She could also smell herself. It was like rotting onions.

She stripped and went directly to the shower. Tillie fought the lethargy and washed her hair. She scrubbed herself with a coarse loofah and water almost too hot to withstand. She dressed in her second favorite pair of jeans and her favorite T-shirt that said **I'd Rather be Reading**.

After making coffee, she stood over the sink and forced herself to eat two grape Pop-Tarts. By the time she finished, she was feeling a little better.

Tillie found her keys on the coffee table. Her phone was usually in her courier bag because it was a glorified purse that also held books.

She began making her bed as she looked there. Pulling the covers back, she saw her phone first.

And then she saw the book.
Tillie's mind raced.
No. Not again. Not… Colin!

***

She rushed to find the shop door intact and locked as usual. Fumbling with her keys, she finally managed to fling the door open so fast it slammed into the counter, and the antique bell flew off. The discordant sound echoed as it tumbled from shelf to counter. It smashed her favorite mug beside the antique cash register and continued to fall.

In a panic, Tillie had scanned all the dark corners of the small bookstore before the bell came to its final rest.

Moving behind the counter, she bent to retrieve the bell and its attached spring arm. Shards of her favorite mug were everywhere. When she stood, Tillie jumped, dropping the bell again. Colin was standing on the other side of the counter.

"Awe, bummer," Colin said. "Wasn't that your favorite mug?"

Tillie burst into tears of relief. She covered her reaction quickly. "Yes, my mom gave me that mug on the day she turned over the bookshop."

Colin stood there looking at the bell in her hand, nodding his head.

"What are you doing here so early?" she said as she laid the bell on the counter and moved to a broom that leaned in the corner.

"I needed to talk to you. It was kinda weird after you left yesterday," Colin said, with reluctance. "I needed a new book to read, and I found an interesting one in the shit shelves." Colin looked into the stacks. "Sorry, you know, that dark corner where you put worthless crap?"

Colin was looking at his feet and didn't see her turn pale.

"Anyway, I was looking at this old book when these two detectives came in looking for you." Colin glanced up. "Apparently, some lady named Audrey Dunn had hung herself. They asked me a bunch of questions. They wanted you to know. Then they got really interested in the book I was reading."

"Why?" Tillie asked.

"They saw what looked like dried blood splatter on some pages or something." Colin paused. "They took the book."

"They what?" Tillie was at the edge of panic again.

"They took it. I figured you wouldn't care cause it was on the shit-shelf." Colin made eye contact for a moment. "But I figured I'd better let you know straightaway. They left a card. It's in the register."

"Thanks, Colin," Tillie said, swallowing hard.

"No problem," Colin said. As he opened the door, he looked up at where the bell used to be. "I'll bring some tools and stuff by later and put the bell back. Place is just not the same without it."

The mailman came in as Colin was going out. Tillie's mind was racing, and she almost didn't notice the postman. He handed Tillie a bundle of mail, including a small package she had to sign for personal delivery.

She was hyper-aware of the weight of the book in her courier bag. She was rapidly digging through her wallet for Ballard's or Townsend's business cards when she saw the return address on the small package. It was just a name.

Audrey Dunn.

Tillie froze, remembering what Colin had said. *"Some lady named Dunn had hung herself. They wanted you to know."*

She let the weight of the satchel rest again on her shoulder. The package was one of those simple "If it fits it ships," boxes. She ripped it open. The box held a note on a single sheet of paper, with a key taped to it. It was an antique key. It had only one tooth.

I had to make sure it would not come back first. Now I'm FREE!

Flipping open the flap on her courier bag, Tillie didn't even need to draw the book out. The latch was facing up. The key fit. It rotated in the ornate lock, and with a click, it felt like her ears had popped. A pressure was gone. The nausea she felt for days drifted away like fog. Suddenly she was starving. She drew the book out of her bag and placed it inside an antique safe she never used under the counter and spun the lock. She closed the shop up and went in search of food and answers.

***

Almost a week of perfect sleep and delicious meals had Tillie feeling right as rain. With a belly full of pizza and an interesting book in her lap, she leaned back on her sofa. Channel 4 News at Eleven had come on, and the lead story was still about the murder of two police detectives while they sat in their car. Behind the reporter, Tillie could see the remains of the now dark, broken neon sign that said, "BLACK MARK." The E and T were gone.

Tillie had made the arrangements for tomorrow. The safe was to be taken out into the ocean and cast overboard. She'd go and supervise the operation personally. She had paid extra for no questions asked. She had the key on a black string around her neck.

The faded leather-bound book she was reading was an odd printing. A collection of poems. Mostly bad poems about lost love. A vanity printing, she was sure. Her antique clock chimed midnight.

The room became cold. She heard a dragging sound. The lights seemed to dim.

When Tillie turned toward the door, she could see her breath. When she turned back, a shadowy figure stood before her, silent. It was different somehow.

"You said you'd never hurt me." She was afraid but still defiant.

The shadow whispered, "I live in someone else's book…"

Tillie looked down at the book of bad poems, open to the cover page. Something began to glow.

Her neighbors heard the screams…

BIO: David Keener is an author and editor who lives in Northern Virginia with his wife and two inordinately large dogs. He writes science fiction, fantasy and mystery but loves the idea of mashing up his favorite genres in new and (hopefully) unexpected ways.

He is the author of novelettes *The Rooftop Game* and *The Whispering Voice*. His first full-fledged novel, an SF heist story called *Clash By Night*, will be published in early 2021. He is the organizer behind the *Worlds Enough* anthology series and co-editor of the first volume, *Fantastic Defenders*. His next anthology will appear in mid-2021, *The Forever House*, about a magical bar that hops across alternate realities.

He frequently speaks at conventions and hopes to again after COVID-19. Find out more about him at his web site:

http://www.davidkeener.org

FINDERS KEEPERS

by David Keener

I. The Case (or, Why Does It Always Start with a Dame?)

Mowbray Lounge, in Little Texas: Sunday, 17:00, 2114 — Missing 16 Hours

The Mowbray Lounge (called the M), more than seedy but less than sleazy, was a restaurant and an entertainment venue with a stage for comedians, dancers, karaoke, you name it. The two things that rescued it from obscurity were the best BBQ and ribs in Little Texas, and the thrice-weekly Dance Nights, where professionals and wannabes strutted their stuff.

The blond woman looked totally out of place sitting alone in one of the back booths, wearing a designer business suit with creases sharp enough to draw blood. She was obviously uninterested in the racy dance routine being enacted on the stage, which I cleverly deduced by the fact that she had her back to the action.

I figured the woman was either my client or somebody had picked a bad place to go slumming.

As I approached, a man sidled up to her table. I'd have recognized that cocky shuffle anywhere, even if his name, alias, and priors hadn't popped up on the edge of my sensorium.

Jaeger, real name Bartholomew Jones.

He'd been out of circulation for a while. He should have stayed there.

Jaeger was dressed street lethal, but flashier than I remembered. He had Snake gang tats entwining his arms, a fluorescent red Mohawk and a crooked nose that looked like it had been broken a few times. He was way out of his territory; the Snakes mostly dominated East L.A. above the 60. He said something to the woman. She obviously didn't like it, because she dashed the drink she'd been nursing into his face.

While he was distracted, I took three fast strides, cupped his head, and slammed it into the table. Hard, like I was dunking a basketball.

And then I did it again, just for good measure.

I shoved him aside. He sprawled on the floor, looked up at me blearily, but still had the presence of mind to extend razor-sharp fighting claws from his fingers.

"Gonna cut you up for that," he threatened.

"Go ahead, tosser, if you wanna lose those claws again."

When I'd still been a cop, Jaeger had used his previous set of claws on one of my snitches and left her face so badly scarred it had taken a couple of years before I could put together a deal with enough of a windfall to get her fixed. Now she was married with two kids and nobody except her husband and me knew she'd ever been a Tinsel Town streetwalker.

Street rules had dictated that I take Jaeger down hard for that. I'd thrashed him within an inch of his life, and then smashed his fingers and claws into splinters with a sledgehammer.

I was disappointed to see he'd apparently done well for himself in the intervening years. Well enough to get all my fine handiwork repaired.

He sneered at me. "You ain't a cop no more."

"You should be afraid," I said, smiling. "Now I don't have to follow any rules." For some reason, nobody except my dog finds my smiles comforting.

Jaeger scuttled backwards without taking his eyes off me. I had cyber mods from my stint in the military; he knew how fast I could move if I needed to.

As it turned out, I didn't have to worry about Jaeger. The bouncer loomed behind him, then reached down and tapped him with a military-grade taser. There was a bright arc accompanied by a snapping sizzle, then Jaeger arched his back in agony before going limp. Out stone cold.

And me without my sledgehammer.

"Thanks, Gavin," I said.

"Don't be startin' stuff in here," Gavin McCloud said mildly. "You'll waste away to a shadow if I have to drop a three-week ban on you, like this loco hombre's gonna get." Gavin was ex-military like me, though he was Republic of Texas and I was U.S.A. His mods were probably better than mine—the U.S.A. was much diminished, in both size and manufacturing prowess, after the Time of Troubles and the Second Civil War.

"Didn't start it," I said. "He was bothering my client here." I turned to the woman. "You're Ester Waynewright?"

"Yes." I noticed she was holding a pulse gun in her lap, a small, easy to conceal gun that quietly fired disabling microwave pulses. Not so helpless, after all. "He asked me if I liked pole dancing. Said he had a pole to show me."

I shot a glance at Gavin. "Eight-week ban…for unoriginality?"

He shook his head sadly. "They just don't make thugs like they used to. Yeah, I think you're right." He looked down at Ester. "Sorry about the trouble, ma'am. The drink is on the house, and I'll get you another one for free."

"No thanks."

Gavin smiled easily. "Rain check, then."

I sat down across from Ester as Gavin effortlessly hoisted Jaeger over his shoulder and carried him away.

"It was actually a very nice Vodka Collins," she said regretfully. "I wasted a perfectly good drink on that idiot."

"So, what brings you to need my services?"

She looked around. "Is there somewhere more private where we can talk?"

"Sure. My office is just around the corner."

A few minutes later we were traipsing around the aforementioned corner. I gestured to a squat, rugged-looking vehicle that looked like the illicit love child of an RV and a U.S. Army troop carrier. Which was a surprisingly apt description; there'd been a lot of surplus gear lying around after the Second War Between the States. It was as long as a bus, but low-slung and slightly wider. It looked like it had seen better days. It had a California license plate that read "GRENDEL" and a bumper sticker right above it that said, "DOG is my Co-Pilot."

Ester shot me a look. "That's your office?"

"Convenient, eh? I can park it anywhere."

I ran my hand over the door access sensor. There was a click as the locks released.

I turned and saw Ester looking at the "BEWARE OF DOG" sticker I'd put right above the sensor.

"I'm guessing you have a dog?"

"You're about to meet him," I said, pushing the door open. "Don't worry, he hasn't eaten anybody in over a week."

"Really?"

"Yeah, I've got him on a diet."

Her eyes widened as my dog suddenly filled the doorway, tail wagging like a propeller. Two hundred and twenty pounds of gengineered canine, part wolf with some Rottweiler and mastiff tossed in for good measure. He had a huge head, an improbably wide chest, legs like furry pillars and scarred ears. Elevated by the two steps that it took to climb into the vehicle, he was basically at eye level for Ester.

"You don't have many problems with people breaking into your office, do you?"

"Not lately," I said. "That was actually the last person he ate. This is Fen, by the way."

She chuckled and held out her hand for Fen to sniff. "Short for Fenrir, right?"

"I guess you know your Norse mythology." I was impressed. Most people didn't pick up the reference to the Norse wolf god. It was a much more suitable name than the nickname he'd had before I got him.

Smiling, Ester brushed away a lock of hair that had fallen across her eyes. "I always liked mythology in general, not just Norse mythology. It made me wonder, though. If that's what people believed in the past, what are they going to believe in the future?"

Fen let her rub his ears and stroke his head, which was even more impressive. He was friendly, but he didn't take to everybody.

"I always wanted a dog," she said wistfully.

"So get a dog."

"Maybe someday." She sounded like she didn't expect that day to ever come, which seemed odd. Judging by her expensive outfit, casual assurance and personal weaponry, she seemed like someone who had both money and connections. Certainly not somebody to be stymied in having a pet if that was what she really wanted.

"Out of the way, you big lug," I said, pushing Fen aside so we could enter.

Inside, you couldn't really tell that the RV was actually a converted troop carrier unless you knew what to look for. Like the low ceiling or the thinly disguised armored doors leading, respectively, to the back compartment of the vehicle and the cockpit.

Otherwise, it had the normal accoutrements of an RV, including a mini-kitchen, a fold-down table with bench seating that I used for a desk and a couch facing a wall-mounted Tri-D projector. The back compartment included a modest-sized bedroom, guest accommodations (bunk beds), the privy, and a secure compartment I used as an armory.

What I really had was a bullet-proof RV with a killer commo suite and the world's worst suspension. And I mean worst. Sometimes I swear it generated bumps if the road was too smooth.

A client hadn't had the cash to pay for a job that had been more complicated and dangerous than expected. We'd agreed that Grendel—that's what I'd named my vehicle—was adequate compensation for the job. I'd been living in it ever since.

I gestured for Ester to take a seat at the kitchen table. While Fen circled three times and then lay down on her foot, I sat opposite her and raised an eyebrow.

"We lost an employee," Ester said. "We need you to get her back."

"Who's we?"

"You don't need to know."

"Name?"

"Claudia Vazquez."

"What's she do?"

"You don't need to know that, either."

I sighed. Sometimes you get clients who think they know best what you need to know. They're usually wrong. "I work better when I have all the necessary information."

"Indeed," she said, smiling. "But you still don't need to know that."

"All right. How do you know she's lost?"

"She's tapped. We have footage that shows her being grabbed by some thugs." She held up a memnode, a shiny device about the size of a fingernail.

I raised an eyebrow. A tap rig meant whoever had the right access codes could see, hear and record everything that the tapped individual experienced. Most people preferred their privacy.

I took the memnode from her. "When was she taken?"

"Last night. Little after midnight."

"So, she's been missing for around sixteen hours," I said. "It's probably going to complicate things." That was an understatement. With any abduction, time is your enemy. Depending on what the kidnappers wanted, she could already have been raped, chopped up for body parts or moved to some remote location. They should have contacted me, or the police, as soon as possible.

"I know," Ester said. "It took too long to convince my employer."

"I have to be honest, most kidnapping cases are solved in forty-eight hours…or they're not solved at all."

"I know the stats."

Flipping open a panel on the wall just above the table, I inserted the device into a slot. Glancing down and to the right, the file list popped into view in my sensorium. There were two files on the memnode, a large video file and a small one. I picked the smaller one, which began playing on the wall above the panel.

POV of someone sitting in a crowded night club with loud, techno-cowboy music. Whoever it was reached for a drink on the bar. A woman, judging by the non-masculine arm, the bejeweled bangles and the cherry-red nail polish. The club's clientele was a mix of men and women, maybe a little on the rough side. I was pretty sure I wasn't looking at a genteel, up-scale establishment.

At my inquiring glance, Ester said, "The Mixie Trixie." I'd heard of it. A pickup club on the edge of Thai Town.

Claudia exchanged some unintelligible words with another woman at the bar. Enhancement would bring out the words later, if they mattered. She got up and walked toward the back of the club, obviously heading for the facilities. After taking care of business, during which Ester and I both studiously looked away from the view, Claudia adjusted her make-up in front of the mirror. There were some good close-ups of her face, so I'd have a good image to show around. A few minutes later, someone hit her with a taser as she came out of the ladies' room.

The view swung wildly as her attackers, and there were at least two of them, carried her down the hallway and though a door into a back alley. The footage never showed a clear view of the attackers, though there was one good silhouette of a man's head outlined in the glare from the light above the back door. He had spiky hair and big ears with holes in the lobes.

The view went away when someone pulled a Faraday bag over Claudia's head.

I looked over at Ester. The corners of her eyes were shiny with unshed tears. "I'll need to see all of the footage of her at the club."

"It's on there," she said. "That was just a clip of the actual abduction."

"She was clearly targeted," I said. "That wasn't a random kidnapping. So, there's something you're not telling me."

"She's a clone."

I raised an eyebrow. Legally, clones weren't people, except in the Republic of Texas.

They'd come into heavy usage before Civil War II, during the world-wide Time of Troubles. It had been a mad, world-wide paroxysm of war that had stopped just short of apocalypse, not that that mattered to the billions that died from conflicts, tactical nukes, man-made plagues, digital assassinations and the like. Fast-grown clones with rough-shod cerebral programming had been used for dangerous jobs like cleaning up plague victims, medical experimentation, cannon fodder…you name it.

Now, clones were too useful for spare body parts, cheap labor, whatever folks needed and didn't want to do themselves. The new slave class. Just like you and me, but not, because of various genetic markers added during the cloning process.

"Is that a problem for you?" Ester asked.

"Not if you pay me enough," I said.

"We can do that."

I leaned back. Whatever her role was with her employer, negotiation clearly wasn't part of her job description. "It just means we're going to be dealing with a rough crowd."

"Is that all it takes for you? Money." She sounded disappointed.

"Money always helps, sweetheart," I said. "It's the universal lubricant. But, no, the way I figure it, anything that can have a meaningful conversation with me is a person. And I don't believe in slavery."

II. First Moves (or, the Hunt Begins)

Little Texas: Sunday, 18:35 — Missing 18 Hours

After Ester had left, I looked over at Fen, still standing next to the door wagging his tail. I said, "Laying it on a bit thick, aren't you?"

"No," he replied, his voice a deep rumble. "I like her, even though she lying. You should mount her soon."

"Thanks," I said dryly, "I'll keep that in mind." He walked over and gently head-butted my leg, which was his signal for me to rub his tattered ears. He'd told me once that the scar tissue itched something fierce, and my fingers were much better at massaging them than his own stubby fingers. "She wasn't lying about everything. I don't know whether Claudia is really an employee, a girlfriend or something else, but I think Ester's seriously worried about her. She certainly paid us enough to keep you in dog food for a couple of weeks."

Whoever Ester represented, and I did believe there was somebody backing her, they'd been generous. They wanted the missing Claudia back. Fen wasn't going to have to worry about eating for a good long time, and neither was I.

"Maybe you could mount both," he said.

I rolled my eyes at his one-track mind. "Let's go for a walk, you clown."

Fen followed me out the door, without a leash, immediately settling into his "well-trained but still just a dog" routine. Nobody needed a reason to suspect that he was anything else, like a military asset—a wardog—that had officially been written off as a "combat loss" on a battlefield in Algeria.

Fenrir, officially "Max," serial number WM-Max-SP34T-017-6, on an equipment list somewhere.

We couldn't talk out loud on these walks. In a digital world, there was too much chance of being observed by security cameras, vehicle cameras, paparazzi snoops, curious bystanders…you name it.

That didn't mean we couldn't communicate, though.

Fen had an augmentation that turned his sub-vocalizations into messages. It's standard milware for wardogs and works just like the same feature in most commercial neural sensorium systems. My sensorium was military-grade, too, but it was reset for civilian use when I left the service, which meant it could now connect to civilian networks but not military ones. Fen's system had needed a hack, an expensive one, so it could connect to the local net.

Baskerville: We sniff where hunters took her?

Sadly, I let Fen pick his own username. I won't be doing that again.

SixGunCal: Later, after dark. I want to find the manager on duty from last night.

We ambled slowly around the block, just a man and his dog going for a walk in the evening. No outward indication that we were silently discussing a case.

Fen left me briefly to range around an empty lot littered with debris and overgrown with weeds, where he did his business. Still a dog, he'd never have the body modesty of a human.

Afterwards, we made our way down the street to Danibelle's Guaranteed Parking. Maybe three or four decades ago, a Texan lady named Danibelle had inherited a multi-level parking garage in what was then one of the worst parts of town. Realizing its lack of salability, and being a bit on the stubborn side, she'd improbably decided to turn it into a viable business.

Lady Danibelle, as she eventually became known, imported other Texans to guard the garage and the vehicles in it, and to escort patrons safely from the parking garage to their homes. Surprisingly, the business had thrived. More Texans moved in, and Little Texas became a neighborhood, supplanting what had once been Little Armenia (though some of the Armenians were still there, too). Now she owned a string of about sixty garages, a taqueria chain and part of a major sports team. She was known throughout California for her flamboyant business style and outrageous comments.

I'd met her once, when I was a cop. She'd been a hoot, practically exploding with outrageous comments and a disarmingly infectious laugh.

Of course, Lady Danibelle would probably be mad at me if you she realized what I was up to.

Maximus Bolt stepped out of the guardhouse as we approached, or the "cage" as he and the other guards called it. He was a fifty-something black man and former pro football player with hulking shoulders, a wide smile and a big belly. He extended a dog biscuit to Fen, who took it eagerly and then went into full-on "happy dog" mode.

Fen likes people who feed him.

"Ready for that rematch yet?" Max asked, as Fen flopped to the ground in front of him and rolled over. Max obligingly bent down and started rubbing his belly.

I'd made the mistake of going target shooting with Max once. While time and pounds had taken their toll, he was retired Canadian Recon. His older mods may not have been as good as mine, but he could shoot a pimple on the ass of a flying gnat at a range that, to my mind, proved that magic existed. 'Cause science certainly didn't explain it.

"Sure," I said. "Let's schedule something for tomorrow."

"Right," he responded, chuckling.

He knew I was echoing a sign posted above the main bar at the Mowbray Lounge:

FREE BEER TOMORROW

The punchline was that if you asked the bartender for your free beer, he'd always reply with: "Aye, no, that's tomorrow." The point being that tomorrow never arrives, which was pretty much how I felt about the rematch Max wanted.

Still rubbing Fen's belly, and with his back to the gatehouse's camera, Max said, "I tagged three cars, but I'm guessing the second one's your client." Sub-vocalizing, he sent three pictures which popped up in my sensorium. He was right, the second one was Ester.

"Thanks, Max."

One of the reasons I liked to meet clients at the Mowbray Lounge was because they invariably chose Danibelle's

Guaranteed Parking for their vehicles. The neighborhood had a lingering bad reputation, which was only augmented by all the expatriate Texans who openly carried guns. Naturally, my clients chose the safest parking arrangement they could find.

A few years ago, Max and I had determined that we both had problems for which the other had an easy solution. Max's problem was that he had eight kids living with him and his girlfriend, plus three ex-wives looking for any money they could find, and a fortune that had evaporated in one of the world's economic fluctuations.

My problem was that many of my clients lied to me. Often about who they were, who they represented or even what they were going to do with the information I provided. Over the years, I'd found it beneficial to find out more about my clientele than they necessarily wanted me to know.

Max and I had reached an understanding. He got a little extra in a Mexican numbered bank account and in return he tagged my clients' vehicles.

Bel Air: 20:07

It was almost after 10:00 PM by the time Ester finally pulled up to the back gate of the estate, some three hours after she'd left McCallister. Ester wasn't her real name, of course, but her Ladyship always said that if you took on a role, you had to fully inhabit it. She'd be whatever she needed to be, for as long as it took, to get her sister back.

She'd driven around aimlessly to confuse any possible tail, then stopped at one of their safehouses to ditch the vehicle, switch clothes and shower.

Just in case the detective had decided to do something tricky to track her.

After that, she'd taken public transit to another safehouse and picked up a new car there. All because Esteban had advised them that, while this McCallister was a good detective, like really relentless, he could also be nosy. Hiring him was definitely a calculated risk.

The gate opened, the two panels rising up six inches with a hydraulic hum to disengage the support bars from their steel-rimmed sockets and then swinging aside in the glow of her headlights. Designed to look like cast iron, the entire gate was made of solid steel.

The whole estate was like that, an ordinary-looking facade hiding the best security features and booby traps that money could buy. The others, all older than her, had been through things that had honed their paranoia to the max. To all intents and purposes, the estate was a fortress. She hoped, like always, that they'd never need all the defensive measures.

She'd do anything to make sure those defenses never needed to be used.

She'd protect all of them, no matter what the cost.

She drove up the back lane in a cocoon of light as the landscape lighting activated due to the car's presence, then shut off as it passed. It was like traveling through a fantastic fairy realm of perfectly manicured foliage created by some fickle god just for her benefit.

The motion-activated lights were another defensive measure, though a more subtle one than the gate.

After a few minutes of winding travel, she pulled into the back garage, which was a small stucco building located about a hundred meters from the main house. Making sure her vehicle was centered on the red rectangle painted on the floor, she activated the lift. It took her down several levels into the warehouse, where she parked near the end of the last row.

There were about forty vehicles in the warehouse. Some flashy ones for her Ladyship, who had an image to keep up. Most of the rest ranged from ordinary down to nondescript. There was no need to draw attention to their activities, most of which were illegal not just in California, but also in the Pacific Union to which it belonged.

Tired, she trudged through the tunnel to the house. Before she could open the door, Bettina pulled it open and greeted her with, "Christ, Baby! What took you so long? Was all that really necessary?"

"Nice to see you, too, Bet."

"Sorry."

"You're not sorry, you're bossy."

Bettina smiled and brushed an errant lock away from her face. "Yeah, that's my job." She was the operations manager for their little organization. Despite being only seven years older than her, and having the same genes, she'd somehow managed to look frumpy.

"Well, this is my job," Ester insisted. "And yes, it was necessary."

"So, you're that sure McCallister can find her?" Bettina asked.

"Yeah."

"Good thing that bouncer stopped the fight, though," Bettina said. "Otherwise, your detective would have been cut to shreds."

She fixed Bettina with an incredulous look. Sometimes she forgot that, thanks to their roughshod upbringing, they all had, well, unusual knowledge gaps. Even her Ladyship, who spent the most time out in the Real World. "You don't really get it.

McCallister is ex-military. Special forces. Wired to the max. The other guy, I looked at his police record back at the safehouse. He's a low-level gangbanger with flashy street mods. It was never going to be a fight, not unless you consider rabbit vs. tiger to be a fight."

"Really?"

"Don't you dare underestimate McCallister. He's dangerous. And smart."

"I thought you said finding her would be hard?"

"For us, yes. We're not detectives. He is."

"Wait." Bettina gave her an appraising look. "Don't tell me you've got a crush on him."

"I do not!" she said indignantly. "And if I wanted to get laid, I'd pick somebody a hell of lot less dangerous than him." She paused, made an attempt to get Bettina back on track. "He'll find her. If anything, it's gettin' her back that's going to be the hard part."

Little Texas: 20:37

After a dozen rings, a woman answered my call cheerfully, if a little breathlessly. "Mixie Trixie, come for the food, stay for the fun. How can I help you?" Despite the energetic greeting, I was pretty sure the club wouldn't meet my culinary standards.

"Hi," I said. "Hey, um, my wife got a call from your manager yesterday. She lost a necklace at your club and apparently somebody found it and turned it in. We were supposed to drop by yesterday and pick it up—"

"Gosh," the woman said. "I'm afraid I don't know anything about it. I wouldn't even know where to look for it."

"That's all right, the manager said he'd keep it safe for us. Um, I'm sorry, I can't seem to remember his name…"

"Yesterday…oh, that was Brian Douglas."

"Yes, that's it. Hey, do you know when he'll be on duty next?"

"Lemme check." I heard the sound of rustling paper in the background; apparently the Mixie Trixie's technology level was stuck in the twentieth century. "He's on duty tomorrow. We open at 11:00 AM, but you could catch him as early as 10:00 if you wanted."

"Excellent," I said. "You've been a big help."

The scam had been pretty easy to discern from the footage I'd been given. Collect a patron's empty drink glass, take it into the back and test it for clone markers. Our man Brian had clearly orchestrated the activities in the club.

I armed an agent with Brian's name and image and sent it out into the Net. After a few minutes, the agent returned with a profile of Brian Douglas culled from public offender services, news outlets and other sources. A list of priors scrolled down the periphery of my vision, including drug possession, intent to distribute (later dropped), DUIs, solicitation and others.

A bad boy, but more of a wannabe than a real threat.

We'd be paying the Mixie Trixie, and Brian, a visit in the morning.

I looked up and saw Fen sitting patiently beside the table, holding a battered copy of *The Complete Sherlock Holmes* in his mouth.

"No," I said. "It's too long for a bedtime story. I am not reading 'The Hound of the Baskervilles' again." I reached out and gently took the book from his mouth.

"Nother one, then?"

Fen couldn't read, though he was struggling to learn. Apparently, reading wasn't an easily learned skill, even for an intelligent dog; their minds differed from ours in a variety of odd ways. But he loved story-time, and at least Sherlock Holmes gave me a break from reading Edgar Rice Burroughs to him.

I moved over on the bench. He jumped up and settled in next to me for his nightly story.

III. The Mixie Trixie (or, Who Really Eats There?)

Mixie Trixie, in Thai Town: Monday, 10:01 — Missing 33 Hours

By daylight, the Mixie Trixie didn't look like much. It was the only business in a rundown, three-story, brick office building that probably dated back to the twentieth century. A neon sign, currently turned off, presided over a battered and rusty steel door, surrounded by wide, dirt-streaked windows that theoretically let passerby see some of the excitement going on within the club.

I wasn't seeing any excitement, but then again it was only 10:00 AM.

The club wasn't officially open for business yet, but the door was propped open.

"Stay," I told Fen, who grumped at me but then circled three times before lying down next to the door.

Entering, I was smacked in the face by the smell, a mix of stale beer, smoke, sweaty bodies and astringent cleaning fluids, which made it clear why the door was open. It was dim inside, with only a few lights on. I was pretty sure that more lights wouldn't improve things.

A feminine voice called out from somewhere in the back, "We're not open yet." The voice didn't sound like the overly cheerful woman I'd talked to last night.

"That's fine," I said, looking around. "I'm not here to drink."

Over there, the bar where Claudia had sat, not realizing that the manager was fingering people like her for a snatch team.

A pretty woman like Claudia. She'd been a prime target.

I wandered over to the back hallway. The back door was alarmed. On the footage, no alarm had gone off when Claudia had been carried through it.

I pushed it open and was unsurprised when an alarm blared out, loud enough to set my teeth on edge.

The alarm ceased when I pulled the door shut. Turning around, I saw a bulky man, who I instantly recognized as Brian Douglas, coming down the hallway with a thunderous expression on his face and a baseball bat in his hand. He was wearing a suit that would have been stylish if he'd been about twenty-five kilos lighter. A twenty-something woman trailed behind him, dressed in the black T-shirt and tan shorts that all of the wait staff had been wearing on Claudia's tap.

She hadn't been featured in the footage I'd looked at.

"Who the hell do you think you are?" Brian shouted. "I want you out of my club now."

I waited until he got close, his expression already faltering at my obvious disregard for the threat he represented. Then I moved, and suddenly the bat wasn't in his hands anymore. I slowed down so he could appreciate just how easily I'd taken his weapon, smiled at him, casually snapped the bat in two, and dropped it at his feet.

"Hello, Brian," I said, putting my hand on his shoulder. "Looks like a sweet gig you've got here. I'd hate, I mean really hate, to ruin it for you. But I've got some questions I need answered." I squeezed his shoulder, something that wouldn't be noticeable in the recording his own sensorium was undoubtedly making, but he could feel the power, the augmented power, in my grip.

"I can't—"

"Can't?" I raised an eyebrow like a macho TRI-D actor I'd watched once. "That's not a word I'm real comfortable with, Brian. Here we are, we've got Proposition 72 on the ballet in October, and you're helping clone hunters snatch people out of your club. I mean, seriously?"

The woman behind him shot an appalled look in Brian's direction.

Clones were legally property, without any personal rights, in most of what had once been the United States. The exceptions were the Republic of Texas, where clones had all the rights that accrued to people; and the Midwest's Freedom League, where clones were considered an abomination to God and subject to immediate execution. The Pacific Union, which comprised California, Oregon, Washington, Hawaii and, rather to a resurgent Canada's surprise, Alaska, had Proposition 72 on the national ballot. If passed, clones would be granted almost the same level of autonomy as they had in Texas.

"I'm calling the police!"

"Go ahead, Fatso," I growled. "But I'm not the one you need to worry about." I leaned over and whispered conspiratorially, "You've really pissed off some powerful people, not to mention the clone rights contingent."

Brian glowered at me as I chuckled and brushed past him. On my way out, I sent my anonymized contact information to the waitress.

Mixie Trixie, in Thai Town: 10:26

When I was a cop, I'd had to go dumpster diving more than once to find a key piece of evidence, from a gun used in an armed robbery to a stolen purse back when I was just starting out. Of course, when I'd been on the force, we'd had these disposable full-body suits we could put on. Hot as hell, though.

Sifting through the dumpster behind the Mixie Trixie, it took us all of fifteen minutes to find what I'd been expecting. Rather than climbing into the bin, I'd chosen the more expedient method of pulling bags out and throwing them onto the pavement, where Fen took delight in shredding them and spreading the contents around.

This advanced detective technique ensured that Fen was suitably entertained and that I didn't end up smelling like I'd been wallowing in garbage.

Amongst all the scattered refuse, it was easy to pick out the blue and white packaging of a bunch of Imogene Clone Identi-Kits, or ICIKs. The kits were intended solely for law enforcement professionals, but they weren't that hard to get on the black market.

I captured a few images of the discarded kits for Ester. It was always nice to have confirmation for my clients.

We left the mess for Brian or one of the Mixie Trixie's other employees to find. Between last night's fake call, today's visit, and the rather obvious dumpster dive, I wanted Brian to be nervous enough to call the real clone takers.

He was too small fry to be running this operation himself. There had to be somebody behind him.

Buck's Chili Bowl, in Thai Town: 10:51

The TRI-Ds have it all wrong. Detective work isn't all action like some Hollywood spectacular. It's mostly about asking questions people don't want asked, and a lot about waiting for things to happen once you've poked the hornet's nest. The way I figured things, if I was going to wait, I'd prefer to be well fed.

Buck's Chili Bowl was a block down the street from the Mixie Trixie, an incongruous but well-known attraction of Thai Town. With Fen at my heels, I took a seat in the restaurant's outdoor seating section, which jutted out into the sidewalk like the shoulder of a hill constricting a river into a stretch of tumbling rapids. A diverse throng of pedestrians vainly attempted to pass by in both directions using the narrow strip of sidewalk that remained.

"No dogs," the waiter said when he arrived.

"He's a service dog," I said without looking up.

"No dogs," he repeated.

I looked up. He was a young Thai, maybe eighteen or so. No gang tats. "You tell him."

Fen looked up, too, baring his fangs and letting a low growl rumble out.

The waiter stepped back a few paces in alarm. I rattled off my order and proceeded to ignore him while I watched pedestrians go through gyrations to avoid stepping off the curb. He left after a moment and returned shortly with a cup of Buck's Fiery Chili, a soda and a breakfast sausage biscuit.

As soon as he left, I fed the biscuit to Fen. I was halfway through my chili when a message arrived:

```
CottonCandyLover3: On brk now
CottonCandyLover3: Not right what happened
CottonCandyLover3: Can we meet?
```

CottonCandyLover3's real-world name was private, but Topaz, a diver I used sometimes, had long ago given me an override hack that showed me the sender's real name anyway. My caller was Caitlyn White, the waitress I'd seen at the Mixie Trixie.

Even in the 22nd century, some people still had a conscience. Made me feel all squishy inside. Or maybe that was indigestion.

It's hard to tell the difference sometimes.

Another message popped up:

Baskerville: Can i have another biscuit?

I sent Caitlyn my location and quietly said "Maybe" to Fen.

Caitlyn showed up just as I was finishing the chili. Once again, Buck's recipe had lived up to its fame. It was a shame I didn't get over to Thai Town that often.

She took a seat next to Fen and put her hand down for him to sniff. He gave it the obligatory sniff and then a friendly lick, which made her smile briefly.

"You want something?" I asked. "My treat."

Caitlyn asked for a coffee and a small Buck's Cincinnati Chili, a milder recipe that incorporated cinnamon with a hint of horse radish, and was served over spaghetti. I'd had it before; it was good, but not in the same award-winning league as Fiery. I signaled the waiter, who reluctantly scurried over, but kept to what he thought was a safe distance from Fen.

I couldn't help smiling. Fen was a wardog. You do not want to piss him off. If he can see you, you're not safe. If you're unfortunate enough to be his target, and he gets your scent, you'll never be safe.

Order safely placed, Caitlyn waited until the waiter was out of earshot. "I didn't know—"

"Not your fault," I said. "Bad boys get into trouble all on their own. It's the missing girl that I've been hired to find." I pulled a flexxi out of my pocket, unfolded it and watched the creases smooth themselves out of existence. I opaqued the back for privacy, brought up a key image from Ester's abduction video and flipped it around for Caitlyn to look at. "Who's that?"

The image showed one of the club's night-time waitresses.

"Is she in on it?"

"Yes," I said. "She was the spotter for the snatch team."

"Shit," Caitlyn said glumly. "She calls herself Tomyris, says her parents named her after some famous warrior queen. As far as I can tell, she spends most of her money on these immersive fantasy games. Fancies herself as some kind of, like, warrior princess. She's been bragging lately that she's got some new source of money. I figured she was hooking on the side."

"She found a more lucrative game."

She nodded. "Brian, the manager, you know, he makes me do most of the administrative stuff. I've seen the employee list…her real name is Elizabeth Hayes."

I smiled.

Caitlyn's eyes widened. "You're not going to hurt her, are you?" People don't seem to like it when I smile.

The waiter chose that moment to arrive with the food: a small bowl of chili and a coffee for Caitlyn, and another sausage biscuit. As soon as he turned away, I passed the biscuit to Fen who wolfed it down in stereotypical fashion.

"No," I said. "I'm not going to hurt her. But the warrior princess is about to get her armor tarnished."

While Caitlyn ate, I gently questioned her and extracted a few more useful tidbits about the operation. After she left a short time later, I set an agent to find out whatever there was on Hayes. It didn't take long; she was a high-school drop-out, a low-level criminal, and apparently the Mixie Trixie was the first legit job she'd ever had. No address, no contact information.

I sighed and blipped Topaz, my one-stop source for anything electronic.

"Hold please," she said a few seconds later, her voice a pleasant soprano. No image, but then there never was. I'd been working with her for more than five years, and I still had no idea what she looked like, or even where she lived. For some reason I couldn't really explain, I trusted her like she was the little sister I'd never had. There was a pause, then she said, "OK, we're fully secure, now. What's up?"

"Need some information on Elizabeth Hayes, a waitress at the Mixie Trixie. I especially need to know where to find her."

There was a pause, probably Topaz doing a preliminary check to see how difficult the task was going to be. "Shouldn't be a problem. Usual rate?"

"Yeah."

"Five minutes."

She was as good as her word. A few minutes later. I got a secure digital package with a hell of a lot more information than I'd been able to find. Hayes wasn't living off the grid, but she wasn't far from it. She was one of those almost nameless people who society barely knew existed.

At twenty-three, the Mixie Trixie had been her first honest, paying job. She'd had a hard life, in and out of orphanages and trouble. Some shoplifting, a couple solicitation arrests when she was in her teens, and then escalation to fraud and more serious crimes. She was a suspect in a series of robberies involving high-end electronics. Serious "fall off the truck" stuff. There were police warrants outstanding for her, none serious enough to make her a prime target for the authorities, but enough that I could collect a small bounty for taking her in.

There was personalized note from Topaz:

```
    Hayes   has   a   serious   online   persona   as
Tomyris,   master   of   hand-to   hand   combat   and
edged   weapons   in   a   bunch   of   different   games.
Her   highest   profile   game   is   "Spirit   of
Bushido."   She's   ranked   277th,   the   highest   non-
wired   person   in   the   game.   If   she   was   wired,
she'd   kick   your   ass.
    I   traced   her   gaming   accounts   and
purchases   to   her   banking   account.   She's   had
some   security   work   done   on   apartment   #5-11,
70526   Trelane   Drive.
    Break   a   leg.
```

Interesting.

I blipped Ester Waynewright. A few seconds later, a head and shoulders view of her appeared on the left side of my sensorium.

"Any progress?" Ester asked in lieu of a greeting.

"Some," I said. "The snatch team's been using the Mixie Trixie for about three weeks, but they've been doing 'tag and bag' jobs for longer than that. So, it's a pro team."

"That's bad, right?"

"Not necessarily," I replied. "Pros means they know what they're doing, but it's just business to them. One option is to just ransom Claudia from them, which is more likely with pros."

"I hate the idea of letting them get away with it, but…safer is better."

"If I find out where she's being held, we'll extract her. I'll hold the ransom idea in reserve, in case rescue isn't an option. Anyway, the manager, a guy named Brian Douglas, is in on it.

He's taking used glasses into the back and running Identi-Kits on them. A waitress named Hayes is working as the spotter."

"You have a next step planned?"

"I'm going to squeeze Hayes for information." There was no doubt in my mind that she was going to be the weakest link. "And I figure that the manager will be contacting the team, so they'll be looking for me soon enough."

If I didn't find them first.

"Be careful."

"Oh, darling, I didn't know you cared."

"I'm not your darling," she said, her brow furrowed in a way that implied more heat than I'd expected my comment to generate. "I just don't want to have to look for your replacement."

"Very efficient," I replied as she broke the connection. I wasn't sure if she'd heard my last comment.

Baskerville: Another biscuit?

Ignoring Fen's message, I stood and dropped some PUDs, or Pacific Union Dollars as the tourists like to call them, on the table. "Let's roll, Fen. We're on the hunt."

Baskerville: The game is afoot

IV. The Spotter (or, Advanced Interrogation 101)

Public Tenements, in Van Nuys: Monday, 12:25 — Missing: 37 Hours

Fen pulled Grendel to a stop in front of the address Topaz had given us. He loved going for drives, even if he did have to contort himself a bit to both steer and reach the pedals. It was safe enough; Grendel's cockpit had polarized windows that appeared as opaque black to outside view, so nobody could see him driving. After all, dogs that could talk and drive weren't something you could buy on the open market.

Hayes lived in a squat, six-story apartment building that was just a step above being classified as "condemned." It was one of about three hundred cookie-cutter buildings, badly maintained cinderblock tax write-offs slathered with different shades of pastel stucco. They'd been built in the seventies as emergency housing after fighting had demolished a major swathe of the city. They were still here forty years later, still earning money for nameless landlords and corporations who resolutely blocked all economic development initiatives for the area.

Made me feel all warm inside, knowing that there were always people to prey on the poor.

Fen followed me into the vehicle's main compartment, then we stepped outside onto a badly cracked sidewalk. A diverse crowd, mostly gathered in small groups or leaning casually against the building, watched us as we exited the RV. I wondered how many drug deals we'd just interrupted.

I could feel them trying to size us up, figuring out if Fen was dangerous enough to worry about, and whether I was a mark, a drug buyer, law enforcement in a plain wrapper, social services or a tourist stupid enough to be in the wrong place.

A Hispanic-looking kid walked up, maybe all of ten years old. He had long brown hair, ragged jeans, a ripped T-shirt and an impudent grin. "Mister," he said with a lilting Jamaican accent, "you shouldn't be here. You too well dressed."

I pulled out a couple of PUDs and handed them to him. I gestured at Grendel with my thumb. "Make sure nobody scratches my paint job." A couple of people in hearing distance snickered quietly. While somebody could damage the painted aluminum panels that made Grendel look more like an RV and less like an Army vehicle, I very much doubted that anybody around here had anything that could even scratch the underlying armor.

"You oughta be scared, seriously," the boy insisted. "All the cameras are broke." If a camera didn't see something, well, nobody in this kind of neighborhood would dare snitch to law enforcement.

While the boy was talking, I studied the crowd, trying to assess who'd make the first move. Too many people about, somebody was bound to have something to prove.

"I never liked cameras, anyway." I brushed past him and headed for the building's entrance, Fen at my side.

As we approached, two Asian teenagers separated from the wall and moved to block our path. One was stocky and muscular, like a weightlifter, while the other was short and wiry. The larger one seemed to be the leader; he was holding his right arm awkwardly behind him as he approached, leading me to suspect that the moron had a gun tucked into the back of his pants. Apparently, he'd never learned anything about gun safety.

I moved as the leader started to pull his gun out. His eyes opened wide in surprise as I suddenly appeared beside him and knocked the gun out of his hand. He fell backwards, sprawling awkwardly on the pavement as his weapon skittered away.

While I was busy neutralizing the one with the gun, Fen chased the other would-be mugger away, barking and snarling in his most theatrical "attack dog" mode, until I called him off.

None of the onlookers had moved, except to get a better view of the, well, for want of a better word, the fight. There was even scattered laughter at the plight of the two teenagers who had been dumb enough to get themselves into a wildly unequal scuffle.

Nobody bothered us as we walked into the building, though I did stop briefly to admire a remarkably good life-size mural that someone had painted on the wall beside the entrance. It showed TRI-D star Adeline Parkes in a scene from *Martian Vendetta*, her latest film, and it was at least as good as any of the professional advertisements I'd seen scattered everywhere throughout the city.

Proof that talent could show up anywhere.

The lobby was a let-down after the mural. It was infested with ratty-looking stained furniture and smelled like vomit. The elevators weren't working, so we took the stairs to the fifth floor, cockroaches scattering before us. I'd have given my eye teeth to live in some place this nice when I was a child.

Hayes' apartment was the fifth door on the right when we exited the stairway. For some unknown reason, somebody had thought it was a good idea to paint the cinderblock walls of the hallway bubblegum pink. Unlike the other doors we passed, our target's door looked brand-new. There was a one-centimeter bubble cam stuck to the wall above the door.

Before I could knock, a female voice said, "I don't know you, I don't wanna know you, so piss off. And the door's a solid steel security door, so don't even bother trying." Apparently, the bubble cam had speakers, too.

So much for the element of surprise.

Baskerville: She don't like us.

I pulled out my pistol and smashed the cam with pistol butt. What can I say? I'm bashful.

Upon closer examination, it was indeed a security door. It had none of the wear and tear of the other decades-old doors we'd passed. It had a scan plate instead of a doorknob and the hinges were on the other side of the door.

Security was only ever as good as the weakest link. One of the useful things I'd learned in the Army.

I took a position to the right of the door, braced myself, and used some augmented force to kick the wall next to the scan plate. The forward edge of a cinderblock smashed apart. Another kick and I had a hole in the wall. I reached through, felt around for a few seconds, unlatched the door and went in, gun drawn.

The apartment followed a typical Public Housing template. It was a rectangle roughly six meters long by four meters wide, with a mini-kitchen on one wall and one corner blocked in for a tiny bathroom. There was a decrepit couch shoved in one corner that looked like it was used as a bed and some folded clothes in neat stacks on the floor next to it.

A state-of-the-art gaming rig dominated the center of the room.

It was a spherical, black, metallic framework anchored to the floor and ceiling. Elizabeth Hayes floated in the center, wearing a black skin-tight sensory immersion suit that left nothing to the imagination. She was suspended by a complex web of cables. The rig allowed her a full range of motion in every direction, applied counter pressure to provide a near-perfect simulation of physical activities such as walking, running, touching, you name it. I suddenly had a pretty good idea of how Hayes had been spending all of her ill-gotten funds, because it certainly hadn't been on the crappy apartment.

Her limbs moved as if she was walking somewhere. She looked surprisingly graceful. I'm not even sure she'd realized yet that we'd invaded her apartment.

A thick cable snaked from the rig to a bunch of complex electronic equipment next to the wall. I nodded in Fen's direction. He extended one wickedly sharp titanium cutting claw and sliced through the cable. A shower of sparks erupted.

Hayes looked around wildly, blind to the outside world and probably stunned that whatever simulation she'd been in had just terminated abruptly.

I holstered my weapon, then reached into the web of cables that kept her suspended and unhooked everything I could reach.

She tumbled to the floor with a dull thud. I dragged her out of the rig, stopping to unhook a few cables I'd missed.

While I was distracted, she kicked me in the stomach. She moved surprisingly fast and was considerably more fit than I'd expected for a gearhead. I backed up with a whoof, more surprised than hurt. I cuffed her upside her head, which had to have hurt despite her helmet, but she still managed to punch me in the face as I hit her.

While she was stunned from the impact, I ripped her helmet loose and tossed it across the room, leaving an angry-looking welt on her neck where the chin-strap had been.

I had trouble feeling sorry for someone who'd helped slavers.

I blocked another punch from her, showing her a touch of augmented speed, saw her eyes widen as she realized how overmatched she was. I shoved her to the floor, hard. Then Fen was in her face, growling and snarling in his over-the-top attack dog persona. She scuttled backward until she came up against the wall.

"Back off!"

On cue, Fen stepped back two paces and sat down. He stopped snarling but fixed a baleful gaze on Hayes as he alternated between light growling and baring his fangs at her. He made a great Bad Cop to my Less Bad Cop.

Not that I was a cop anymore.

I approached and knelt on the floor in front of her. "Elizabeth," I said calmly. "You have been a bad girl."

Tears slid down her face. "Wh-wh-what do you want?"

"You have warrants out on you," I replied. "I can collect a nice bounty on you."

"But my…my…gear." She gestured at the hole I'd smashed in the wall. "They'll take my stuff." She was right. If I took her away, this apartment would be empty by the time she made bail and got back.

"Tough luck, then." I paused, as if considering an alternative.

Despite the tears, I could see her sizing me up, trying to figure out if she could escape somehow. Her first move was an obvious one.

"If you try to kick me again, I'll break your leg," I said mildly. "And I'll let my dog take a couple bites out of you. He'd like that." Fen stood and snapped his fangs in her direction.

"Or…" she said, wiping her eyes.

"How do you know there's an 'or'?"

"There has to be, or you woulda already taken me in."

"You're smarter than you look," I replied. "Tell me about the snatch team you've been working for."

"They'll kill me."

I pulled out a flexxi, unfolded it and showed her a picture of Claudia. "Two nights ago, you targeted her for a snatch. She's got connections, serious connections, and they want her back. Bad. The snatch team might kill you, but my client assuredly will if they don't get her back." I grinned at her. "I get a bigger payday for getting the lady back than I do from your bounty. But, hey, I get paid either way. Your call."

"Shit." She looked away. "OK, what do you wanna know?"

"What's your involvement?"

"The team's run by the Snakes, they're a—"

"I know who they are."

"I was with one of the guys." I raised an eyebrow at the euphemism. I barely knew Hayes, but Topaz's profile had hinted at a streetwise girl who'd been smart enough to stay away from gang affiliations. Detecting my hesitation, Hayes said defensively, "The Snakes run this area. They point, you lay down, if you know what's good for you. At least Carlo bathes. And he gets distracted easily by anything with boobs, so I don't gotta do him that often."

"And?"

"After a while, they noticed I was smarter than their usual conquests. So, they started using me for things. Courier work, at first. And then they arranged the job at the Mixie Trixie. Taught me what to look for."

"The clones they capture…do you know where they keep them?"

She looked at me for a moment, and I knew I'd hit pay dirt. "Yeah," she said, finally. "The Snakes, they like action, they're not so good at the, you know, the boring stuff. There's a couple of us, we take turns babysitting the targets, like feeding them, emptying waste buckets, the stuff the guys don't wanna do."

"What happens to the clones?"

She sighed. "They got different buyers. The biggest is Halkronen—"

"Konrad Halkronen?"

"Yes."

"Jesus." Halkronen was a big deal in the legitimate clone exchange trade. When I'd been a cop, there'd been rumors that he dabbled on the black market side, but never any proof. Halkronen was a careful man, with a lot of money and powerful connections.

"He's real particular, though."

"I bet." He'd be taking the cream off the top, taking only the illegal clones that he could get top dollar for. "So how does it work?"

"Halkronen's buyer gets first dibs, then there's maybe eight others that might buy. Anybody that's left, they disappear…I don't know what happens to them." She probably didn't want to know.

My guess was that any left-over women ended up as low-level street walkers somewhere foreign like Mexico or the United States or the Federation. Anybody else probably got sold either for hard labor or body parts.

I held up the flexxi. "And her?"

"She was in the warehouse this morning," Hayes replied. "And the buyers usually come around on Saturday morning. So, she should still be there until next weekend."

"You know the next question."

"Yeah." She wiped her eyes again and gave me the location. "So, you won't take me in?"

I smiled and stood up. "I never promised that." She looked alarmed as I pulled my gun out. She tried to scramble away, but I caught her with a tranquilizer round. She crawled almost all of the way to her gaming rig before she collapsed.

Surprisingly, I felt a little bad for her. But now that she'd told me where Claudia was being held, I couldn't afford for her to tell the Snakes what I knew. I needed to put her on ice until tomorrow, and the easiest way to do that was to turn her in for the bounty. I knew a couple guys on the police force who would keep her away from comms overnight for a bit of cash.

Tough luck for Hayes, though.

V. The Blight (or, Demolition Central)

The Blight: Tuesday, 00:08 — Missing 48 Hours

Claudia and the other captured clones were being held in an abandoned warehouse in the Blight, in what had once been East Los Angeles before the whole area had been bombed into oblivion back when the United States still thought it could hold on to both California and its vanished dreams of glory. East of the 110 and below the 60, it was just block after block of demolished buildings, rubble and twisted steel wreckage going south almost as far as the 405. The Blight was like a gaping wound gouged out of the city. Sometimes it seemed like the city had been so damaged that the wound had turned gangrenous.

But the Blight wasn't empty. People lived there, scrabbling a meager living out of the scraps of civilization. They were the castoffs of society: illegal immigrants, runaway clones, gang members, prostitutes, drug dealers, drug users and more.

I'd grown up in the Blight.

"If you need more help—" Max said, turning from the wheel of the van to shoot me a glance.

It was 2:08 AM, and Fen and I would be hitting the collection point in about ten minutes. A collection point was the nicely sanitized euphemism clone hunters bandied about to hide the fact they were really slavers. It sounded clean and modern, but really it just meant the location where they brought their victims to cage them or chain them up.

Technically not illegal. Wrong, in so many ways, but not illegal.

For the registered clones, what was actually illegal was reselling them rather than returning stolen or lost property to their owners. It was worse for the unregistered clones. Their very existence was illegal, and the law permitted only euthanasia. The reality, though, was that unregistered clones would be sold on the black market.

Although Ester hadn't spelled it out, I was sure that Claudia was unregistered.

"No," I said. "You're doing more than enough." I was so deep in mission-think that it took me a minute to realize that Max was probably worried because he thought I was going in alone. "I've got a partner on this. He's been scouting the situation for a couple of hours, now."

"Oh," he said, looking relieved.

Since we were hitting the collection point, Fen and I had resolved to rescue all of the victims that were being held. Accordingly, we'd have to transport them. Grendel was too conspicuous, so I'd scored a gray van with clean papers from a contact of mine. For a fee, of course. The papers were fake, but they'd pass any light scrutiny.

But the Blight wasn't the kind of place where you parked a vehicle and expected it to still be there when you came back later. Especially in this area of the Blight, southeast of the wall that protected Downtown, all bright and shiny, from the people that society pretended didn't exist. This part of the Blight was Snake territory, so I'd brought Max in as our getaway driver and designated vehicle minder.

I'd known Max could use the money, and Ester was footing the bill. It was nice working for someone with deep pockets for a change.

"Here is good," I said. Max obligingly brought the van to a stop and I hopped out. The van was moving again before the door had finished closing. I watched as Max pulled the vehicle into a side street, backing it into the shadows and mostly concealing it behind a pile of debris. I strode twenty meters down the street and turned into an alley.

A shape coalesced out of the darkness and said, "Took you long enough."

Fen was in full war dog regalia. When I'd liberated him from the military, we'd gotten all of his custom equipment, too. Form-fitting combat suit with quick-response impact nullification armor—still not widely available even for special forces; helmet with AI-assisted threat recognition and combat controls; shoulder-mounted, auto-controlled guns; titanium claws; and, best of all, comprehensive chameleon camouflage. I couldn't even begin to guess how much Fen's gear had cost.

My combat suit was anemic by comparison, though it had been the best gear I could buy on a civilian budget. No camouflage or power assist, either.

We walked side by side down the alley, skirting around piles of rubble. "Sitrep?"

"Shift change 'bout two hours ago," Fen replied. That was good. It meant we were unlikely to be surprised by reinforcements. "Three Snakes inside, one on watch on the second floor of the building across the street. No sensor net. Squirrels." To Fen, anyone who didn't meet a military level of professionalism was a squirrel.

"Can you take out the watcher?"

"Alive?"

"Yes," I said, "and without being seen." While I didn't have much use for the Snakes in general, leaving a trail of bodies was the kind of thing that attracted law enforcement scrutiny, something we didn't need or want.

"You're no fun," Fen grumbled. "Yes, I do that."

Fen had sent me images of the warehouse earlier. I brought one up on the left side of my view, so it didn't block my straight-on vision. The front of the one-story, flat-roofed building was a collapsed ruin, but the back was intact. The Snakes' holding area was accessible via a double-wide metal door that looked like it dated back to the warehouse's original construction. Nothing I couldn't break through with relative ease and speed.

"Fast is good, I'm thinking. Straight through the door and then I deal with whatever I find. Any problems with that?"

"Me Tarzan, you Jane," Fen replied.

I chuckled softly. This is what I got for reading stories to him. "We already discussed this, Fen."

A full-frontal assault was a viable attack strategy for taking on a small group of gangers, especially with surprise on my side. Not so much, though, if there was anyone inside wired up to military or mercenary levels.

Still, all of life was a risk. You just had to pick and choose your risks as best you could.

"Your armor stinks," Fen insisted. "Should be me."

Logically, he was right, of course. Except for the fact that he was a wardog, and as far as anybody knew, there weren't any wardogs outside the military, and certainly not lurking about the City of Angels. We needed to keep it that way.

That relegated Fen to scouting, with full camouflage enabled, and backup in case the brown stuff seriously impacted the rotating oscillator.

I followed Fen to a position just around the corner from the area the Snakes' lookout could watch from his second-floor vantage point.

"Good hunting," I whispered, as he faded out of sight. I heard him take a few steps away, and then his presence became undetectable. Not for the first time, I found myself missing the military-grade combat suit I'd had in the Army. Chameleon mode seriously rocked.

The Blight: 00:13

Fen padded silently down the alley behind the building where his prey huddled inside his temporary lair. He sniffed the air, grateful as always that the designers of his suit had understood how important scent was to dogs. He picked out the earthy smell of the weeds and grasses that steadily encroached on the urban wasteland and the sharper odor of rodents lurking prudently out of his sight. From further away, the sweet but cloying scent of decaying garbage.

No human had come this way since he'd last scouted here.

When Fen had observed the enemy's shift change earlier, he'd had a chance to study his prey as he'd taken up his guard position and knew him to be lightly armed and armored, at least by his standard. But even low threats could be dangerous, especially if alerted and acting in a pack-like manner.

Cal was right, at least on this matter. The guard needed to be taken out, or he could put his adopted human at risk. And that was not acceptable. Cal was pack, after all.

Pack, above all else.

Fen stopped under the second-floor window he'd chosen earlier as his entry point into the building. His night vision made the scene almost as clear as day, if green-tinted. The window had been smashed sometime in the past; only a few shards remained around the edges of the frame. Considering the angles, he backed up two body lengths.

He charged at the wall of the building, then jumped when he got close. He hit the wall above the height of two humans. Leveraging his momentum, he ran up the wall to the broken window. Balancing for an instant on the edge of the frame, he picked his landing point to avoid anything that could make noise and then flowed silently into the room.

He padded stealthily through the corridors until he came to the room where his prey was on guard duty. He sidled through the doorway slowly so his prey wouldn't see even a flicker in his camouflage. He might as well have not bothered.

The guard was looking through a window, his back toward Fen. The man's automatic rifle was leaning against the wall next to him.

Fen looked at him in disgust. Even squirrels were more worthy as prey than this human.

He triggered a Bedtime Special and a gun on his shoulder spat a pellet at the guard. His vision darkened automatically as a miniature lightning storm briefly enveloped his target. Fen didn't understand tech, but he understood the effects. The lightning disabled his prey's gear, and the dart at the center of the pellet put his prey to sleep for at least eight hours.

Baskerville: Squirrel down.

As soon I got the all-clear from Fen, I jogged around the corner, my Heckler-Koch SP-47x Smart Pistol in my right hand. My night vision made the scene as bright as day, so I didn't have any problem navigating across the cracked and buckled asphalt of the access road behind the target warehouse. I passed a loading dock with a concrete platform and three wide pull-down doors that were currently closed. Beyond the platform was a stairway with six steps that led up to the double-wide doorway that was the only entrance Fen had seen the clone takers using.

I knew Fen was watching me from the other building, ready to take out any threats that might pop up unexpectedly. In a weird way, it felt like Algeria all over again.

I mounted the steps and stopped on the small landing at the top. Someone had used spray paint to stencil a skull on the door, with a snake coiled underneath. Nice decor.

Now for the fun part.

Shifting into overdrive, I yanked the door open and went in, pistol first.

The space beyond was cavernous. My black market Zeus 4.6 combat mod informed me the dimensions were fifty meters wide, extending twenty-two meters to my left and twenty-eight meters to my right, past the loading dock doors, and twenty meters deep. Zeus also helpfully highlighted the visible Snakes and assessed their threat level.

My first three targets were playing cards and drinking beers at a makeshift table to my right and about three meters away. Two of the Snakes were just noticing my presence. The third, a wiry Asian with ornate facial tattoos, must have had some good street mods. He was already rising, his chair tumbling backwards in slow motion. He was still reaching for his pistol when I shot him.

Lightning flashed around him, illuminating his two slower-moving companions. Still moving forward at high speed, I shot the other two Snakes, then scanned for more targets.

My speed saved me as I heard a round whing past my head. Something I learned in Algeria, movement is life. If you're not under cover, speed is your friend, especially against potentially wired foes.

Zeus highlighted where the shot had come from. Spotting the Snake, still firing his pistol in my direction, I snapped off a burst that took him out. He reeled backward, outlined by lightning.

He'd been standing in front of a makeshift pen, with a female behind him chained to a ring in the floor. One of my shots hit the clone, too. I hoped I hadn't hit Claudia.

Couldn't worry about that right now. I needed to make sure the place was clear. Fen had estimated three Snakes inside, and I'd already taken out four.

I was turning when the fifth Snake shot me in the back. The pain was intense; I couldn't tell whether the round had penetrated or not. My combat suit reacted to the impact, doing its level best to spread the force around as much as possible. The stiffening armor impeded my movement and I slipped as I tried to pivot to face my attacker.

Falling actually helped, at least somewhat. Two more shots went above me as I slammed into the concrete floor and slid for ten meters. The downside was that falling at enhanced speed hurt and drove all the air out of my lungs just when I needed it the most.

My vision was darkening around the edges when I fired my next round. The shot didn't pass that close to my attacker, but

Zeus had selected a micro-grenade round and automatically optimized its trajectory in flight as much as it could. It would have missed him by about two meters, but instead the directed explosion sent most of the titanium slivers in a fan that shredded the unarmored Snake.

Oops.

So much for my goal of no casualties.

I wasn't sure, but just before the round hit, I'd caught an impression of spiky hair and big ears. I thought he might have been one of the men who'd grabbed Claudia at the Mixie Trixie.

It took me a moment to recover my breath, almost an eternity in overdrive. Since nobody else shot me while I was sucking concrete, I was pretty sure I'd gotten all the Snakes. It finally registered that somebody was shouting at me.

"She's not breathing!"

My first thought was: Of course, he's not breathing…he doesn't even have an intact torso anymore. Then I realized the voice, a female voice, was coming from behind me…and had to be describing the clone I'd accidentally shot, not the dead Snake.

Alarm spiked through me. I seriously hoped I hadn't shot Claudia.

Some goddamn rescue.

VI. Oops (or, Friendly Fire Isn't)

The Blight: Tuesday, 00:19 — Missing 48 Hours

I lurched to my feet, my back screaming in protest. I slung my rifle over my shoulder, then felt my back where my Zeus indicated maximum damage. My hand came away red with blood.

Shit. Not good.

First things first. I limped toward the comatose clone.

The Snakes had confined the clones using prefab wooden fence sections, which were crudely nailed to the wall and the concrete, forming open-fronted pens. Each pen had a steel ring embedded in the center, with a chain attached to a metal ankle band for each captive. A bucket for sanitary purposes, some cheap sleeping pads and dirty blankets completed the picture.

Activating the command channel, I said, "Site secured, five by one. Send the bus." I'd just told Max and Fen that there'd been five zeds, or bad guys, and one of them was dead.

"Roger," Max said. "Moving out."

"Help her," a woman said over the fence, having presumably climbed as high as she could while encumbered by her chain. Whoever she was, she wasn't Claudia, nor was the lady I'd accidentally shot. She had startlingly light blue eyes that glittered in the fluorescent overhead lighting.

"Working on it," I said, coming to my knees next to a vaguely Italian-looking woman in a postage-stamp-sized nightclub dress that had been ruined by her capture and incarceration, as well as the scorching it had received from my round. Er, rounds, I realized as my sensorium helpfully pointed out the impacts. I'd hit her in the chest and leg, so she'd been electrocuted and hit with a double dose of a drug designed to take out wired soldiers.

No wonder the poor woman had flatlined.

I ripped her blouse open and her breasts bounced out. Apparently, bras weren't part of nightclub attire these days. I grabbed my Trauma Kit from my belt, a black square about the size of an antique wallet—she needed it way more than I did.

My system had already primed the TK with situational data so it started working as soon as I dropped it on her chest. Medical actions scrolled past in a window at the bottom of my vision as it hit her with adrenaline and an antidote for the sleepy-bye drug, then shocked her heart back into activity.

It sealed itself to the lady's chest and then dropped into monitoring mode.

The woman asked, "Is she—?" Her blue eyes glittered in the harsh overhead lighting.

"Yeah, she's alive," I responded. "She's going to be out for a while, though, and she'll be a hurtin' puppy tomorrow." Not that I was exactly in great shape myself; the pain seemed to be hitting me in waves.

TKs were a relic of the modern battlefield. In war, you died, or you lived…even if they had to regrow pieces of you later on. Anything in between was rare, which made battle both more lethal and, incongruously, safer than it had ever been.

The TK was the most expensive single piece of tech I owned, not that I'd actually paid for it. This one had kept me alive once, and Fen alive once. Now it was keeping Miss Italy alive.

I pulled out a vibroblade and cut the chain attached to the steel cuff around Miss Italy's ankle.

I stood, fighting off a wave of dizziness, just as the door behind me opened. I knew it was Max without turning because nobody else would have lived long enough to get to the door with Fen on overwatch.

I limped out of the pen, stepping over the comatose Snake, so I could get a perspective on the other pens. It turned out there were seven clones present, two per each occupied pen except for the one with the woman I'd shot. Miss Blue Eyes had jumped down from her position on the fence and stood defiantly in the middle of her pen, standing protectively in front of another woman who I suspected might be her partner. She looked like a slightly plump housewife, but I couldn't help thinking there was some iron to her.

The other clones were looking at me with a mixture of fear, uncertainty and hope. There were more women than men, but they were all so disheveled that I couldn't tell if Claudia was among them.

Max stopped beside me, wearing a black security suit and helmet. He'd used black tape to hide the security company logos on his helmet.

"You're bleeding," he said, looking at my back and ogling the blood trail I'd left behind. He pulled a trauma patch out of a pocket and gently smoothed it over the hole in my armor. Though it would seal the armor and the wound, it wouldn't do much for internal bleeding if I had any.

I turned and handed the vibroblade to Max. "Free them."

"Listen up!" I shouted. "This is a rescue." I pulled my flexxi out of my pocket, opened it and held it up as I shuffled past each pen in succession. "We're here to rescue Claudia, but we're taking all of you with us no matter what."

Miss Blue Eyes said, "What if we don't want to go with you?"

"You're being held in the middle of the Blight." I shrugged. "We're not slavers. You can do whatever you want. We won't force you to get into the van outside, but I'm telling you that you'll be a lot better off if you do come with us."

I watched as Max cut Miss Blue Eyes and the other woman in her pen free and then hurried down the line to the next pen. "Is one of you Claudia?" Nobody answered me.

Miss Blue Eyes walked barefoot out of her pen, the few remaining chain links clanking against her ankle cuff as she moved. She stopped at the Snake and stamped on his face hard enough to make me wince. Then she circled him and kicked him in the crotch. She looked up at me, smiling. Leaving the Snake behind, she stopped in front of me. Nodding towards the flexxi, she said, "They took her this afternoon."

"Who?"

"According to him," she said, pointing her thumb back at the Snake she'd just attacked, "it was a buyer from Halkronen. He was bragging about it, said there was some special event going on Tuesday night."

Peachy, just peachy.

The Blight: 00:31

Max did most of the work of herding the rescued clones into the van, while I haltingly made my own way in that direction.

He'd tried to help, but I waved him off. As soon as I got outside, and it was obvious I was injured, Fen started messaging me:

Baskerville: Me Tarzan, you Jane

"I know," I muttered.

Baskerville: You almost dumb as squirrel

"Bite me."

Baskerville: Good plan

I was trying to think of a good comeback when Miss Blue Eyes came up behind me, tucked my arm over her shoulder and started helping. A moment later, her companion did the same thing.

"I don't bite," she said.

"Sorry, not aimed at you. Talkin' to someone else."

Together, the three of us stumbled toward the van. Max passed us carrying the woman I'd shot in his arms.

"So, there's three of you that pulled this off?"

"Yeah."

"Thanks," she said. She started to say something else but choked up.

By the time she got herself under control again, we'd arrived at the van, where they half-lifted, half-pushed me into the passenger seat. Then they helped me recline the seat as far back as it would go.

Max looked in briefly. "Gotta torch it," I said. "Can't leave the blood evidence behind." He nodded and left. DNA was not your friend when you crossed the legal line. I found it ironic that slavery effectively fell on the right side of that line, though I still held out hope that Proposition 72 might change that.

Things got a little fuzzy for a while after that, until I heard Max say, "Where we goin', boss man?" Opening my eyes blearily, I saw Max strapped into the driver's seat.

"Watts." Even deeper into the Blight, the demolished neighborhood known as Watts was where a lot of clones congregated for safety. And they took their safety seriously. The gangs didn't mess with them, and neither did the police. In fact, that entire area had a history of violence and riots that went further back than the existence of clones.

I sent Max a map of the route I'd prepared before the mission. We'd be moving slowly because of the bad road conditions, which would allow Fen to parallel us in an overwatch role, then he'd egress on his own after we'd dropped our rescuees off. We'd pre-positioned Grendel west of Watts, as close as we could park it without being in the Blight.

"They know we're coming?"

"Not yet."

He shot me a look, but didn't say anything.

The Blight: 00:52

Fen sat on the corner of the roof of a three-story ruin, waiting for Cal's slow-moving van to catch up. He was about two short blocks ahead of it. As far as Fen had been able to tell, the van's path was clear, at least up to his position and then for the next block. He'd detected no sign of any sentries, nor had he smelled any hint of booby traps or explosives.

When it got close, he'd race ahead again to make sure the path remained clear.

He cocked his head as he heard a sound coming from his right.

Engine noises, coming from the cross-street.

Motorcycles.

He sub-vocalized a question and Oggie spoke up and told him the range and showed him a map. They were about five blocks away.

Probably a Snake patrol, since they were near the edge of what Cal had said was the Snakes' territory.

Silly squirrels.

Fen was here, so it was his territory, now.

He leaped off the building, landed with a solid thud and started running. Not too long after that, he was safely hidden in an alley a few blocks down the cross-street when three motorcycles went past at a leisurely speed, about thirty klicks according to Oggie, their headlights bobbing as they traversed the rough terrain. Snakes, as he'd guessed.

Fen charged out of the alley, the staccato pounding of his footfalls obscured by the sound of their engines and camouflage mode turning him into nothing more than a blurry streak. They might have seen him in their rear-view mirrors, if they'd been looking. But they weren't.

He caught up to the hindmost cycle in seven seconds and swatted the rider from behind at the juncture of the skull and spine. With Fen's augmented strength, it was an instantaneous "lights out" strike.

Fen slammed the dead Snake's cycle sideways, where it clipped the rear wheel of the next rider's cycle. The rider tried to compensate for the impact, then hit a big pothole, crushing the front wheel and flipping the rider over the handlebars.

While that rider was still airborne, Fen surged past both tumbling cycles, leaped and knocked the third rider off his cycle. Fen rotated in mid-air, came down backwards and slid to a dusty stop.

The third rider rolled in good form when he hit the ground, nicely diffusing the impact—he'd obviously had some race training. After he stopped rolling, he slid for a short distance, his leather outfit taking the brunt of the damage. He was moving weakly when Fen got to him and ripped out his throat with titanium claws, something that leather outfits emphatically did not protect against.

Fen bounded over to check on the second rider, the one that had gone over the handlebars. He needn't have bothered. The man had snapped his neck when he face-planted into the pavement.

Snakes should learn not to mess with his pack.

The wardog stalked away, confident that the remaining Snakes would be too stupid to understand the insult he'd just left behind. They were squirrels. You didn't waste ammunition on squirrels; you saved it for real threats.

The Blight: <times not specified>

The rest of the night was a blur to me, except for brief patches of lucidity. I remember Max shaking my shoulder. I'm not sure, but he might have been shaking it for a while. "Your partner says there's a roadblock ahead."

I fixed my blurry gaze on Max's face. "Where are we?" I croaked.

"Near the old Watts boundary."

"Turn on the running lights, approach really slow, and when someone questions you…tell 'em we've got a boxcar." I started to fade, but then another thought hit me. "And tell…" I almost said Fen's name, but just barely caught myself in time. "…my partner what we're doing, or he'll kill everybody."

"Boxcar? Oh, you mean…I get it now, the Underground Railroad…"

My next memory was of someone shining a flashlight past Max into the back of the van. There was enough ambient light for me to see that the man holding the flashlight looked familiar.

I said, "Ernie?"

"No," the man replied, "I'm Bernie." Looking again, I saw that he didn't have the facial scars that marred the right side of Ernie's face.

"Ernie knows me," I said wearily, and then I was out again.

The noise of the van's main door sliding open woke me again. I heard voices, multiple voices, but I was too out of it to associate meanings with what they were saying. The voices echoed a little, like the van was in a building.

A light played over my face. "Damn, he looks like shit." The voice sounded like Bernie's, but raspier. Same model as Bernie, but with a voice damaged from inhaling riot control chemicals a few too many times…had to be Ernie.

"Man don't know his limitations," Max said.

"True that," Ernie replied. "Never did."

"You owe me a beer," I said.

Ernie laughed coarsely. "Screw you, lightweight, how 'bout I pass your ass over to the Doc instead. Or maybe the glue factory if you keep pissin' me off."

"S'all right," I said, and was gone again.

My next bout with consciousness was when they moved me from a vehicle to a stretcher. I remember pain, and an Asian man shining a light in my eyes.

"I've seen worse," the man said. Noting my eyes tracking him, he added, "I'm Doctor Octo, I'll have you patched up in no time."

I'd heard of Doctor Octo, and their hidden clinic in the Blight. Dr. Octo was an experimental batch of clones who had been created with built-in augments that did their level best to stitch eight people into a single hive mind. It had been highly illegal experimentation that had unquestionably succeeded and also scared the hell out of whichever corporation had done the work. Rightfully fearing imminent euthanasia, Doctor Octo had escaped from captivity.

Trained to be a battlefield medical unit, Dr. Octo had quickly found their purpose within the illegal community of free clones. I was out again, I think, as soon as I realized I was in good hands.

Thai Town: 01:28

Ester sat in the dark, her sensorium illicitly tied into the apartment building's fifth-rate security system, worrying about why she hadn't yet heard from McCallister. Those worries were temporarily pushed out of her mind when Brian Douglas appeared in an outside camera view, looking tired after his shift at the Mixie Trixie. He was carrying a Shop-n-Go bag and a Slurpee cup. She switched to another view after he entered the building and watched him trudge up the stairs.

The security system didn't have a view that covered his apartment door, but that didn't matter. He was a heavy man, and she heard his dragging steps stop outside the door. She shook her head in bemusement as she heard his keys jangling—the building was so decrepit that it didn't even have automated personal lock controls. She'd come equipped with all sorts of fancy burglary gear and software hacks, and all she'd really needed was a hair pin.

She heard him curse at the lock, then he finally got the door open. Stepping inside, he shut the door behind him and came down the hallway, still in darkness, and into the kitchen.

"Lights," he said. When nothing happened, he started cursing again. It was easy to tell from the increased volume of his cursing when he discovered that his sensorium had just crashed. All of the normal telltales, the time, location, the reminder panel, the side menu. All gone.

"Lights," Ester said. As the illumination came on, his eyes almost bulged out of his head when he realized there was a woman in a form-fitting, black combat suit sitting at his kitchen table with a pistol pointed at him.

"Wh-wh-who are you?"

"I'm not happy with you, Brian," she said. "Helping the Snakes with their little slavery ring."

"It's not illegal," Brian replied, his eyes shifting from side to side as if looking for an escape route that would get him out of this predicament. "They're just clones. In fact, I could cut you in on the deal." And now, the little weasel was trying to figure an angle to talk himself out of trouble.

"Really?"

"Yes, I—"

"I don't think so," the woman said. "Three nights ago, you picked up my sister." He gaped at her. Even he was smart enough to understand that that meant she was a clone, too. He looked like he was still trying to think of an angle when she shot him in the chest.

VII. With Morning Comes Pain (or, Being Shot Sucks)

Little Texas: Tuesday, 08:15 — Missing 56 Hours

I came awake again as Fen pulled Grendel to the curb in one of our regular overnight spots, which amounted to anyplace where we didn't have to worry about Grendel being towed. As soon as I opened my eyes, I wished I hadn't awakened.

I had a splitting headache, my entire back felt like somebody had beaten me with a baseball bat and the bullet wound was a sharp spike of pain despite the drugs I'd taken. If that wasn't enough, I had six unanswered calls from Ester and a host of increasingly frantic, and strident, messages. To top it all off, the rescue had been a bust.

I hated failing.

There was some consolation, though not much, in rescuing the other clones. Max had told me that they'd been grateful to be rescued and safely given into the care of other clones, though understandably shell-shocked about losing whatever lives they'd built for themselves. The woman I'd accidentally gunned down had been stirring when we arrived, and safely out of danger, so Max had been able to retrieve my Trauma Kit. Soon enough, our rescuees would either be on the Underground Railroad to Texas, or else they'd have new identities and better training to evade detection.

That was something, at least.

Seven souls slaved from slavery.

Just not the one we'd been looking for.

Max had accompanied me to Doctor Octo's clinic, while Fen had made his own way through the Blight and back to Grendel. After being patched up, Max had dropped me off at Grendel and then taken the van away.

The shot had penetrated my armor but most of its power had been spent doing so. My whole back was a bruise; the bullet wound was about four centimeters deep, just enough to penetrate into my body cavity, but not deep enough to do any significant damage. It hurt like a son of a bitch, though, and left me with internal stitches and a small drain underneath a bulky dressing. Doctor Octo had also told me I'd be pissing blood for a week thanks to the impact, then smiled and helpfully added, "That'll teach you not to get shot."

He'd told me to take it easy for a few weeks, too. I turned to Fen and said, "I guess it's time to face the music."

He growled at me in response, still angry that I'd been shot. He'd get over it, but, frankly, it didn't bode well for any Snakes that might cross his path in the future.

I looked through Ester's messages. Interestingly, I also had some surveillance alerts. She'd been out and about doing something last night. I knew this because she'd been driving around in the same car that Max had tagged for me back at Danibelle's Guaranteed Parking on Sunday.

I blipped Ester and got an almost instant response, sans image, probably because she didn't want to give me a clue as to where she was or what she was doing. "Where have you been?"

"Hey sweetheart, nice talkin' to you, too."

"Don't 'sweetheart' me, Mr. McCallister, did you get her back?" So now I was Mr. McCallister; somebody was seriously peeved with me. I often had that effect on women.

"No," I said bluntly, figuring there was no easy way to break the news. "We hit the collection point and rescued seven clones, but she wasn't there. We dropped—"

"Took them to Watts, I know," she said brusquely. "We've been known to send some funds their way."

"Oh."

"Where's Claudia?" she demanded.

"They sold her to Halkronen, sometime around 4:00 PM yesterday. He's—"

She cursed for a moment, fluently and in both English and Spanish. She'd have fit right into the military; she certainly had the salty language down pat. "This is all your fault."

"You want fault, how about this," I responded heatedly. "You and your people sat on your asses for over sixteen hours before you even contacted me. I told you then that most abductions are solved in forty-eight hours or less. So, don't give me any bullshit about this being my fault!"

"You took our money!"

"And I took a bullet for you, too," I countered. "Eight hours, that's how much we missed her by."

"Then we hit Halkronen next," she insisted.

I exploded, "Are you kidding me? Halkronen's seriously dangerous. He's got mercs working for him, not street-level wannabes like the Snakes. Real mercs, real gear, real training. He's a hard target. Even if he does still have Claudia, you don't have the firepower to hit him. Face it, your sister is lost."

"I don't accept that…wait, how'd you know?"

"I didn't, not for sure," I said. "Thanks for admitting it, though."

"Dammit."

I thought I heard part of a sob before she abruptly ended the call.

"Hell," I said. "What are the odds she's going to give us the second half of the payment?"

"She wants her pack mate back," Fen replied. "She stubborn like you."

I shot Fen an annoyed glance. His tongue was hanging out of his mouth in his version of an impudent grin. I didn't care what he thought, Ester and I were nothing alike.

"Shit!" I said, rubbing my forehead tiredly. "She didn't let me finish. Halkronen still has Claudia, at least until tonight." I took the safer, more expedient way out and blipped Ester a message:

```
SixGunCal: H. is going to have Claudia at some
Event tonight.
```

The Blight: 08:35

By the time Jaeger got to the warehouse, Big Red was already in a screaming rage. When Jaeger rounded the corner on his Matsumoto Skirmish 7500 cycle and cruised down the access road behind the warehouse, he spotted the gang leader striding back and forth in front of some gathered Snakes and waving his arms angrily. Jaeger stopped just beyond the edge of the sludge zone, put down his kickstand and hopped off the motorcycle.

Apparently, the Snakes had had a bad night. At least, that's what he'd gathered from his early morning wake up call, as well as his quick catch-up on the overnight online gang chatter. A triple-tap—their collection point had been destroyed and that useless, self-important manager from the Mixie Trixie had been killed. And someone had whacked one of the gang's night patrols, as well.

Dammit, he reflected sourly, even the shadows are on the wrong sides of everything. Noon was early enough to crawl out of bed. Mornings were for corp drones, not street entrepreneurs such as himself.

The warehouse was a wreck. The front had been demolished long ago in the war, but the rest was now a charred ruin. Well, at least, anything he could see through the congealed sludge looked charred.

Adhering to their normal protocol for the Blight, the fire department hadn't even sent any trucks or police, just a fire suppression hovercraft to drop enough fire-retardant chemicals to smother the flames. Typical dump and scoot maneuver, with never even a pair of boots on the ground.

Stepping carefully through the sludge on the pavement, Jaeger found Big Red and some other Snakes standing around a pile of unconscious men. The four guards from the collection point had literally been stacked on top of each other; not posed or anything, just thrown carelessly into a pile.

Jaeger raised an eyebrow. "Hell," he drawled. "That's something you don't see every day." A bunch of heads swiveled in his direction, probably eager to have someone else divert the gang leader's attention.

The interesting thing to him was that the unconscious men were still alive.

Conflicts between gangs usually ended in bloodshed, while conflicts with the cartels always ended up that way. This was neither, because somebody hadn't wanted to break the law. He gave the warehouse a considering glance. Or, at least didn't want to break the law too badly; nobody was going to complain too much about an already wrecked warehouse burning in the Blight.

"Is that everybody?" Jaeger asked.

"No," said Bek, an angry-looking, scar-faced Snake. He was one of Big Red's go-to warriors, the elite of the Snakes. He aimed his thumb over his shoulder at the adjacent building. "Knocked out the lookout, too. But we still got one missing."

"Collateral damage, then," Jaeger responded. Someone had taken down five out of six street warriors, then gotten unlucky enough that they'd had to kill one. Impressive. Pointless, but impressive. Personally, he didn't mind bloodshed, as long as it wasn't his.

Big Red fixed his gaze on Jaeger. "You got an idea who done this?"

"Yeah," Jaeger said, "there was a guy pokin' around the Mixie Trixie yesterday, asking about our operation there. I know him, and this looks like his handiwork."

"Do tell," Big Red said with a predatory grin.

"Cal McCallister," Jaeger said. "He's an ex-soldier, ex-cop, and all-round pain in the ass." Inside, he exulted. His head still ached from being slammed into a table by McCallister at the Mowbray. The ex-cop had some serious payback coming.

"Do you know where he lives?" the scar-faced Snake interjected.

"No," Jaeger said, smiling, "but I know what he drives." An idea struck him. "And I know how to find him."

Little Texas: 09:02

I unwrapped the end of my breakfast burrito, a fiery special from Jackson's Burritos, and watched Fen dig into his bowl. I'd gotten him a breakfast steak, which I'd cut up into small pieces and mixed in with Kibbles & Bits. It was one of his favorite meals.

Before I could take a bite, somebody started pounding on Grendel's door. I brought up an outside view and spotted Ester standing outside in a sharp-looking gray and white ensemble that managed to be sexy and business-like at the same time. I thought about not answering. But that seemed impolite, since I'd gotten an alert a short time before regarding her final payment hitting my bank account. On the other hand, I'd already gotten shot working for her.

I opened the door anyway.

"You're an asshole," Ester said, peering up at me.

"Sweetheart, you're not even close to the first person that's told me that." I stepped back and let her climb the steps into the compartment.

"I'm not your sweetheart," she said, brushing past me. I got a whiff of some kind of expensive-smelling perfume.

"No accounting for taste."

Ignoring my response, Ester sat down at the table and said, "As a hypothetical, what would it take to get Claudia back from Halkronen?" She reached down and rubbed Fen's head while I sat down across from her.

If she still thought hitting Halkronen was a viable option, she was crazy. Suicidally crazy. I decided to humor her by laying out why taking him on was a crazy idea. "First, we'd need to know where Halkronen is holding her. Second—"

"He's definitely still got her," Ester insisted.

"How can you be so sure?"

"Your tip matches some things we already knew. There's a big Chamber of Commerce event tonight. Brings in a lot of upper crust folks, people with more money than God and not a lick of sense to go with it. Halkronen usually boozes it up with the rich and famous, then sells his…special…merchandise at a private event afterwards. He calls it his Midnight Extravaganza."

"And you know this because?"

"He's a slaver…we watch all of the big, successful slavers." I tried to wrap my mind around who "we" was in this context, and why they'd want to keep tabs on slavers. And how they, whoever they were, were also helping to back the clones in Watts.

"Assuming you're right, we still need to know where she's being held."

"I'm pretty sure I already know," she replied. "But my organization can find that out for sure."

"How?"

"Look, people like Halkronen, they don't advertise what they do," she said in an exasperated tone. "But they don't go out of their way to hide it either, because it's technically not illegal. And they all have support staff they don't even think about…janitors, caretakers for the clones, you name it. We've checked and we have…someone…we can lean on for confirmation."

"Floor plans?"

"We have…sources," she replied. "Staff like I just mentioned. Plus, people that Halkronen bought and sold, before we rescued them."

"OK, that brings me to my second point. Halkronen's hardcore. You're going to need some serious muscle. That'll cost…a lot. You're gonna pay through the nose for a team that can go up against that kind of competition and is willing to do so. Especially on short notice."

"Yes," she said. "We want you to put the team, and the plan, together."

"Look," I said, "You paid me to find Claudia. I found her. You didn't pay me for this."

"Agreed," she said, with a hint of a smile, and proceeded to give me a number that had a lot of zeroes in it.

"Dammit," I said heatedly. "This is insane. Especially on such a tight timeline."

"We have the money, and we can get you some shooters and transport. Plus, a distraction to keep Halkronen's emergency response team off your back."

I raised an eyebrow. "You can get shooters?"

"CRAG," she answered. "The Clone Rights Action Group. They hate Halkronen."

"Ah," I said. "All right, then. We'll need somebody more tactical—I have someone who owes me a favor." Gavin McCloud had the chops to do this, and he owed me for getting his little sister out of serious trouble. "But we're going to need cyber help, too." I'd approach Topaz about the job, but this might be too far into the gray for her.

"Contact them," Ester said. "Offer a fair price, and we'll cover it." There was a pause, then Ester added, "How badly were you shot?" Surprisingly, the ice queen seemed genuinely concerned about my well-being.

"I've been hit worse," I responded, "but not in a while. I'll show you the scar the next time we're in bed together."

She snorted in an unlady-like manner and stood up. "You'll be all right for tonight?"

"Eighty-five percent, you betcha." Well, probably, anyway. Let's hear it for applied chemistry. I was going to miss the pain drugs, though, because I'd need to be sharp for another rescue attempt. If, and it was still a big "if" in my mind, all the pieces came together in time.

I stood up, suppressing a groan, then followed her to the door.

Ester stopped, her hand on the latch, and turned to face me. "We've got work to do if we're going to hit Halkronen tonight. I'll get back to you with an intelligence packet as soon as I can."

"We'll need that ASAP," I said. "And just be forewarned, I'll be dealing with pros. If they don't think the op is doable, they won't go. And you'll be paying them a kill fee, too."

She chuckled. "You hold up your end, I'll hold up my end." With that, she opened the door, hopped down to the pavement and walked briskly away.

I stood there for a moment, enjoying the view, then shook my head. No way. She was pretty, but I'd bet her middle name was Trouble. I stepped back and closed the door.

"Dammit," I said, "this is a bad idea."

"We goin' after Haki-prey?" Fen asked.

"Apparently," I said, absently. "Not him, but we'll be hitting one of his facilities."

Fen cocked his head. "Snakes part of his pack?"

"Yeah, basically."

"Got shot 'cause of him?"

"Kind of."

He bared his fangs and said, "I not like Haki-prey."

VIII. Full Contact Game (or, Are You Crazy?)

Little Texas: Tuesday, 09:21 — Missing 57 Hours

I had Gavin's number; he and I had gone drinking a few times. Not surprising. After all, we had similar backgrounds and we ran into each other all the time at the Mowbray Lounge. I knew a little bit about the problems with his father that had driven him away from Texas and the family business, a well-regarded mercenary unit known as Heavy Metal. And he knew something about my time in the police, my service in the military and my tours overseas. Most of that was surface stuff, though.

We were friendly, but not quite friends.

But he'd known enough about my investigative skills to seek out my help when his younger sister got involved in some trouble. I solved the case and kept his sister out of jail, so he owed me for that.

From my time in the police, I knew that he sometimes worked with independent merc crews in Los Angeles, though law enforcement had never had any real evidence against him.

We'd certainly never talked about his extracurricular activities. But those were what I needed right now.

I blipped him.

There were about ten rings before Gavin answered in a voice still thick with sleep. "What the hell, hombre? You know what time it is?"

"Morning, sunshine," I said in my best mock-cheerful voice. "Things are happening, my man. I'm putting a full-contact game together and your name came to mind."

There was silence on the other end. I'd bet his mental circuits were busily processing the fact that I knew about his other life, calculating the odds that a relatively straight-and-narrow schmuck like me might actually have a need for over-the-line skills like his, and then trying to figure out if it was some kind of setup.

"I need some players on short notice," I added. "Thought you'd be interested."

"I might be."

"I gotta be honest," I said. "Might be a lot of fun, or it might not pan out." A professional wasn't going to do a half-assed mission. Ester needed to come through with the necessary intel, or the mission was going to be still-born.

"When?"

"Tonight."

Gavin whistled. "Jesus H. Christ on a crutch, you ain't kiddin' 'bout the short notice."

"I'll be over in fifteen minutes," I said. "I'm bringing breakfast."

Little Texas: 09:43

Gavin lived on the third floor of a modestly upscale condo complex about two blocks from the Mowbray. Fen padded after me as I mounted the stairs, navigated down the hallway to his door and knocked. Fen sniffed the air a few times, then messaged me.

Baskerville: He's alone.

Gavin pulled the door open as soon as I knocked. "Well, you're just chock full of surprises, ain't'cha?"

"Keep 'em guessin', that's my motto."

Gavin laughed. "You're an asshole, you know that?"

"Strangely, you're not the first person to tell me that today." I held up a bulging bag of breakfast burritos. "And yet, I bring sustenance." I'd gone overboard with the quantity because, well, I'd seen Gavin eat before and it wasn't a pretty sight.

He ushered me and Fen in. It was a nicely designed two-bedroom condo decorated in contemporary bachelor, which meant battered, comfortable furniture and surprisingly artistic paintings on the walls. Gavin led us to the living room, then reached down to scratch Fen's ears, who responded by wagging his tail excitedly.

"Fen," he said in a mock-serious tone, "I'm so glad you brought your pet human with you. It's important to have somebody along to carry the food." He straightened up and turned to me. "What the hell are you calling yourself nowadays, anyway?"

Baskerville: He smarter than he looks.

"Private security consultant," I said. "It looks good on a card."

Baskerville: My pet.

"I bet," Gavin said. "Cal, we gotta get some stuff settled up front. I trust you, or we wouldn't be having this discussion. But this is business, and if you burn me in any way, it won't go well for you."

"Understood," I said.

"All right." He gestured at a gray couch. I sat down while he settled in an armchair. Fen did his usual three turns and then lay down at my feet. "So, what's the job?"

"My client's mission is a simple snatch and grab from a secure facility. The ramifications, well, they could be high profile. Forget all about bragging rights." Sometimes, if you hit big enough targets, you seriously wanted to keep quiet about it afterward.

"What about intel?"

"In progress."

Gavin shot me an incredulous look. "You're kidding? Right?"

"Nope," I said. "Number one thing that could abort the operation is not getting the proper intel in time."

Gavin frowned. "You expecting it anytime soon?"

I shrugged. "You'll know when I know."

"I'm interested," Gavin said, "but..." He held up a hand and frowned. "The intel is a show-stopper. Plus, I'm going to have to know more about the target."

"Halkronen."

Gavin steepled his fingers and rested his chin on them for a moment. "Well, you don't think small, do you?"

"It's the client, not me," I replied. "I just followed a trail and that's where it led."

"What kind of team?"

"Six," I replied. "You, me, three more shooters, and cyberwatch."

"This is more than a favor, you know."

"Yeah," I said heavily. "But we'll be saving the life of a woman who doesn't deserve the trouble she's in." He'd used the same line on me to convince me to help his sister.

His eyes bulged a little, but he managed to control his temper. "You really are a pain in the ass."

It was tough to argue with a man when he was right. "Give me a price, and the client will pay it."

Gavin named a price. It was high. When I questioned him on it, Gavin snapped, "Look, Cal, take it or leave it. Honest to God, nobody you can trust will do it for less. Especially on such short notice."

"I'll get back to you," I said, as Fen and I left to go break the news to Ester.

Baskerville: I like him. He smells trusty.

On the 5, near Glendale: 11:20

Fen was driving us to Jo Jo's Ironmongery, which was one of my favorite places to shop. Their inventory was both vast and top-notch, up to the limit of what the law allowed them to sell. And if they didn't sell it, and they classified you as valued (and trusted) clientele, then they could probably point you to whoever did sell it.

My plan had been to hit Jo Jo's when it opened at 11:00 AM. I needed a replacement for the armor section that had been compromised in last night's operation.

Oh, sure, armor could be repaired.

Theoretically.

Call me paranoid, but it hadn't escaped my notice that the people who repaired armor didn't have to go into combat situations with it. And since modern suits were modular and I was flush with money thanks to Ester, I decided to splurge and buy a whole new back panel. Besides, Jo Jo's already had my measurements on file.

We were late getting to the shop, though, because traffic had been terrible. Apparently, morning rush hour traffic all over the city had been disrupted by flash mobs of clone rights protesters.

Left with dead time on my hands, I decided to make the best of the situation. I blipped Topaz. "Hey, Tops, you wanna go out tonight?"

"Maybe," she replied. No image, as per usual. There was a pause, then she said, "OK, we're fully secure, now. What's up?"

"Got a mission going on today, early evening. Could really use somebody for cyber watch. But I gotta be honest. It might not be your kind of mission."

"Why not?"

Topaz wasn't somebody you lied to. I gave her the low-down on everything that had happened so far. "So, we've got five ground-pounders going up against potential merc-level heavy response. And there may be casualties on both sides."

"Damn, Cal," she said. "I thought you preferred finesse?"

"This ain't that kind of job."

We talked over the particulars for a few more minutes, including the target being Halkronen, which didn't seem to faze her at all. Then again, she wasn't going to be physically present and getting shot at. Presently, she said, "All right, I'm in."

Which was when I spotted the flashing lights behind us.

"Unbelievable," I muttered, shaking my head in disgust. "Hey, I've got to go. Apparently, we're about to be pulled over by the cops."

"Good luck," she said, chuckling.

IX. Payback is a… (or, Gosh, so Many Choices Here)

On the 5, near Glendale: Tuesday, 11:35 — Missing 60 Hours

Fen pulled Grendel to the side of the road while the police car, a plain wrapper, pulled in behind us.

I turned to Fen, who'd bared his teeth at the cops. "Did we get some parking tickets I don't know about, or what?" For Fen, this was a threat display by another pack, and he didn't like it.

"Not know what they want," he rumbled, halfway to a growl.

I reached over and scratched beneath his ear. "Well, whatever's going on, I'm pretty sure I can talk my way out of this." I unbuckled my seat belt. "Time to switch seats, Fen."

After we'd exchanged places, I checked the side mirror again. I was expecting somebody to get out of the car, but they waited until two more police cars, black and whites this time, pulled in front of me.

Well, that was unusual. I had trouble imagining that this was about the Snake I'd killed last night. And I couldn't think of anything else I'd done recently that would warrant this amount of attention.

A tall black man in a sharp-looking suit got out of the driver side of the vehicle that had pulled us over. I recognized him as Rickles, a homicide detective I'd met a few times when I was on the force. His partner, a thin but well-built Hispanic lady named Moretti, exited the passenger side and they approached side by side.

I de-opaqued the window so they could see into Grendel's cockpit and cued the external intercom. "What can I do for you, Rickles? Moretti?" They looked a little surprised at the external audio.

"Morning, Cal," Rickles said. He looked grim, but then again, that was how he always looked. "You want to open the window?"

"No can do, sir, the windows don't open." Thanks to Grendel's heritage as an armored military vehicle, all of the windows were trans-steel plates as strong as the rest of vehicle's armor. Being able to open them had not even remotely been a design parameter.

"Can you come out, then?" Rickles insisted. "I prefer to talk face-to-face."

"Sure thing," I said cheerfully.

I glanced out the windshield at the two other police cars and saw two cops per car standing behind open doors, ready for trouble but with guns undrawn. I guess they thought I was dangerous.

I shook my head; I'd never be dangerous to a police officer. Not ever.

I made my way to the exit door, which opened street side. I came through the open door slowly, hands up, making it clear to anybody watching that I wasn't combative in any way.

I walked slowly forward and met Rickles and Moretti in front of Grendel. "Can I put my hands down? Or are these guys—" I nodded towards the other cops. "—gonna get all jumpy?"

"I don't know," Moretti said, smiling in a predatory way. "Are you going to be a bad boy?"

"Maybe later," I responded, chuckling. I swiveled toward Moretti. "When do you get off?" Moretti glared at me. Hard to believe I'd actually slept with her once a couple years ago. Then again, we'd both been really drunk.

Rickles rolled his eyes. "Put 'em down, Cal. We just need you to answer some questions."

"Fine by me." I lowered my arms and leaned back against Grendel. "Besides my number, for Moretti here, what do you need to know?" Moretti's eyes flashed with quickly concealed anger.

"You know a guy named Brian Douglas?"

If Rickles was asking me about him, then they already knew that I'd met him yesterday. No sense in lying. "Yeah. Slimeball manager for a club called the Mixie Trixie." This was not good. I had a feeling I was about to find out what Ester had been doing on her solo excursion last night.

"Somebody took him out last night," Moretti said. "Very professionally, too. Shot him and then hosed the electronic evidence…the residential control system, his personal mods, you name it."

Peachy. Thanks, Ester. It wasn't like I had a real alibi. Yes, officer, I couldn't have whacked the victim last night because I was all the way across town whacking some Snakes instead.

Rickles gave me a smile that didn't reach his eyes. "What was your interest in Douglas?"

"None," I answered. "I had a client who thought there was some funny business going on at the club. There was. I reported in. Done deal."

Moretti snorted. "We're supposed to believe that?"

I shrugged. "Not my problem what you believe."

Rickles exchanged a skeptical look with her. "This client have a name?"

"Doesn't work like that," I said. "A good percentage of my cases are anonymous. You have a problem, you pay me to investigate it. As long as the money's good, you get a solid investigation."

"Yeah, right," Moretti said. I was getting the strange feeling she didn't like me anymore.

"So," Rickles drawled, "was there any funny business going on?"

"Yeah."

His brow furrowed when I wasn't immediately forthcoming. It was actually kind of amusing to have a captive audience. I waited just long enough to let him know that I was playing games with him, then said, "He ran drugs in the bathrooms for the party crowd and, as a bonus, fingered clones for a snatch team. If I had to guess, I'd say that last is probably what got him dead. Those are some mean hombres when they get crossed."

Moretti glared at me and said, "So where were you last night?" I think she was trying to play Bad Cop, but it didn't come off well.

"You haven't told me when our dearly departed, well, departed."

"Around 1:30 AM," Rickles replied.

"He defend himself in any way?"

"No," Rickles replied. "Took a bullet in the chest, then a double-tap to the head. No sign of a struggle."

I beckoned towards Grendel's open door. "Can you step into my office for a minute?" Nobody made any move to stop me, so I climbed into the vehicle, Rickles following right behind me. Moretti started to follow, but I shut the door in her face. Petty, perhaps, but it felt good.

I pulled up my shirt, as much as I could with my left hand. With the gun wound, I didn't have much mobility on my right side. Rickles whistled when he saw the bandages wrapped around my torso. There was even some blood leaking through the bandage, which made it look suitably dire.

"I didn't kill your guy," I said. "I was too busy getting shot. Who and why is none of your business. But I wasn't in any position to terminate your zedbag."

It wasn't really an alibi per se, but there's only so many hours in a night. The odds of me getting shot at one location, getting medical attention at another location, and then murdering dear old Brian at another location all in one night—well, it started to look improbable pretty quickly, no matter what order you arranged the events in.

"Hell," he said, which was the only swear word anybody had ever heard him use. "We had a tip." He shook his head. "Not that I really wanted it to be you, but I guess this isn't going to be a simple case, after all."

"Not my fault." It was Ester's fault, and in a little while she was going to be getting a piece of my mind.

I followed Rickles out. As he stepped out onto the pavement, he told Moretti, "It's not him."

"He knows something," Moretti insisted. "I can tell."

I held out my hands so they could cuff me.

Neither of them moved.

"Been nice talking to you." I turned around, got back into Grendel, and then Fen drove us away.

Jo Jo's Ironmongery, in Glendale: 12:07

Jo Jo's Ironmongery was housed in a large, flat-roofed building that had once been a supermarket. The plate-glass windows were long gone, replaced by bullet-proof TRI-D screens offering the finest in modern weaponry, armor and hardware of all sorts. Given the paranoia of the owners and the value of their merchandise, I suspected some substantial improvements had been made to the building's defensive posture. The parking lot was surprisingly full, so Fen parked Grendel at the back of the lot. I left Fen in the RV and was halfway across the lot when the Snakes came gunning for me.

My first indication of trouble was the sound of revving motorcycles. I looked up and saw three riders accelerating in my direction, largely anonymous in full leathers. I spotted a tuft of red underneath the helmet of the largest rider, maybe a beard, but I didn't get a good look because I was already diving for cover.

I caught a glimpse of weapons being pulled just before I hit the pavement between two parked cars. Gunfire provided a staccato counterpoint to the dull impact of bullets smashing into the car I was using for cover and the tinkling sound of broken glass showering down on me.

Landing hurt, and I felt something rip in my side. Ignoring the pain, I scuttled forward over the broken glass. Several rounds punched entirely through the car and passed above me with angry hornet-like sounds. I needed to get out of this narrow aisle between the cars before the riders came abreast of my position and I became the star attraction of the ensuing turkey shoot.

While my attackers continued perforating the vehicles around me, I reached the end of the car sheltering me. I surged up into a crouch and started zig zagging between the parked cars. I heard cursing when the Snakes reached where I'd been and realized I wasn't there anymore. I pulled my gun out, then popped up and demonstrated why it was unwise to attack a military vet with a Zeus Mark 4.6 integrated combat mod, a Heckler-Koch SP-47x Smart Pistol, SOS (Selectable, Optimized, Smart) ammunition, and enhanced reflexes.

The smallest of the three must have had enhanced reflexes himself—he dropped behind his bike as I fired. Zeus optimized my round trajectories and adjusted their explosive spread for maximum damage against unarmored combatants, as well as minimal velocity to prevent collateral damage in an urban environment. I didn't see the rounds take out the other two riders, including the big one with the beard, because I was busy ducking.

While I was firing, Zeus had picked up a reflection in a car window showing a couple cars and some additional riders entering the battlespace behind me, something I hadn't been aware of because of sheer adrenaline and the ambient noise of gunfire. Zeus reacted instantly and dropped me to the ground before I knew what was happening.

The Zeus override saved my life—gunfire smashed the windows above me as I was going down and sprayed glass into my face. But I could take some facial cuts a hell of a lot better than I could take being dead.

I rolled under a car and started crawling.

Many things happened after that, much of it extremely loud and confusing from my vantage point. Piecing it together, and looking at some of the video later on, it went down something like this...

Fen saw me being attacked and, being a wardog, decided to Do Something about it. The new wave of Snakes was so focused on me that they didn't even notice Grendel moving until Fen started plowing across the parking lot to get to them. There were cars in the way, which didn't matter at all, because Grendel weighed eighteen tons and either crushed them or knocked them out of the way like bowling pins.

Grendel took fire from the riders, but that didn't matter, either.

Grendel wasn't a tank, but it was a distant cousin. The vehicle's custom aluminum facade, which made it look more like a commercial RV, got shredded pretty badly. But Grendel itself, not so much.

So, while I was crawling under cars, Fen turned six Snakes into bloody pancakes then did a wide turn, through more cars, and came back for another round of carnage.

But that didn't matter, either, because after Fen's first attack run, the customers and staff of Jo Jo's came out armed, and the staff at least were linked to Jo Jo's command/control AI...which helpfully pointed out, as if that were needed, that the Snakes were facing the wrong direction. They were still trying to deal with the Grendel situation when everybody started firing at them.

All in all, there ended up being nine dead gang members. Everybody who came out of Jo Jo's, which was about half the customers and most of the workers, was focused on maximum lethality. Justifiably, since the AI had almost instantly classified the firefight as a Level One Multiple Active Shooter event and then notified the local authorities.

After the shooting stopped, I slowly stood up, with my bloody hands and arms clearly above my head. One of the staff called out to me, "You're clear, Cal, we got you ID'd as Friend, not Foe." At that time, I hadn't yet had a chance to piece together everything that had just happened, but you'd have to have been blind to not understand that Fen had gone all Demolition Derby on the parking lot.

I lowered my arms and then blipped Fen.

```
SixGunCal: I'm safe, but you need to get the
hell out of here.
Baskerville: Where?
SixGunCal: Find an alley somewhere. Make it
look like a human passenger abandoned Grendel
and went running. No witnesses. You get to play
the panicked dog.
Baskerville: You owe me biscuits.
SixGunCal: Yeah, yeah, so what else is new…
```

Which is how Fen ended up driving Grendel through a hedge and a couple of small trees to get out of the parking lot just as the first police cars entered the other side. I think my jaw dropped open as the first two cars raced past me in pursuit of Grendel, apparently not noticing the, ahem, crime scene that they had to roll over.

An aborted car chase ensued. I say aborted, because the first police car went through the hedge and got stuck on the stump of one of the trees Grendel had knocked down. And the second car ran into the back of the first one.

I shook my head in disbelief, then let the staff corral me and the armed customers into the store before the police accidentally shot anybody. Inside, it was party time (which doubled a short time later after the authorities verified that, while a few pedestrians and passing motorists had received minor injuries, nobody except the bad guys had been killed).

A bald, pot-bellied customer clapped me on the back. "This is so ace," the man said, "we've already gone viral with the news outlets. They're calling it the 'Shoot-Out at Jo Jo's.'" He held up a shiny, new Desert Phoenix with the price tag still on it and practically chortled with glee. "And I got one of them bastards with this thing, too. On film." He let out a yell, and went off to tell somebody else.

I had a feeling some of these people weren't going to be so happy when they realized that their insurance wasn't going to cover the damage to their vehicles. One of the side effects of the global Time of Troubles and, in North America, the second Civil War, was that insurance companies seriously took it in the shorts. Modern insurance policies covered accidental damage, not damage due to violence—that was a special rider that almost nobody ever purchased.

They could try a civil suit against me, but that was a losing proposition, too. Hard to prove my culpability for the Snakes committing an illegal act. And, as the victim, I clearly hadn't been driving Grendel. Yes, I was the owner of Grendel. But thanks to the sheer amount of terrorism during the Time of Troubles, there were liability protections in the law to cover individuals acting against public threats.

I shook my head. What a mess.

Bowing to the inevitable, and figuring rightly that everyone would be stuck here until the police were done with them, the management got the staff circulating with trays of refreshments and set up tables with ice and various (non-alcoholic) drinks. They also put replays of the firefight from various angles on all of the screens around the store.

I went looking for the manager, but apparently I was the man of the hour. I must have ended up posing for photos with ten or so customers; apparently the fact that I was bleeding was a plus. I put up with it because, well, they had helped save my ass. And besides, it was good advertising—you never knew who might need a private investigator in the future.

I finally found the manager, a stocky lady with a big bosom and a glorious smile named Sherill MacKenzie who I'd worked with before. "Hey," I said. "I've got a shopping list. It's—"

"Jesus, Cal," she said, eyeing my bloody arms and hands. "I been running around so much, I didn't realize you were injured." She barked some orders and one of her workers went to get a first aid kit for my various cuts and scrapes while another went to retrieve a chair for me.

I handed Sherill the list I'd quickly scrawled out. "It's a bit on the urgent side. And I'm going to have to get the stuff from you…discreetly."

"I bet," she said, perusing the list and chuckling. "We can do that."

We caught up for a few minutes, until I heard a man clear his throat behind me. I turned and found Rickles glowering at me, shadowed by the inimitable Moretti.

"Officers," I said. "Fancy meeting you again."

JoJo's Ironmongery, in Glendale: 12:19

More police cars raced by on their way to Jo Jo's as Jaeger continued his slow fade backward through the crowd of onlookers. He'd ditched his leathers back in the parking lot, revealing a nondescript outfit of jeans and a black T-shirt, and he'd zeroed out his facial tattoos—a nice mod, that—so it wasn't hard to pass as a relatively ordinary citizen. Well, at least, his spiky hair hadn't been unusual enough to attract undue attention.

In the confusion of all the shooting, when he'd run out of the parking lot, hunched over and obscured by a row of bushes, nearby pedestrians had helped him get undercover, believing him to be a refugee from the gun battle rather than a participant.

Now, as he made his way unobtrusively away from the crime scene, he was seething with anger, not so much at McCallister, who he already knew was both dangerous and wicked fast, but at Big Red, who'd managed to totally screw up a perfectly good plan.

At least the bastard was dead.

Him and Bek.

Elite warriors, my ass, he growled under his breath. *I could stop at any goddam kindergarten and find smarter thugs.*

And it really had been a good plan.

Jaeger had called in a police report, his voice suitably disguised, and fingered McCallister for Douglas' murder. Plausible, of course, because the detective had been sniffing around the Mixie Trixie. Then all they had to do was wait for the police to find him. Public scrutiny of the police was intense; they'd learned McCallister's location within minutes of his being stopped.

But then Big Red had decided to ambush McCallister as soon as they caught up to him, ignoring Jaeger's warning that a parking lot with lots of cover, and in front of Jo Jo's Ironmongery, was a Bad Idea. At which point, the moronic gang leader had dragged Jaeger along with him in the first wave.

At least he'd had time to swap bikes before they headed off after the detective—you didn't bring a flash bike like his Matsumoto Skirmish 7500 on a gang hit. Losing that cold, untraceable bike at Jo Jo's wasn't such a big deal.

Finally reaching the back of the crowd, Jaeger turned into an alley. A short time later, he was two streets over and safely away from the site of the disaster. He took the opportunity to delve into the Net for reports of the incident and was appalled to discover both how much notoriety the gun battle had already achieved and that McCallister had survived.

An idea came to him and he blipped the anonymous number he'd been given for Halkronen. A moment later, a female voice answered, "Yes?" It sounded like Halkronen's daughter, Helga, though it was hard to be certain. He'd only met her that one time, when the Snakes were originally setting up the deal to be suppliers for Halkronen.

"There's a potential problem coming your way," Jaeger said. "Somebody hit our collection point last night. I think they might have been looking for the clone we sold to you."

"And you think they might hit us?" There was a note of incredulity in her voice.

"Yeah. That's what I think."

"Seriously?"

"I wouldn't put it past them. Evidence I saw, they're swinging some pretty serious firepower."

"Thanks for the update."

X. Pre-Game Preparations (or, the Frenzy Before the Calm Before the Storm)

An Alley, in Glendale: Tuesday, 15:23 — Missing 63 Hours

I winced as Sherill pulled her car to a stop behind Grendel. My ribs hurt from slamming into the pavement, my side ached from being shot, my arms were sore from the various glass cuts, and my face was numb from whatever the medics had put on it. And, thanks to the Snakes, I'd just had three hours excised from my day thanks to the police, though I'd successfully resisted being taken, alternatively, to the police station and the hospital.

At least Ester had come through with the necessary intel.

Her packet had come in while Rickles and Moretti had been interrogating me in Sherill's office. I'd surreptitiously passed it on to Gavin in between questions, though I hadn't had any time to examine it myself.

I hadn't heard any complaints, yet, so I figured that was good news.

I turned toward Sherill. "I'm sorry about—"

She let out one of her big hearty laughs. "Don't be. You have no idea how much free publicity we're getting out of this. I'm just glad nobody except the bad guys were really hurt. That was an awful lot of ammunition headin' downrange." She smiled brightly. "Plus, at least my car didn't get turned into tin foil."

I sighed.

"Come on," she said, "I'll give you a hand with the packages."

I got out of the car. Fen had pulled Grendel into an alley behind a run-down shopping center. I grimaced at the damage. The front half of Grendel's after-market aluminum shell had been largely shredded, and what hadn't been shredded had been perforated with bullet holes. Grendel's drab gray armor showed through the rips.

Fen went wild when we carried the packages into the APC, only partly an act for Sherill's benefit. While he ran in circles around us, we set the new gear on the table.

"Good dog," I said, as I bent down and hugged Fen, reassuring him that all was well.

Baskerville: Stupid human. Who feed me if you gone?

I just hugged him tighter.

Baskerville: You owe me steak. With Charlotte's Web again.

I couldn't help chuckling. If Fen wanted steak and story time for saving me, he could have them. We'd both be dead a couple of times over without each other.

"Got some things to discuss," Sherill said, after allowing us a moment. "I know you've got something going on, and I don't need to know the details. It's obvious it's some kind of hostage rescue, though. And the timeline is tight?"

I stood and gave her a curt nod.

"OK," she said. She opened the biggest box. "Armored long coat, heavy as shit, presumably for protecting the hostage. Off the books, in case the police come back calling. We'll just call that an exchange for the free publicity." She gestured at another box. "General-purpose helmet, also presumably for your hostage." She pushed a smaller box toward me. "Special ammo for your HK, from my own private stock. Illegal as shit, just like the ammo you lit off in my parking lot. Also, off the books. You owe me double in replacement, so you better damn well survive."

I nodded. "That's my plan."

"Next, your armor plate replacement." She opened another box for my inspection.

My eyes widened. The plate was bubblegum pink. Looking up, I caught her grinning.

"Pink?" I asked incredulously.

"That's all we had in your brand and size."

"Pink?"

"Spray paint is your friend."

"Who the hell makes pink armor?"

"It was a special commission for a rock band."

"They never picked it up?"

"All paid for," she said, "but the lead singer OD'd before he could take possession. So, half price, to you."

"Fair enough," I said. "I'll find some black spray paint."

"The rest of the boxes are the electronic gear you wanted. All attributed to a fake company in San Jose. For the usual extra charge, of course."

"And this level of service," I said, "is why I keep coming back to Jo Jo's."

"Damn tootin'."

Danibelle's Guaranteed Parking, in Little Texas: 16:31

"I no like you no more," Fen said.

I'd had a chance to look at Ester's intelligence packet and I'd thrown together the outline of a plan. Fen hated it.

On the face of it, the packet was comprehensive. The intelligence was first-rate. Halkronen's special merchandise was kept in Encino, in a complex on Balkan Street. We had floorplans and guard details, although we didn't know what cell Claudia was in. We even had specifics for the diversion that Ester would be running. Despite all that, I couldn't help feeling that something was missing.

Like I was seeing part of the big picture, but not all of it.

It was something I'd felt a few times in the military, when the high-ups were trying something fancy or ill-advised, and hiding the details behind "need-to-know."

So, I'd detailed Fen to follow Ester, rather than participate in the operation against the Balkan Street facility.

"Sorry, Fen, this is the way it's gotta be."

He growled at me, but didn't say anything else as I got up from the passenger seat, walked out of the driver compartment and exited Grendel. Fen sped off as soon as my feet touched the pavement.

Max came out of the guard shack as I walked into Danibelle's Guaranteed Parking, a big smile on his face. An expression that faded as he took a better look at me and spied the glass cuts on my face, covered with skin sealant. And even with a fresh, long-sleeved shirt, I had bandages on my arms that extended down to my wrists.

"Damn," he said, "you look like shit." He gave me a thoughtful glance. "More alert than last night, but twice as beat up."

"The Snakes decided a little payback was in order."

"The hell?"

"What can I say? They caught up to me at Jo Jo's."

Max's eyes just about goggled out of his head. "That was you?"

"Yeah," I said. I saw his attention wander for a moment as he checked the news feeds.

"Shit, I didn't realize," he said. "Looks like your name hit the news about thirty minutes ago." Frankly, I was surprised. I'd figured my name would have been out there even sooner.

"I need the gray van, Max." He'd stashed the van on one of the lower levels of the parking garage, not so much with the expectation that I'd need it again, but more so that I could dispose of it at some chop shop at my leisure and recoup some of my investment in a "clean" vehicle.

He stared at me for a couple seconds. "You ain't serious."

"Yeah."

"You're goin' again?"

"That's the job, Max," I said. "That's what I get paid for. I don't ever stop 'til the job is done."

"You're crazy." Max shook his head. "Some jobs ain't worth it."

Business Park, in Korea Town: 17:51

I turned the gray van into the parking lot of a low-rent business park full of Asian wholesalers, body shops, construction suppliers and the like. I was late. I was supposed to have been there at 5:30 to meet with Ester before the others showed up at 6:30, but traffic had been terrible again.

Apparently, while I'd been busy being hassled by the cops, being shot up by Snakes, and being hassled by the cops again, the morning's flash-mob demonstrations for clone rights had continued throughout the day. Traffic was snarled up across the city. The news was even showing growing crowds of protesters around the new Civic Center where today's Chamber of Commerce activities were going on.

I cruised slowly past the long front extent of Building D, a warehouse-style building almost three football fields long and one football field wide, until I got to the back of the lot. It felt weird driving without Fen beside me.

I turned into the wide lane that went around the short end of the building, then pulled around to the back side where the loading docks and garage-style entrances were.

I stopped in front of Unit J. I knew Ester was already there because she'd come in the car Max had tagged for me on Sunday. An operational security flaw on her part, but one that helped me keep tabs on her.

I was unsurprised when the garage door rose, revealing Ester standing, arms akimbo, in a sleek, black, form-fitting combat suit. Without her helmet, her blond hair hung free to her shoulders. I pulled the van into the cavernous space, coming to a stop just in front of her, and the door closed behind me.

She said, "I saw the news—" as I got out of the van.

"It's your fault," I said, marching up and putting my hands on her shoulders. "You almost got me killed."

"What?"

"You wanna tell me what you were doing last night?"

"I—" She stopped and took a deep breath. "That bastard…he took my sister from me, and he didn't even think twice about selling her into the worst kind of slavery." She looked away, took another deep breath. "I couldn't…I couldn't tolerate him existing in the same world as me, not after what he did." She looked at me, eyes glistening in the overhead lights. "You might not understand, but as far as I'm concerned, I'm at war with monsters like him."

"Well," I said, sighing and taking my hands off her shoulders, "you triggered Cal's First Law of Criminal Dynamics…for every action, there's a reaction. I got pulled over by the police today as a suspect in your little escapade last night. Besides the fact that my only real alibi is that I was killing somebody else in another part of the city—"

"Oh, shit."

I chuckled. "Oh, it gets better. Because then the Snakes ambushed me at Jo Jo's today, which you saw in the news."

"Yes."

I smiled. "I don't believe in coincidences. I'm guessing one of the Snakes figured out who I was from my visit to the Mixie Trixie. So, they reported me as a suspect in your little adventure, and then waited for the police to find me. Then they hit me after the police cut me loose."

I saw a range of emotions cross her voice. Finally, she said in a low voice, "I'm sorry."

"Sorry doesn't cut—"

She kissed me.

It was a good kiss. Maybe a little clumsy on her part, but, yeah, it was good. For about two seconds, and then I stepped backward like I'd just touched an electrical wire. "What the hell?" I rubbed my forehead. "Jesus, do you think I'm that easily manipulated?"

Her face turned red and her expression turned hard. "Jesus never helped me or my kind," she spat. "We're just soulless pieces of meat to most people. And, yeah, I kiss all the guys I meet, so you're nothing special." She turned and stalked away.

Business Park, in Korea Town: 18:40

"All right," Ester said. She was wearing her helmet to preserve her anonymity. "Thanks, everybody, for agreeing to do this."

We all nodded politely.

The whole team was present, sitting on metal fold-up chairs, except for Topaz, who was present virtually. Gavin McCloud sat poised and alert, already in his top-of-the-line combat suit, but helmetless. Bernie and Ernie sat next to him, acting laid back and nonchalant, in serviceable but relatively low-tech gear, identical twins except for Ernie's facial scarring. The third CRAG-supplied shooter sat next to them, a hulking combat clone named Later.

And me. Not dressed yet because I was waiting for the second coat of spray paint to dry. My pink armor plate had been a point of hilarity with the others as they'd shown up. I'd already had to reject "Pink One" as my call sign for the mission.

A couple of fold-out tables set up against the wall held the gear the others, mostly Gavin, had brought. Plus, my suit and new armor plate. The gear from Jo Jo's was already stored in the van. Thanks to Gavin's mercenary connections, we were bringing some seriously heavy weaponry with us. Hopefully, we wouldn't need it.

"Topaz, show us the target," Ester said. A wireframe of the target building appeared in all of our views, rotating slowly to show the general layout of the building's grounds.

"The building has three levels," Topaz said in her melodic voice. "Plus, a basement level. They've got holding pens in the basement and first floor levels. Laboratory and medical facilities on the second floor, and administrative facilities on the upper level."

"Right," I said. "Our primary objective is getting Claudia back. I'll be carrying the protective gear for Claudia. Secondary objective goes to Gavin, who will clear the top two floors and set the demolitions. The rest of us will focus on taking the control room. We'll be freeing all the clones, partly as a distraction, partly because it's the right thing to do, and partly because we don't want Halkronen focusing on why Claudia was the target."

Gavin said, "That's new, freeing the clones?" He frowned. "Without any prep or training, they're just going to get captured again."

"Flash mob to the rescue," Ernie said, smiling with the one side of his face that still functioned well enough to do that. "Call will go out about thirty minutes before we go. Just the general area; the mob'll get the specifics after we go in."

I wasn't sure I liked that, and neither was Gavin. As far as I was concerned, we were going to be in and out with Claudia as fast as we could. Anything else was not our problem.

I was also beginning to get the sense that all of today's flash mobs and protests were actually cover for tonight's operation, which gave me the willies. Whoever Ester worked for, they'd made a deal with both CRAG and their more publicity-oriented parent organization, Free Clones Now (FCN). I wondered what they'd promised to get this level of cooperation.

I had the sense of vast forces moving, unseen, around me. And I didn't like it.

Topaz went through the official floor layouts, adding that, "These are the official plans, but Halkronen may have made changes without going through the permitting process."

Ester said, "Based on our sources, Claudia is probably on the first floor. The basement is primarily for exotics." I wasn't quite sure what she meant by exotics, and I wasn't sure I wanted to know. "There's also some temporary holding pens on the lab level."

"By the way," Topaz interjected. "The first floor looks like it has dark, tinted windows—it doesn't. They're a facade." It was a good detail to know. No easy alternate egress from the first floor.

"Guards?" Gavin asked.

"Six guards in the building," Ester said.

Topaz added more detail. "They're Ace Security Services. Military vets. Effective within their limits, but not equipped to face you guys. The real problem is—"

"Xenophon Services," Ester said.

"Right," Topaz said matter-of-factly. "Halkronen has a Quick Reaction contract with Xenophon Services. They can be on site in ten minutes."

Gavin and I exchanged a glance. Xenophon was hardcore. We did not want to mess with them.

I pointed out, "Ten minutes should be enough for an in-and-out, but Xenophon could certainly cramp our escape."

"We've got two things going on to deal with that," Ester replied confidently. "First, the flash mob which should give you plenty of cover. Second, we're staging a distraction at Halkronen's home across town." Halkronen's late night event was being held at his home, so that would really get his attention. "We expect Xenophon to go there, instead."

She was too confident.

If there's one thing I learned in the service, no plan survives contact with the enemy intact.

I asked, "What does a Quick Reaction force look like?"

"I don't know," Ester replied.

Gavin said, "It varies between merc units, depending on contract and circumstances. Generally, a VTOL craft, armed and armored, with ten troopers and a pilot. All equipped a notch or two down from my gear, so no camouflage and only light strength enhancement. Well trained and dangerous."

Bernie and Ernie stared at him.

"He comes from a mercenary family," I explained.

"A distraction sounds good," Bernie said.

"Yeah," Ernie echoed him.

"Plus, we'll have Topaz on oversight, with eyes in the sky," I added.

We spent another hour hashing out more details, including ingress, egress, backup plans, and call signs. We were Red Team. I was Red One, Gavin was Red Two, and Bernie, Ernie and Later were Red Three, Four and Five, respectively. And Ester was the Red Queen. It was a pleasure working with professionals.

When it was clear that everything was settled that could be settled, I stood up. "It's time for a final decision. Go or no-go?"

Topaz said, "Abstain. You all are taking all the real risks."

Bernie and Ernie looked at each other and said in unison, "Go."

Later said, "Go." His voice was incongruously high-pitched, like a young girl's soprano.

I looked at Gavin. He nodded. "Go."

I said, "Go." I turned and looked at Ester. "See you on the other side."

As the other team members stood, grabbed gear from the tables, and headed for the van, Ester touched my arm, stopping me.

"That other problem," she said. "I will fix it. I promise you."

I nodded curtly, then walked off and joined the others, collecting my own gear on the way.

XI. Assault (or, Things Start Badly)

Encino, near the Balkan Street Complex: Tuesday, 20:49 — Missing 69 Hours

We'd been waiting for about twenty minutes when Ester said on our general channel, "Diversion is in progress." I felt more than heard the others perk up at the idea of eminent action. Somewhere on the other side of town, CRAG had launched an attack on Konrad Halkronen's home, the planned site for this evening's planned festivities.

I had thought that Ester was running the diversion, but apparently I was wrong. Her tag had her parked somewhere in Downtown, kilometers away from Halkronen's residence.

More confirmation that there was more going on than what I'd been told.

I didn't like being kept in the dark, which was why I had Fen following Ester.

While I waited and worried, a swarm of fast-moving, agile buzzbombs was converging on the Halkronen complex from all directions. Tiny little drones carrying a variety of payloads: small but surprisingly powerful explosives, stink bombs, noisemakers, you name it. Lots of sound, smoke, confusion and damage.

I'd parked the van on a side street about a block and a half away from our target building. I turned half around to face the back seat. "Let's do it."

Reclining comfortably in the driver's seat, I watched as Bernie exited the van, leaving the sliding door open. He walked around the vehicle, sans helmet, and into an alley, then casually relieved himself against the side of a warehouse.

This was just a show, in case we were being observed by anybody. What had really happened was that Gavin had exited the vehicle after Bernie, in camouflage mode and with thermal nullification engaged, and was slowly making his way to our target building.

He was our scout.

"Next," I said.

In the back of the van, Ernie opened the box containing the electronic equipment I'd bought at Jo Jo's based on Topaz's specifications. Two eyeballs, which were state-of-the-art, four-centimeter, air-propelled globes filled with sophisticated electronics and sensors. Probably better than the ones I'd linked with in the military, although not hardened to military standards. And a swarm of thirty flybabies, which were tiny drones about half a centimeter in diameter that floated on a tiny air jet.

On our private channel, Topaz said, "Diversion confirmed. Halkronen is gonna be seriously upset when he finds out." I hadn't really doubted that Ester would hold up her end of the operation, but I always, always verify.

I sub-vocalized a confirmation.

Topaz had explained that the first eyeball was for "situational awareness" of the battlespace, with the second one stationed further away as a backup in case enemy action took out the first one. The flybabies didn't have all the sensor gear that the eyeballs did, but could operate in a harder-to-detect passive mode that augmented the eyeballs. Topaz could also use them for some degree of oversight if both eyeballs were destroyed. The flybabies were also faster and much harder to take out than the eyeballs were.

Yeah, Topaz was seriously professional. Even her redundancies had redundancies.

On another private channel, one that Topaz didn't know about, Fen said, "She's out and hunting. Full gear, stealthed. Me trailing."

Interesting.

There was a whining sound as the air jets on the eyeballs kicked in. The first one lifted out of the box and then did a slow donut around my head, Topaz showing off a little. Then it floated out of the open door of the van in company with the second eyeball. A moment later, all of the flybabies except one followed them, looking absurdly like little ducklings floating out into the night.

The last flybaby settled on my outstretched hand. After the air jet shut off, I put it in a pocket for later use.

"Assets are all nominal," Topaz said.

"Now what?" Bernie said, jumping back into the van and sliding the door shut behind him.

"We wait some more," I answered. We couldn't engage until Red Two had a chance to scout things out and Topaz got her drones on station.

"Xenophon is in the air," Topaz announced a few minutes later. Clearly a response to Ester's diversionary attack, or Topaz would have said something. So that part of the plan was working.

I couldn't help wondering what Ester was doing, but it wasn't like I could ask her without giving away that Fen and I were tracking her.

Balkan Street Complex: 21:12

"Red Two, in position, all clear."

"Red One, we're heading in," I said.

I pulled the van out of the alley and drove to Halkronen's facility by a circuitous route that didn't expose the van to view from the building until the last hundred and fifty meters.

Topaz chimed in, "Nothing in my detection envelope, and I'm pretty widespread right now." Good news, because if she had detected other drones in her ops space, then it would mean Xenophon was present, and that would be...bad.

I gunned the engine and headed for the gate. This wasn't like the TRI-Ds, where the heroes just crash through the gate. Halkronen invested in better security features than that, which was why Ernie hung out the passenger window and fired explosive rounds at the barrier from his Samson X4 Rifle Launcher.

Surplus military gear that Gavin had brought to the mission.

Jo Jo's was great but sometimes I envied Gavin his mercenary connections.

Ernie hastily pulled himself back in and belted up just before we smashed through the weakened gate. The van veered widely as one side gave way slightly before the other, but I managed to keep us from going sideways and rolling.

Gavin would never have let me live that down.

I looked over at Ernie; he had a manic grin on his face.

I floored the pedal and headed for the front entrance. The building only had three entrances: a back door, the loading dock next to it, and the front lobby, which unsurprisingly faced the gate across a span of parking lot.

"Plan B," Gavin said. "Xenophon is already here."

I veered right as armed troopers boiled out of the lobby doors. The van bounced over an ivy-covered island with a gut-wrenching jolt and past the front corner of the building. A couple rounds punched through the back part of the van and then all hell broke loose behind us as Gavin unleashed against the response team with everything he had.

Gavin and I had figured that, in the unlikely event that security was on high alert or already reinforced, they'd come at us from the lobby. Which was why our invisible scout had been stationed just to one side of the lobby entrance.

"Everybody all right?" I yelled over the battle noise. I was gratified to hear affirmative responses from both Ernie and Bernie, as well as a grunt from Later which I assumed meant he was unhurt.

Some Snakes too smart for his own good must have warned Halkronen of potential trouble coming his way. Not good. After Jo Jo's and now this, street rules called for some serious payback later.

If there was a later.

I screeched to a stop about two-thirds down the side of the building, positioning the van so the front faced the building about five meters away, and the sliding door of the van faced away from where Gavin had just ambushed the Xenophon troopers.

A fireball lit up the night, and everything went silent for a second afterwards as my helmet's sound suppression blocked most of the otherwise deafening boom. No more front lobby, no more problem. At least not from that quarter.

Topaz cut in, "Analysis: Red Two took out at least five X's and three R's." Xenophon troops and regular guards. "Probably five X's and two R's left. Be careful."

"Red Two, secondary mission in progress."

I responded, "Red One confirms Topaz and Red Two. We're executing Plan B now."

Ernie slammed the van's door open and then he and Bernie jumped out. Later landed with a thud behind them, carrying the biggest gun we had with us. I slid into the back, grabbed my HK, shouldered the gear pack, and followed them.

"Do the honors," I said, looking at Ernie and gesturing toward the wall between two of the fake windows.

Baskerville: `Ester go in high bldg`

I took a second and glanced at the images accompanying Fen's communication. Ester had entered a high-rise building from a utility door in an alley.

No time to worry about Ester's escapades as Ernie grinned lopsidedly, then turned and fired five explosive rounds at the wall of the building, arranged in a pretty half-circle that was almost instantly engulfed in smoke and flame. Debris pelted my combat suit as the three of us ran through the hole into a demolished office. Flames flared up one of the walls and loose papers from a shattered file cabinet fluttered around us and then we were in a hallway.

Competing alarms were going off, probably both fire and intrusion alerts, a jangling cacophony that was thankfully mostly suppressed by my helmet. Later surged through the room, opened the singed office door, then yanked it off its hinges and threw it aside. This was now one of the possible exits for escaping clones.

While the others headed into the hallway and turned left, I pulled my own Samson X4 off my shoulder and covered our rear just as the sprinkler system suddenly drenched us.

Civic Center, Downtown: 21:16

"I apologize, gentlemen," Konrad Halkronen said. "And lady," he added, inclining his head ever so politely in Genevieve DuCalle's direction. It wouldn't do to offend her. With her rather… unusual… appetites, and the immense fortune she'd inherited, she was one of his best customers. "Duty calls, I'm afraid."

Halkronen disengaged after exchanging a few more platitudes and waded across the main ballroom, discretely followed by his security detail. The going was slow, propriety requiring him to exchange a few words with various notables on the way, including Mayor Franks, Congressman Stevens and Adeline Parkes, the famed Tri-D star.

He spotted Lady Danibelle in the crowd and made a point of staying far from her. She wasn't one of his fans, and it would take too long to disengage from her if she did manage to intercept him.

Once free of the ballroom, he strode down a hallway, his guards closing ranks around him. Approaching the room where his staff members waited, one of the guards checked the room first before allowing Halkronen to enter.

He came into the spartan back room like a dragon about to breathe fire. As soon as the doors closed behind the last of his detail, he exploded, "What the hell is going on?"

Captain Evans, his Xenophon liaison, heavily tanned and sporting a military crewcut, said mildly, "Sir, you're being targeted by CRAG for sure, and almost certainly the FCN. They've just hit two of your facilities."

Halkronen grimaced. FCN was bad enough, but that was mostly a publicity problem. CRAG were the ones with the guns. "How bad?"

"Your house…basically a Denial of Service attack," Evans said. "No way you're hosting an event there tonight. Casualties were minimal compared to what CRAG is capable of…only five people. Oh, and maybe about ten servant clones." He shrugged. "As far as damage, the fires are out, but the stink won't go away for about a month. Lots of broken windows. Driveway's cratered like the moon. And the grounds look like a war zone."

He cursed at the imminent publicity disaster with his clients. His was not a profession where one wanted to look weak or ineffective.

"And the other target?"

"The Balkan Street facility, just like you were warned."

"Hell," Halkronen responded. "Somebody needs to be swatted. Hard. How are we doing with that?"

"In your neighborhood, our Response Team cut off the escape of the zeds, then we mousetrapped them between us and your regular security. We'll have that mopped up shortly." Evans paused for a moment to send him an image of an overturned, bullet-riddled white van with a plumber's logo on it. "Don't expect survivors, they don't seem to be inclined to surrender."

He chuckled. "I'm down with that."

"At Balkan Street, they came in hard," Evans said, frowning. "About forty percent casualties on the interior contingent in the initial attack."

"Jesus."

"Yes, sir," Evans replied, frowning, "But the reinforcements are about to kick ass, and we've got another Response Team on the way, just in case."

"Good," Halkronen said. He turned to one of his staff members. "Lewis, make the rounds and give my apologies to our clientele. The rest of you, we've got just under three hours to move the festivities to our Halkronen Show Room." It was the main sales point for their conventional products, but they could re-purpose it for the night. He smiled, seeing in his mind how they could still pull it all off. "We'll set up catering in the main showroom, maybe put the special merchandise on the upper levels." To Evans, he added, "Let's get me out of here, there's organizing to be done."

"Yes, sir."

Balkan Street Complex: 21:18

The lights went off as we raced down the hallway past cells full of clones in gray institutional uniforms—proof that Gavin was busily knocking back his mission objectives. The emergency lighting kicked in with a dim reddish glow that made the water from the sprinklers look like falling blood.

Our own objective was the control room that regulated access to all of the cells. From there, we could release all the clones at once. Much better than our backup plan, which was to use vibroblades to open cells—no way we'd have time to get them all open, especially facing serious opposition.

I figured that some of the remaining guards were probably holed up in the control room, while the rest had likely been stationed near the back entrances. If I was right, we were smack-dab between the two groups, with the possibility of defeating them in detail.

Or getting crushed between them.

One or the other.

We'd know soon enough.

I skidded around the corner, cursed as I almost fell. Would have fallen, but Ernie reached out a steadying hand. Bernie and Later, watching our six, exchanged fire with somebody behind us. The boom from Later's mammoth weapon made Bernie's sound like a weak echo.

We'd gotten out of that long hallway just in time.

One more dogleg and we'd be at the control center.

"Red Three, guard the back door," I said.

"Red Three, yeah." That long hallway worked both ways. Bernie hung back to harry anybody trying to assault us from behind.

Ernie, Later and I ignored the gunfire behind us and advanced on the next corner. I looked over at Ernie. "Time to knock on their door."

We both pulled out flash bangs and lobbed them around the corner. Three seconds later, there was a noisy blast, a modest amount of acrid smoke and a whole lot of gunfire. Zeus indicated conventional caseless slugs, probably because destroying the client's property was generally a big no-no for mercenaries.

We didn't have that limitation.

"Red One, activate the last flybaby." I pulled the little drone out of my pocket and threw it past the corner, figuring that it would likely be lost in the confusion.

"Two guards in the control room, three in the hallway in front of it," Topaz said, and the drone's view appeared in a window for me. Only one of them was Xenophon; he was in the hallway.

I leaned out, holding my Heckler-Koch Smart Pistol and snap-fired three bursts. I got hit maybe six or seven times, felt the impact driving on my armor, and then I slipped on the wet floor and sprawled on my back.

27th Floor - Unicide Tower, Downtown: 21:19

"He's left the ballroom," her eldest sister said, "should be heading out soon."

"Acknowledged," Ester replied.

She lay on the floor of an expensive office, looking down at the alley behind the Civic Center through the scope of her state-of-the-art rifle. She'd drilled a hole through the floor to ceiling plate glass window and was waiting patiently for her target.

If Bettina and the FCN had coordinated the protests properly, then there should be only one exit that her target—

A knot of people came out of the expected door into the alley. Guards surrounding a man with mostly gray hair.

Her target.

She exhaled slowly, then took the shot.

Ester had just enough time to see the splash of her target's head exploding. Then she was on the move, dropping her rifle and rolling away from the window.

She scuttled through the doorway, then leaped up and sprinted for safety as the office blew up behind her. The force of the blast slammed her against the wall, then sent her tumbling down the hallway until she slammed through the plate glass wall that separated the offices from the company's foyer.

XII. Rescue (or, Things Get Even Worse)

Balkan Street Complex: Tuesday, 21:20

I winced at the pain in my chest, wondering if I needed to add cracked ribs to my litany of injuries. My front armor could generally take conventional slugs, but that didn't mean it was an enjoyable experience.

I looked at my handiwork. All three guards outside the control room were, well, dead was an understatement. Splattered was perhaps a better word. All over the walls, ceiling and dripping down the bullet-proof windows of the control room.

Bullet-proof glass that had been starred by the explosive ammo I'd used in taking out the companions of the two guards left in the control room. Not Xenophon, just regular security guards, staring wide-eyed at me through the blood-stained glass as I stood up.

"We've got trouble," Topaz said. "Somebody just took out my—" There was a burst of static. "Repeat, somebody just took out my eyeball, working on—" Another burst of static.

"Topaz, you there?" Nothing. "Topaz?"

"I'm back," Topaz said, "fighting off an HK swarm." Not good. Hunter/Killer drones hunted down other drones, which meant we had company. "Somebody's got some good countermeasures. I lost both eyeballs."

"Understood," I said.

Survivability had just dipped to a new low, but maybe we could still get Claudia sprung. I'd hate to go through all this trouble for nothing.

I looked over at Ernie.

"Go help, Bernie," I said. "I got this." Glancing over at Later, I added, "Take the hallway on the other side, make sure nobody sneaks up on us."

Ernie nodded and trotted back towards Bernie's position, where a whole lot of firing seemed to be going on. Later headed the other way.

Topaz broke in again. "Something's happened at the Civic Center, something bad."

Switching to our private channel, I said, "I need you to coordinate with Red Zero. He's keeping tabs on Ester."

"Red Zero?"

"Need to know," I said, sending her Fen's sanitized contact information. "Now you need to know. He's full mil-spec, like Red Two." Although Topaz didn't need to know that Red Zero was a rogue wardog in full battle gear.

I walked up and tapped on the glass of the control room with my smart pistol.

"Can you hear me?"

One of the guards nodded nervously. They had to know that I could take them.

"I need in there. I want to see what clones you have, and I want to open all the cells. You can give me what I want, and you can live. Because I've got no burning desire to kill you. Or I can force my way in there. In which case I guarantee that your families are gonna get some bad news tonight.

"Your call. I'm gonna count down from ten."

I didn't even get to seven before the door clicked open.

19th-27th Floors, Unicide Tower, Downtown: 21:20

Ester groaned and slowly got to her knees, glass shards tinkling as they fell off her and landed on the floor. The air was hazy with smoke, the fire alarms were wailing and the sprinkler system had gone off.

She hurt all over, but her armor had done its job. Her system showed all green, with no breaches. And her internal air supply—a whole ten minutes—had kicked in because of all the smoke.

A realization struck her and she cursed. If the fire alarm was going off, then there went her plan to egress by elevator. She'd anticipated return fire, but not explosive return fire.

Cal probably wouldn't have made that kind of mistake.

Ester painfully stood up and staggered through the foyer, past the tumbled furniture, to the glass door that opened onto a publicly accessible hallway. The building had four stairways; she headed for the one furthest away from the blasted office.

She needed to get down twenty-seven floors and disappear before Xenophon got in place and trapped her in the building.

As she walked, she found her legs starting to respond more effectively. Less stagger, more speed, that was good. She rounded a corner, spotted the stairway and threw open the door. There were people on the landing, looking curiously in her direction…and reacting to her presence.

Shit, her camouflage wasn't working. Ester brushed past them, almost knocking a middle-aged woman down, and started running down the stairs. She ignored the protests coming from behind her.

There were more voices echoing in the stairway, from both above and below her. With the fire alarms going off, it made sense that people were evacuating. But why the hell were so many people working this late?

Ester tried to toggle through her suit's controls to find out what had happened to her camouflage, which was difficult while she was running pell mell down the stairs. It wasn't until the nineteenth floor that she realized the camouflage sub-system had crashed. It must have happened when the suit responded to the impact of the explosion.

She initiated a reboot, then ran through another group. This time, a man tried to stop her. She snapped an elbow into his face, breaking his nose, and kept moving.

Speed was life.

Maybe.

If she was lucky.

Near the Balkan Street Complex: 21:20

Jaeger fidgeted in his seat, trying to get comfortable in the form-fitting combat suit that the response team had insisted he wear, while not jostling the troopers next to him as the APC moved out of its hidden position down the street from Halkronen's building. Xenophon had brought him in as a subject matter expert—even paid him a modest amount—to provide background on what they'd described as the "potential threat" that had been brought to their attention by Halkronen's daughter. He'd seen in their faces that they hadn't really believed a cobbled-together rescue attempt was all that plausible, but they'd taken precautions nonetheless.

He figured they might be more willing to believe him now that McCallister's force had just blown through forty percent of the reinforced guard force in Halkronen's facility.

Certainly, the men, and a few women, around him were out for blood.

Apparently, they hadn't appreciated their companions being taken down.

He studied Lieutenant Leonard Blix and Sergeant Martin Wilsey, standing in the middle of the compartment holding on to the drab netting that covered the ceiling and swaying with the movement of the vehicle. The young, fresh-faced lieutenant added occasional commentary as Wilsey, a stocky, gray-haired man with a bulldog face and a crewcut who couldn't have ever been anything but a hardcore military vet, briefed the troopers.

Jaeger couldn't even imagine Wilsey ever wearing civilian clothes. What really struck him, though, was the stark contrast between the professionalism of the Xenophon mercenaries versus the rank amateur theatrics and tactical idiocy of the Snakes.

"Intel says we've got five attackers," Martin said, "four in the group that blew their way through the side of the building, and one wildcard in full stealth gear." He turned to Jaeger. "You got anything to add?"

"Yeah," Jaeger said, unclipping his harness and standing up. "They're probably working with the Clone Rights Action Group." There were some nods around the compartment. Any mercenary organization working for a client had to have some familiarity with the client's likely enemies, and CRAG was an obvious one for Halkronen. A sudden lurch as the APC hit a bump caused him to grab the netting to keep from falling. If he was interpreting the unit's data stream properly, they'd just driven over the gate McCallister's team had blown up. "They're military veterans—"

"So are we," a woman interrupted, and a wave of laughter broke out.

Jaeger stared at them until the laughter died down, and then waited another few seconds until it was painfully obvious that he hadn't joined in their laughter. "They're probably tougher man for man than you guys are—I know you guys don't want to hear that, but it's true. And their leader is a mean, tricky son of a bitch who can hit you out of left field when you ain't expecting it. Do not underestimate them."

"Not tougher than me," said Anderson, the sole trooper wearing an advanced, powered battlesuit. Another wave of laughter, quickly extinguished, went through the group. The rest were wearing light mil-spec combat suits, which Jaeger had been informed meant no enhanced strength and no camouflage mode.

"There is no such thing as overkill," another trooper intoned, to a chorus of "Oohrahs."

"Anderson, you cool your jets," Wilsey said, fixing the hulking trooper in his blocky armor with a mean-looking glare. "Lieutenant Blix says you're in reserve until we figure out where best to apply you to cause the most trouble."

"Plus," Lieutenant Blix interjected, "I don't want you destroying too much client property, like last time. My father's still mad at me about that." Jaeger had been told that his father was a high-ranking Xenophon officer.

The APC came to a quick halt.

Looking around the compartment, the sergeant continued, "We got no rules of engagement, except to kill these hombres, so let's make sure they die for their cause.

"Let's go," Wilsey thundered, and the clamshell doors at the rear of the APC, facing away from Halkronen's facility, began to open.

Jaeger knew he wasn't any sort of military genius—he was gaining a new respect for true professionals—but he'd have gone in fast and hard, with that big guy right in front.

Downtown, near the Unicide Tower: 21:21

From his position in the shadows of an alley, Fen tried to make sense of what was going on. A good portion of the twenty-seventh floor of the building that Ester had entered earlier had been blown up. That looked like a response to—what?

"Red Zero, this is Topaz, need your sitrep?"

"Waiting," Fen growled, sending Topaz both his own position and video of the strike against the building. "Maybe response to sniper?"

"Shit," Topaz said. "That makes sense. Checking something…"

"Not know if Ester live."

"Xenophon and Black Label Security both deployed response forces east of you, like they're blocking somebody heading east from Downtown. There's more forces moving from the Civic Center coming your way." There was a pause. "Holy shit. I think she killed Halkronen."

If Fen could smile, he would have. He'd been right all along.

Ester was a hunter.

First Floor, Balkan Street Complex: 21:21

"Red One, this is Red Four, we are pinned in Hallway A by the rearguard."

"Red One here," I said on the tacnet, responding to Ernie while keeping my attention on the screen where one of my disarmed security guards was flipping through views of the cells.

"Understood."

Based on the battle noise I was hearing in the background, it sounded like the Halkronen's welcoming party was really unhappy with us.

"Red Two, be nice if you'd stop sightseeing and do something about the problem in Hallway A."

"Red Two on the way," Gavin responded. "Confirmed target is not present." So, Claudia wasn't on the second floor. "Also, boom-booms are laid."

Topaz broke in, "Flash. Got an APC just stopped in the parking lot." An aerial view appeared in a window, showing troopers boiling out of the vehicle. At least one of them was excessively large—

"Shit," I said, feeling a cold finality in my bones, although I kept my expletive off the tacnet. "They're got a battlesuit." Not much any of us, including Gavin, could do against a battlesuit. This was the mission I wasn't walking away from. The end of the line. Fen was going to be disappointed in me.

"Red One here. Red Two, take the rearguard and open up the escape route for the escaping hostages. Three, Four—" Ernie and Bernie weren't cybered up, they'd be seeing the tacview in their helmets. "—hold position and delay new force, designated X."

On a private channel with Topaz, I said, "Now tell me some good news."

Topaz answered, "In addition to the APC, Xenophon had a VTOL heading for your location…but it's been diverted—"

"Thank God for small things."

"—because Ester just assassinated Halkronen at the Civic Center."

"What?"

"She's being chased by more mercs than you can shake a stick at," Topaz said, "including Xenophon elements at the Civic Center, the VTOL that was heading for your location, Black Label Security, and some other companies that have been asked to assist."

"Jesus."

"Red Zero and Ester are trapped between the forces."

"Nothing we can do from here," I said, feeling sick. I didn't want to lose Fen. Or Ester, either. And, much to my surprise, I didn't just mean because she was my client.

Just then, I thought I spotted Claudia on the screen. "Stop," I said to the guard. "Go back. Go, go. Yeah. Where is that?" It was her, sitting on a cot, looking out through bars at a hallway.

The guard looked up at me, his forehead shiny with sweat beneath a receding hairline. "Basement, cell eight."

"This place got an intercom?"

"Yeah," he said, and showed me how to operate the mic.

"This is a breakout," I said over the intercom, signaling my pet security guard to open all of the cell doors. "Repeat, this is a breakout. Head to the first floor and out the back doors as fast as you can. Keep going until you see cars—they'll pick you up and take you someplace safe." Screens showed cells opening and clones running out into the hallway.

On my private channel with Topaz, "The mob?"

"They're close."

Hell. Civilians on a battlefield. This was going to be ugly.

In a moment, I had both guards out of the control room, with their weapons and badges left behind. "Run," I told them, and they obliged, happy to escape with their lives. Then I jogged down the hallway to help Ernie and Bernie with Hallway A.

We needed the hallway clear long enough to get to the stairway heading to the basement. Even if we couldn't get out, at least we could get Claudia free. Xenophon was going to be worrying about people with guns, not unarmed, panicked clones.

"Hey Topaz," I said on our private channel. "I just want you to know…it's been a pleasure working with you." I chuckled mirthlessly. "And you have a sexy voice."

XIII. Fighting (or, Where the HELL did all these Shooters Come From?)

Downtown, near the Unicide Tower: Tuesday, 21:22

"Red Zero," Topaz said. "She's alive. There's been 911 reports of a woman in a combat suit in one of the tower's stairwells."

"Too slow," Fen said, watching troopers unload from a transport in front of the building. They weren't Xenophon—wrong uniform colors. Fen was camouflaged, lying in a tiny section of decorative landscaping across the street from them.

Oggie helpfully read the name off the transport for him: "Black Label Security." Xenophon must have called in help from other companies.

That was bad.

"Blocking forces in place," Fen said. "She needs working escape route…"

"Understood, I'm trying to contact—" Topaz's signal cut out at the same time that a blinking icon appeared in Fen's view indicating the presence of enemy jamming.

That was more bad. The enemy was getting organized.

Fen moved out of his observation point, padding slowly but steadily to minimize blur. He edged carefully around people who'd stopped to gawk at the troopers unloading with their full combat loadouts. He headed across the street at an angle, wanting to get a view into the boxy troop transport.

As the last of the troopers jumped down and moved out of the way, Fen saw two things of note. First, the main compartment was, as expected, empty. Well, empty of people anyway; it looked like the troopers had left behind a lot of heavy gear. But more importantly, the hatch to the driver's compartment was open. Something that would never have been allowed in a combat zone but then, obviously, they didn't think they were in a combat zone.

Not Fen's fault they hadn't realized they'd entered his territory.

As the troopers headed left to go into the tower and the rear door of the troop transport started sliding down, Fen blurred into motion. He leaped into the transport just before the door closed, hurriedly swishing his tail out of the way so it didn't get crushed as the door settled into place with a solid, metallic thunk.

Fen huddled in place for a moment, waiting for any indication that his presence had been noticed by the driver. It quickly became apparent that the driver was too busy talking on comms to have heard anything.

Studying the gear around him, it looked like Black Label Security had brought enough gear to fight a pitched battle with well-equipped CRAG fighters. Since such no battle had appeared, or seemed imminent, and since their current mission was just to hunt down a lone assassin, the unit had left the heavy gear in the transport.

That provided interesting…possibilities.

He padded silently up to the doorway and looked into the driver compartment, where the driver was clearly doubling as the unit's communications officer. The curved dashboard of the vehicle showed dozens of screens, including POV imagery from some of the lead troopers, building floorplans, and an overhead street map of where forces were being positioned to prevent Ester's escape.

"Roger," the thin, pasty-looking driver said. "The reports say she's in the north stairwell. Block north and west stairwells. Xenophon just got here, they'll take south and east. And put eyes on the skyway exit, which is third floor, east side, it gives access to the Holloway Building."

If Ester was smart, she'd get out of the north stairway as soon as possible. If she wasn't, well, she might not live long enough for Fen to assist her. As soon as Fen got some indication of where she was, he'd take out the driver and see if he could cause enough trouble to help her escape. Right now, though, it was time to absorb as much situational information as possible.

If the enemy takes away your intelligence capabilities, use theirs instead. That seemed fair to Fen.

First Floor, Balkan Street Complex: 21:22

As fast as I raced to the corner to back up Ernie and Bernie, I never quite caught up to Topaz's flybaby zooming along ahead of me. Then again, her little drone didn't have to worry about slipping on the treacherous footing.

The good thing about losing my race with the flybaby was that by the time I got there, Topaz was able to show me a view of the hallway. I wish it had shown me better news. To the left, we had Xenophon troopers at the far end of the hallway, as well as halfway down the hallway in the office we'd re-architected into our grand entrance. In between our position and the troopers, there were an ungodly number of clones in the hallway, screaming and huddling on the floor desperately trying to stay out of the gunfire. Other clones were still trapped in the open cells, afraid to come out.

For sure, no clones were escaping while the hallway remained a combat zone.

Enough zigging, it was time to zag.

"Red One here," I said, coming to a stop behind Ernie and Bernie. At intervals they'd lean into the hallway to send more fire downrange. "Red Four step back and make us a hole in the wall."

Ernie pulled back and looked at me as I pointed to the wall on my right.

"Break through into the cell," I said, "then the next wall is the stairway. Our target is in the basement."

Ernie nodded, then moved further down our cross-hallway, presumably to play with explosives as far from us as possible.

"Red Two, in position, on my count…"

I tapped Bernie on the shoulder, he looked back, nodded at me.

"…three…"

I took up a position on the right wall of our cross-hallway. Bernie, Red Three knelt across from me.

"…two…"

I gripped my HK tightly. Just about time to put Zeus to work again.

"…one!"

There was an explosion in the distance, presumably Gavin's flanking attack on the zeds at the end of the hallway, followed by more gunfire. Hoping that Gavin's attack distracted our closer contingent of troopers at least a little, I leaned out high while Bernie went low. Zeus already had the targeting information from the flybaby. Almost without any conscious effort on my part, rounds poured out of my HK in a staccato rhythm, then the expensive, brilliant ammunition did its work.

I saw two of the Xenophon soldiers torn apart. Another one might have taken lighter damage while diving for cover. The others managed to duck back into the demolished office before the storm arrived, though I was sure they'd taken some shrapnel hits—the explosions had been shaped to send shrapnel into the office rather than into the huddled clones.

I got hit by an explosive round that shredded the armor on my right arm and side and ruined the HK. A couple lighter rounds hit me, too, which hurt, but didn't penetrate. I especially disliked the one that pinged off my face shield and left a star-shaped crack. I dropped the damaged weapon and fell back behind cover, just as Bernie's head disappeared with a splash.

I found myself lying on the floor, half-unconscious from shock, unable to move, my thought processes too fuzzy to figure out what to do next. I couldn't feel my right arm. There was a dull ache in my side that I knew I should be worried about. I was having trouble seeing because of the water on my face shield; at least that's what I thought the problem was.

For some reason, I felt cold.

I became dimly aware of moving, as if someone were dragging me down the hallway, and then darkness closed in.

4th Floor, Unicide Tower, Downtown: 21:23

Ester struggled to control her heavy breathing as she timed her movements to ghost through the glass door of Leonard, Renault & Associates behind a FedEX delivery woman. She hoped her camouflage would continue working; it had already cut out twice since she'd rebooted. Moving slowly to minimize blur, she edged around a group of people milling around waiting for some meeting, then hurriedly dodged out of the way of a fast-moving young intern. A moment later, she was through the lobby, around a corner, and moving down a long hallway.

She stopped in front of the fifth door. She was annoyed to discover that the door was closed and that there were voices coming from the office beyond.

Why couldn't anything be easy?

She waited for a woman carrying a satchel of legal-size folders to pass. Once the hallway was empty again, she opened the door, stepped in and closed the door behind her. There were four people in the room, all looking toward the open door. Three were sitting in comfortable looking chairs in front of a mahogany desk behind which sat a man in an impeccably tailored business suit.

"What the—" the man behind the desk said.

Ester drew her pulse gun out of a pocket, which drew everyone attention because it wasn't camouflaged like the rest of her gear, and shot the lawyer.

While the others were still processing the existence of a disembodied gun, and reacting in horror to the lawyer slumping in his seat, she quickly shot all three of them. Then thanked her own foresight in bring a non-lethal weapon along…just in case.

Beyond the desk, the roof of the skyway ran from the Unicide Tower to the Holloway Building across the street. Pocketing the pulse gun, she got down on her knees by the window, pulled out a vibroblade and cut herself an Ester-sized hole in the glass.

Just as her camouflage died again. This time, rebooting didn't seem to be an option.

Parking Lot, Balkan Street Complex: 21:23

Jaeger stood next to Anderson, feeling tiny next to the hulking presence of the trooper. It must be an incredible feeling, wearing a battlesuit like that and knowing you were virtually invincible on the battlefield. Well, maybe not a real battlefield, but certainly any combat zone Anderson was likely to encounter in Los Angeles.

Anderson's unhappiness at being kept in reserve was almost palpable, which was probably why the first thing the trooper had done after jumping out of the APC was to blow up the gray van McCallister's crew had arrived in. Now they were both here watching as the other mercenaries filed past the smoking remains of the van and entered the hole in the building.

Jaeger shook his head. Lieutenant Blix was an idiot. Personally, Jaeger would have sent Anderson in the first wave, rather than keeping him in reserve. Screw the breakage. Wilsey should have overruled Blix, or quietly "advised" him, maybe.

If Jaeger was properly reading the heads-up view of the "battlespace," as Wilsey had called it—the Xenophons had hooked him up as a courtesy—they'd just lost two troopers at the hole that had been blasted in the building. As for the back door, there'd been three Halkronen security guards and four Xenophons from the original on-premises group holding the rear entrance…and it looked like they'd suffered some serious casualties, too.

Which meant that McCallister and company were probably planning to exit from there.

Just as he'd figured that out, Wilsey's voice said on the tacnet, "Vulture 2 here, Vulture 10 to the back door."

Anderson took one step forward, then there was a sharp, flat crack that echoed around the parking lot, and the big trooper toppled forward, hit the pavement with a crash, and was still.

Jaeger was already moving as a second sniper shot blew through the space his head had occupied just a quarter second before. His augments kicked in with superhuman speed as he sprinted for cover behind the APC.

Huddling behind the vehicle, he heard a whirring noise as the cupola on top of the APC rotated. Jaeger knew just enough to not look directly at the gun. He heard a barking cough and was thankful that the sound of the blast was mostly suppressed by the helmet the Xenophons had provided him. A wash of heat rolled over him as the cyan flash of the APC's main weapon lit up the parking lot. The retaliatory shot smashed into the sniper's position in a neighboring office building.

Watching military-grade heavy weapons in action was a new experience for Jaeger, but what really made his eyes goggle was how the flash of light had illuminated a stream of cars—just regular, everyday vehicles—speeding into the parking lot. In the brief flash, Jaeger couldn't even begin to count how many cars were coming, but he knew it was lots.

Downtown: 21:25

Fen sat just outside the hatch of the transport vehicle's driver compartment and watched the driver coordinate the activities of the Black Label Security mercenaries. They'd divided up, with a pair on each of the two stairways they were covering, another pair making sure nobody escaped via the skyway, and two pairs actively hunting for Ester. It looked like Xenophon had done something similar.

"Wolf Seven," a female voice said, "the chicken has flown the coop. Repeat, the chicken has flown the coop. She's in the Holloway Building."

"Wolf Zero," Fen's pet driver said, "how'd the chicken get to the other side of the road?"

"Jesus Christ, Nimitz," another voice cut in, "this isn't a goddamn joke!" Sounded like an irate sergeant to Fen.

"Wolf Seven, she cut the glass and egressed using the roof of the skyway."

"Wolf Zero, copying Xenophon—"

No, you're not, Fen thought as he shot the driver with a Bedtime Special, choosing the non-lethal round because Cal would have wanted him to be as non-lethal as possible and because he didn't need blood messing up his camouflage. As soon as the electrical effects dispersed, he undid Nimitz's harness, yanked him unceremoniously out of the seat, and then took his place.

The transport was still running, so he put it in gear and drove away.

Basement, Balkan Street Complex: 21:25

Zeus had some difficult decisions to make. Its programming dictated that it do everything possible to save the life of its Principal. Unfortunately, said Principal was currently both weaponless and in a non-combat-capable state, apparently being moved to relative safety by a designated Friendly, identified as "Later." Drugs were presently being administered in accordance with doctrine, both to handle pain and to bring the Principal back to limited combat capability.

Zeus still had access to incoming signals, including the tacview and various drone views that its Principal had instantiated. Of primary importance—a view from the damaged and non-flight capable drone lying in a puddle of water on the first floor. That view showed Enemies following the path of its Principal, approaching the corner where another Friendly had been terminated.

The struggling combat system also had a weak signal from its Principal's weapon, which was damaged and unusable as a weapon, but which still contained brilliant, explosive ammunition. The damaged weapon was located next to the corner the Enemies were approaching.

Further analysis revealed that two of the Enemies appeared to be high-value Targets—one was apparently a lieutenant and the other a sergeant, though Zeus could not identify the military force in its database. It calculated a high probability that the two Targets might be the leaders of this unit of Enemies.

This datum tilted Zeus into action. It detonated all fourteen remaining explosive rounds a meter away from Sergeant Wilsey, blowing him into pieces along with Lieutenant Blix and two other troopers. The carefully shaped charges injured several other troopers and also blew a hole through the ceiling.

XIV. Escape (or, Maybe Some of Us Might Get Out Alive)

Parking Lot, Balkan Street Complex: Tuesday, 21:26 — Missing 69 Hours

Jaeger tried to move toward the building, then cursed as another car almost clipped him. Dodging left him right back where'd he'd started—next to the APC. As best he could tell, it looked like the cars were trying to hem in the APC it so it couldn't move without rolling over them.

Other cars were driving in a big circle around the building.

His suit alerted him to a signal being broadcast in the clear. "ATTENTION XENOPHON!" The voice was vaguely female, but obviously obscured to avoid identification. "This is a flash mob of unarmed civilians protesting for clone rights. All your activities are being broadcast live on the net."

There was flurry of outraged comments on the Xenophon tac channel.

"ATTENTION XENOPHON! There are unarmed civilians in your battlespace. Any endangerment of civilians is grounds for legal action. You are live on the net. STAND DOWN or pay the legal consequences."

Clones started running out of the building, streaming from the hole that had been blasted out of the side, and, it was hard to tell from his angle, but it looked like from the rear of the building, as well. Jaeger's jaw dropped as he watched clones getting into random cars and being driven off.

Jaeger shook his head. He had to hand it to McCallister. He hated the damn bastard, but he had to admit that it was a stunning escape plan.

Leaning up against the APC, listening to the Xenophon chatter on the tacnet, it quickly became apparent to Jaeger that, with Sergeant Wilsey dead, nobody knew what to do. Except the troopers who were still in close combat with the rescuers.

"Reinforcements to the basement," Jaeger said on the tacnet. "Don't worry about the escaping clones, too much of a PR problem. Just get the attackers, and let the high-ups deal with the customer later."

He had no authority, but somehow they started doing what he said anyway.

Downtown: 21:27

Ester ran down the sidewalk. She knew she was being herded by multiple teams; all she could do was try to get out of the box before her pursuers closed it, but it was looking increasingly unlikely that she'd be able to do that.

She needed to do something unexpected or they'd have her, and soon.

Two security vehicles, not Xenophon but another company, zoomed into the intersection about fifty meters ahead of her.

She pivoted and used her suit's augmented strength to drive her through the plate glass window of a restaurant. Customers screamed as glass shards flew everywhere. She skidded on a tabletop, knocked plates off with a crash, landed on her feet, and accidentally slammed a customer out of her way—he went flying and knocked some other tables over.

She kicked another table out of the way as she made a beeline for the restaurant's exit into an indoor mall occupying the first floor of a multi-story office building. Then she was running through the mall, dodging through people.

"You're an idiot," Topaz said.

Ester grunted. "Little busy right now." She needed to find an exit before she got trapped indoors.

"Go right at the fruit stand," Topaz said. "There's a utility door behind it. Probably locked, but you need to get through it."

"How?" Meaning, how was Topaz getting through to her? Her pursuers had imposed some sort of communications black-out on her.

"They're blocking the usual tactical channels, got some serious gear involved, too," Topaz said, "so I'm piggy-backing off the commercial nets."

Ester skidded to a halt at the aforementioned fruit stand, spotted the utility door, and used her suit's augmented strength to pull the door open.

The knob came off instead, so she punched the door jamb into splinters and yanked the door open. She sprinted down a no-frills utility hallway with concrete floors and cinder-block walls painted light yellow, turned a corner, then burst through a metal door into an alley.

"You've got to keep going southeast," Topaz said. "It's the weakest point of the trap you're in. And Red Zero is headed that way to back you up."

"Red Zero?"

"Red One had a backup plan to cover you being stupid," Topaz said. "Personally, I'd have just let your useless ass die. Now, shut up and run, fool."

Basement, Balkan Street Complex: 21:28

Clarity returned slowly, like a fog slowly receding in the morning sun. Bringing with it the enervating keening of dueling alarms, intermittent gunfire and…rain? No, the damn sprinklers had gone off, I remembered. I was lying in a cell, in a puddle of water. My helmet was off.

I felt a tugging at my neck.

Turning my head, I saw Claudia looking down at me, kneeling beside me and working at my suit's catches. She was soaking wet, her hair straggling down around her face. She looked a lot like Ester, but her face was a little narrower, her cheekbones not as pronounced, her eyebrows more stylized. "Hey there," she said, and her voice was exactly like Ester's. "Ernie told me to get you out of the suit."

"Claudia," I croaked, raising my left arm slowly to help her with the catch, because I couldn't feel my right arm. Suits were tricky to get out of. "Nice to finally meet you."

Her lips quirked up into a brief smile.

My brain may have still been a little fuzzy, but I was surprised that Ester and Claudia didn't look exactly alike (like Bernie and Ernie), because I was pretty sure they were both part of the same clone family. That meant one or both of them had undergone some body sculpting work.

I made the mistake of looking at my wounds. The part of my right arm closest to my side looked like raw hamburger, but with a plastic sheen that told me that somebody must have found time to apply some emergency sealant to stop the bleeding. I assumed my side looked the same, but all I could see was the shredded armor.

As Claudia managed to get the top of my suit unbuckled, I sat up, felt only a few twinges from my right side. My right arm was just a dead weight.

No pain translated to better living through applied chemistry, I assumed, drugs deployed automatically by the suit at the behest of Zeus to get me operational again. A hyped-up, artificial alertness that I'd pay for threefold when this was all over.

If we got out of this mess.

A moment later Claudia had my top off, then she helped me stand up so I could get the lower half off, including my boots. Leaving me standing in nothing but my soggy boxers. I was a little wobbly and I had a thundering headache, but I was mostly functional. The fuzziness was clearing quickly.

That was when I noticed the boy sitting on the cot, rocking back and forth. He was young, perhaps twelve or so, tall and lanky like a colt.

When he saw me looking in his direction, he stopped rocking, fixed his unblinking eyes on me and said, "You want yum yum?" He repeated the same phrase five more times and then went back to rocking when I didn't respond.

"Special merchandise," Claudia said.

"Jesus."

Technically legal, but obscene—the part of the clone industry that polite society didn't talk about.

I found myself glad that Halkronen was dead.

"Screw Jesus," Claudia said bitterly. "You can have him. He's never done anything to help out us clones."

"We have to get him out."

"Already tried." Claudia shrugged. "He's so programmed, there's really nobody home. He's a meat robot. You can't even reconstruct a personality matrix on top of what's left."

She walked over to the cot, picked up a wet, blood-stained clone uniform and held it out to me.

That had been one of our contingencies, to discard our gear and try to get out posing as escaping clones.

Things obviously hadn't gotten any better while I'd been unconscious.

"Red One," I said, as I took the uniform from her. "Back online."

"Nice to hear from you again," Topaz said, a hint of relief evident in her voice.

"'Bout time you joined the party," Ernie drawled. "You get the package and the other clones out the back door, me and Later'll keep the fleas off'n you." Their positions appeared in one of my views, on the same side of the hallway as the cell I was in, but further away from the rear exit and closer to our pursuers.

"Roger."

As I pulled the clammy, sodden uniform on, Claudia said, "The big guy took your suit and blew it up already."

I nodded. It was nice of Later to make sure my DNA traces were scrubbed, but ouch, suits were expensive to replace, even civilian jobs like mine.

Once I had the uniform on, she handed me my vibroblade. "They said you'd want this."

I accepted the weapon from her with my left hand.

"Not with the power source in it," I said. Careful not to hit the safety, I shifted my grip and used a fingernail to pry open a compartment at the bottom of the weapon's haft. I shook it until the finger-length energy unit dropped out. "Not if we have to go past any mercs." Without its power source, it was a wickedly sharp knife, not a universal can opener.

Parking Lot, Balkan Street Complex: 21:29

"Is that sniper still around?" Jaeger asked on the command channel.

"Vulture Zero, no sir," the APC's driver said. "The drones show him buggin' out. He's pro, he won't be back now that he knows the APC's defenses are up." There was a pause. "By the way, you're supposed to use your call sign on comms."

"What's my call sign?"

"Vulture Zero here, it's Baggage One, sir."

Jaeger rolled his eyes. The hell with that. The only thing he was going to answer to was his own street name. "New call sign is Jaeger, so get used to it. How do you know he was pro?"

"It was a miracle shot, 'cause that's the only way you could take out a battlesuit with a simple, old-school rifle."

"Jaeger here, attackers are probably—"

There was a rolling series of booms, almost instantly reduced in volume as his helmet's sound suppression capabilities kicked in. He watched in surprise as most of the windows on the second and third floors of the Halkronen building blew out. Flickering orange and red flames were visible through the shattered windows. Even in the half minute or so that he was paralyzed by surprise, it was obvious that the flames were spreading quickly and that it wouldn't be long before the upper floors were fully engulfed.

What finally broke Jaeger's paralysis was the realization that the protesters had been even more surprised than him. All over the parking lot, the vehicles circling the building had stopped.

Some deliberately, some as the result of minor collisions brought on by drivers reacting in unexpected ways to the explosions and falling debris.

Seizing the opportunity, Jaeger began weaving through the vehicles, heading for the rear of the building.

"Jaeger here, attackers will be leaving from the rear exit. Press 'em hard and we can stop them there."

"Vulture Seven, understood. We are blocking the rear exit."

"Hornet Four, we are in contact with Alpha Force, sending the shitstorm now."

"Jaeger here, Vulture Zero…Can I get some backup at the rear exit? And I want you to set up some views for me…"

Jaeger pulled his pistol out of its holster as he ran. Sergeant Wilsey had warned him that if he so much as touched the pistol during this op, the sergeant would personally frag him. But Wilsey was dead, so screw him.

Rear Stairway, Balkan Street Complex: 21:29

"It's time," I said, as a cacophony of heavy gunfire started up—Ernie and Later had popped smoke and then opened up with everything they had, all to cover our escape attempt.

"Are you sure?" Claudia asked, eyes wide. She looked scared, as any sane person would be if asked to run through the middle of a firefight.

"It's the only way," I said gently.

Claudia nodded, then we ran out into the smoky, red-tinged hallway. We headed right, away from the gunfire and toward the building's rear entrance. Ernie and Later were firing from positions in cells on the same side of the hallway as the cell we'd just left, so we hugged the opposite wall to hopefully avoid any overshoots aimed at my other team members. As much as possible, I tried to stay between the Xenophon shooters and Claudia, a strategy that might help her but not me, seeing as I was unarmored.

Made me feel naked, to tell the truth.

I needed to get the other freed clones moving. "We've got to get out of here!" I bellowed. "Head for the exit. Move! Move! Move!"

The building shook as a series of explosions temporarily drowned out the sound of gunfire. I slipped, reflexively tried to put out my right arm to catch myself and, well, that didn't work so well. I ended up falling and landing on my injured right arm instead. The pain was so intense I almost blacked out, then Claudia and another clone helped to my feet again.

If those explosions had been Gavin's "incendiaries" going off, then I'd hate to find out what his idea of serious demolition work was.

A little further down the hallway, I almost tripped over someone huddled against the wall. My only good hand was holding the vibroblade, so I put it in my mouth, biting down on the haft, while I yanked the clone to his feet and then shoved him down the hallway ahead of us.

While the firefight raged behind us and stray shots passed us with angry whines, Claudia added her yells to mine and others started joining us. The smoke thinned out as we progressed down the hallway, revealing that our group had grown to maybe twenty or so clones. The more cover we had, the better chance that Claudia and I would be able to get out.

I felt a twinge of guilt at that thought. All of the clones were people, just regular people, but treated like slaves. They didn't have the advantages that Claudia and Ester possessed. Nobody would have rescued any of them if Claudia hadn't been here.

"When we get outside," I shouted, "find any car and get into it. They'll take you to safety."

"Thanks," yelled a woman, loping along next to me. I caught a flash of her smile, then most of her head disappeared as a stray shot caught her.

I sped up, nudging Claudia along so we were in the middle of the pack by the time we got to the stairwell. I palmed the vibroblade, with the blade stretching up under my sleeve. There were Xenophon troopers on the first-floor landing, looking professional and dangerous in their black combat suits with gold trim. Two of them were facing us, scanning us as we climbed the stairs. There were others beyond them. One was facing up the stairs where Gavin had been exchanging fire with them earlier; now there was smoke drifting down

"Red Two, I'm outside, will be at the back door in a minute." That made sense. If I'd been Gavin, I wouldn't have wanted to be on the second floor when the explosives went off, either.

As expected, the Xenophon troopers were letting us pass by, clearly under orders not to damage the merchandise. After all, maybe the "products" could be retrieved later. Six or seven clones filed past, followed by Claudia, then another clone. As I approached, something changed, I'm not sure what. I noticed a sudden alertness in the two mercs checking me out.

Somehow, they'd been warned.

I was closest to the merc on my left, so I stepped into him as he was trying to point his rifle at me. Despite the warning, he hadn't realized I had augmented speed and reflexes, at least until I drove my vibroblade up under his chin. I twisted behind him as his partner opened fire.

Hey, if you don't have your own armor, borrow somebody else's armor. My makeshift two-ply armor (front and back, with meat padding between the layers) took the shots while I dropped my blade, reached around, and grabbed the dead merc's hand, his finger still on the trigger of his rifle. I swiveled to point the rifle at the other guard, and then yanked the man's trigger finger to fire a long burst that stitched my opponent from crotch to helmet.

There were screams as gunfire broke out. Ricochets whined off the concrete walls like angry hornets and the air filled with flying concrete chips. Clones desperately went prone for relative safety as the remaining troopers responded by shooting at me. The armored corpse I was using as a shield took more hits while I hosed down the landing above me on full automatic. Not that I wanted full auto, but that's the setting the merc had chosen and I couldn't change it one-handed without dropping the weapon.

Memo to self: Never, never, never engage in a full-fledged firefight in a confined, concrete stairwell.

The noise was deafening. After a few seconds, I couldn't even hear the screaming anymore. I saw another trooper go down and then my weapon clicked empty and I figured I was a goner.

And then I saw a blur moving behind the troopers and they all went down in quick succession.

"Red One, you OK?" Gavin asked. I couldn't hear his communication, of course, because my I'd been mostly deafened by the close-quarters gunfire. But Zeus helpfully provided a transcript.

"'Bout time you showed up," I responded, letting my shield slump to the floor. "Let's go," I shouted. When nobody moved, I realized they were all as deaf as I was.

"Where's Claudia?" I asked, suddenly panicked. I'd momentarily lost track of her.

I surged up the remaining steps to the landing. Claudia was slumped against the wall to my left, holding her hand tightly over a shoulder wound that was still oozing blood. Since she still had a shoulder, I deduced that she'd been struck by a ricochet.

I wished I still had my Trauma Kit, but that had been attached to my combat suit. I tore a strip off my uniform, bound it around Claudia's shoulder and arm, and tied it as tight as possible. It was the best field-expedient care I could give her. She'd need medical attention soon, though.

"Keep pressure on it," I said to her, and then Gavin helped me get her on her feet. With one of us on each side of her holding her up, we exited the stairwell, then followed a short hallway to the rear exit door.

XV. Rendezvous (or, It Ain't Over 'Til It's Over)

Downtown: 21:30

Fen drove the stolen troop transport down a main road, studying the array of screens and considering his options for causing the most trouble for Ester's pursuers. From listening to the comms, he'd learned that the unit of Black Label troopers had discovered that their transport was missing, but were still thinking that Nimitz had gone "off the reservation" somehow, whatever that meant. They were trying to fix the situation without having to admit some sort of screw-up to their leadership.

Of course, both the transport and the troopers were tied into the same tacnet, so the unit knew his position just as he knew theirs. They were following him, albeit more slowly because they were on foot.

There had to be some way he could use that.

Meanwhile, he'd dumped the unconscious Nimitz in an alley and spent a few minutes rigging the gear the troopers had left behind. The transport was basically a rolling bomb.

All he needed was the right… Oh, that looked good. There was an intersection two blocks away cordoned off by Phelps Security Services where a Xenophon VTOL craft was in the

339

process of landing. And it looked like a Gray Mountain transport was headed there, too.

Looked like they were getting ready to set up a cordon to block Ester's escape.

Fen made a hard-right turn at the next intersection, tires screeching as he rolled through a red light. He clipped a car crossing the intersection, sending it careening into a parked car and snarling up traffic behind him.

He slowed down a little, watching the dots on the Black Label tacview screen that represented his pursuers adjust to his new path.

"Red Zero, they're getting close to Red Queen," Topaz said. "Camo's not working, so they've got her location pretty well fixed. They just haven't caught up to her yet. Parse the squeal for encoded situational data." There was a loud blip after she stopped speaking.

"Diversion soon," Fen said. "Busy now." Off comms, he told Oggie to parse the data and was rewarded as Ester's position and estimated positions for some of her pursuers showed up on his own tacnet. She was only a few blocks behind him, heading southeast as Topaz had directed her. She was being pursued by Xenophon troopers and the Black Label unit he'd stolen the transport from. They had her largely boxed in on three sides and were herding her to where a cordon was obviously about to be set up by Gray Mountain, PSS, and the troopers about to unass from the Xenophon VTOL.

Technically, Fen was in the box, too, but he was ahead of all the pursuers and the cordon wasn't quite set up yet.

As Fen came up on the next intersection, the light turned green. The cars stopped at the light were slow to start off, so he dodged into an empty turn lane, sped past them, and then cut off the lead car as he shot across the intersection.

Halfway down the block, traffic was stopped because the next intersection had been blocked to allow the VTOL to land. Fen spotted the aircraft about sixty meters up and descending. He jinked right and the transport bounced over the curb and onto the sidewalk. Pedestrians scattered to get out of the transport's way.

Fen opened the back door, then made sure the transport was lined up on his target, the gap between the Gray Mountain and PSS transports. Twenty meters from the target, he hit cruise control and used combat speed to race out of the cockpit and through the main compartment. On his way, he grabbed a loop of rope that he'd duct-taped to the wall, and jumped out.

At combat speed, he was going almost as fast as the transport, but in the opposite direction. Velocity mostly canceled, onlookers barely even saw a blur from his camouflage as he landed on the sidewalk. Of course, as he'd leaped, the loop had pulled out the pins of several hand grenades. Knowing what was coming, he dove for cover in a doorway alcove.

Without a driver, the transport angled slightly left and hit the rear panel of the Gray Mountain transport rather than the gap Fen had aimed at. The back-end of the transport slammed sideways into the PSS vehicle, knocking it into some of the Gray Mountain troopers. That didn't do too much except make noise, because they were all lightly armored mil-grade vehicles and the troopers that got slammed were wearing combat suits.

Then the grenades went off, demolishing the interior of Fen's rolling bomb and spraying shrapnel out the back door and into the crowd of Gray Mountain and PSS troopers in the intersection. The grenades lit off a secondary explosion that tore the Black Label vehicle apart, badly damaged the other two transports and sent pieces crashing into the Xenophon VTOL, which had been at about eight meters when the collision happed.

The right engine of the VTOL flamed out. The pilot didn't react fast enough—a hard pancake landing had been his only viable choice—and the right wing dipped and hit the ground hard. It crumpled and jet fuel spurted out onto the flaming debris of the vehicle collision. This was not good news for the troopers who'd just unloaded from the transports.

And even worse for the VTOL, as the wing burst into flame and the aircraft crashed upside down into the middle of a flaming pool of fire. Black smoke and flame rolled into the air.

"Holy Mother of God, Red Zero, what the hell did you do?" Topaz said.

"Diversion complete," Fen said, extremely pleased with himself. Despite the mayhem, their gear would ensure that most of the troopers would survive, but they'd be in no condition to put a cordon in place.

Parking Lot, Balkan Street Complex: 21:30

Jaeger rounded the corner and couldn't believe the sight that greeted his eyes, even though he'd half expected it. McAllister was there, exiting from the rear door along with a crowd of clones. He was helping a female clone toward a waiting car.

How the hell did he get past the Xenos? He'd warned them that McAllister was posing as a clone when he'd seen him coming up the stairs in one of the real-time views from the troopers.

Jaeger extended his pistol with two hands, lined everything up, and fired five shots at McAllister. He'd have sworn they were all hits, but McAllister didn't go down, though he did look up in surprise at the sound of the shots.

Instead of hitting his nemesis, it was almost like they'd hit some sort of invisible shield—

Oh shit. He'd hit a soldier in a top-of-the-line camouflage combat suit…he knew McAllister's team had a guy like that. With a pistol that could only make him angry.

Jaeger dove for cover behind one of the circling cars, just as bullets ripped through the space he'd occupied. He found himself thankful for the first time that the parking lot was full of moving vehicles. Then two Xenos rounded the corner just in time to start shooting at where the camouflaged guy had been.

He didn't think they hit anything. He'd bet anything the guy had just ghosted away.

Jaeger was seething inside as he watched one of the cars drive away with McAllister and the clone he'd rescued.

Stepping in front of one of the cars, he screamed and brandished the gun. When the driver didn't stop quickly enough, he put a round through the windshield close enough to let him know what was going to happen next if he didn't stop.

Jaeger climbed into the passenger seat and discovered that the driver was a young, terrified woman with wide eyes and close-cropped, blue-dyed hair.

"What's your name?" he asked, waving the weapon in her general direction.

"Anna," she said, her voice quavering.

"Well, Anna," Jaeger said, "these clones are being taken somewhere and I want you to take me there. Do you understand?"

She nodded, tears streaming down her face.

"Then, drive!" Jaeger snarled.

Ester ran down an alley, gasping for breath. She was so tired she could barely lift her legs. She'd broken contact with her pursuers, but they'd find her again soon enough. There certainly were enough of them. And unlike her, most of them had useful combat augments, like speed or strength, and combat drugs to enhance performance.

All she had was some cosmetic enhancements that let her change the shape of her face within certain practical constraints, so she wasn't a dead ringer for her Ladyship. Drugs were out, too; combat drugs had to be tailored to the metabolism of the user, and her family couldn't afford to have that kind of information out in the wild.

She came across a niche set into a building that held three battered dumpsters and ducked in beside the last one. She bent over, hands on her knees and tried desperately not to throw up.

Something you definitely didn't want to do in a combat suit.

"Red Queen, why are you stopped?" Topaz asked.

"Can't...run...any...more," Ester gasped.

"Thirty seconds, that's all you get," Topaz snapped. "Then it's run or die, bitch!"

At the allotted time, Topaz hounded her into motion. Ester stumbled out of her hiding place and started jogging, gun in hand. She needed to get out of this alley before her pursuers caught up to her. She rounded a corner to another alley and literally ran into a Black Label trooper. As they collided, she fired an explosive round at point blank range. The round penetrated his front armor but not the back and the resulting explosion shredded the soldier within his suit.

344

The blowback damaged her own front armor and knocked her backwards. From a prone position, she spotted the dead trooper's companion behind the trooper she'd just shot and exchanged fire with him. Multiple impacts struck the pavement around her, and she was hit twice, in the torso and helmet, but both shots ricocheted off her sleek, curving armor. She only got two shots off, but he disappeared from her view.

She rolled to the side, in case he was still active, and spotted his body sprawled against the wall. She wasn't sure at first where his head had gone, but then she spotted his helmet further down the alley. Damage analysis scrolled in a view. Apparently one of her shots had missed, but the other one of had hit the second trooper in the throat. The explosion had decapitated him.

She was lucky, though. If he'd been using the same ammo as her, she'd be dead.

"Took out two zeds," she said for Topaz's benefit as she climbed to her feet and started running again.

Rendezvous: 21:37

"This is so ace," the driver said. "It feels really good to actually do something about the clone situation. That's what we really need, more action."

I shook my head tiredly. Five minutes ago, I was getting shot at. Now I was listening to an amiable Hindu chatterbox excitedly talking about social justice issues. The gunfire just outside his car had practically scared him shitless, but at a distance of six blocks or so, he was already starting to focus on the exciting story he'd be able to tell his friends.

The rendezvous turned out to be a parking lot. As the driver turned in, Cal could see a line of cars ahead of them. Apparently, not even clones rights activists were immune to traffic jams. Beyond the line of vehicles, Cal could see organizers in black T-shirts putting groups of clones in an eclectic collection of vans and driving them away.

"Thanks," I said, "you've been a great help. We're going to get out here."

He was still chattering away as I exited and then helped Claudia climb out of the passenger seat. Arm in arm, like two walking wounded, we stumbled toward the vans.

The way I figured it, we had priority. This whole escapade had been set up to rescue Claudia, after all.

Somebody shouted, "Hey, McAllister!"

I should have recognized that grating voice instantly, but I didn't. I turned and saw a man in a gray combat suit pointing a pistol at us. I had no weapons. He was four meters away and could easily kill me before I got to him.

I stepped in front of Claudia to shield her.

The man said, "It's payback time, asshole!" That's when I recognized Jaeger's voice. Like a thunderbolt, I realized that Jaeger must have been a complication all along. He'd fingered me for the Snakes, probably warned Halkronen, and now he was here to kill me.

Persistent son of a bitch.

"If you were a real man," I drawled, "you'd take me on hand-to-hand."

Hey, it always worked in the TRI-Ds.

Jaeger laughed. "I don't think so." He assumed a classic two-handed shooting stance. "Goodbye, mother—" And that's when a car swerved suddenly swerved out of the line and ran him over.

The impact slammed Jaeger forward into another car. I saw the gun go flying away with the unexpected impact. Jaeger screamed as the two vehicles collided with a solid crunch and crushed his legs to a pulp. Steam swirled out from under the hood of the car that had struck Jaeger, half obscuring the man slumped over the front of the vehicle. I couldn't tell if Jaeger was alive or dead, but he certainly wasn't a threat anymore.

A thick-set man in a black combat suit with strategically placed black duct tape got out of the passenger side of the vehicle and said, "Hey, hey, hey, my man, you look like shit."

"Hell," I said tiredly, "I suppose you still want that rematch, too."

"Indeed, I do."

Downtown: 21:39

Fen was stalking Ester's pursuers now, which had to be creating a panic within the two teams, Xenophon and Black Label, as team members steadily disappeared from their tacnet.

This was actually the job that war dogs had been created for, going behind enemy lines and creating mayhem. And Fen had been one of the best war dogs ever.

Fen was having fun. It had been a long time since he'd been able to hunt like this.

"Red Queen is trapped," Topaz said.

Fen didn't bother responding. He was in hyper mode now, and slowing down enough to talk was difficult.

According to his tacview, nicely updated by Topaz, Ester was stuck in a narrow alley and taking fire from two groups. They had her mousetrapped between them. He was already close to her location. If she could hold out for another thirty seconds, he'd be there.

The first group had a lookout posted to make sure nobody came up behind them. Moving at better than forty kilometers an hour, Fen was on her almost before she had a chance to realize there was a threat. Lightning flashed as Fen bricked her at close range with a Bedtime Special.

The others in her group were still reacting with ineffectual fire as Fen blurred past them, Oggie assisting with the targeting of his shoulder-mounted guns. Lightning crackled against both sides of the alley as four more zeds got bricked.

Cal was going to be annoyed with him for running through almost all of his Bedtime Specials. They were expensive and hard to replace.

Ester was sheltering behind a delivery van that looked like it had seen better days. It was riddled with holes, both large and small. "Supremely perforated" was a phrase Fen remembered Cal using in a similar situation back in Algeria. Shots were still impacting the vehicle from the second group positioned at the end of the alley, where it intersected with a cross-alley. Four shooters, two on each side periodically leaning out and shooting at Ester's position.

Guess he was in time after all.

Still moving fast, but starting to zigzag now. If the other group was smart, they'd know that somebody else had entered the battle space. And now, almost right on schedule, gunfire came his way. They didn't know precisely where he was, but they certainly knew he was there.

He was so hyped that he could see the vortex trails the rounds made through the air. Oggie backtracked the rounds for him, and Fen sent four cluster rounds back.

Fen deliberately aimed high and watched the clusters shatter against the wall behind the shooters. A firestorm enveloped the alley at a height of about ten meters, but the residual effects at ground level had to be severely uncomfortable for the troopers. It was also a blatant warning that he could kill them any time he wanted.

Now they had a choice. Come after him and die, or let him and Ester escape. Additionally, if any of the troopers he'd bricked were using internal air, then somebody needed to open their helmets or they'd suffocate in their now-dead suits.

Fen had been hit only once, a glancing shot that bounced off his armor and mostly exploded behind him. His armor had been singed a little, but all his status icons still showed green.

Coming down from hyper mode, and still in camouflage, he stopped next to the vehicle and said out loud, "Come with me if you want to live." With that, he blew a hole in the wall to give Ester a new escape route.

He hoped somebody would be stupid enough to follow them. He'd like to have some more fun.

Epilogue (or, Cal Figures Stuff Out Despite all the Really Good Drugs)

For the second night in a row, I found myself under the tender ministrations of Dr. Octo. "You again?" Doctor Octo said, in the guise of Jane, their red-headed unit. "I don't give discounts for repeat customers, you know."

"Oh, hell," I said. "Can I pay you on the installment plan, then?"

I spent the next three days in Doctor Octo's clinic, being drugged up in different ways and undergoing more medical procedures than I really wanted to think about. During my periods of alertness, I thought hard about everything that had happened since the case had started.

It should have been a simple case, except for two things. Ester and her clone family had waited too long before they got help. Just eight hours earlier and we'd have rescued Claudia from the Snakes. We'd never have had to deal with Halkronen. The second complicating factor was Jaeger. Unbeknownst to all of us, he'd been throwing a wrench in our plans every time he could.

He'd sicced the Snakes on me after our raid on their collection point, most likely after hearing about me from the manager of the Mixie Trixie. He'd put enough together to figure out that we might be going after Halkronen to rescue Claudia, so he'd obviously warned them.

Without the Xenophon reinforcements, we'd have been in and out of the Halkronen facility in record time. And probably with no casualties.

On the second day of my incarceration, Ester showed up with Fen, who promptly put his front paws up on the bed and started licking the side of my face. Ester was dressed down, at least for her, in gray leggings and a long, loose blouse. Her blond hair was pulled back in a ponytail. To me, she looked like a vision.

Baskerville: Stupid human.

"Hey," she said, taking a position on my left side where there was less medical equipment and no dog in the way. "You're awake."

"Yup," I answered, while scratching behind Fen's ears. "I'm just enjoying the general ambience of this five-star resort." As clinics went, Doctor Octo provided top-notch care. They just didn't have much in the way of amenities. On the other hand, unlike hospitals, they didn't report to the police.

SixGunCal: Love you too, Fen

Ester snorted in an unlady-like manner. "Well, I've got a present for you." She set my Trauma Kit down on the table next to me.

"Where'd you get that?"

"Ernie." At my inquiring glance, she added, "He's down the hallway. Told me to thank you for it. He says it kept him alive."

"Later?"

She shook her head. "Shot to death. Ernie got shot, too, but he had your kit." She angled her head at the device. "Xenophon pulled back and guarded the exits while the building burned and then collapsed. Ernie found a way into the front lobby." I remembered the front lobby as a one-story add-on to the front of the building, though Gavin had pretty well demolished it.

She was smiling, so I figured there had to be more. "So, how'd he get free?"

"He stole the suit of a dead Xenophon trooper then waited to be rescued." She laughed. "Hijacked the damn ambulance during his escape."

I shook my head. "You have to give him points for style."

"You, too," she said.

"Well," I said, "I make a terrific trouble magnet."

She laughed.

"More seriously, though," I said, "you kept me in the dark about a few things, didn't you?"

She looked more sober, now. "I had to."

"Your…family…is influential, but they're not all that close to CRAG and the FCN. Those groups wanted more than money in exchange for their help on short notice, so you made a bargain."

"Not me, personally, but yeah."

"Your family needed help to rescue Claudia from Halkronen, including intelligence, extra shooters, and a diversion. CRAG wanted action—they wanted to make a clear and unequivocal statement that no matter how prominent you were, if you dealt in clones then CRAG could take you down. And FCN wanted fuel for their ongoing public relations battle in favor of clone rights. Of course, FCN would decry the violence of the CRAG, as per usual."

She nodded.

"So assassinating Halkronen was the price you paid for Claudia's rescue."

"Yes."

"How…are you handling it? I mean, you've killed two people now."

Baskerville: Squirrels don't count.

"Four," she answered, with a hint of resignation in her voice. "I ran into two Black Labels." She shrugged. "I think…killing is too easy. Pull a trigger and a target goes down. I don't feel too bad about Douglas and Halkronen. But the troopers, they were just regular guys doing a job. They were both married, you know. One of them had kids."

"They were professionals in a violent business," I said. "Sometimes you pay the price of the business you're in." For a moment, I flashed back to the fellow soldiers, and often close friends, I'd lost in Algeria. "But, you lose that regret, you lose something core about yourself." It was the same way I felt about the guards, both Halkronen and Xenophon, at the Balkan Street facility.

Baskerville: Humans think too much.

Ester gave me a sad smile. Then she leaned down and kissed me.

She let out a surprised squeal as I used my good arm to tumble her into the bed beside me on my right side. She didn't notice that Fen used a little augmented speed to get out of her way. The activity hurt a little, but it was totally worth it. With a really bad fake leer, I said, "I told you I'd get you into bed."

"Jerk," she said, then kissed me again. She propped herself up on one arm and looked down at me. "We fixed the Douglas thing. The police found a neighbor with surveillance camera footage of a woman in a combat suit entering his apartment building, so you're off the hook. It's being treated as a CRAG hit. And the Snake attack on you is being treated as a case of mistaken identity—the Snakes struck back at the wrong target for the Douglas hit."

"Nice."

There was a polite cough. I glanced up and saw Claudia, looking somewhat the worse for wear with a bandaged shoulder and her arm in a sling, standing in the doorway with a big grin on her face.

"My, what an interesting shade of pink," I said, as Ester blushed. Some antics ensued as she climbed over me to get out of the bed.

As soon as her feet hit the floor, Fen jumped up on the bed and settled in beside me.

Holding back laughter, Claudia said, "Ester, you dawg! I didn't think you had it in you. I had you figured for some kind of warrior nun." She glanced at me. "And thank you for rescuing me, Cal." As Ester came up beside her, she said, "Should I give you two a moment so you can get some tongue action in?"

Ester clouted Claudia in her good arm.

"Ow," she exclaimed. "That hurt."

"Good," Ester said, laughing. "Come on, Fen, we've got to go."

I smiled as Fen pointedly ignored her. He clearly had no intention of leaving.

"He might as well stay," I said. "I'm sure I can get somebody to help me feed him and take him out for walks."

The two sisters walked out of the room together, though Ester turned back in the doorway, shrugged and said "Bye" before continuing down the hallway with her sister.

I had a feeling I'd be seeing her again.

With more time on my hands before Doctor Octo was willing to let me leave, I worked on the puzzle that was Ester's family.

Ester and Claudia were part of a very wealthy clone family. That much was both obvious and also highly unusual.

Their names had to be fake, but probably followed a typical clone pattern. Due to their unconventional upbringing, clones aren't usually very good with names. I recalled a fellow cop who came across a clone called Bering Sea—he'd just liked the sound of it. Another pattern was that a group of related clones would often name themselves alphabetically, generally by age.

My best guess was that Ester was part of a clone family of at least five clones from the same line, with Ester being the youngest. Her real name probably wasn't Ester, but I'd bet it was Elizabeth, Emily or something like that. In such families, where all of the members have the same basic intelligence and innate capabilities, members will often specialize.

For a high-functioning, wealthy and well-hidden clone family like Ester's, I'd bet on specialization. I made Ester out as the family's defender. Claudia's "warrior nun" comment tended to bolster my hunch. Other family members might specialize in making money, general management, public relations, etc.

So, we had a well-hidden but rich clone family. They had influence because of their money, but the need for secrecy would understandably keep them at arms-length from the FCN and CRAG.

As clones, Ester and Claudia didn't look exactly like one another because one or both of them had undergone some cosmetic changes. I could only see two reasons for that. The simplest was that sometimes the clones appeared in public together, so they couldn't look like each other without giving the game away. But this was L.A., so the other possibility was that one of them, most likely the eldest, had somehow become a celebrity. And celebrities couldn't be in two places at once, or it would be noticed.

I'd bet on the celebrity option, though I had no real evidence.

If I ran with that idea, though, some other things followed from it.

Like the plan for the assassination.

The bombardment of Halkronen's home was a diversion to assist the raid to rescue Claudia. But together, the assaults were intended to convince Halkronen that his organization was under attack, so that he'd leave the Civic Center. Meanwhile, FCN's flash mobs had ensured that the only viable exit was the one where Ester was waiting to shoot him.

If I'd planned that operation, I'd have wanted an inside person if it was at all possible. Someone to tell me when the target was on his way. That would have been hard to arrange on short notice.

But a celebrity could get themselves invited to an event at the Civic Center.

It wasn't hard to score a list of attendees. In fact, the Civic Center had posted the list themselves.

With the pool of possibilities reduced to the community of attendees, discovering Ester's family was both anti-climactic—because it was so easy—and shocking.

Her eldest sister was Adeline Parks, the world's foremost Tri-D star.

I couldn't help but marvel at the family's sheer audacity. Who else but a superstar actress could travel the world without the checks that other travelers would be subjected too? Who else but Adeline could escape a police clone check…by signing an autograph? Who else but a celebrity like Adeline could be rightfully paranoid about protecting her DNA? After all, illegal clones of celebrities were big ticket items on the black market.

I didn't spend all of my downtime working out things that puzzled me. I also thought about how good it was to have friends, people who cared about you. And how good it was to be lucky. And how dangerous it was to depend solely on luck.

Because with all of the opposition we ran into, and with the roadblocks that Jaeger threw in our path, we should have failed.

We absolutely should have failed.

Ester's escape plan for her assassination attempt was weak, and didn't cover the necessary contingencies. She should have died or been caught. But I cared enough about her to divert Fen to watch her back, even though I didn't know what was going on.

The assault on Halkronen's Balkan Street facility should have failed. Even if Fen had been there, we'd have been overmatched by the battlesuit. But Max was worried enough about me that he tagged our van and showed up on his own to watch my back. And it took a sniper of Max's caliber to exploit the tiny flaw in the battlesuit's neck connection necessary to kill the man inside.

Yes, we gave Max a share of the money. He totally earned it.

Friends and luck. That's what it came down to.

ACKNOWLEDGEMENTS

A surprisingly large number of people helped with this anthology in one way or another, including the members of the Hourlings Writing Group and the Loudoun County Writers Group, who were gracious enough to critique many of these stories.

Thanks go to David Keener and his unwavering eye for details. Thanks also go to Martin Wilsey for the final assembly and publishing. Finally, special thanks go to Erica Rue for managing the production of this anthology. Raising a family, writing her own novels, all while herding cats that love the sound of those deadlines as they go whistling by…

The First Anthology

The Second Anthology

The Third Anthology

The Fourth Anthology

www.ingramcontent.com/pod-product-compliance
Lightning Source LLC
Chambersburg PA
CBHW051304300726
48976CB00002B/268